PLEASE! NOT ME! NOT ME!

Hank heard McDuff's voice echoing in the open bay of the car wash, then a woman's panicked plea.

"Please! Not me! Not me!"

The strangled cry caused Hank to whirl. McDuff strode towards the car, a small attractive young woman dangling in his grip, her feet several inches from above the ground. One of his massive hands held her off the ground, the other held her hands behind her back.

"Dear God, don't let this happen to me," the woman prayed aloud. "Please let me go. Please don't let this happen to me. Not me!"

"You're going with me," McDuff said.

Kicking at her captor, she managed a hoarse, whispered plea to Hank. "Help me!"

"Get in and hold her," McDuff demanded, stuffing the helpless woman in the backseat of his Thunderbird.

Hank hustled into the car, pinning the woman against the side with his hefty body while holding her hands immobile.

"Please let me go. Please don't let this happen to me," she continued to beg.

McDuff jumped behind the wheel and eased the vehicle out of the car wash, going the wrong way on a one-way street. Several cars had to brake to keep from hitting him.

"Please, not me. Not me," the woman pleaded over and over. "Help me."

But there was no help for twenty-eight-year-old Colleen Reed that night. Once again, Kenneth Allen McDuff had plunged over the edge.

It was not the first time, nor would it be the last.

ORDINARY LIVES DESTROYED BY EXTRAORDINARY HORROR.
FACTS MORE DANGEROUS THAN FICTION.
CAPTURE A PINNACLE TRUE CRIME . . . IF YOU DARE.

LITTLE GIRL LOST (593, $4.99)
By Joan Merriam
When Anna Brackett, an elderly woman living alone, allowed two teenage girls into her home, she never realized that a brutal death awaited her. Within an hour, Mrs. Brackett would be savagely stabbed twenty-eight times. Her executioners were Shirley Katherine Wolf, 14, and Cindy Lee Collier, 15. *Little Girl Lost* examines how two adolescents were driven through neglect and sexual abuse to commit the ultimate crime.

HUSH, LITTLE BABY (541, $4.99)
By Jim Carrier
Darci Kayleen Pierce seemed to be the kind of woman you stand next to in the grocery store. However, Darci was obsessed with the need to be a mother. She desperately wanted a baby—any baby. On a summer day, Darci kidnapped a nine-month pregnant woman, strangled her, and performed a makeshift Cesarean section with a car key. In this arresting account, readers will learn how Pierce's tortured fantasy of motherhood spiraled into a bloody reality.

IN A FATHER'S RAGE (547, $4.99)
By Raymond Van Over
Dr. Kenneth Z. Taylor promised his third wife Teresa that he would mend his drug-addictive, violent ways. His vow didn't last. He nearly beat his bride to death on their honeymoon. This nuptial nightmare worsened until Taylor killed Teresa after allegedly catching her sexually abusing their infant son. Claiming to have been driven beyond a father's rage, Taylor was still found guilty of first degree murder. This gripping page-turner reveals how a marriage made in heaven can become a living hell.

I KNOW MY FIRST NAME IS STEVEN (563, $4.99)
By Mike Echols
A TV movie was based on this terrifying tale of abduction, child molesting, and brainwashing. Yet, a ray of hope shines through this evil swamp for Steven Stayner escaped from his captor and testified against the socially distrubed Kenneth Eugene Parnell. For seven years, Steven was shuttled across California under the assumed name of "Dennis Parnell." Despite the humiliations and degradations, Steven never lost sight of his origins or his courage.

RITES OF BURIAL (611, $4.99)
By Tom Jackman and Troy Cole
Many pundits believe that the atrocious murders and dismemberments performed by Robert Berdella may have inspired Jeffrey Dahmer. Berdella stalked and savagely tortured young men; sadistically photographing their suffering and ritualistically preserving totems from their deaths. Upon his arrest, police uncovered human skulls, envelopes of teeth, and a partially decomposed human head. This shocking expose is written by two men who worked daily on this case.

NO REMORSE
BOB STEWART

PINNACLE BOOKS
KENSINGTON PUBLISHING CORP.

PINNACLE BOOKS are published by

Kensington Publishing Corp.
850 Third Avenue
New York, NY 10022

Pinnacle and the P logo Reg. U.S. Pat. & TM Off.

First Printing: February, 1996
10 9 8 7 6 5 4 3 2 1

Printed in the United States of America

To the men and women of law enforcement who selflessly serve to protect; may God always bless their efforts.

In a few passages this book contains the graphic language common to the lost souls of a degenerate subculture found in the bars and dives and cheap motel rooms and crack dens of the underworld. It was with great difficulty that I elected to use it in this book since I neither condone its use, nor use it myself. The language remains in documented quotes, however, to illustrate a world, often devoid of hope, where base vulgarity and obscenities are the commerce of language. To do otherwise, perhaps, would be dishonest.

The names of many of the people who met or knew Kenneth Allen McDuff have been changed.

Acknowledgments

Without the cooperation and encouragement of many people this book would not have been possible. It is drawn from many sources. Perhaps the most important source is the memory of the men and women who lived it. The quotes and recollections of some events are as accurate as memory allows.

I would like to acknowledge, and thank, the following people for sharing their memories with me and for helping me with critical research:

Lori Bible, former Tarrant County District Attorney Charles Butts, Rhonda Chamberlain Chandler, Travis County Assistant District Attorney David Counts, Beatrice Dwunam, McLennan County District Attorney Investigator George Foster, Roy Greenwood, McLennan County Assistant District Attorney Mike Freeman, McLennan County Assistant District Attorney Crawford Long, Major John Moriarty of the Internal Affairs Division of the Texas Department of Criminal Justice, Lori Elmore-Moon of the Cleburne *Times,* former Waco Police Department Special Forces Sergeant Mike Nicoletti, Assistant U.S. Attorney Bill Johnston, Waco Police Department Legal Advisor Annette Jones, Mayor's Crime Victim Director for the City of Houston Andy Kahan, Assistant U.S. Marshal Mike McNamara, Assistant U.S. Marshal Parnell McNamara, Bureau of Alcohol Tobacco and Firearms Special Agent Charles Meyer, Travis County District Attorney Investigator Allen Sanderson, Waco Police Department Public Affairs Director Sergeant Malissa Sims, Bell County Criminal Investigation Division Inspector Tim Steglich, U.S. Marshal Service Inspector Dan Stolz, Austin Police Department Sergeant J.W. Thompson, Austin Police Department Sergeant Sonia Gill Urabek, and several street people and officers who prefer to remain anonymous.

And finally, I would like to acknowledge and thank Martha Ann; my inspiration, my life, and my wife, who happily endures my gypsy life as a writer.

—Bob Stewart

There are six things the Lord hates . . . Haughty eyes, a lying tongue, hands that shed innocent blood, a heart that devises wicked schemes, feet that are quick to rush into evil, a false witness who pours out lies . . .

—Proverbs 6:16-19

Scripture taped to the cover of the case book of McLennan County Assistant District Attorney Mike Freeman during the trial of Kenneth Allen McDuff for the murder of Melissa Ann Northrup.

ONE

Everyone called him Mac. Some called him Cowboy. Lanky and raw boned in his western shirt, blue jeans, and boots, Kenneth Allen McDuff looked the part. But on this blustery December day in 1991, if a working cowboy saw the light-colored straw hat pulled down over McDuff's deadly brown eyes, he would recognize the leathery-faced man as one of the drugstore variety. A real cowboy or a true aficionado would wear a felt hat in winter and a straw hat in summer. But McDuff wasn't wearing the hat just to keep his head warm.

Image was important to the forty-five-year-old parolee. Not one tattoo marred his muscular body. Towering at six feet, three inches tall, with two-hundred forty-five pounds spread evenly over his large frame, McDuff strutted arrogantly, starched and clean, among the pimps, prostitutes, junkies, drunks and bikers who populated The Cut, an underworld haven on the northern outskirts of Waco, Texas. On casual glance his pristine appearance made him appear out of place, but Kenneth McDuff was very much at home in this shadowy subculture. From Waco his tentacles stretched nearly two hundred miles north to Dallas and a hundred miles south to Austin in one bloody year of beatings and rapes and murders that forever would change the parole laws governing the Texas penal system.

Kenneth McDuff would carve out a unique niche in American and Texas penal history. He would become the first person ever to be given two death row numbers in Texas. He would become the first person in Texas, perhaps the United States, to be convicted and sentenced to die for three separate murders in three separate incidents. He would become the first person in Texas history to be sentenced to die by two different methods; electrocution in 1966, and lethal injection in 1993 and 1994.

Behind his back Kenneth McDuff was derisively known as Crack Mac for the form of cocaine he had discovered after his release from prison. One year later, on December 29, 1991, McDuff was barrelling along Interstate 35 toward Austin to find prostitutes, drugs, and a good time. He had with him a new sidekick, thirty-four-year-old Alva Hank Worley, a some-time drywall worker whom McDuff had met in October through a mutual acquaintance. Hank was in high cotton as he sipped beer and looked out the window of McDuff's 1985 beige Thunderbird speeding south along Interstate 35 between Waco and Austin. He was on his way to high adventure with someone whom he considered a big man. Worley had already joined his buddy on several exciting forays into the Central Texas underbelly, drinking with McDuff in bars such as He Ain't Here, Dundee's and Poor Boys.

Although McDuff claimed to be a full-time student at Texas State Technical College in Waco, he always had time for "hell-raisin' " and long hours on the road. One November night around Thanksgiving, McDuff drove twenty-eight miles to Belton to pick up Worley, then drove right back to Waco. The pair hit a couple of beer joints before scoring some speed, the drug McDuff preferred when he could not obtain crack, then they swung by Whore Alley on The Cut. The street, normally populated with eager women, was empty.

On the way back to Belton, where the divorced Worley lived in the S&S Trailer Park with his sister, the men talked coarsely about drugs, guns, whores and sex, McDuff's favorite topics. The convict sounded like a foul-mouthed teenager parading his machismo. Cowboy also mentioned a "damn good lookin' girl" who worked at a convenience store near the college he attended.

"I'd like to take her," McDuff said.

Worley understood his friend. McDuff was talking about

abduction. But then McDuff said something that would come to haunt Alva Hank Worley.

"I'd like to take her and use her up."

Worley dismissed the statement. Whenever McDuff was tilted on dope he talked about "taking" women and "using them up." Worley would admit later that he understood the deadly meaning of those words, but he just could not bring himself to believe that his new buddy was seriously proposing to commit rape, much less murder. He attributed the talk to a vulgar tongue loosened by drugs and alcohol.

That November evening ended when McDuff's maroon pickup truck quit running. Stranded, Worley had to telephone his ex-wife, Janice Worley Jewold, to come pick them up. Janice's present husband, Elroy Jewold, would become fast friends with McDuff.

But this December night was different. Ken had new wheels; a massive Thunderbird. Already the pair had consumed one six pack of beer and were sucking on longnecks from a second that Worley had purchased at a truck stop. As usual, the men soon turned to talking about finding prostitutes, maybe even kidnapping one.

The obvious spot to score drugs in Austin was on the outer edges of the sprawling campus of the University of Texas, a few blocks off Interstate 35. Hank was surprised when McDuff wheeled on past this familiar outlet. McDuff shrugged. They still had beer, why get the dope now? He reasoned.

The men cruised the streets of downtown Austin before stopping at a Dairy Queen on Congress Avenue to eat a hamburger. Back on the prowl, McDuff guided the Thunderbird onto South Sixth Street, where he pulled the car alongside a man standing on the curb.

"Where are the whores?" McDuff asked.

"Down on Congress," the stranger said, referring them back downtown to a boulevard running north through the inner city to the domed state capitol building.

McDuff gunned the big car into motion and wheeled the

wrong way onto Powell Street, a one-way street. When they passed a car wash, Worley noticed someone washing a light-colored sports car in one of the bays. It was the only car there. Worley checked the time: nine-thirty.

McDuff circled the block twice, still going the wrong way. Michael John Goins, a driver on Sixth Street who had to brake for McDuff at the Powell Street intersection as he was trying to make a legal turn, noticed that the driver of the Thunderbird appeared indecisive.

Finally, McDuff guided the Thunderbird into a bay at the car wash at 1506 West Fifth Street. Later, Worley would tell police he thought his friend was going to wash the car or get rid of the growing cache of empty beer bottles. Without a word, McDuff got out of the car, and disappeared into one of the bays. Worley exited the car to dump some of the trash they had generated. He heard McDuff's voice echoing in the open bay, then a woman's panicked plea.

"Please! Not me. Not me!"

The strangled cry caused Hank to whirl. McDuff strode toward the car, a small, attractive young woman dangling in his grip, her feet several inches above the ground. One of his massive hands held her off the ground, the other held her hands behind her back.

"Dear God, don't let this happen to me," the terrified woman prayed aloud. "Please let me go. Please don't let this happen to me. Not me!"

"You're going with me," McDuff said.

Kicking at her captor, she managed a hoarse, whispered plea to Worley.

"Help me!"

"Get in and hold her," McDuff demanded stuffing the helpless woman into the backseat.

Worley hustled into the car, pinning the woman against the side with his hefty body while holding her hands immobile.

"Please let me go. Please don't let this happen to me," she continued to beg.

McDuff jumped behind the wheel and eased the vehicle out of the car wash, again going the wrong way on a one-way street. Several cars had to brake to keep from hitting him.

"Please, not me. Not me," the woman pleaded over and over. "Help me."

But there would be no help for twenty-eight-year-old Colleen Reed that night. Once again, Kenneth Allen McDuff had plunged over the edge.

It was not the first time, nor would it be the last.

TWO

All his life Kenneth Allen McDuff lived on the edge, a half-step ahead of the law, and out-of-step with respectable society. To his doting mother he was "Junior," her favorite since his birth, but to the townspeople of tiny Rosebud, Texas, he was a bully, a troublemaker in school, and a thorn in the side of the county's law enforcement officers.

If not wealthy, exactly, the family was amply provided for by its patriarch, John Allen McDuff, a successful concrete contractor. Kenneth and his older brother, Lonnie, labored at back-breaking construction work as soon as they were old enough to hold a shovel. It was a thankless job for the two brothers. They seldom heard a word of praise from their father. More often they got a cuff to the head for the smallest mistake.

At home it was a different story. Tart tongued Adilee "Addie" Howard McDuff ruled like a queen, and her prince was Kenneth, who was catered to by his four older siblings. Louise, Lonnie, Mary Lee, and Geraldine. There was a younger sister, Carolyn, but Kenneth was pampered as though he were the baby of the family. His mother described him as "the tenderest-hearted of my children." John McDuff, a quiet man, left the family to Addie while he concentrated on making a living.

Kenneth McDuff still speaks fondly of his formative years. The family lived in the country, where he attended a school that had two or three grades in one room. There were never any problems, he says, until the family moved to the "city"— Rosebud, population 1,638. There he was the new kid in school. His grades were below average, and he made sure his fellow students knew he did not mind the failing grades. It was all a big joke, as far as he was concerned; the townspeople were just envious of his family's success.

When he turned sixteen, McDuff's parents gave him a new car. He acquired a Harley-Davidson motorcycle a year later.

"I was somewhat disrespectful of authority," McDuff admitted in an interview, before adding, "I was *really* disrespectful to authority."

The rebellious teenager delighted in high speed chases with law officers. He claims he was caught twice, but only because he ran into a ditch one time and one of his tires went flat the other time. He saw each chase as a game between himself and the law officers near his age.

It was an idyllic life in his eyes. He was dating a majorette at Cameron High School. They planned to marry.

But to others in Rosebud, Kenneth McDuff was a bully who terrorized the small Falls County farming community thirty-nine miles southeast of Waco, stealing his classmates' lunch money or forcing them to gamble with him by flipping quarters until he had won all the shiny coins.

Martha Royal, McDuff's fifth-grade teacher, remembers him as a loner.

"He did not get along with other children really well," Royal recalled in a Dallas *Morning News* article. "He was kind of a bully as he got older."

Big for his age, he used his size and demeanor to try to intimidate teachers. He was not the only McDuff to have trouble with the school authority. Lonnie once pulled a knife on Rosebud principal D.L. Mayo, who proceeded to throw the self-named "Rough Tough Lonnie McDuff" down the stairs.

When, at fifteen, Kenneth received a sound licking from Tommy Sammon, one of the eighth grade's most popular and athletic students, it was the talk of the town. McDuff called Sammon out for a well-attended after-school fight that lasted only a few minutes. Not long after the embarrassing whipping,

McDuff quit school to go live with his older brother in Fort Worth.

Teachers in the school system cheered. Letters to prison authorities would later verify the troubled times during his school years. The letters, required in Texas upon entry into prison, would state that the young man's parents could never accept the fact that their son was involved in any wrong doings, and constantly took his side against school officials.

Kenneth idolized Lonnie, who was six years his elder.

After living with Lonnie a year, McDuff returned to Rosebud. Then the real trouble started. Drinking. Fighting. Late-night high-speed car racing with the cops. Burglarizing. He burglarized again, and again, and again, until finally he was tried and convicted for fourteen different burglaries in Bell, Milam and Falls Counties.

This time his mother could not stop the inevitable. McDuff was eighteen years old, no longer a juvenile, and on March 3, 1965, he was sentenced to fifty-two years in the Texas Department of Corrections. He received a cumulative sentence of two years for his crimes. The sheriff delivered McDuff to the TDC on March 10, 1965, eleven days shy of his nineteenth birthday on March 21.

McDuff cockily admitted to prison officials that he was well known to Falls County law enforcement officers who had detained him numerous times for fighting, disturbing the peace, and possession of alcoholic beverages. But boys will be boys in Central Texas, and local officials released him with stern lectures, hoping somehow that a second, third, or fourth chance would give the teen incentive to go straight.

Perhaps the judge viewed McDuff as a fresh-faced teenager who was feeling his oats; perhaps the judge divined a spark of decency in what he thought was just another teen on the verge of going wrong; maybe the judge hoped that this first-time offender would find religion and straighten up and fly right.

Whatever the reason, it seemed for the first time Dame Justice had turned a blind eye on Kenneth Allen McDuff. But it was brief as the incorrigible teen was sentenced to serve the burglary terms concurrently instead of consecutively, a form of legal philanthropy that cut the actual time he served in prison to mere months instead of years.

On his first day working the fields, McDuff got into two fist-fights with an inmate leader, then he claimed the prison guards beat him unconscious with "slap jacks," a form of billy club. After that day the teenager determined to show no weakness.

"It toughened me up, somewhat," he said.

But McDuff made outside trusty in three months and was soon freely roaming a farm where he watered hogs. In less than ten months, he was back living with his parents and terrorizing his hometown. But now, it was different. He went into prison a young boy convicted of a dozen burglaries, but on December 29, 1965, he emerged a broad-shouldered, ham-fisted, two-hundred-pound man, now a remorseless and eager student of the malevolence nurtured behind prison bars.

Ironically, the day of his first parole from prison fell twenty-six years to the day that Colleen Reed would be kidnapped from an Austin car wash.

About six months after his parole, in June, 1966, McDuff picked up a new buddy. At a street dance in nearby Bremond, he met eighteen-year-old Roy Dale Green, a high school junior and a natural-born follower who worked as a carpenter's helper. McDuff, then twenty, was always seeking hero-worshiping, weak-willed followers he could manipulate. So, it was a perfect match when a mutual acquaintance, twenty-year-old Richard Lee Boyd, introduced the pair. Each provided an emotional need that welded the friendship. Green had been living with his mother but moved out after she remarried. He had been living with Boyd since the school year ended several weeks earlier.

Kenneth bragged that he had raped and killed women the night they met, Green would later testify. McDuff even told his new pal that he was looking for a victim that summer night.

"Have you ever killed anybody before?" the wide-eyed Roy Dale asked.

"Yes," McDuff answered, indicating there had been several.

"What did you do with all the people you killed?" Green asked.

"I got them buried in shallow graves," McDuff answered, but Green would later testify that his friend had never shown him any shallow graves.

The pair became fast friends. They shared long rides together, and rowdy adventures. Once Green watched in awe as McDuff raped a girl in his buddy's home, then squirted Deep Heat into her vagina.

"Killing a woman's like killing a chicken," Green said McDuff told him. "They both squawk."

Another time McDuff used the same analogy, telling his buddy that "Kidnapping a woman is just like killing a chicken. You got to shut the hen up before you get the rooster."

It was not unusual for McDuff to spot a girl, as the pair roved the county, and suggest they kidnap her. Green would quote his friend as saying, "It's just like stealing chickens."

Richard Boyd accompanied McDuff on one of his long rides that fateful summer. McDuff picked up Jo Ann Polka, a sixteen-year-old girl he was dating in Bremond, and the trio wandered along back roads until they stopped at a baseball park in the nearby hamlet of Hearne. Boyd spotted a broken broomstick which he snatched up to play with before tossing the jagged pink stick carelessly into the back seat of McDuff's car when they left. A simple act that would have tragic consequences.

Green was too mesmerized by the rebellious McDuff to flee the budding friendship. He refused to accept the truthfulness of all of McDuff's stories, as other buddies would do in the future. They were too fantastic to take seriously. Roy Dale credited many of the claims to youthful braggadocio. Instead of distancing himself, sometimes Green would spend the night as a guest in the McDuff home, basking in McDuff's aura of invulnerability. This was a man of the world. He raped with impunity, tortured with glee, and he had even spent time in prison. His brand new Dodge automobile and money-filled pockets were just icing on the cake.

Roy Dale was only too happy to oblige when Kenneth asked him to spend the night and pour concrete with the McDuff men Saturday morning, August 6, 1966. That Friday night the convict proudly pulled a thirty-eight caliber pistol from the automobile's glove compartment. Boyd and Green were impressed by the long-barreled gun even if the steel-blue tint was dotted with rust. Kenneth proudly told them the pistol belonged to "Rough Tough Lonnie McDuff."

When Roy Dale Green awoke that Saturday morning he was only a few hours from discovering that his hero spoke the evil truth. As the morning progressed, Kenneth proposed a trip to Fort Worth where, he told Roy Dale, he knew some girls. The men finished pouring concrete by noon, and after lunch with the McDuff family, the two left in mid-afternoon. They stopped in Waco to buy alcoholic beverages, then sped one hundred and twenty-five miles down the back roads toward Fort Worth.

The two friends stopped at Everman, a tiny bedroom community some fifteen miles outside Fort Worth. Danny Turner, a nineteen-year-old minister's son whose eighteen-year-old sister, Edith, Kenneth sometimes dated, joined them in a leisurely joyride around the southern portions of Tarrant County.

"I'm tired of the girls in Rosebud," Kenneth complained to Danny.

As evening approached Danny left to go on a date. Kenneth and Roy Dale stopped at the local Dairy Queen. As his buddy became more and more obnoxious, McDuff seemed to go into a shell. By yelling at girls, Roy Dale thought he was flirting. By challenging the boys, he thought he was emulating his idol. Kenneth left Roy Dale to bluster by himself for an hour before reappearing with Edith Turner.

The couple sat in the backseat as Roy Dale drove around the area, occasionally getting instructions from Kenneth. After several hours, the pair dropped Edith at her sister-in-law's home. Kenneth lingered on the porch with Edith for a long goodbye.

The couple took a brief walk while Roy Dale waited in the car. Then it was back to prowling the streets.

A drowsy, half-drunk Roy Dale Green saw three teenagers illuminated in the headlights of McDuff's new Dodge Coronet. Two boys and a girl were at a car parked by a baseball field. One of the boys was wearing a white sailor hat, Green would later say. McDuff drove past, stopping about one hundred fifty yards beyond the chattering teens.

"What are you gonna do?" Green asked.

"I'm gonna get me a girl," McDuff replied.

Robert Hugh Brand, a seventeen-year-old from Bethany, and his sixteen-year-old sweetheart from Everman, Edna Louise Sullivan, had already planned to go to a movie that Saturday night. John Marcus Dunnam, Brand's fifteen-year-old cousin visiting from Tarzana, California, wanted to turn the evening into a double date by escorting Louise's best friend, sixteen-year-old Rhonda Chamberlain. Louise and Rhonda lived only a few houses apart on Marlene Street in a new subdivision of brick homes in southwest Everman. Rhonda had introduced Louise to Robert, a distant relative. Rhonda considered it a perfect match since Robert was as happy-go-lucky as Louise.

When Marcus called Rhonda that Saturday morning to make it a double date, she innocently asked how Marcus was going to get from his grandmother's house in Fort Worth to Everman.

"You don't have a car," she said.

"I'm going to hitchhike," Marcus told her.

Instantly, an icy foreboding gripped the girl. The word "hitchhike" chilled her.

"No!" she exclaimed, a bit surprised at herself. "You can't come over here. You can't hitchhike."

"But . . ." Marcus began.

"If you do, I won't go with you tonight."

"Okay," he said, deciding to placate her. "I'll get a ride with my grandmother."

"Just promise me that's what you'll do," Rhonda insisted.

"Okay. I will."

"I won't go out with you if you hitchhike," she warned.

It was a bad feeling she could not shake, although in hindsight she says it was not a premonition that something would happen that Saturday night, but one of an unexplained pending doom: *Something bad is going to happen if he hitchhikes.* She could not push the thought from her mind.

Trembling, Rhonda left her home on Marlene, and walked to Louise's home a few houses away, where she blurted out her fears.

"I've got a bad feeling about Marcus hitchhiking over here," she told her best friend. "If he hitchhikes—and I believe he's going to although he said he wouldn't—something bad is going to happen to him. I'm not going to the movies with y'all tonight if he hitchhikes. It just gives me the creeps."

Rhonda devised a plan. She would hide in the hallway near the front door of Louise's home. When Marcus arrived, Louise would meet him on the porch. She would ask him how he got there as Rhonda listened.

In Fort Worth, Marcus awoke from a troubled nap, muttering, "They're doing something terrible to one of the girls."

Startled, Gertrude Dunnam asked her grandson what he meant.

"Nothing," he said, still sleepy. "I don't know. I guess I was just dreaming."

The loving grandmother would remember the words in the hours to come, and she would repeat them to her daughter-in-law, Beatrice.

True to her word, Louise met Marcus on the porch when he arrived. Casually, she asked Marcus how he had come to Everman.

"I hitchhiked," he told Louise with a shrug. Rhonda peeked out the doorway as the friends talked.

I'm out of here, Rhonda thought, heading through the back door, goosebumps covering her arms. *There's no way I'm going.*

It is possible that Rhonda may have misunderstood Marcus. The boy's mother says that her son had ridden to the Sullivans with his cousin who also lived in Fort Worth.

Rhonda had instructed Louise to tell Marcus that she had a headache if he told her he had hitchhiked. She felt a little sheepish about it, but it was an intuition she had to trust. The girls, however, would go ahead with their plans to spend the night together at Rhonda's home. As often happens, one falsehood leads to another, however. The fast friends knew that Louise's mother would not allow her to go to the movies with two boys, so the unsuspecting mom was told that Rhonda would be with the trio. It was a double lie that would haunt Rhonda within a matter of hours.

Beatrice Dunnam had just purchased a charm on Catalina Island, off the coast of California. It was a likeness of the ship that she had ridden to the island. On the back was the date 8-6-66. In light of the evil deeds that August 6, she would find it ironic in years to come that the day and the year engraved on that charm would be 666, the Biblical mark of Satan.

Robert, Louise, and Marcus decided to follow their original plans and go to the drive-in movie. The trio climbed into Robert's 1955 Ford and headed for the outdoor movie at the South Side Drive-in. Dusk would not fall until around nine o'clock that summer evening so the teens would probably not return until nearly midnight.

But, at ten o'clock, an excited Louise returned several hours before the drive-in movie should have ended. They had left early because Marcus was not feeling well, Louise told her friend. He was lying down on the backseat of the car. Robert stayed with him while the teenage girlfriends talked.

"Some car tried to sideswipe us," Louise blurted out excitedly. Rhonda noticed that her friend was "kind of shaken and still a little scared," but there were few details. The vehicle came out of nowhere, and then disappeared. Was it accidental or deliberate? It would remain a mystery.

Louise told her friend that they had stopped at a gas station, and were now headed for the high school.

"I'm going to take my driver's test Monday," Louise explained. "I'm going to practice parallel parking at the school."

The high school was less than a mile from where the girls lived. The secluded baseball field was only a stone's throw from the high school. She could practice parking there, Louise said, then the trio would hang loose until it was time to take Louise back to Rhonda's house. Louise promised to return before midnight.

It was the last time Rhonda would see or speak to her best friend.

"Get your stick and come on," McDuff ordered Green, taking the thirty-eight revolver out of the glove box. When they neared the car, Green told authorities that McDuff instructed him to stay back.

"I'll handle it from here. Just come when I call you."

He heard McDuff order the trio from the car. As commanded, Green waited alongside the road until he was called. There were no people in sight when he walked up to the 1955 Ford.

"I have three people here," McDuff said. "They're in the trunk."

He held a pair of billfolds in his hands. "You boys don't have very much money," he yelled at the closed trunk.

McDuff walked away from the car, motioning Green to follow him.

"They got a good look at me," he said. "I'm going to have to kill them."

"Kenneth, why don't we just . . ." Green began before being cut off.

"Get in the car and come on," Kenneth commanded.

The pair drove Brand's Ford back to where they had parked. McDuff fished in his pocket and tossed the keys to the new Dodge to Green with instructions to follow him.

After a bit, McDuff pulled off Highway 81 South onto a dirt road. From there he pulled into a pasture.

"This is not the right place," he said, apparently looking for a predetermined spot. "Back up. Follow me."

Back on Highway 81 South the men continued on to Farm Road 1017. McDuff exited and drove about a mile west before turning into a hay pasture. Green eased the Dodge behind the Ford, the front bumper several feet away from the trunk.

"I just want the girl out," McDuff told the three in the trunk as he opened it.

"I just want the girl out," he ordered again.

Louise, clad in a blouse and blue jean shorts, quietly got out of the truck. Green recalls being struck by her beauty although her light brown hair was mussed, and fear clouded her blue eyes. McDuff told Green to put the one hundred ten pound girl into the trunk of the Dodge. Roy Dale opened the trunk and the frightened girl meekly climbed in.

McDuff kept the gun leveled on his captives in the Ford.

"I'm going to have to kill them," he told Green after Louise was secured. "We can't leave any witnesses. I'm gonna have to knock them off."

"What you want me to do?" Green asked.

"Just stand there," Kenneth answered. He stuck the pistol into the Ford's trunk. Roy Dale Green saw the trunk light up from the flash of the first gunshot.

Suddenly the night was aroar with thunder as the pistol bucked in McDuff's beefy hand. Startled, Green flinched, then turned his face from the carnage a few feet away. Stepping backward he bumped into McDuff's car, then vaulted onto the hood, his body twitching at each shot as his feet beat a jerky tattoo on the thin hood of the car.

The first shot drilled into Robert Brand's head, the force of the impact shoving him backwards off his knees. The second shot into the head ended his life. The third bullet slammed into Marcus Dunnam who instinctively threw up his arm to ward off the next lethal projectile. The flesh slowed the bullet's passage so that when it struck Marcus's head, it knocked him unconscious. Green would later tell dismayed lawmen that McDuff coolly walked over to the fifteen-year-old victim and shot him between the eyes. The heartless killer then turned Dunnam's bloody head to one side and shot him behind the left ear lobe, execution style.

Green leaped off the hood of the Dodge and grabbed McDuff by the arm. "Good God, Kenneth, what you do that for?"

"I had to," McDuff said simply.

Green would later testify in court that his buddy was "cool, calm and collected. He act like he ain't done nothing," while Green was "almost dying of fright."

McDuff did become upset when he tried to close the trunk lid on the bodies and it kept springing open.

"Trunk won't close," McDuff grunted angrily before handing Green the gun. He gave the lid one more mighty shove. It was the only time he showed emotion, Green would recall.

McDuff ordered Green to get something to wipe the fingerprints from Brand's Ford. Green put the pistol in McDuff's glove box, then searched the Ford. He found a freshly laundered blue and white striped shirt neatly packed in a paper sack that Marcus's Aunt Louise Ruth Brand had given him before the trio left that afternoon.

McDuff instructed Green to wipe the Ford's trunk lid and whatever he had touched in the car. Roy Dale carefully ran the shirt over the dash and the door handles, inside and outside. McDuff then got into the car and backed up, jamming the rear of the vehicle into a fence. Roy Dale could only guess that his friend hoped the position of the car against the fence would hide the butchery from anyone who drove by the pasture.

"Help me wipe these tire tracks off," McDuff demanded as he bent to swipe at the tracks left by his Dodge. He used Marcus Dunnam's now dirty shirt. Green backed the Dodge

Coronet onto the gravel road, then joined his friend in wiping away tire tracks. The pair tried to erase any sign of their presence in this pasture of death.

What must have passed through Edna Louise Sullivan's mind as she heard the gunshots and the frantic effort to rid the area of evidence while she remained a prisoner in the trunk of McDuff's car?

Midnight. Rhonda Chamberlain awaited the return of her friend. She knew Louise would be punctual because Robert Brand's parents enforced a strict curfew on their son. She felt confident that the three teenagers would arrive momentarily.

Kenneth McDuff and Roy Dale Green drove south along Highway 81 South with Edna Louise Sullivan still locked in the trunk of the car.

"What are you going to do with the girl?" Green asked.

"I don't know," was the curt reply.

They drove in silence. Kenneth turned onto Ethane Allen Cutoff Road and followed it to a sandy road that led to a pasture in adjoining Burleson County.

"I'm going to get the girl out," McDuff told Green, pulling the car onto the side of the road.

The lanky killer put the girl into the backseat, then ordered Green out of the car. "He made the girl undress and he pulled his pants off, I think his underwear down," Green would later testify. "And then he raped the girl."

When he finished, he offered the girl to Green, who declined.

"Why not?" McDuff demanded to know.

"I just don't want to," Green insisted. McDuff pushed the front seat forward to get out of the car.

"I want to talk with you . . . ," he started before Green interrupted.

"I think I will screw her, Kenneth," he said, claiming that he feared for his life because he knew his friend had a gun. He took his clothes off and raped Louise in silence.

"All the time I was on top of the girl I kept my eye on him," Green would say in his confession. "She didn't struggle or anything, and if she ever said anything I didn't hear it." Green would try to justify his actions by claiming the rape was accomplished without a full erection because of his fear.

When Green was finished, McDuff ordered him to start the car and drive as McDuff resumed violating Louise. Green listened, knowing that McDuff had a soft drink bottle and the broken broom handle with the jagged end in the back seat—handy instruments of torture.

At one point Louise cried out in pain. "Stop! I think you ripped something."

McDuff directed Green back to the paved road until he spotted a white crushed-rock road and ordered his lackey to turn onto it. A short while later he told Green to stop the car, then the rapist ordered Louise to put her clothes on and get out of the car. The three had wandered more than twelve miles from where the bodies of the boys had been left.

"What are you going to do with me?" she asked, beginning to beg for her life as she dressed.

"I am going to tie you up," McDuff answered.

"Tie me up?" Louise asked. "What for? I'm not going nowhere."

McDuff wanted something to tie her hands. Green offered his belt but the convict threw it back into the car before ordering Louise to stand in front of the vehicle. Green noticed that McDuff had the broomstick in his hand.

Curious, Green exited the car to watch as McDuff ordered Louise to sit down on the ground. McDuff decided he wanted the belt after all, so Green turned to get it.

As he walked to the car, Green heard an explosion of air, "something like air escaping from a balloon," he would tell officers. Green turned to see McDuff straddle the helpless girl, now flat on her back. McDuff was mashing the broomstick against her throat. Louise's hands waved wildly in the air. She grasped the broomstick, pushing vainly against it. Her legs were flailing behind McDuff's back as he rode her bucking body.

"No! Kenneth!" Green ran back. He was weeping. "Leave her alone."

"Grab her legs," Kenneth ordered the stunned man. Green complied briefly, then let go.

"It's gotta be done," Kenneth insisted. Again he ordered Green to grab the dying girl's legs, and, again, Green complied, this time holding them until she no longer struggled.

The killer demanded that his follower help him push the broken broomstick against the helpless girl's throat. Green followed orders.

"Let's put her over the fence," Kenneth finally said. "Grab her by her head."

Green reached under her arms as McDuff grabbed the feet of the tiny one hundred ten-pound girl, then the two heaved the light, lifeless body over the fence like a sack of potatoes. They jumped the fence. McDuff dragged her limp body into a clump of bushes. Once again, he pressed the broomstick against her neck. He seemed to have an insatiable appetite to kill, Green would testify. McDuff ordered Green to take the broomstick and once again press it against her throat. The follower complied. McDuff snapped some necklaces from Louise's neck, shoving them into his pocket.

Kenneth stayed with his trophy as Green turned the car around and came back to pick him up. He found McDuff still pressing the broomstick against the girl's crushed throat when he returned.

One o'clock. Rhonda faced a major dilemma, alone and worried. It made no sense that her three friends had forgotten the time. Rhonda had stayed with her younger siblings as her parents enjoyed a rare night out. They had just returned and were preparing for bed a few feet down the hall. She debated telling them that Louise was late. But, she could not confide in them without revealing the lies and deception the girls had woven. Loyal, she did not want to get her friend in trouble.

One-thirty in the morning. Rhonda tried to sleep but worry kept her awake. She had a babysitting job at six o'clock that Sunday morning so she needed the rest. Finally, she drifted into a fitful sleep only to dream of solid blackness that gave birth to a pistol floating on nothingness. It fired six times. "Louise. Louise," she screamed in her dream, stumbling frantically in the darkness, unable to locate her friend.

Rhonda awoke in the dark saying Louise's name, and to the relief of sounds in the kitchen. *Thank God,* she thought. *She's back!* Rhonda hurried to the kitchen only to find her younger sister standing on the countertop, rummaging for something to eat.

Peering outside, Rhonda saw the family car, door open, overhead light shining. Louise could not get in and was sleeping in the backseat of the car, she decided. But when she slipped out the door and ran to the car, her friend was not there. Apparently Rhonda's parents had accidently left the car door open. The worried girl checked the garage. No Louise.

Maybe Louise decided to go on home for some reason. It was worth a try. Rhonda walked to Louise's bedroom window and rapped sharply. No response. She waited a few seconds and rapped again, careful not to wake the family. No answer.

Rhonda looked at the starry skies.

Louise, she asked silently. *Where are you?* An aching dread had now begun to fill her troubled soul.

The murderers hurried down the gravel road putting as much distance between themselves and the carnage as possible. McDuff fished into his pocket to hand Green the necklaces with orders to dispose of them. Green tossed them out the window at the intersection where the white gravel road began.

McDuff ordered the interior of the car wiped clean of potential fingerprints, especially the glove box that held the pistol. Green wiped frantically as they hurtled down the highway.

Next came the broken pink broomstick. Green rubbed it clean then hurled the murder weapon spinning into the night and into obscurity. It was followed by the cleanly-wiped soft drink bottle.

"Hey! Stop!" McDuff hollered a few miles down the road, pulling the car to the side of the road.

"Get the gun," he instructed, leaping out of the car. "Get the gun out of the glove box for me."

Green handed it to him, and McDuff swore as he popped the revolver chamber open. He wanted to know if he had any bullets left. But, he had had only six cartridges that day, and he had fired all six into the boys. A grateful Green would discover that there were no others in the glove compartment before they took off again. The spent cartridges followed the other evidence out of the speeding automobile window.

"Keep your mouth shut," McDuff warned his nervous friend on the ride back to Marlin. "Don't say anything about them. If police beat on you, it's better than what'll happen if you tell them.

"They'll try to put you in the electric chair," he threatened. "Plead not guilty, get a good lawyer, and find an eyewitness. Because when the jury goes to retire they always have that little doubt in their mind about whether you're guilty or not guilty."

Near a population sign at the Hillsboro city limits, McDuff buried the wallets belonging to Robert Brand and Marcus Dunnam.

At a Marlin service station McDuff instructed Green to check his underwear for blood. Both discovered dark ugly stains. McDuff attempted unsuccessfully to flush his bloody underwear down the toilet.

They would end the night in Marlin sleeping in the same bed in Roy Dale's old room at his mother's home.

Three o'clock. Jack Brand arrived at Rhonda's home looking for his son, Robert. The couple had a strict curfew for their children. Robert's mother had awakened crying from a bad dream, fearful for her son, Brand told Rhonda. When Brand arrived home from his job at Bell Helicopter at about two o'clock, he found his wife pacing the floor. The boys had not returned.

The frustrated father wanted to know where Everman teenagers would go parking on dates.

"We don't do that," sixteen-year-old Rhonda maintained. "We don't go parking."

Although the couple had only been dating a little more than a month, the father wondered if Robert and Louise might have run off to get married.

"Louise would never do that," the loyal friend insisted, still trapped in the web of deception. "There's got to be something wrong."

Rhonda knew that her friend was close to her family. Louise was especially fond of her stepfather, E.R. Hughes, whom her mother, Edna Ruth, had married seven years earlier. Louise and her family had plans for her to go to college. It was a carefully charted life that Rhonda knew her friend wanted to follow. Louise worked extra hard to keep some of her grades up and was excited about becoming a junior at Everman High School that fall where she played basketball.

When Rhonda went into her room to try to sleep, she prayed that her friends would be found alive. Perhaps she was getting worried over nothing, she reasoned. They were only a few hours late from the curfew. Still, it was not like them to miss curfew, especially by several hours. No matter how she tried to reassure herself, Rhonda knew that something was wrong.

Had her premonition come true? It was more than she could consider at that moment.

Lonely in her secret and horrified by her growing fears, the teenager even crossed her fingers as she prayed to show God her sincerity.

It would be days before she would confess the truth to her parents.

THREE

A little before six o'clock that Sunday morning Rhonda Chamberlain called Louise Sullivan's parents to tell them that their daughter had not come in that night. She made up a new story in which the four teens had gone to the drive-in and Louise had dropped her off after the movie because Rhonda was not feeling well. She said the three other teens had decided to go riding around until the midnight curfew. The troubled teen then left for a baby-sitting job.

Exhausted from searching all night, Jack Brand lay down for a few hours rest at his Bethany home.

Bill Sanders was going fishing Sunday morning when he spotted a car parked in a pasture off Farm Road 1017 shortly before seven o'clock. The Burleson native suspected that someone was having car trouble; perhaps teenagers had run the automobile battery down while parking and listening to the radio. It was not unusual for necking teens to use these back roads for romantic interludes, so he investigated to see if he could be of help. From a distance he could see there was no one inside the vehicle. Maybe someone was asleep on the seat. He called out as he approached the front of the vehicle. No answer. The trunk was open. Sanders peered into the automobile interior. It was empty.

The trunk was not.

Badly shaken, Sanders dashed to farmer Raymond McAlister's nearby farm house to report the horrifying tragedy.

Scrawled across the rear window in black mascara was the name "Louise." Did the sign tell of a harmless lover's interlude shared with Robert, or a prank played by Marcus, or had the girl tried to identify herself to whoever found the vehicle and its grisly contents?

That would become another unanswered mystery.

Inside the car investigating officers found Louise's white straw purse, hair brush, and tennis shoes. Her parents had filed a missing person's report only a few hours earlier. Edna Ruth Sullivan was not concerned about her daughter until Rhonda had called. She had no reason to be worried. Until that moment she had assumed the girl was safely tucked in bed at Rhonda Chamberlain's home.

"She's a good girl and always comes home on time," she told officers in making out the report.

As the massive manhunt for Edna Louise Sullivan began, Jack Brand went to All Saints Hospital in Fort Worth to identify the bodies of his son and nephew. Marcus did not have on a shirt, but his mother would tell police officers that he often went without a shirt in warm weather.

When he awoke, Kenneth McDuff decided to hide the murder weapon. Green fetched it from the car. McDuff put it in a cigar box after wrapping it in a rag. He dug a hole by the garage, buried it, then sprinkled leaves to camouflage the freshly broken ground.

A car wash was next on McDuff's busy agenda. As he cleaned and wiped the interior he came across a long brown hair lying on the backseat. He held it up.

"You see this?" he asked his buddy.

"Yes."

"That could get me convicted," McDuff answered. He threw

the strand of hair into the air, and watched as it floated to the ground to disappear.

Icy cool, McDuff picked up Jo Ann Polka that Sunday morning around 10:30 a.m. Jo Ann had been on the trip to Hearne when Boyd picked up the pink broomstick that would become the murder weapon.

Polka rode with McDuff and Green to Bremond where McDuff dropped Green off at Richard Boyd's home.

The killer then doubled back to Green's home in Marlin where he had spent the night. He sent Polka into the house. Curious, she watched through the window as he dug up a pair of white pants and a plaid shirt. He put them in the trunk of the car before summoning her from the house for a drive across town to Lonnie's home. There, she watched as the brothers disappeared behind a barn.

Rhonda's parents came to tell her the sad news in person. The bodies of the boys had been found in a pasture. Louise was missing. The Chamberlains went on to the Brand's home to see if they could help.

Rhonda crossed her fingers, and prayed more fervently. She certainly felt thankful because she knew that her unexplained premonition had spared her from whatever had happened to her friends. Then she felt shame for being thankful and guilt for not being with her friends, then a desperate hope that Louise would be found alive, then remorse, and finally, she mourned the loss of young Robert and Marcus. It was a circle of emotions that would consume the young girl for months to come. Well-meaning friends would tell her that God had a special purpose for her life. *What purpose that would kill three other people?* she wondered. Words that were meant to encourage her turned her against religion for more than a year.

"All three of my friends had been baptized and were saved," Rhonda would reflect. "I determined I would not be baptized if that was the reason God allowed me to live. It was too much."

But a little more than a year later she was baptized.

"There were a lot of different emotions," a mature Rhonda says nearly three decades later. She still deals with twinges of guilt. "I felt guilt because I lied. If I had gone with them, maybe they would not be dead now. Maybe I could have saved her. I can't explain how horrible I felt."

It was months before the teen-age Rhonda could once again date and reenter life's mainstream.

Newspaper accounts of the day reflect the story that she had concocted with Louise. True to her friend's memory, Rhonda would tell reporters that she did not go with the trio that night because of illness; the same story she told the police. Charles Butts, one of the district attorneys who prosecuted the case against McDuff, was amazed to learn the truth.

"I don't know if it would have made a difference in what we did," Butts said of the revelation, "but it surely is interesting. The young girl bore a real burden."

"There's seldom a day goes by that I don't think of Louise," Rhonda now explains. Louise is forever a happy-go-lucky teenager, frozen in time, as Rhonda grows older cherishing the memory of a light-haired, blue-eyed beauty who "was always laughing, vivacious, real sweet, and loved kids. She was always happy."

Richard Boyd noticed that Roy Dale Green was more highstrung than usual that afternoon of Sunday, August 7, when the pair went cruising around town. Several times Roy Dale cried without apparent reason.

"You're sure jittery," Boyd said.

The pair drove in silence for a few minutes. Concerned for his friend, Boyd stopped the car.

"Let's walk," he said.

"I can't stand it any longer," Green wailed, breaking into heaving sobs.

"What's the matter?"

"You know those two boys they found in this field south of Fort Worth?" Green managed between sobs. Boyd nodded. "Well, Kenneth killed them."

Boyd was silent as he took in the information.

"Well, let's go turn him in," Boyd finally said.

Soon Robertson County Sheriff E. Paul "Sonny" Elliott and Falls County Sheriff Brady Pamplin were questioning a fidgety Roy Dale Green. He tried to help searchers locate Louise's body, but all the roads looked the same in daylight.

Meanwhile hundreds of volunteers scoured the back roads and pastures as the temperature rose to a sweltering ninety-four degrees. A team of skin divers was dispatched to a nearby stock tank, where Bill Sanders had been going when he discovered the bodies. Searchers had discovered that a fence near the tank had been cut and fresh footprints dotted the area. The search was abandoned by mid-afternoon.

Roy Dale Green was taken to Fort Worth Sunday afternoon for an all-night interrogation at the Tarrant County Sheriff's Office.

Sheriffs Elliott and Pamplin were waiting for McDuff when he returned with Jo Ann Polka around 11:30 that Sunday night. When the headlights of his car fell on the lawmen standing in the Polka driveway, weapons at the ready, McDuff jammed the vehicle in reverse and roared backwards out of the driveway. Jo Ann dropped to the floorboard. At first, Pamplin watched in amazement. He had never seen anyone drive that fast in reverse.

Fearful that the girl might be harmed, the veteran lawman darted alongside the car calling for McDuff to stop as the vehicle wheeled backwards into the street. When McDuff did not respond, the crusty lawman fired a round of buckshot at the front tires and radiator. Sheriff Elliott opened fire with his pistol.

On the street McDuff changed gears. The car leaped forward as Pamplin unloaded another round from the shotgun. The riddled car disappeared into the darkness, scraping the street on metal rims that shredded the deflated tires.

McDuff would later claim that he feared the men were Jo Ann Polka's relatives who had warned him not to date her.

Within minutes, the sheriffs located McDuff in nearby Franklin. The killer had jumped into a pickup driven by Jo Ann's twenty-year-old brother, Richard Polka. McDuff asked Polka to take him to the constable's house because someone was shooting at him. As Polka drove away, the sheriffs spotted the pickup and pulled along side it.

"Stop!" Pamplin shouted through his window, presenting his shotgun. Polka pulled over

"Get out," Pamplin barked.

This time McDuff followed orders, meekly stepping from the pickup truck with his hands in the air. Polka would testify that he feared McDuff would use him, or his sister, as human shields because he knew the shots at the Polka home were fired by lawmen waiting in ambush.

In years to come, some would wonder aloud if it wouldn't have been better if the lawmen had killed McDuff in the Polka family driveway. Some would wonder if the presence of the innocent girl had saved McDuff's life.

Had McDuff died that night, nearly a dozen lives—maybe more—would have been saved.

Perhaps, for the first time in what would become a pattern, some twisted, evil fate had preserved McDuff's life.

Brady Pamplin would devote the rest of his career to keeping McDuff behind bars, a legacy he would pass on to his son, Larry, who would follow in his father's bootsteps to become sheriff of Falls County. As a teenager, Larry had helped his father and Sheriff Elliott capture McDuff that night.

After a night of "no comments" in the sheriff's office, McDuff had only one arrogant question. "When can I post bail up here?"

* * *

Jack and Beatrice Dunnam left for Texas immediately upon learning of their son's death. They stopped briefly in Arizona to pick up Beatrice's sister. Exhausted, Beatrice took a nap as the car rolled through New Mexico, only a few miles from El Paso. At a red light, she awoke only to see her son standing beside the car, silent, clad only in blue jeans, a belt, and white socks.

"There he is," she said, pointing out the window.

"Who?" her sister asked.

"Mark!" she said her son's name quickly. "Mark!"

Her companions could see no one.

"No, no, it's him," she said, describing the way he was dressed. It was a memory that burned in her mind during the remainder of the trip. Consumed with concern she went straight to the funeral home upon arriving in Alvarado, where she was met by funeral director Arrdeen Vaughn.

"Arrdeen Vaughn gave me his clothes," she would later recall. "It was a pair of blue jeans, white socks, and a belt and buckle that I had bought him. It was his buckle. A big silver square with a bucking bronco on it. It was the very clothes I had seem him wearing when I woke up." Beatrice noticed that her son's clothing had grass on it.

Vaughn also gave her the clothing worn by Robert Brand. She called the Fort Worth police and turned the boys' clothing, including the belt and buckle, over to two officers who came to the Dunnam home.

Tarrant County Sheriff Lon Evans and Deputy Sheriff Earl Brown picked up McDuff. On the way back to Fort Worth, the killer dozed. McDuff roused once to hear a radio report about Charles Whitman, the University of Texas tower sniper who had killed fifteen people less than a week before.

"That guy must have been crazy," he commented.

The brutal deaths of the three teenagers horrified even hardened criminals. A few days later, Sheriff Evans was approached by a delegation of trusties working in the jail kitchen.

"We don't want their kind up here [working in the kitchen]," one of them told the sheriff.

Another inmate threatened the safety of the murderous duo in a conversation with Deputy Brown, suggesting that McDuff and Green not be put in the jail tank where he and other prisoners were held.

"They wouldn't come out of here alive," the deputy quoted the inmate.

An autopsy confirmed that both young boys died of gunshot wounds, but the wound on Marcus's hand indicated that he may have put up a fight. Beatrice Dunnam believes the two boys were killed elsewhere and that her son resisted the attackers.

"Obviously Marcus was resisting," she said years later. "From the look of the body, and from the fact that he had the bullet wound in his finger, I would have said he was outside the car."

She believes the boys were placed into the trunk after they were killed. "His socks had grass on the bottom of them," she said. Marcus's shoes were with the clothing she had turned over to Fort Worth police.

Robert Brand and Marcus Dunnam, inseparable cousins who were like brothers, were buried in identical pale blue coffins in Glenwood Cemetery in Alvarado after joint services Wednesday morning in an overflowing First Baptist Church. The chief of police in the small town led the mile-long procession to the cemetery.

Vaughn Funeral Home handled the service. Parked behind the stately white Victorian residence-turned-funeral home, where the boys would lie in state, was the hearse that carried President John F. Kennedy's body from Parkland Hospital to Air Force One in Dallas in 1963. Funeral director Arrdeen Vaughn later would acquire the bullet-riddled car that desperados Bonnie Parker and Clyde Barrow were driving when they were killed May 23, 1934, in an ambush near Arcadia, Louisiana.

Funeral services for Edna Louise Sullivan, who had been found on Monday, were held later in the day at a First Baptist Church in Cleburne. She was buried at Godley Cemetery about 10 miles away. Students at Everman High School would dedicate the yearbook in honor of the popular student.

The day after the funeral service Governor John Connally revoked the parole that had allowed McDuff to leave prison seven months and eleven days earlier.

That same day an Assembly of God minister said that McDuff had given his heart to Jesus at a worship service several weeks before. McDuff had been reared in the Assembly of God faith. He was baptized at twelve. He attended services regularly in Rosebud until he turned fourteen when his attendance became irregular. By the time he entered prison on burglary charges he would tell prison officials that he went to church about once a month or less.

Meanwhile, hardened lawmen laughed at the minister's announcement, which garnered headlines in the local newspapers. They knew that Jesus Christ was in jail. He had to be, because so many prisoners found him there.

FOUR

Kenneth Allen McDuff followed his own advice and pled not guilty, got a good lawyer, and maintained that the only knowledge he had of the murders "is what I read in the papers."

"He's got dead eyes," Assistant District Attorney Charles Butts, 45, and a veteran prosecutor, told his colleagues. His would be the responsibility of questioning McDuff under oath.

The evidence against McDuff built quickly as the trial moved toward a November start.

- Green's confession and eyewitness account was the centerpiece of the case as he nervously told his story with fluttering hands. At the trial, McDuff would stare emotionless at his former follower.
- The boys' wallets were recovered in a cotton field near Hillsboro where they had been buried under the city limits sign.
- Several shell casings were found on the side of the road.
- On the night that McDuff was apprehended, Sheriff Pamplin discovered Marcus Dunnam's dirty blue and white striped shirt in the trunk of McDuff's automobile along with a pair of blood-stained underwear.
- Raymond McAlister, whose farm lay about four hundred yards from where the bodies were discovered, remembered seeing McDuff and a male buddy walking in the pasture sometime the previous May. When McAlister approached them, the boys jumped into a blue Mustang to flee.

McDuff's face was clearly illuminated in the headlights of the farmer's automobile. McAlister testified that the man with McDuff had his arm wrapped around a girl. The farmer said he saw her undergarments in the back seat of the Mustang. McDuff went "barreling out of there" as McAlister tried to block the vehicle. He clipped the rear of the speeding Mustang with his car.

- Edith Turner verified that McDuff used to drive a blue Mustang before getting the Dodge Coronet. She also verified that the murderous pair had been in Everman and left her about 9:30 or 10:00 on the night of Saturday, August 6, 1966.
- McAlister's wife saw two cars pull off the road about 10:35 that Saturday night. She awoke her husband, but he was too tired to investigate what had become a weekly irritation. The couple had had trouble with teenagers using their land for parking. "I'll check it in the morning," he told her.
- Boyd confirmed Green's story that McDuff had shown his two friends a blue steel, wooden-handled pistol the night before the teens were shot to death.
- Two witnesses said they saw McDuff and Green at a service station in Hillsboro shortly after midnight.
- Green's crude map put the searchers in the general vicinity, and Edna Louise Sullivan's battered body was subsequently discovered in a clump of bushes late Monday night, August 8, about six hundred yards off Farm Road 917.
- An autopsy revealed that the girl was strangled. She died when the tiny hyoid bone in her throat was snapped and the thyroid cartilage crushed. The report also showed that the girl had bled internally.
- Lonnie McDuff was arrested in Rosebud and charged with concealing and destroying evidence. Lawmen said they discovered the charred remains of a western-style shirt with metal snaps in the driveway of the McDuff farm. They believed it was the shirt McDuff wore the night of the murders. The officers also charged that Lonnie was con-

cealing the thirty-eight caliber weapon used in the murders. Bond was set at $20,000. Lonnie was out of jail in time to attend the November trial of his little brother.

However, searchers would fail to find either the pistol or the pink broomstick with the jagged end as they fanned out along the roads and highways Green said the pair followed back to Marlin.

A few days after McDuff's arrest, reporter Robert Mann wrote about an altercation he had with young McDuff in Cameron, Texas, when the two were high school students. McDuff dated the sister of Mann's best friend.

"I remember him as tall, lean and tough," Mann wrote in a Fort Worth newspaper. "He generally was quiet around me, but not always." Mann went on to describe a heated exchange he had with McDuff at an intersection following a minor automobile accident. That meeting led to a fistfight several days later.

"Kenneth and I argued about some insignificant matter that seemed important to boys trying to be men . . . and then we both swung. A Cameron policeman ended the bout but each of us vowed a return match. The next day we fought again, this time on an isolated road. The fight ended like most teenage scraps. Kenneth and I shook hands and became friends."

Mann was surprised when McDuff went to prison for burglaries. He was just as surprised to see McDuff in a Cameron pool hall a month or two before the murder of the three teens. There had been a change in McDuff.

"Kenneth appears more 'clean-cut' than I remembered him from high school days. He wore a button-down collar shirt, slacks and had short hair. Before I had always seen Kenneth in jeans, a T-shirt, and he usually wore a narrow-brim hat on the back of his head."

After a few minutes, "Our eyes met for just an instant and then, without even nodding, he turned back quickly to the table."

Addie McDuff, in interviews with the news media, waged a campaign to exonerate her son as the trial began.

"If I knew he was guilty of such a thing, I couldn't turn him loose if I was on the jury," she said on the eve of the trial. "Don't ask me how I know. I just know he is not guilty."

She said her son was "too good for his own good" because "He was always loaning people his shirts." The loyal mother claimed that her son was keeping mum to protect the reputation of a girl he had dated that night.

"This girl has a real good reputation. I think she is studying to be a missionary, and he wants to keep her name out of this.

"If he is willing to go to his death to protect her, I guess that's his business," the mother sniffed.

"Right after this happened he told me, 'Mother, I've done some things I'm not proud of, but I would never hurt a girl'."

His father was more matter-of-fact, according to a *Texas Monthly* story by Gary Cartwright.

"If I believed he did what you say, the state wouldn't have to kill him," he told a lawman. "I'd do it myself."

McDuff maintained his innocence throughout the sensational trial which attracted an international audience. He steadfastly blamed Green.

"Roy had a problem with girls. Very much so. He did not know how to act around girls," McDuff explained. "Roy got mad because he didn't have a date. He wanted me to wait some place. He said he knew a girl and thought that if I was along I'd have some influence on her. I was tired and didn't want to do anything."

McDuff said he was asleep in a burned-out building at an Everman strip center when Green killed the three teenagers after borrowing his new car. McDuff also claimed that he once sat in the living room of Green's home and listened as Green raped a fourteen-year-old girl he had taken into his bedroom. A thirteen-year-old girl corroborated McDuff's story in court. She said she asked McDuff to help the girl as they listened to her struggles.

"He said he didn't think we should, that it wasn't any of our business," the girl testified.

McDuff dismissed his burglaries as "just stunts," the actions of a bored teen.

"Smaller towns are different from big ones. There are no drive-ins and things like that and there isn't much to do," he said under Assistant District Attorney Charles Butts's questioning. The burglaries sprang from the bored minds of a group of boys who were "just standing around without anything to do."

McDuff admitted that he had stolen rifle shells from one store. He vandalized another with a sledge hammer because he found no money inside. One Falls County store yielded money, checks and "quite a bit of merchandise" he said.

Asked if he considered the crimes a "stunt," McDuff replied, "No, sir. I do not."

As the trial came to a conclusion, Sheriff E.P. "Sonny" Elliott dropped his own bombshell in a newspaper article that would cause many readers to wonder about Green's sincerity. Green told the sheriff that he was a reluctant participant in the rape and murder because he feared for his life.

"Roy Dale Green told me he and Kenneth McDuff went to Bryan, on Highway 21 West and saw two girls around ten years old [playing] in front of a beer joint.

"He and McDuff got out of the car and slipped up on the little girls with the intent of kidnapping and raping them. But a man walked out and both went back to the car and left."

The date of this trip to Bryan? August 5, one day before the three teens were slaughtered. McDuff had a gun, according to Green.

District Attorney Doug Crouch, in delivering the concluding arguments, addressed the issue of Green's truthfulness.

"The difference between Roy Green and the defendant is that Roy Green has a conscience. The defendant, behind that icy look, does not have a conscience. You have to take Green as he is—a person of weak will—but you also have to take him as a man with a conscience."

Godfrey Sullivan, McDuff's attorney, challenged Green's claim that he feared for his life by noting that the sidekick was given the car keys and told to move the car. It was an opportunity to escape, but Green did not.

"Why didn't you?" Sullivan asked.

"I . . . I . . . I just don't know," Green stammered.

Over and over Green would claim that he thought what was about to happen was a joke.

"All the time until he started shooting I thought he was joking, and then . . . Oh God, yes, I was scared to death," he had said in his confession. "The only reason I screwed the girl was because I was scared. He had killed two and I was looking to be next.

"I just didn't believe what he said was going to happen," Green testified. But at the time of his arrest he told newsmen and lawmen that the pair had driven around talking about a sex escapade with a parked couple.

Veteran reporters wrote about McDuff's cold, emotionless expression throughout the seven-day trial. The expression did not change when the jury of nine men and three women found him guilty of murder with malice aforethought on November 15. The jury recommended death in the electric chair for the capital murder. The jury of nine men and three women returned the verdict in less than three hours, deliberating forty-five minutes the day the trial ended, and one hour, fifty-two minutes the next day, when it delivered the verdict.

Assistant District Attorney Charles Butts asked several jurors after the trial what may have tipped them to McDuff's guilt other than the evidence presented. Several believed they had found a tip-off to his truthfulness in McDuff's massive hands.

Although his hands could not be seen from the spectator's gallery, the witness stand was open on the side facing the jury box. McDuff remained in full view of the jury as he testified. Whenever McDuff answered nonthreatening questions, the jurors noticed, his imposing hands lay placid in his lap. But when he denied the crime or when the prosecutor's questions produced stress, McDuff kneaded the knuckle of the index finger of his left hand.

"It was the most perceptive jury I've ever seen," Butts said.

Rhonda Chamberlain, also, remembers Kenneth Allen McDuff's cold, emotionless eyes which she caught fixed on her several times during the trial.

"I wondered if he realized that he missed getting me, too?" she mused.

But perhaps the most poignantly ironical reflection came from Green when he was asked by Fort Worth *Star-Telegram* reporter John Tackett what his reaction would be if he received the death penalty in a later trial.

"I'd probably lose my mind. It's a hard thing for someone to face . . . knowing you're going to die."

Tackett later said he could only think of the helpless girl entombed in the trunk of the automobile.

In June, 1968, nearly two years after the fact, after his testimony put Kenneth McDuff on death row, Roy Dale Green received a five-year prison sentence when a jury found him guilty of murder without malice in the death of Marcus Dunnam.

"I thought I'd get life, not five years," an incredulous Green said.

Unsatisfied with the light sentence, the state decided to seek the death penalty for Green's part in Robert Brand's death. Fearing the electric chair, Green eventually pled guilty. On April 1, 1969, he was given a twenty-five-year sentence to run concurrently with the five years he received for Dunnam's murder.

Beatrice Dunnam had moved from California to Little Rock, Arkansas, after Marcus's death. She attended Green's trial for her son's murder and she was quite vocal in her displeasure at the light sentence received by the killer's apprentice.

A week later she received a ghoulish package in the mail at her new home. Inside the neatly wrapped package was a white sailor hat similar to the one Green said her son was wearing the night he was murdered. Beatrice Dunnam denies her son was wearing a sailor hat that night, although Green said he saw one. Marcus had been playing with one prior to leaving his grandmother's home that day, but "that hat was still at the Dunnam house."

Meanwhile, newspaper reports said that it was a blood-soaked sailor hat similar to the one worn by Marcus the day he died that had arrived in the mail. "That was just bad reporting," she says. The white hat was unmarred.

Assistant District Attorney Truman Power assured the horrified woman that the cap could not be the one her son had on when the bullets tore into his head. The state had kept the cap and other clothing worn by the hapless victims.

"We've already been through a great deal, why do they want to harass us?" Beatrice asked.

"I don't believe there is any justice in Texas," she said. "This is adding insult to injury."

Only a handful of people in Fort Worth knew her new address, she said.

"If anything like this happens again, I'll prosecute to the fullest letter of the law," she promised.

Several weeks later a second, a more horrifying package arrived in the mail bearing a Fort Worth postmark.

She unwrapped it with trembling hands to find Marcus's belt and western belt buckle, a large silver square with a bucking bronco on it.

"It was his belt. The one he wore the night he was murdered," she said. "I know it was his, because I bought it for him."

The last time she had seen it was when she turned it over to Fort Worth police. An investigation failed to turn up any suspects; all fingerprints on the package were smudged.

It was another one of the many mysteries enveloping the case that would remain unanswered.

* * *

Kenneth Allen McDuff's death penalty was automatically appealed, as are all such cases in Texas. It would take the Court of Criminal Appeals fifteen months before it ruled on February 21, 1968, that no trial errors had occurred in the carefully prepared case presented in the Tarrant County Criminal District Court. McDuff was ordered to pay with his life as judge and jury demanded.

It would be another eight months before McDuff once again stood before District Judge Byron Matthews on October 8, 1968, to receive a formal sentencing to death.

"Stand for the sentence, please," Judge Matthews instructed the convict before beginning.

"I'd rather sit down for the sentence," McDuff replied coolly.

"All right," the judge said.

"Have you anything to say why the sentence of the law should not be pronounced against you?"

"No."

Judge Matthews began reading the formal sentence which included the words McDuff's mother feared to hear.

". . . and shall, on December 3, 1968, before sunrise cause to be passed through the body of you, the said Kenneth Allen McDuff, a current of electricity of sufficient intensity to cause death, and shall apply and continue the passage of such current of electricity through the body of you, the said Kenneth Allen McDuff, until you are dead; and may God have mercy on your soul."

McDuff, by now twenty-two years old, stared directly into the judge's eyes. He did not change expression. Behind Kenneth his mother closed her eyes at the words, "until you are dead." Tears formed in the corners of her eyes and began to slide down her face.

McDuff rose to leave, then said, "Goodbye, Mom." Addie McDuff sat weeping as the sheriff led her doomed son away.

In a jailhouse interview McDuff would continue to staunchly deny any crime.

Asked if he would deny the crimes, even if he had done them, the raw-boned concrete worker said, "That's something I don't know, so I'll just leave that blank."

McDuff spent the time reading western stories and the Bible, he told reporter John Tackett. But he denied giving the impression of discovering religion or repenting. A person should be as religious outside bars as inside, he insisted.

"I won't do it [be religious] anymore in here. I'll do it less than outside," he said.

His main concern, however, appeared to be his family.

"I'd never say I did something like that," he said. "It's so bad . . . it would make my parents look so bad."

Did he feel sorry for anyone as the result of his murder conviction?

"The hardest part was for my family."

He paused before conceding that, also, "It was bad for those kids' parents."

FIVE

Nineteen sixty-six was a difficult year in an even more difficult decade for the Lone Star State. Maybe it was the times—bloody times, not only in Texas but across the nation. It seemed the world was turning upside down as America's young men marched off to war in Vietnam amid turbulent protest while Lyndon Baines Johnson, a Texan, served as president.

Earlier in the summer a drifter named Richard Speck sneaked into a nurses' dormitory in Chicago and massacred eight nursing students. It was the "crime of the century" until Charles Whitman took to the killing tower later that summer, on August 1 in Austin. The twenty-four-year-old ex-Marine slaughtered his wife and mother, then climbed to the top of the University of Texas victory tower to kill another thirteen and wound scores more. In Dallas a jury had ruled that Jack Ruby was sane when he gunned down Lee Harvey Oswald, the accused assassin of President John F. Kennedy.

Maybe Texans were ready to forget. Maybe the murders would have faded into the past, anyway, as public attention turned to the next bizarre event; so many brutal deaths seemed to dominate the news. As time passed, so did public interest in the triple murder and in McDuff and Green. Although both faced charges of rape and murder in Johnson County for the torturous death of Edna Louise Sullivan, the pair would never be brought to trial in that county. The cases involving the death of the teen-age girl would disappear from memory and subsequently be dismissed years later for the failure of the courts to pursue a swift and speedy trial.

McDuff entered the Texas Department of Corrections system less than two months before his scheduled execution date, December 3, 1968. Despite that, he seemed unworried about his pending death, according to a confidential evaluation conducted at the prison.

"His attitude toward the sentence imposed is one of disbelief, and apparently he feels that it will never be carried out, as he does expect a reversal in his case," the report read. "Apparently Mr. McDuff is something of a manipulator and is apparently convincing himself that he will have no difficulty in shaking off the penalty imposed.

"The instant offense is his only recorded involvement in assaultive behavior; however, his reported involvement in numerous fights would indicate that he was somewhat of a 'bully' and impulsive in nature.

"Mr. McDuff impresses as being an individual who has resented and rejected authority figures from early childhood, and one who has been unable to relate satisfactorily not only with authority, but with his peer group. Information would indicate that his parents supported him in his rejection of authority, and while it would appear that they did offer some form of adequate control and guidance, he even rejected their assistance."

A psychiatrist examined the killer in October.

"This patient is free of any thought disorder and shows no evidence of digressive illness," the report read in part. "He exhibits a dyssocial personality. He is of average intelligence and completed the ninth grade. His fund of information is compatible with his background and his personal history indicates that he left school because of much difficulty with teachers, school principals, and others who were responsible for his conduct . . ."

The report went on to note that McDuff's relationship with his peers was not always wholesome.

McDuff claimed that in 1968 he did not use narcotics but

said that he had consumed an average of three beers each evening since he was seventeen years old. He did admit that he occasionally overimbibed.

Perhaps the most chilling psychological tipoff came as the convicted killer coldly tried to convince the psychiatrist of his innocence while remaining indifferent toward the man whose testimony put him on death row.

"When discussing the present offense, [McDuff] went into considerable detail of what was alleged, also giving details of how he felt the offense in itself was committed by one Roy Green," the report read. "No animosity [toward Green] was noted; however, it is felt that Mr. McDuff is convinced that his attorney will succeed in obtaining a reversal in his case."

The convicted killer apparently had trouble in relationships with women. He had been engaged to a woman prior to his first imprisonment for burglary but her family insisted that she break the engagement, McDuff told prison officials. He said that he was continuously searching for a "nice girl" but "was never able to make a go of the relationship, mostly due to the girl's parents learning of his prior convictions," the report stated. "His statement, and the fact that he dwelled on this subject would indicate a belief on his part that had he been able to find this 'nice girl' he would have married and settled down and . . . not be in his present predicament."

In the admitting interview, McDuff mentioned that he was alleged to have killed Edna Louise Sullivan, then he told the interviewer that he was charged with the deaths of Robert Brand and Marcus Dunnam. Ironically, he was sent to death row for the murder of Brand, yet the boy's death appeared to be of secondary importance to him since he first mentioned Edna Louise Sullivan.

Although he had an IQ of 92, about average, it was obvious to prison officials that they had a master manipulator on their hands.

McDuff settled back into prison life. In a way, it was a return home, although the homecoming was intended to be a short one since he had a date with death. McDuff was to die before dawn, December 3, and as the day approached his actions became more and more bizarre.

Death row guards began to find blankets and shoelaces and articles of clothing tied together and threaded through McDuff's cell door in what appeared to be an effort to barricade himself. Guards also noticed that the twenty-two-year-old man was stuffing tissue and paper into his nostrils.

For the first time, Kenneth McDuff escaped the deadly embrace of Ol' Sparky, the nickname inmates had given the electric chair. Only days before his death, McDuff received a stay of execution. The new date was January 2, 1969.

This time the death ritual began as lawyers frantically sought to keep McDuff alive. Normal procedures called for McDuff to make a decision two weeks before his execution as to who would receive his personal property upon his death. The warden asked for a list of people McDuff wished to watch the execution. He was allowed up to five witnesses. The condemned man decided who should receive the money in his prison account.

As the date neared, McDuff continued to loop shoelaces and blankets and clothing together to turn his cell into a safe haven.

Meanwhile, an execution log book was to be begun on the final day, January 1, 1969. Each of his actions and words were to be recorded during the last hours; every morsel of food noted. In Huntsville most executions occur at 12:01 a.m. since the official decree calls for the act to be completed before the hour of dawn.

But on New Year's Day, with only hours to spare, District Judge Woodrow Seals of Houston issued a stay of execution. Twice in less than a month, McDuff had escaped the retribution of the State of Texas for his crime.

Only a few days after his near brush with death, McDuff's bizarre behavior was enough to warrant an evaluation by an outside psychiatrist.

"He relates to me having gone through an episode of being fearful that some of the building tenders were trying to kill him, at which time he tried to lock up his cell door by wrapping blankets around it, shoe strings, and other articles of clothing," the confidential report read in part. "He further stated he had been having some thoughts that what was going on in his mind was being broadcast through his nose and that he couldn't keep this under control and made an effort to stuff up his nose with paper and other bits of material."

Having safely passed through two execution dates, McDuff told the psychiatrist that most of this outlandish action was imaginary and not real.

The psychiatrist added, "He indicates no delusional thinking at this time, nor is he hallucinating." The medical expert believed that McDuff's "stream of thought and speech" was appropriate, but, "His judgement was pretty much that of a sociopath."

The psychiatrist asked McDuff what he would do if he found a letter, stamped, addressed and sealed. "He answered he'd probably open it, which is a common answer for impulsive sociopaths."

"The expert concluded that McDuff used auto-suggestion to talk himself into fantasies that had become real. It is not uncommon, the report added, for a sociopath to become paranoid when unable to control the environment. The threat of reality is more than a sociopath can bear, so he manipulates himself into a paranoid state.

"I have seen this many times," the psychiatrist noted. "If the imminence of their environment controlling them continues for long periods of time, they may acquire this paranoid state in a fixed manner, and this will become persistent and will actually become a delusional system. However, in this young man, he is not now confronted with imminence of death and is back in contact with reality in all areas.

"It is my prediction, however, that since this man has been able to incite such a state in himself, he will do this again, and if he is threatened with execution again, he probably will incite

such a state, and my prediction is that he will make it a fixed
state and will become psychotic at some time in the future."

On February 21 Judge Byron Matthews decided to move the
execution date to April 1, 1969. But on March 25, a week before
McDuff's scheduled death, the convicted killer was granted his
third stay of execution by U.S. District Judge Leo Brewster.

Tarrant County Assistant District Attorney Truman Power an-
nounced in June 1970 that McDuff would face a second murder
trial for killing Marcus Dunnam as "insurance" in case the U.S.
Supreme Court would eventually declare the death sentence a
"cruel and unusual punishment" and abolish it. Power noted
that at that time there was no provision in the law to change a
death sentence to a life prison sentence without a new trial.

On July 30, 1970, Judge Byron Matthews again sentenced
McDuff to die, this time on September 9, 1970.

The judge overruled a motion to quash the second trial on
grounds that McDuff was denied the right to a speedy trial.
If McDuff lived to face the charges, Judge Matthews would
grant a change of venue, moving the case to Judge Jon Vance's
criminal District Court 194 in Dallas. In essence Judge Matthews recused himself because he had been the presiding mag-
istrate at the 1966 trial for the murder of Robert Brand.

The American legal community cherishes the theory that
Justice is blind, but in the case of convicted mass murderer
Kenneth Allen McDuff, she was a deaf mute, not only once,
but an astounding four times. His fourth stay of execution
came about through a unique combination of beginner's audac-
ity and veteran experience. The fourth time McDuff's life was
saved by a man who was not yet a lawyer.

SIX

Dr. George Beto was already a Texas legend when he thundered into the small office that housed a staff of two attorneys hired to help inmates file the hundreds of habeas corpus writs that had begun to plague Texas prisons. The director of the Texas Department of Corrections (TDC) had found himself in a unique position in early September 1970.

Although it had been in law books for close to two hundred years, thousands of prisoners across the nation had discovered the writ of habeas corpus in the 1960s. The law was originally established by America's Founding Fathers to protect a citizen's Sixth Amendment rights against illegal imprisonment. The intent of the writ was to bring a party before a court to prevent unlawful restraint; but, in the past few years it had been twisted by jailhouse lawyers to apply to almost any imprisonment. State courts were flooded with writs scribbled by diligent inmates who used the vast law libraries common in the prison system. Then, these self-educated legal eagles eagerly helped others to do the same. It was the constitutional right of each prisoner to file a writ and a handful saw to it that it was done with a vengeance.

In an effort to stanch the torrent of writs flooding its courts, the State of Tennessee had ruled that no inmate could help another prepare the legal document. But in 1969 the United States Supreme Court ruled that Tennessee could not discipline prisoners who broke the rule against helping others, unless prison staff attorneys were hired to help the inmates prepare the writs.

To ward off similar potential problems in Texas, in the summer of 1969, Dr. Beto hired an experimental staff of four law students, among them twenty-four-year-old Roy Greenwood, who had helped found the Criminal Law Association at the University of Texas in Austin that year. Greenwood spent the summer in Huntsville interviewing hundreds of convicts and writing writs for the successful experiment. It was a heady experience for an eager law student.

However, fate found Greenwood without a job shortly before taking the bar examination on June 25, 1970. A coveted position with the attorney general's office in Alaska had melted away like the winter snow in a spring thaw when the attorney general who had promised Greenwood a position had been defeated in an election. His successor asked for everyone to reapply. The recent law graduate did not have enough time to comply.

Roy Greenwood was contemplating his next step when Professor Bob Dawson, his counselor at the university, called for him.

"Dr. Beto still needs help," Dawson told his student. "Assuming you pass the bar examination, he's ready to hire you."

Dawson went on to explain that in the fall of 1969, Beto had hired Harry Walsh, a young attorney with several years experience, but the case demand was too heavy for one man. Greenwood would start at guard's pay until Beto could get authorization for the second attorney and the corresponding salary. Dr. Beto asked Greenwood to go to work the Monday after he took his bar examination. Both Greenwood and Walsh would report directly to Dr. Beto as members of his staff.

"Why not?" Greenwood said. The internship the previous summer had been hectic, but fulfilling. Dr. Beto was recognized as an expert in religion, education, and prison management. It was an opportunity to renew his work for this unique man. As an assignment his senior year in college Roy had prepared a brochure on habeas corpus that could be used in the prison population. It was a chance to test his work. But, he was not prepared for what would happen shortly after he reported to Huntsville.

"Kenneth McDuff is scheduled to die next Monday," Dr. Beto told Greenwood on Wednesday morning. The death watch had already begun when the prison administrator approached his legal staff. "I understand his attorney died a month ago. He doesn't even have anyone to represent him."

The legendary minister, educator, and prison administrator paused. He wanted no misunderstanding.

"The lawyer's dead," Beto added. "He's without counsel. It's about a week before the execution. No one is going to be executed on my watch without proper representation."

The last time someone had been strapped into Ol' Sparky was July 7, 1964, when thirty-year-old Joseph Johnson from Harris County was electrocuted for murder. Since then a series of legal maneuverings had stayed the electric switch.

"Do something!" Beto demanded, tossing a sheaf of papers on the young man's desk.

Do what? was Roy's first thought. Helping inmates file a pesky writ of habeas corpus was one thing, but fighting for the life of a killer was another. He vaguely recalled hearing something about McDuff and a teenager—*or was it two, or three?*—several years before.

Roy glanced at his wristwatch. *Mid-morning on Wednesday. Execution is to be Monday. We've got a little less than six days to work this.*

Nervous fingers flipped through the documentation before chilling reality sunk in. Kenneth McDuff was to die at 12:01 a.m. Monday night, one minute after the end of the Labor Day holiday. Suddenly, Saturday, Sunday, and Monday disappeared into the long holiday weekend.

Less than three days to get this done—more like two and a half because everyone will take off early Friday, he thought realizing that his time had been cut in half.

Unexpectedly, the life of a man—albeit, that of a brutal murderer—was riding on Greenwood's young shoulders.

What kind of a monster would kill three teenagers? Green-wood wondered as he settled in for a quick read of the documents that detailed McDuff's criminal history.

The attorneys were stunned to discover that McDuff did not know that his court-appointed attorney, George Cochran, had died. For some unknown reason no one in the family had sought other counsel or told the TDC that their kin no longer had legal counsel.

Greenwood used the telephone to confirm the attorney's death. Roy discovered that before McDuff's attorney had died, he had started a habeas corpus petition that had gone through the trial court. The petition was in the state Court of Criminal appeals when McDuff's attorney died, and shortly thereafter the petition was denied. Cochran had also raised a unique case called *Witherspoon v. Illinois,* which eight months before had challenged the constitutionality of jury selection in Illinois, a procedure followed by most states in the union. If a prospective juror admitted even the slightest aversion to the death penalty, he was excluded from the panel.

"Bang! You have a killer jury that the defense can't do anything about," Roy said, explaining the ruling. "If a prospective juror says, 'Yeah, I could give the death penalty but I don't like it,' then they are excluded."

"This guy was good," Roy said as a plan began to form. He and Harry Walsh did not have time to check the voluminous *Witherspoon v. Illinois* transcript so they decided to gamble on the deceased attorney's having done his homework. The men decided to take the state writ prepared by Cochran and mirror it into a federal writ of habeas corpus.

"What about McDuff?" Harry Walsh asked. "Don't we need his permission?"

"To heck with him," Roy said. "Dr. Beto is our boss and he told us to get a stay of execution until McDuff can get an attorney. This guy doesn't have a lawyer and we can't go around hunting him a lawyer for two days.

" 'Do something!' " Roy said, quoting Beto. "We've got to scramble if we're going to get it done."

Roy spent hours on the telephone as harried law clerks read him the lengthy petition transcripts of state proceedings along with the technical pleadings. The pair did not want to go into court with something new until state avenues had been exhausted. Once there were no state legal avenues available, then the habeas corpus case could be brought into federal court and a stay of execution won.

As Wednesday drew to a close, Greenwood's frantic statewide investigation produced a telephone call from D.K. Calhoun, an attorney who told Greenwood that he might be representing McDuff.

"Just what do you mean you *may* be representing McDuff?" Greenwood asked.

"Well, I'm talking to the family," Calhoun explained.

"Are you going to file something?"

"I don't know."

Greenwood passed the attorney on to Walsh, who passed him on to Dr. Beto, who passed him back to his staff attorneys.

"This guy doesn't know what the hell he's doing," Greenwood told Walsh, holding his hand over the receiver.

"He sure can't guarantee us he's going to do anything," Walsh replied.

"I wish he would," Greenwood said. "Then we could wash our hands of this mess."

The two co-workers fell silent. "It's like he's negotiating with the family," Greenwood finally said, rage growing with each passing second. *I'm not a lawyer,* he thought. *I could just walk away from this.* But abandoning someone—especially a man on death row—was not one of the principles he had come to cherish as a law student.

"Do you see any ethical problems with me going ahead and doing this?" Greenwood asked.

Walsh shrugged, and shook his head no.

"If his attorney was alive he'd be doing this, presenting the same thing," Greenwood muttered, half to himself. "What the hell's the harm? McDuff sure isn't going to gripe about it. And no one else has a right to gripe. Since he was not an attorney, he added, "I'm not under constriction to the state bar."

Greenwood put the telephone back to his ear.

"Look we've got one perfected issue, and that's *Wither-spoon.* I'm not going to start trying to give legal advice to a defendant I've never talked to, who I don't have a right to talk to anyway—because I'm not a lawyer—about going back and trying to perfect new state issues and get a trial judge to reconsider. We're having enough trouble just getting this thing into federal court.

"I'm going to Fort Worth to represent McDuff," he told Calhoun. "You do whatever you have to do."

As he hung up Roy looked at Harry. "That's the last we'll hear of him."

The team worked until the morning hours of Wednesday, grabbed a few hours sleep, and finished the presentation by Thursday afternoon. Federal District Judge Leo Brewster was going dove hunting Friday afternoon. Greenwood was advised by the judge's secretary to be in court first thing Friday morning so as to not miss him.

One chore remained before leaving. He had to have McDuff's signature on the documents. It was a brief meeting.

"You've already been told your lawyer died," Greenwood told McDuff. "I'm going to Fort Worth to try to get a stay of execution. I need you to sign this."

McDuff mumbled something under his breath.

"What did you say?"

The convicted killer leveled cold, emotionless eyes on his potential savior but said nothing else. McDuff signed the documents. The meeting had no special meaning for Roy Greenwood. He was just doing a job. He viewed the McDuff incident as just another foul-up in the criminal system.

So it was that at eight o'clock the next morning a bemused law clerk found Greenwood seated on the steps of the federal building. After driving the two-hundred-fifty miles to Fort Worth and spending the night with a cousin, he filed the petition for a stay of execution, then settled down to await the judge, whom the law clerk expected around nine o'clock that morning.

For the first time in two days the young law student relaxed. His obligations to Dr. Beto and the legal system were about to end. Idly, he watched the law clerk studiously reviewing the inch-thick petition.

Two hours later, the judge was not there.

Still plenty of time, he told himself. *Don't panic.*

Ten o'clock. The time began to drag, each minute longer than the last. Roy was tired, and not a little bit annoyed by the judge. *I made it on time. Why can't he be on time?* he wondered. The waiting exacerbated his weary psyche. He was ready to get it over with. On the long drive to Fort Worth he had had time to consider the McDuff case. The man deserved legal representation; he was not so sure he deserved life. *But that's not my decision,* he thought, relieved of the burden of the law.

The telephone brought him out of his reprieve.

"It's for you," the law clerk said, offering the telephone.

"How . . ." he started before realizing that Harry and Dr. Beto knew where he was.

"Mr. Greenwood, this is Will Gray." The voice on the other end of the telephone was all business. "I'd like to help you."

Will Gray? Roy was surprised. He was talking to the state's acknowledged expert on the death penalty. Gray detested the death penalty and would go on to spend his career representing death row inmates at no charge.

"Did you raise the issue that the death penalty constitutes cruel and unusual punishment?" Gray asked the younger man.

That thought troubled Greenwood, who as a student had just studied constitutional law.

How can you consider the death penalty unconstitutional when the Eighth Amendment allows for it, he thought. *Of course it can't be unconstitutional because the Constitution provides for it.*

"What about . . ." Roy began.

"I wish to raise this issue," Will Gray interrupted the younger man. "And what I am going to do is file a writ of habeas corpus on McDuff's part, raising that question."

Gray went on to ask about *Witherspoon*. When Roy assured him it was the centerpiece of the pleading, Gray insisted that the issue of cruel and unusual punishment be added to Roy's pleading.

"How do you expect to do that?" Roy shot back.

"From what you tell me, Judge Brewster is not there in court, and you've got some time to kill," he said.

"Well," he paused. "Sure, I guess."

Gray suggested that Greenwood go to Judge Byron Matthews' state district court, which was also in Fort Worth.

"You've got thirty minutes to get there. In thirty-five minutes I'll call and dictate a writ of habeas corpus to his law clerk. Then you present it to Judge Matthews, and he will promptly deny it. Then you call me back at this number, collect. I have a runner in Austin who has the very same writ and he will immediately present it to the Texas Court of Criminal Appeals."

Roy Greenwood began to understand that Gray had carefully calculated every move before calling him.

"You take a copy of the writ of habeas corpus that the court reporter in Judge Matthews's office has done for you," Gray continued, "and you type it up and add that as a federal writ. Also, I'm going to pursue another avenue."

Cruel and unusual: This is a bullshit issue. I'm not going to do it, Roy thought, rebelling at the older man's interference. *But you're not a lawyer, yet. This guy is volunteering to do this. Why not!*

True to Will Gray's predictions, Judge Matthews denied the thirty-two-page writ on the spot.

"Okay, it's denied," Greenwood told Gray over the phone.

"Go back to Judge Brewster's office."

Within an hour Will Gray called with the news that the writ delivered by the runner had been denied in the Court of Criminal Appeals.

I'm going to double check that, Roy thought as he telephoned Austin for confirmation.

Quickly he wrote up a hand-written attachment to his federal pleading. It noted the exhaustion of state remedies and conveniently gave a list of the cause numbers. He tucked it into the file.

High noon. Roy had been so busy the past few hours that the time had slipped by. Judge Brewster had not come into the office and it was only three hours until the judge would leave for his hunting trip.

What if he decides not to come in? Greenwood wondered. The fear of failure rankled the lanky young man.

"He's got to come to the office," the law clerk said, trying to assuage his fears. "He's got some of his hunting gear here."

"I don't know what his schedule is," Roy replied. "He may decide he doesn't need that gear; or, he may not want to talk to me at all."

Judge Hughes! Greenwood suddenly thought. The name came from the recesses of his subconscious. Judge Sarah T. Hughes. The famous federal judge who administered the oath of office to Vice President Lyndon Baines Johnson in Air Force One within minutes of President John F. Kennedy's assassination. She was thirty miles away in Dallas. Like any other federal judge in 1970, she had the power to stay an execution in any state in the United States.

"I'm with the inmate attorney's office of the Texas Department of Corrections," Roy told Judge Hughes' secretary when she answered the telephone. "I'm trying to get a stay of execution. I'm in Fort Worth and Judge Brewster is not here. Is Judge Hughes available?"

"Just a moment." A pause.

"This is Judge Hughes," a soft voice floated out of the telephone. He had been introduced briefly to this historical figure at a law function in college but in his wildest daydreams the young man had never anticipated practicing law before her, and without a license at that.

Quickly, he ran through the unique circumstances surrounding the McDuff case. "It's a *Witherspoon* issue judge. It's just been perfected, and we need a stay."

He then pointed out that all state remedies had been exhausted.

"Okay. I'll grant this stay for you," Judge Hughes said. "But you must be here by three o'clock."

Thirty miles. Forty-five minutes to make the drive, another ten to fifteen minutes to find parking, his mind raced. *If the time gets away from me I can always call her and ask her to wait once I'm downtown.*

"I have to catch a plane," she added.

"I'll be there before three," he reassured her, relieved by the promised stay. Hanging up he turned to the law clerk.

"If Judge Brewster isn't here by one-thirty, I'm going to Dallas," he said.

"I can't imagine why he's not already here."

Chips and a soft drink placated him as, once again, he settled in to wait. Within minutes a well-dressed man entered the office and identified himself as D.K. Calhoun, the attorney on the telephone. Obviously he had decided to represent McDuff.

I'm off the hook, Roy thought. He discussed the case with Calhoun until Judge Brewster came roaring into the office shortly after one o'clock. Roy decided that the federal judge's appearance matched his demeanor. He estimated that the massive judge weighed nearly three hundred pounds. Fierce eyes peered out from under bushy eyebrows near the crest of a frame that towered several inches above six feet. Wild hair and a face that Roy could only describe to himself as "mean" completed the presentation.

"What are you doing here?" the judge challenged Calhoun with barely a glance at Roy.

"Well, judge . . ." Calhoun began.

"Shut up!" Judge Brewster growled, pointing a beefy finger at the door. "I want you out of here. Out of this building. Right now!"

"But . . ." Calhoun started again.

"If you're not out of here in thirty seconds I'm having the marshals throw you out of this building," the judged snapped.

"Here," Calhoun said, opening his briefcase to grab a stack of papers and shove them into Roy's hands, before scurrying down the hallway to safety.

Greenwood would later discover that someone—perhaps Calhoun—had earlier approached Judge Brewster on the McDuff case claiming that state remedies had been exhausted when they had not. The judge issued a stay of execution on the tainted information which had kept McDuff from dying the previous April Fool's Day.

"Come in here," Judge Brewster demanded. "Now. How do you know Calhoun?"

"Judge, I don't know anything about him," Roy explained. "I just met him. I've never seen these papers before. All I know is that I'm trying to get a stay of execution for Kenneth McDuff. I'm using *Witherspoon*. I want you to know I'm not a lawyer. Dr. Beto ordered me to get a stay of execution because McDuff's attorney died."

Judge Brewster questioned the young man for more than thirty minutes as Roy kept an eye on the clock. Obviously the judge was not pleased to have to deal with the McDuff case once again. Roy glanced at his watch. It was nearing two o'clock. The judge had to give him an answer. He could not wait much longer. He knew a stay of execution order awaited him in Dallas. He regretted that he had not gone on over to Dallas. It would be done by now.

Precious seconds ticked away. After several more minutes of negotiations the judge signed a show cause order, which called for the attorney general's office to establish the validity of the claim that state remedies had been exhausted as well as review the legal facts of the case. The order gave the attorney general's office twenty days to complete the work, but it did not stop McDuff's pending execution.

"Okay, judge, here's the motion and the prepared order for the stay of execution," Roy said, sliding the papers across the glass-topped desk.

Immediately Judge Brewster put a finger on the papers, deftly turned them around, and slid them back.

"I'm not going to sign this," he said quietly.

"Sir?"

"I'm not going to sign this," Judge Brewster repeated in a deadly quiet voice.

"Why? You just gave the attorney general twenty days to answer. You can dissolve the stay order at any time. At least give the attorney general time."

"I'm not going to sign it. This guy has had habeas corpus proceedings up here before," the judge answered.

Roy paused, sizing up the situation. *He believes that McDuff ought to die.* The thought came as no surprise considering the brutal triple murder occurred on the judge's home turf. It was the same cold reception he had received in state court from Judge Matthews, who had been the presiding judge at McDuff's trial. *He's personalizing this case.* Roy had read the case documents. He knew the brutality of the murders. *That's not my personal concern. The law has to be served.* He made a decision that would have the rippling effect of a rock tossed into a placid pond, the repercussions eventually affecting the lives of nearly a dozen families.

"I don't need this," Greenwood said. Judge Brewster looked up, startled, as Roy began to sweep the documents off his desk; originals, new pleadings, anything in front of the judge. He stuffed his briefcase, clicked it closed, and rose to leave.

"Where you going?"

"I have to get to Dallas. Judge Sarah T. Hughes has already told me that she would grant this stay, and I've got to be there by three o'clock," he said. "I'll probably kill myself driving too fast to get there in less than an hour, but I'm gonna try."

Roy Greenwood wheeled to leave.

"Wait a minute!" the judge barked, motioning to the chair when Roy turned back. "Sit down." This time it was more of a request than an order.

The young man cringed inwardly. He had been impressed by the way Judge Brewster dispatched Calhoun. Now it was his turn. He had never dealt with a federal judge but he did not doubt that Judge Brewster could do anything he wanted to do. Roy Greenwood anticipated federal marshals bursting through the door any minute to whisk him into custody. Mentally, he was already composing the plaintive phone call he would place to Dr. Beto from the county jail.

Judge Brewster smiled and patiently asked, "Now tell me once again what you are?

"You said you were not an attorney," he added before Roy could answer.

"I am an employee of the Texas Department of Corrections, a member of Dr. Beto's staff," Roy recited patiently. "Dr. Beto told me to bring this stuff up here. Dr. Beto said that if you want to call him, then call him." He quoted the telephone number, then added, "They'll put you straight through to him because he's expecting the phone call when I get this stay."

"Why isn't your name on these papers as a lawyer?" the judge countered.

"Judge, I thought I told you this," Roy answered, checking his watch as fear gave way to urgency. "I am not licensed to practice law—yet. I am just a law clerk right now awaiting the results of my bar exam, and I don't have time for all these questions."

The two stared at each other for long seconds.

"All right, I'll sign the stuff," Judge Brewster said, quietly. Within minutes the paperwork was done. The stay of execution order was being sent by teletype to Dr. Beto as Roy called Judge Hughes.

"I was wondering what happened to you," she said.

Greenwood was unable to get through to Will Gray but left word with his secretary.

An emotionally drained Roy Greenwood staggered out of the courthouse, went straight to the nearest bar, and celebrated.

He telephoned Dr. Beto upon returning to Huntsville Saturday night. The administrator wanted to know everything that happened, exactly as it happened.

"Good job," he acknowledged. "By the way. We received a second stay of execution about eight o'clock Friday night that was signed by Justice Hugo Black."

So that's what Will Gray meant by another avenue, Roy thought. *The United States Supreme Court.*

Greenwood whistled when he hung up the telephone.

"Two stays of execution in the same day," he marveled aloud, shaking his head in amazement. "That man has phenomenal luck."

Later, he would learn that Will Gray had not received his telephone message that the stay had been ordered, so the older attorney had contacted Justice Black at his Maryland home because the Supreme Court justice, too, was leaving on a three-day holiday.

Four days after Roy Greenwood won the dramatic stay of execution, prison business caused him to place a telephone call to Texas Supreme Court Chief Justice Robert Calvert.

"Congratulations," the judge told the law clerk a week before the list was posted. "You've passed the bar exam."

Roy Greenwood was licensed to practice law on September 18, 1970, almost three weeks after he helped keep Kenneth McDuff from dying in the electric chair.

SEVEN

This time it was truly an indefinite stay of execution for the convicted killer. The mood of the country was tolerance, and after four tries, the State of Texas seemed to run out of resolve for, or interest, in McDuff's execution. The attitude seemed to be that Kenneth McDuff was safely tucked behind bars; why worry with him?

While it has been generally accepted that McDuff spent six years on death row, this was not the case. He spent two years in the Tarrant County Jail safely awaiting the result of the appeal of his murder conviction to the Texas Court of Criminal Appeal. Technically he was sentenced to die, but no date had been set and he was in a county jail. Once that court ruled that there had been no error, McDuff was moved to the Texas Department of Corrections in October 1968, where he was put on Death Row and lived through the four execution dates in less than two years.

However, two years after Greenwood's work, the Supreme Court did rule that the death penalty was cruel and unusual punishment, a ruling that ultimately commuted the death sentence of one hundred twenty-seven death row inmates to "life" terms. They would be eligible for parole after serving twenty years, according to an Associated Press dispatch.

With a stroke of the pen, McDuff's death sentence was reduced to life imprisonment on September 18, 1972, and with it came the right to eventually apply for parole.

* * *

Roy Greenwood studied the story in the morning Austin American Statesman. On June 27, 1972, the U.S. Supreme Court had ruled that the death penalty was cruel and unusual punishment in a landmark case that would come to be known as *Furman v. Georgia*. It had been a split decision, five to four. Death penalty cases were to be commuted to life sentences in all fifty states.

"I guess it wasn't a bullshit issue," Greenwood said to no one in particular.

Since the precedent-setting case came out of Georgia, he was relatively sure that it had nothing to do with his pleadings of cruel and unusual punishment on behalf of Kenneth McDuff.

Although, he remembered, *Supreme Court Justice Hugo Black had been involved in that case.*

Former Tarrant County Assistant District Attorney Charles Butts was distraught when he heard the news about *Furman v. Georgia.* The memory of the pure savagery of the three deaths in 1966 overwhelmed him with rage as he recalled the tragic days following the murders. A young McDuff had sat in the witness stand, ice cold, deadpan. He remembered McDuff's deadly eyes, which held no emotion. Several times during the trial in Fort Worth he felt as if McDuff stared straight through him. "There was no sense of remorse," Butts told his colleagues during the trial. "I can tell, because he has dead eyes."

Butts had tried many cases since McDuff, but he still rated it as the worst crime he had ever seen. And now, McDuff's sentence would be commuted to life. It hardly seemed fitting.

"It was the most heartless case I ever prosecuted," Charles Butts says in later years. "My personal impression was that McDuff was a heartless, cold-blooded, methodical killer."

It was almost as if McDuff did not exist during those death row years when he wore Execution Number 485, which meant that he was the 485th person sentenced to die on death row since the state legislature outlawed execution by hanging the summer of 1923. Prior to this reform law, convicted capital offenders were executed by public hanging in the county of the offense, and under the supervision of the sheriff. By design, the death penalty was resurrected on February 8, 1924, with the execution of Charles Reynolds by electrocution, the new method authorized by the state legislature. The twenty-seven-year-old Red River County man had been convicted of murder. His execution was followed within minutes by the deaths of three other men; a fourth was executed several hours later for a total of five executions in one day. Since then, death row inmates have been issued numbers. Ironically, Reynolds was the first to die that day but he had been issued Execution Number 5. Mark Matthews, a Tyler County man, had been given Execution Number One, and was the fourth to die by electrocution that day in the Roaring Twenties.

During his years in the prison population McDuff rose in the ranks to become boss of his tier of cells in maximum security with his own punk, or cellmate, who provided whatever drugs or sex the killer demanded. He took correspondence courses to impress prison authorities, and although not a model prisoner, McDuff knew how to teeter on the edge of acceptability. He would never give the establishment reason for much retribution but he never submitted totally to the system.

The Supreme Court would eventually reinstate the death penalty in 1976, four years later, but by then McDuff was safely serving his commuted life sentence. There seemed to be little effort to make him pay the extreme penalty for the lives of Edna Louise Sullivan and Marcus Dunnam, two deaths still demanding justice. With the Brand sentence commuted to life, he could have been tried for the murder of either of the other victims. Perhaps authorities believed that McDuff would never be paroled.

McDuff's prison life really began the day his death sentence was commuted. Until September 18, 1972, Kenneth McDuff was a "dead man walking," the term inmates use to refer to convicts sentenced to die. They were dead in everything but the truest sense. Hope was rare. It was a barren existence. There was nothing to live for, no incentive for good behavior, no ability to accrue the accumulated good time that came with good behavior. Nothing would hurry the date of a death row inmate's release, so they were guarded as if they were mad dogs ready to attack at no provocation.

Because his sentence was commuted, McDuff would eventually receive good time credit for his two years in Tarrant County Jail awaiting the results of the appeal, and the four years in the Texas Department of Correction on death row. Suddenly in 1972, the game and the rules had changed. Kenneth McDuff was no longer a "dead man walking." According to Dr. James Grigson, a psychiatrist who specialized in death penalty cases, McDuff now lived for one reason: "He lived to get out of prison and kill small women."

His native cunning told McDuff to play the game, and he tried. By spring 1974, he had enrolled in a college program, followed by another in the summer. He would eventually earn forty-five hours college credit, although a 1990 IQ test would reveal a score of 84, a considerable drop from the 92 he registered in 1968.

The killer made prison trusty, only to lose the privilege in 1976 for false soliciting of money. That same year McDuff received a minor punishment for creating a disturbance and possession of contraband. He became weary of the college classes and dropped them.

By 1977 the McDuff family had hired an attorney, Gary D. Jackson, of the firm of Colvin and Jackson in Dallas. Kenneth would no longer be represented by pro bono lawyers paid by the court.

Jackson was a hard worker and a man with a cause. Jackson was going to prove to the world that McDuff was innocent. Furthermore, he was going to see to it that a movie-of-the-week would tell the tragic story of a man falsely imprisoned.

"Justice for McDuff," a corporation that listed Kenneth as vice president, was established to seek out a movie contract, perhaps even a book on the alleged miscarriage of justice.

But first Jackson had to get his client out of prison. His first step was to write a lengthy petition echoing McDuff's claims that Roy Dale Green committed the crimes. Jackson appeared to be a true believer in his client's innocence.

He arranged for the firm of Leavelle-Hillard & Johnston to administer a polygraph test on September 6, 1977. A polygraph—sometimes called a lie detector—measures physical response to questions by measuring heart beat, pulse, and respiration on the theory that normal involuntary physical functions are affected when a subject lies. For the most part the device is considered an acceptable screening tool for lawmen. The results of a test are not permissible in a court of law because some psychopaths have been known to pass the test while being untruthful. Their understanding of reality is often so distorted that lies become truth.

"You know how to tell he's lying?" goes the old joke among law officers.

"Sure, his mouth's open," is the familiar answer; or "Sure, his lips are moving." Lawmen find a bitter truth hidden within the biting humor.

The polygraph test was given by veteran law enforcement officer Gene Johnston, who had retired in 1974 after nineteen years with the Dallas Police Department. He became a certified polygraph operator in April 1976 after attending a school operated at Texas A&M University.

Johnston designed a series of questions for McDuff to answer yes or no. The first set of questions concerned the murders in 1966.

"Do you actually know, of your own personal knowledge, anyone who caused the death of any of the victims?

"Did you yourself, in any manner, cause the death of any of the victims?

"Did you actually know that any of the victims had been shot before you were arrested?

"Did you yourself shoot any of the victims?"

The second set of questions concerned the attack on Edna Louise Sullivan.

"Did you yourself force the girl to have any sex relations with you?

"Did you have any sex relations with the girl we discussed?

"Do you remember actually being present when any sex relations were had with the girl we discussed?"

McDuff answered no to every question. Johnston carefully noted "no deceptive criteria" by each question.

"It is our conclusive opinion that no deceptive criteria is indicated to the relevant questions in either examination conducted. Therefore, it is our conclusive opinion that the subject has been truthful to these relevant questions," the polygraph examiner deduced in a letter to Jackson which was used in the court pleadings.

Jackson immediately fired off a six-page motion-to-dismiss the charges of rape and the murder of Edna Louise Sullivan in Johnson County using the polygraph as the centerpiece of the document. Furthermore, he requested that the charges be dismissed because his client was denied the right to a speedy trial after the murder and rape indictments were returned on August 23, 1966. Jackson even offered up McDuff for another polygraph test in the document dated September 15, 1977.

District Judge Byron Crosier of the 18th Judicial District did not buy into the polygraph argument which claimed to prove McDuff innocent. On March 8, 1978, he dismissed the cases but "for the following reason only: the defendant has been denied his constitutional right to a speedy trial."

It was a sad day for E.R. and Edna Ruth Hughes. Eleven years after their daughter, Edna Louise Sullivan, had been tortured and murdered they learned that Kenneth McDuff would never have to answer for the death of the vivacious teenage girl he had tossed over a fence like a discarded rag doll.

Yet once again, the man with the massive killer hands had quietly slithered through the delicate fingers of justice.

McDuff's first parole hearing came April 14, 1976. In early March, Parole Board Commissioner Helen Copitka wrote a letter to Tarrant County District Attorney Tim Curry requesting information on McDuff. Curry replied immediately with a detailed description of the triple murders and rape in 1966 before adding:

"We wish to protest parole for this individual as strongly as possible. As you are aware, we seldom protest parole, deferring judgment to your department," Curry concluded. "We wish to make a strong exception to this case."

McDuff was denied parole unanimously by Copitka, Edward Johnson and Paul Mansmann.

The convict needed two out of three votes to be freed. There was never a face-to-face meeting between McDuff and the entity called a "parole board." In most motion pictures, a parole board hearing is a dramatic scene. The criminal is escorted in to meet the parole board as sobbing family members protest his release. Grim-faced lawmen add their support to the protesting family as they stare down the criminal in this emotionally charged moment.

But, in real life in Texas, eighteen people are appointed to the board by the governor of Texas. Only three are required to rule on any one parole, and this is done individually, not collectively. The first person goes over the hopeful's prison file before making a recommendation. It is then passed on to the second board member who either agrees or disagrees with the first recommendation. If both agree that the inmate should be paroled, then the parole process is started. If they disagree, however, a third parole board member must make a ruling to break the tie. Therefore a parole would require the favorable vote of two out of three.

The file should contain a record of the instant offense, which is the reason the inmate is incarcerated. It should also contain letters of protest from the victim's family or law enforcement officials involved in the case. Occasionally a parole board member or an inmate might ask for a personal meeting, but these are rare. In Texas the prisoner usually remains in his cell as the three commissioners study his records.

Edward Johnson cast the first favorable vote for McDuff in 1980.

Gary Jackson pitched a fit in the media, singling out Judge Byron Matthews and Falls County Sheriff Larry Pamplin as "authorities hindering McDuff's parole" that kept the inmate from receiving a second favorable vote which would have freed him.

The next year Helen Copitka believed McDuff was ready for release, but Ruben Torres and Connie Jackson disagreed.

The killer had been one vote away from freedom two years in a row.

In 1982 McDuff asked for a private meeting with a parole commissioner. Instead of seeing the person who voted for him the previous year, McDuff asked to speak to Glenn Heckmann, a relatively new member of the parole board and a man reputed to have the Governor's ear.

"If you can get me out of this pen, I guarantee that ten thousand dollars will be left in the glove compartment of your car," McDuff is quoted in a *Texas Monthly* article as telling Heckmann. "I know you're the governor's man. Word is, I get your vote, I'm out of here. My family's got the money."

Heckmann immediately reported the offer of a bribe. Once again, McDuff was brought to trial for breaking the law. At that time Texas had a three-time loser law. He had been convicted of burglary in 1965 and murder in 1966. A bribery conviction could result in a life imprisonment term under the old habitual felon act. Another life imprisonment term would have pushed McDuff's parole eligibility back to 1992. Instead, McDuff was given enough leeway by the judge to tell his story unencumbered and without the details of his 1966 murder spree. It followed the familiar theme established by his mother: The world—especially law enforcement—was out to get Kenneth McDuff. The jury found him guilty of bribery on July 30, 1982. But, under the penalty phase of the trial the jury misunderstood the legal instructions and instead of giving the killer another term of life in prison—which would have effectively pushed back his parole date—the jury sentenced him to two years in prison, an ineffective penalty since he had that much time already accumulated in good time incentives. In effect McDuff had offered a bribe and gotten away with it.

Good luck? Fate? Special protection by an evil force? Whatever the reason, Kenneth Allen McDuff once again eluded the intent of the law.

His parole was denied unanimously in 1982, 1983, and 1984, perhaps as a testimony to the bribery attempt. But in 1985, only three years after attempting to bribe a parole commissioner, he once again received a favorable vote. Sue Cunningham also voted favorably in 1986 and 1987. It had to be frustrating to be only one vote from freedom for three years in a row.

Kenneth McDuff was introduced through prison bars to a striking young woman, blonde and pinup beautiful. She claimed to be his daughter, the product of rape and attempted murder about two decades before in Marlin. Although family members were skeptical, McDuff never denied Teresa Ann Allen's claim that her teenage mother had been raped, had her throat cut, and been tossed aside by McDuff as carelessly as a used-up beer can.

Teresa said her mother was walking home from a school event when she was attacked. The ravished girl survived but never reported the incident to the police. A child of poverty, she feared the McDuff clan. To her they were wealthy, and with wealth came power. Any claim of rape would be denied.

"She felt like in a small town, you know, they wouldn't

believe her," Teresa would later explain. "[Kenneth] was wild and unruly and his parents had a little bit of money and all that so she was kinda left alone."

The hapless teen married a young sailor when she was seven months pregnant. Teresa was reared knowing only this man as her father until she turned twenty-one. Her mother's revelation turned Teresa's world upside down.

"Everybody thought I was [my father's]. So, all of this has really come as a shock to them. It's like waking up in a nightmare, an old nightmare."

Consumed by curiosity, Teresa badgered her mother until she named McDuff as the rapist/father. Her mother then called the prison system to locate her daughter's biological father. Teresa wrote him a letter. He put her in touch with his sisters.

The rapist seemed content to claim her as his daughter; no proof was demanded, no blood tests performed. McDuff accepted her on blind faith. Addie McDuff was not quite so charitable.

He enjoyed Teresa's visits, often reacting toward her more as a girlfriend rather than a daughter, Teresa would tell lawmen. But with McDuff behind bars the pair seemed to hit it off.

Meanwhile, McDuff walked a thin line between open rebellion and hostility. He was punished for refusing to obey orders in 1985. He was demoted in January 1986 for possession of alcohol and received a minor punishment in each case for refusing or failing to obey an order, possession of unauthorized drugs, and fighting without a weapon.

The same month McDuff learned that the older brother he idolized had been killed. On January 5, Lonnie had died in a fight over a woman or drugs, or both. Kenneth elected to believe his brother had been killed in a drug deal gone bad, according to authorities.

Later that year a frightened inmate approached officials. On March 4, McDuff had demanded that the inmate smuggle drugs, specifically marijuana, to him when he returned from furlough, or suffer the consequences. Fearful for his life, the inmate asked not to be assigned to the same prison unit as McDuff.

In 1987 McDuff was punished for being "out of place." That same year he forfeited 550 days good time for destroying state property. He eventually won it back as he did with all docked good time.

McDuff straightened up and good time rolled in as the TDC allowed forty-five days for every month served. This policy would cut any jail sentence by more than half. Prison officials argue that such incentive helps control inmate conduct.

In January, March, May, and August he received the equivalent of eighty-five days of good time for each month, all in 1989. Although his parole hearing was near, he could not keep from receiving minor punishments for possession of contraband, failure to work, and gambling.

As he patiently worked his way through the system, once again, the federal government seemed to come to the convicted killer's aid. An inmate had filed a federal suit charging that the state prison system was overcrowded. The federal courts had ruled in 1972—the same year the death penalty was nullified—that the state had to either build more prisons or incarcerate fewer prisoners. A succession of governors delayed as long as possible. The state had to either find the money to build more prisons or empty the ones that were then overflowing. Finally, Governor Bill Clements started his second term in office by giving the order in 1987 to begin emptying Texas's terribly overcrowded prisons. The federal ruling stated that Texas could not have more than 94.5 percent occupancy without conflicting with federal law. The generous parole standards were viewed as a delaying tactic to allow the state time to build more prisons.

Soon the system had released those convicted of nonviolent and white collar crimes. The standards were lowered. By 1989 the parole board was scraping the slime off the bottom of the barrel but it still was not enough.

And by then, twenty-three years after the brutal murders, McDuff had faded into anonymity. He was just another number on the hastily scanned parole list.

It appeared that McDuff had struck pay dirt in 1987 on his thirteenth attempt to win parole. Ken Casner and Chris Mealy voted for parole while Neal Pfeiffer voted to deny. McDuff had his two votes! The parole process was started but denied after the board received additional information; lawmen and officers of the court protested. On the second vote composed of a new board—Pfeiffer, Wendell Odom and Henry Keene—all were unanimous opponents.

The next year, Ken Casner would again vote favorably for parole and two administrative reviews would follow, but McDuff's release was denied.

McDuff's fifteenth petition proved to be the charm. The families of the three murder victims were not notified, so no one showed up to protest. Letters of protest from Falls County District Attorney Tom Sehon and District Judge Byron Matthews apparently were not read. Telephone protests from Falls County Sheriff Larry Pamplin apparently went unheeded. These may not have been in McDuff's file since the records of old-time convicts seemed to sometimes disappear.

"You don't have to read *Silence of the Lambs* to know his potential if he was paroled out and set loose in Falls County, or anywhere else, again," Sehon said, underscoring his concern in a television interview.

A report compiled for parole commissioners to consider during the fifteenth parole petition stated in part, "The case reports from the initial report through the seventh parole reviews were not in available file material."

There is a list of thirty-five reasons for denying a parole and in McDuff's case this time, seven significant factors were listed for consideration, included numbers:

2. Criminal behavior pattern.
3. Nature and seriousness of offenses.
6. Multi-offender.

10. Parole violation.
16. Delinquent sex behavior.
21. Use of weapon in current offense.
22. Assaultive in the instant offense or in past offenses.

The employee who worked out the supplemental case summary also pointed out that while McDuff's victims were teenagers, there would be no juveniles residing where he would live.

In an interoffice memorandum Dr. James Granberry, an orthodontist who was chairman of the Texas Parole Board at the time, and a member of the panel chosen to review McDuff's case, disqualified himself from voting because of his life-long friendship with Gary Jackson, McDuff's attorney.

Although Henry Keene voted against parole, McDuff received approval from Cora Mosley and Chris Mealy.

McDuff was on his way to freedom until letters of protest from Tarrant County District Attorney Tim Curry and Brazoria County District Attorney Jim Mapel struck a nerve. These letters arrived sometime between June and September as the three parole commissioners considered McDuff's parole request and voted individually. It was decided to review the approved parole in light of the strongly worded letters.

This time the administrative panel would consist of Chris Mealy, Henry Keene and Dr. Granberry, who had changed his mind about serving on the panel. The trio was charged with reviewing the additional information as well as the entire file going back to McDuff's original incarceration. They could vote only two ways—either to "withdraw parole recommendation" or "to continue parole planning."

Mealy and Granberry voted to continue parole planning. As he did before, Keene cast the dissenting vote, this time to withdraw parole recommendation.

Chris Mealy, the sole parole board member who cast a vote to free McDuff in both sessions, would say later that he was impressed by McDuff's correspondence courses and the fact that in six of the fifteen years McDuff was eligible for parole the inmate had received one affirmative vote.

Eight out of every ten convicts up for parole were released in 1989 and Kenneth McDuff was among them as he wormed his way through the legal system, although district attorneys and lawmen howled in protest.

As his parole date neared, McDuff called Teresa to prison, she told officers. He offered to take her to Las Vegas upon his release where he would be her pimp. She declined her father's offer. Disgusted, she moved away but not before alleging in the news media that a $25,000 bribe had been offered to an unidentified parole board member to get McDuff paroled.

On October 11, 1989, twenty-three years and two months after entering prison on a death sentence for murder with malice aforethought, a savage killer walked out of prison on parole.

EIGHT

Falls County Sheriff Larry Pamplin wears a white hat. It isn't one of those drugstore cowboy felts, but a large-brimmed beaver of the type favored by working drovers in the Old West, one that snaps down in front and back to protect face and neck from the blistering Texas sun. Pamplin fits the image of the Texas peace officer: laconic, prickly as a cactus, tough as a bull, swift as a rattler, yet soft as rabbit's fur under a granite exterior.

Angrily Pamplin grabbed the telephone and began punching in numbers. Intense, prickly, his emotions were awash in disbelief; at that moment he was all business.

"Yeah," he said tersely when a secretary answered. "Is Parnell there?"

He waited until his childhood friend, Parnell McNamara now a deputy U.S. marshal in Waco, came on the telephone.

"You're not going to believe what happened, Parnell," Pamplin said immediately, not waiting for a reply. "They've paroled Kenneth McDuff."

There was silence for long seconds. Finally, McNamara asked a simple, troubled question.

"Have they gone crazy?"

Pamplin shook his head.

"I don't know if it'll be next week or next month or next year, but one of these days, dead girls are gonna start turning up, and when that happens, the man you need to look for is Kenneth McDuff," Pamplin said. "It will happen."

"What about your family?" Parnell asked. McDuff had threatened to kill the Pamplin family after his arrest by the late Falls County Sheriff Brady Pamplin, Larry's father.

"I'll keep watch on them," Sheriff Pamplin said. As a young man near McDuff's age, he had helped his father arrest the accused killer in 1966 in the blazing gun battle that nearly destroyed the criminal's automobile.

"We'll all keep watch on McDuff," Parnell assured his friend. All included Mike McNamara, Parnell's younger brother by a year, also a deputy U.S. marshal.

The men hung up the telephone to contemplate the situation. A sadistic killer was on the loose, someone, both law officers agreed, who should have died for his sins. Obviously the system had failed, miserably.

And if Sheriff Larry Pamplin was right, very soon that failure would be underscored by the grisly deaths and disappearances of young women.

Three days after McDuff's parole on October 11, 1989, the body of diminutive Sarafia Parker, a twenty-nine-year-old suspected prostitute, was found in a field of weeds in Temple, Texas, the city to which McDuff had been paroled. She had been beaten and strangled.

Rhonda Chamberlain Chandler and her mother, Betty Chamberlain, were on their way home from a happy-go-lucky weekend of bingo in Choctaw, Oklahoma, when memories of her dead friend, Edna Louise Sullivan, overwhelmed her without apparent reason. She pulled to the side of the road and began weeping. Within the next few days she would discover that McDuff had been released from prison and she would relive the old anxieties all over again.

"It just broke my heart."

Had her subconscious picked up on a newscast during her

Oklahoma trip? Perhaps. But her anxiety was real that night, as real as it has always been when a pop song—Louise and Robert considered "When a Man Loves a Woman" to be their song—or news of another brutal killing or a sweet recollection would send her mind down a torturous memory lane.

For a fleeting moment Rhonda recalled Kenneth McDuff's dead eyes. She wondered if he would come for her now that he was free. She dismissed the possibility as remote, but it lingered in her subconscious.

It would have startled her to discover that the Brand family had the same fears with the killer on the loose.

In Central Texas, Tommy Sammon, who had whipped McDuff in the eighth grade, heard the news and worried about the safety of his family.

Charles Butts, whose prosecution got McDuff his first death sentence, shook his head in amazement.

"A person of that bent should not have been paroled," he said.

Meanwhile the citizens of Rosebud locked their windows and doors.

"I had a loaded gun at every door," a man would say in a television interview.

Sheriff Pamplin simply evaluated the situation: "The system has totally broke down."

Kenneth McDuff was welcomed home with a big party and a brand new Mustang. Several months later, in early December he would meet with producers to discuss a movie based on his life. The parole certainly strengthened interest in a movie. It was a dream scenario—convicted but innocent man paroled after two decades in prison.

McDuff was paroled to live with his sister, Louise Parker, in Milam County, but by January 1990 he had moved in with his parents without informing parole officers.

Later that month, McDuff was removed from sex offender supervision and placed on intensive supervision.

"McDuff gets upset upon being referred to as a sex offender," parole officer David Darwin explained in a confidential report that was revealed on WFAA-TV by reporter Robert Riggs. "Seems that could be very dangerous or explosive if the wrong button is pushed."

July proved a fateful month for McDuff. On July 10, he applied for, and received, food stamps. A day later the quarrelsome convict was seated on a curb in downtown Rosebud talking to musician Robert McBee during a break in a rock band's practice session. Sixteen-year-old Lafarrel Holman was walking by when McDuff challenged him.

"I said, 'What's up?' as I walked by and this man said, 'Hey, nigger, do you like white people?' and I said no because I was [offended] by the way he said, 'Hey, nigger,' " the high school student told police. "He got up and got in my face, wanted to fight me. Then he walked over to his car, gray Ford Mustang, and got a large pocketknife out of his door pocket.

"He opened the large knife and started at me. I was backing between the building. I said, 'Man, what are you going to do?' He said 'I will kill you. I will kill you, nigger.' So I picked up a brick and kept backing up. Some of my friends came around the corner and the white man turned around and left. This man was about six foot, one inch and had on a cowboy hat."

Several other teenagers, McBee, and a police officer who saw the incident from an intersection where he was working radar, all verified the story. The teens added that McDuff, in a fit of temper, threatened to fight them all.

McBee described the knife as brass with a wooden handle and six inches long when closed. McBee said he locked McDuff out of the building where the band was rehearsing. He told him to leave and not return to hear the rest of the band's practice session. But when the musician returned from the police station that night, McDuff was back, harassing band members.

"He said he could and would go anywhere he wanted any-time he wanted," McBee would add to the police report.

It had not been difficult for McDuff to drop into his old ways, but he had forgotten many of the back roads he had travelled. He totaled his Mustang five days later on July 16 when he approached a T-intersection and failed to negotiate the turn. Two days after that he was taken into custody for parole violation and terrorist threat. By that evening he was in the Bell County jail. He had been free nine months and ten days.

A parole revocation hearing was held September 11. The hearing officer, as well as the field officer, recommended revo-cation. A parole analyst in Austin concurred. McDuff's parole was revoked.

He was returned to prison on October 11, 1990, for the terrorist threat, exactly one year to the date after he had been paroled.

Amazingly, McDuff did not try to alibi his way out of the terrorist threat charge. A case history notation states "Of these revocation allegations he admits such to be true and correct."

The final sentence gives a chilling insight into the man. What was the rationale of his return to prison?

"It just happened."

On October 16, five days after McDuff's return to prison, a startling interoffice memorandum was issued by William H. Brooks, deputy division director of the Texas Department of Criminal Justice, Pardons and Paroles Division. It was later fished out of a trash bin behind the TDCJ in Austin. Two of the points had been underlined.

Addressed to Bob Owens, division director, the memo ad-dresses the subject of "Releasee population and release pro-jections."

Please refer to your memo on scheduled releases dated October 12, 1990.

There were two primary areas of concern that you cited in the above noted memo. I will attempt to clarify each issue separately.

I. Utilization of the Institutional Division percentage capacity in calculating the number of releases per day.

Staff is not withholding releases based on the percentage capacity of prison capacity. Staff is under standing orders to issue certificates on every inmate that is eligible.

The number of certificates produced and their projected eligibility is monitored daily when the 150 per day quota is consistently being met. If the 150 per day is not being met, [certificates] produced is monitored a minimum of twice a day and hourly if necessary. Once the certificate issuance is authorized, the certificates are printed in Huntsville. Certificates are printed and delivered to the Institutional Division twice a day, the Institutional Division recalculates parole eligibility and either prepares the inmate for release or returns the certificate to Joe Moore with the recalculated release date noted. Certificates for inmates in disciplinary status, administrative segregation or with a detainer for an offense committed within the institution are also returned, regardless of legal eligibility. Mr. Moore screens the returned certificates and decides whether to suspend release or return the certificate to the ID with a memorandum to release despite the detainer, disciplinary or segregation status. If the inmate is not parole eligible or ready for mandatory release, the certificate is held for approximately two weeks prior to the projected eligibility, then returned to the Institutional Division to be prepared for release. Certificates are also occasionally held because additional information such as additional commitments or a protest has been received.

Therefore, it can be difficult, on any given day, to predict how many certificates will be rejected by the ID or to predict the actual day the inmate will be released once the certificate is issued.

Thus, the safest course of action is to release everyone eligible. However, if the quota starts to continue to show a deficit, we start to release TP 2's inmates in disciplinary status, etc. I do not consider this 'holding back' cases.

Also, according to Mr. Claymon [a parole analyst], he did have a conversation with Dr. Granberry earlier in the week in which he mentioned he was issuing certificates on inmates in disciplinary status. Mr. Claymon also informed him that the ID capacity increase would end on Monday, October 15, 1990 and that additional inmates would be accepted to raise the percent of capacity to about 94.4%. He also mentioned that on October 2, 1990, the population dropped to 93.98% even though we had not released 150 per day for almost two weeks. (This information is available to everyone on the Case flow Daily Report distribution, which includes all Board offices.) It is unknown how Dr. Granberry interpreted this information, but according to Mr. Claymon he did not say the quota was not met because any releases were being held or that the percent of prison population had anything to do with the number of releases needed.

II. A report with recommendations to ensure the release of 150 inmates per day.

You verbally asked me for the above recommendations on Wednesday, October 10, 1990. I met with Dr.

Martinez [a parole analyst] on Thursday, October 11, 1990 to discuss your request. We formulated five recommendations that we both considered feasible. In that you had already asked him to submit a report on parole released, I asked him to incorporate the recommendations into that report. Dr. Martinez informed me you would receive the report on Monday, October 15, 1990. *Since you did not give me a due date,* I assumed that October 15th was a reasonable time frame.

What may have confused this issue is that on October 11, 1990, you also asked me for a statistical report to show that staff was providing the Parole Board with a sufficient number of cases to achieve their quotas. That report was provided to you on Friday, October 12, 1990. Perhaps you thought that was the only report you were going to receive.

Also, I had informed you verbally on several occasions prior to October 15, that increasing the Fl rate was the only real solution to this problem.

Regardless, I do not understand why this has become a major issue. Although, we may not release 150 cases every single day, *we do achieve it, and occasionally exceed it,* on a monthly basis. (Please refer to the attached memo from James McGaffigan dated October 16, 1990).

I believe I mentioned to you that we have temporary computer break downs, etc. that prevent us from consistently reaching that daily rate. However, we usually make it upon the weekly average. Sometimes, we do not achieve our goal until the end of the month. But we achieve it and that should matter.

Again, permit me to reaffirm the critical elements of the October 12, 1990 report submitted by Dr. Martinez which must be accomplished to maintain our monthly averages:

1. Subsequent review cases must be considered for parole every six months. The approval rate for these cases must be a minimum of 72%.

2. A minimum of 2800 initial review cases must be considered by the Board every month. The approval rate for these cases must be a minimum of 83%.

3. The Board needs to consider a minimum of 980 cases a week for a 750 FI rate.

4. Anytime the parole approval rate drops below the percentages indicated above, or the case considerations do not reach the level stated above, the division will not achieve our release goals.

WHB
cc: Ben Gallant, TDCJ Board
    James Lynaugh, Executive Director

The mind-set in 1990 was to release as many inmates as possible to keep within the federal guidelines. There seemed to be little concern about the quality of releasees; a goal had to be met with little concern for public safety. Seven hundred and fifty inmates had to be released each week; 1,500 every two weeks; 2,250 every three weeks; 3,000 a month. The monthly figure is almost twice the population—1,638—of McDuff's hometown of Rosebud.

Andy Kahan, a former parole hearing officer, is now the Mayor's Crime Victim Director for the City of Houston and an expert on Texas' parole system. Appointed by Mayor Bob Lanier as a crime victim's advocate, he holds the only such post in a major city in America. In a special report concerning parole, he wrote:

"In a three year comparison of 1987 through 1990 one can

easily see the progression of inmates paroled. The parole percentage rate for the fiscal year 1988 was 43%. In 1989 the percentage jumped to 56% and during the boom year 1990 parole approval rates leaped to 79%."

Few people understand the system better than Kahan, who watched helplessly as hardened criminals were released onto the streets.

Kenneth McDuff's return to prison was a bureaucratic nuisance. The parole board and the TDCJ were attempting to keep people out of prison, not put them in. It stands to reason that if the prison capacity was to hover at 94.4 percent capacity, then the prison system would have to continue to parole one-hundred-fifty inmates a day to offset the one-hundred-fifty a day going into the prison system.

There was a trickle-down effect onto the county jail system. As criminals were convicted, the local county jails were often forced to keep them rather than send them on to the already overcrowded prison system, which was accepting only one-hundred-fifty prisoners a day to stay within federal guidelines.

McDuff's return undoubtedly bumped one of the one-hundred-fifty prisoners stuffed into already crowded county jails, possibly an inmate who had been waiting months for his turn in the big house.

McDuff had added to the problem of the overburdened county jails. Although he had been out of prison a year, he had been free only nine months and ten days before he was arrested for the terrorist threat in July 1990. The rest of the time he had been in a county jail. At this point he was seen more as an aggravation to the system rather than a threat to society.

District Attorney Tom Sehon dropped the terrorist threat charges against McDuff because the witnesses and victim were unwilling to testify. Before McDuff was even returned to the Texas Department of Criminal Justice, and almost as if penning a prophecy, Sehon warned in a letter dated August 3, 1990:

"The above is probably the most extraordinarily violent criminal ever to set foot in Falls County, Texas. Currently, he is being detained on a blue warrant because of an attempt to attack a young boy with a knife in the City of Rosebud, Texas.

"McDuff has made other threats against persons in Falls County. He has both the capability and the will to carry out those threats.

"Should McDuff ever be restored to parole status, and I hope that he is not, I respectfully request that a parole condition prohibit McDuff from ever entering Falls County, Texas, for any reason whatsoever."

Sehon received a reply dated August 15, 1990.

"Your letter of August 3, 1990, has been received. Please allow this to serve as a response.

"Your concerns are acknowledged. Your letter will be placed in the subject's permanent file."

The letter was signed by Jim Fitzgerald, analyst for the Communications Unit, written on behalf of Ronald L. Valladares, director, Hearing Section.

What happened next is still being debated in Texas.

A few weeks after McDuff reentered the TDC, his attorney submitted a motion to reopen McDuff's hearing. He also wrote a letter to his childhood friend, Dr. Granberry. It is dated October 31.

"Kenneth McDuff's 'Releasee's Motion to Reopen Hearing' requesting that a parole revocation be set aside was dispatched to the board on 23 October 1990. The revocation resulted from an incident at a rock concert which was nothing more than bad manners on the part of both McDuff and the longhaired hippie complainant. Neither the prison system, the parole system, McDuff nor the complainant is benefitted by sending McDuff back to the prison population.

"McDuff was unable to find steady work in the Temple area. We found a job for him in Denton County with a client of ours who also found him a home to share with another man. However, the parole officer would not approve McDuff's relocation. If the Board sees fit to re-examine the revocation proceeding and to set it aside, my suggestion is that the supervisory staff be instructed to give McDuff some latitude to relocate in pursuit of a job.

"Please share these facts with the remainder of the Board and restore Kenneth McDuff to parole status."

Briefly, the petition noted that the investigating officer, the complainant and two witnesses failed to show up for the revocation hearing. It also states that the only evidence produced was hearsay. There was no evidence that Lafarrel Holman was in imminent bodily harm.

"Wherefore, for reasons shown, Kenneth Allen McDuff requests that this Board reopen his hearing and, after which, continue supervision of Kenneth Allen McDuff in a parole status," the petition concluded.

McDuff's attorney noted that the terrorist charges had been dropped by the Falls County district attorney.

All Jackson had asked is that the hearing be reopened for further consideration.

McDuff had already admitted during the previous parole revocation hearing that he had brandished a knife, and threatened Lafarrel Holman with violent harm.

That admission alone breaks Parole Rule No. 5 on the standard certificate signed by McDuff upon his parole. Rule No. 5 states, "I shall not own, possess, use, sell, nor have under my control any firearm, prohibited weapon or illegal weapon. . . . nor will I unlawfully carry any weapon nor use, attempt or threaten to use any tool, implement or object to cause or threaten to cause any bodily injury."

But there would be no new hearing. Instead a parole subordinate identified as Bettie Wells, the staff counsel, made a bureaucratic decision to release McDuff. She had the sole responsibility for reinstatements under these conditions. There would be no review by parole board commissioners, nor would the hearing be reopened, nor would any parole board commissioner read Sehon's strongly worded protest.

"The Releasee," Wells wrote, "Kenneth A. McDuff, TDCJ# 227123, was released from the Texas Department of Criminal Justice Institutional Division on October 11, 1989, with a scheduled discharge date of Life and an instant offense of Murder with Malice and Bribery. The Releasee administrative release status was revoked based on the following violations(s): Rule #2(n) Terroristic Threats.

"The Releasee's attorney is requesting that his parole be reinstated because the violation arose from an incident where both parties made threats against each other.

"Recommendation: Reinstate administrative release status."

McDuff was paroled to his parents home on December 18, 1990.

McDuff worked briefly in the Dallas area as a forklift operator before he moved back to Temple to live with his parents. He continued to receive food stamps.

McDuff's movie deal moved a step closer to reality in January 1991. Gloria Jackson, Gary's wife and law partner, wrote Kenneth that a movie deal was nearing with United Screenwriters Production Partners in Dallas. She asked Kenneth to make himself available for a stockholder meeting of Justice for McDuff, Inc., between February 4 and 18.

In a separate letter, Jackson wrote out the details of the proposed venture with United Screenwriters, then she went on to warn McDuff about moving his residence without permission from the parole board. As if writing a recent high school graduate, Gloria outlined plans for McDuff to live at home with his parents while commuting to school. She encouraged him to learn a trade to promote his long-range objectives.

She warned, however, that McDuff faced immense obstacles

because of his age and imprisonment, which kept him out of society. Gloria expressed her husband's confidence in McDuff and cited the convict's native cunning and determination as tools other inmates might lack.

His biggest asset, Jackson wrote, was his family and their support for more than twenty years. She sympathized with the forty-three-year-old man by noting that she was nearly his age when she entered college.

Enclosed was a letter that brought him up-to-date on the movie project with the wry note that it might be finished when he completed his schooling.

By March McDuff was enrolled in Texas State Technical College (TSTC) in Waco. He decided to live in the dormitory—a man in his forties living the life of a young college student. He applied for, and received, an eight hundred dollar student loan.

In May McDuff took a job at Quik Pak No. 8, a convenience store on New Road near TSTC and Interstate 35. The application form asked if he had ever been convicted of a felony. He checked the box marked "No." According to the application McDuff was quite a student. He said that he attended Alvin Junior College for one year and had forty-four college credits.

He worked the graveyard shift beginning May 9, but in less than a month the responsibility was more than he could bear. A group of friends decided to go to the lake one summer afternoon and McDuff walked off the job to join his beer-drinking buddies. He was terminated on June 2, 1991, for failure to return to work when scheduled. It was noted that he was not eligible for rehire.

The next month petite twenty-one-year-old Melissa Ann Northrup would sign up with Quik Pak No. 8. Her first day was July 22, 1991. She had been introduced to McDuff by her husband, Aaron, who had trained him for the Quik Pak job. The couple had two children.

Kenneth McDuff also discovered The Cut, Waco's bawdy

underbelly. He had finally arrived in an area that would tolerate his violent mood swings and cultivate his drug habit, as he spewed forth a spate of violence that would erupt in a savage orgy of brutality, rape, and murder. International fame for Kenneth McDuff was only eight months away.

About that time Falls County Sheriff Larry Pamplin made another telephone call to his childhood buddies.

"McDuff has enrolled at TSTC," he told Mike.

"You've got to be kidding."

"Wish I was," was Larry's laconic reply.

"He's right here?" Mike was incredulous. "He's right here? Next to someone's daughter?"

"Doesn't make any sense, does it?" Larry asked. He did not have to point out that McDuff was on the government dole as a student.

"It sure doesn't make sense."

The McNamaras and Pamplin had been friends as long as they could remember, and all three had a particular interest in the criminal. As was Larry, the McNamaras were second generation lawmen. Their father, the late Deputy U.S. Marshal T. P. McNamara of Waco, was a well-known federal law officer in Central Texas who wore a brace of pearl-handled pistols. His sons had followed in his footsteps, working for the U.S. Marshal's office for more than two decades. The McNamara boys were about McDuff's age, teenagers, when the criminal was brought to justice. It was then that they started working for the U.S. Marshal's office as special deputies.

Sheriff Larry Pamplin remembers McDuff's evil demeanor in the Falls County jail. He even served the killer a few meals. As a young boy, Larry Pamplin was reared in housing quarters in the back of the Falls County sheriff's office and jail. It was not uncommon for lawmen to house their families in such special living quarters at the county facility.

Larry's news that day had disturbed Mike. He immediately notified the campus police about McDuff.

"This is like having Jack the Ripper sitting next to you," Mike warned the campus police.

Thanks to Pamplin's sharp eye and law enforcement connections, the three men were only a few jumps behind McDuff as he meandered across the countryside. County boundaries kept Sheriff Pamplin at bay, and the McNamaras could do nothing until McDuff broke a federal law. They knew he would eventually; they just had to keep watch and wait.

Meanwhile, the destiny of a handful of people would be irrevocably affected by life on The Cut and the parole of Kenneth Allen McDuff.

NINE

She was one of the most beautiful women Frank Pounds had ever seen. Whip slender, with a mass of hair colored somewhere between cornflower blonde and golden hue, it framed her pale face with a soft honey glow. Dancing along the side of the highway, her head filled with some unheard music, she was a study in perpetual motion. As he drove past her, the tiny woman flicked her thumb.

Hitchhiking? Frank could not keep his foot off the automobile brake. *Or something else.*

Maybe it was her wistful face, or the slight slouch of the shoulders, perhaps a hint of despair hidden by her incredible animation; whatever, he was instantly drawn to this slender girl as he pulled to the side of the road. Much later, he would ponder on that split second of decision and wonder why he stopped, but Frank would never come to a satisfactory conclusion. He watched her trotting toward the car. *A hundred pounds, soaking wet,* he thought, estimating her weight. There was no hint that at that moment his life would take a bizarre twist that would plunge this gentle academician into a world he had only read about.

Earlier that year, Frank Pounds had separated from his wife. He moved to Las Vegas where he lived off modest success at the craps tables. Tiring of that life after several months, he had moved to Waco to live with his mother—at least that was the reason he told his mother he was moving in with her. It was his first day in town; maybe he was a little bored after the bright lights in Las Vegas.

"Where ya goin'?" Frank asked as the young woman crawled into the truck. He noticed that her tight dress hiked seductively along her thighs. He was glad that he had decided to go get a newspaper on this bright May afternoon.

"The Cut," she grinned. "It's not far from here. I live there."

"The Cut?"

"Yeah," she said, nodding her head rapidly. "That's over off the Old Dallas Highway."

When Frank gave her a blank look she started giving instructions, nodding her head up the road, jabbing the air with a finger. "Take the first right, then go three blocks . . ."

"All right," he chuckled. "You can tell me as I drive. What's The Cut?"

"You're new, ain't ya?"

"Yeah. I was in Vegas for awhile."

She nodded. "I'm Regenia."

"Well, Regenia, it's nice to meet you," Frank said holding his right hand out across the seat.

"Me, too," she said, firmly taking his hand. Frank noticed her hand was warm. *Fever?* he wondered. She looked a little flush, but not feverish. She let her hand linger in his, slightly moist, soft; just long enough to be confusing.

An awkward pause followed. He could still feel the tingle of her touch. *Don't be a school boy. You're just giving her a ride.*

"What's your name?" she asked.

"I'm sorry. I'm Frank. Frank Pounds."

"I've always wanted to go to Vegas."

"There's nothing there you can't get right here," he said before shaking his head. "Well," he added, "maybe you can gamble a little easier."

"All those bright lights," she sighed. "And free booze. It sounds like paradise."

"Maybe," he said. "But it can surprise you."

"How?"

When he paused to consider how to answer, she jumped to a conclusion. "You didn't get in trouble with nobody? Somebody ain't after you?"

Frank grinned and shook his head. This girl had an imagination.

What actually drove him from Las Vegas was a unique mixture of superstition and bad luck. Surprisingly, he found himself telling this total stranger about the night several weeks before when he decided to pick the daily double in a horse race and win a large amount of money.

"I knew I could do it," he explained. "So I got racing forms, results, tout sheets, anything I could find about this one race."

By morning he had several lists of figures scrawled across the coffee-stained hotel stationary where he was living. It came down to two horses, Five and One; but which order? One would start strong and fade in the backstretch, according to his figures, and Five would run behind the pack and close strong.

"I knew that Number Five would not only come from behind that day, but would pass Number One in the backstretch. They would finish Five and One," Frank explained.

"Take a left here and get on the bypass. That takes you to The Cut," she instructed, before adding, "So, what happened?"

Bleary-eyed from the all-night session, Frank took a shower, dressed and went to the track where he ate breakfast with plenty of time to place his bet. Roughly ten minutes before the race started, Frank purchased his ticket with $168, clearly telling the clerk his picks, then put the ticket in his shirt pocket.

It was as thrilling a race as he had seen. Horse Number One shot into the lead. True to form, Number Five trailed the pack. Frank kept waiting for him to make his move.

"I didn't think he was ever going to come on," he told his spellbound listener. "Finally he did make his move."

He knew he had her when he paused and she impatiently waved her hands in the air, beckoning his reply. He noticed a tattoo on her left hand.

"And . . . ?"

"And he won," he said triumphantly, hearing a sigh of relief from his appreciative audience. "But I didn't," he quickly added. "When I looked at the tickets I had Six and One."

"But . . ." she began.

"I don't know what happened. I don't know if the teller made a mistake, or if I told her Six and One," he said, now able to chuckle about it. "That little mistake cost me sixteen thousand dollars."

"Sixteen thousand dollars!" she repeated.

"Yeah, so I decided then and there it was a sign for me to get out of Vegas," he said. "And I did. That's why I'm here."

"Lucky me," Regenia teased.

"No. Lucky me," Frank replied, surprised that he was more serious than not. "What's that on your hand?"

Regenia laughed. "That's a tattoo," she said holding up her left hand. "It says 'RAT!'," she explained.

Frank saw an exclamation mark on her little finger.

"I done it when I was a kid—twelve or something like that," she said. "Me and a girlfriend. That was my nickname back then. The other kids gave it to me."

Frank nodded. They rode in silence.

"My last name is Moore," Regenia said unexpectedly, as if offering a gift. "You gave me your last name when you introduced yourself. Out here, we . . . on The Cut, some things are private. We . . ." she let the thought die.

"This is it," she said, changing the subject.

She directed him off the Old Dallas Highway. A bypass that was once a main thoroughfare, the highway had been mostly abandoned when Interstate 35 was constructed several blocks east. They passed several bars, each a little more seedy than the next, each identified by Regenia by type: "Bikers. Cowboys. Rockers." She directed him to turn right onto Faulkner Lane, a sharp turn—*The Cut,* he surmised—that led back into a modest subdivision. The place was teeming at the turnoff.

More than a dozen women stood along the curbs, mostly black women, with a smattering of Anglos and Hispanics.

A small, unkempt lot with chest-high weeds ran alongside The Cut. Frank would learn that paths led into the interior of the weeds like hallways where prostitutes stomped out small cubicles to ply their trade. In two blocks he was past The Cut and into the neighborhood.

"Where do you live?"

"Back there, in the Sleepy Time Motel, across the street. Want to see my room?" she smiled, inviting.

Frank looked at her. "Sure, why not?"

He was not particularly surprised to learn that she was a prostitute. What surprised him was that he did not care. Somehow she had reached into the aching recess of his heart and rekindled a golden glow that had been missing. It felt good. It felt right.

"How old are you?" he asked as he traversed The Cut, then under the bypass he had just exited to an access road that was home to several seedy motels.

"Twenty-one. Why?"

"I just wanted to know," he said, thinking that at fifty-five, he was old enough to be her father.

The Sleepy Time Motel looked like any other no-tell motel. Rundown from lack of maintenance, it needed holes repaired in a few doors, a coat of paint, and attention to a scraggly patch of grass, green more from weeds than grass. Regenia directed Frank around to the back. She explained that otherwise they would have to walk through the building to reach the stairs to the second floor where her room was located.

"No sense paradin' through there when you can go right up," she said.

Like its outward appearance, the room was not much. A small table, a pair of chairs, a shabby chest of drawers missing one of the drawers, and a double bed.

Regenia was ready to make her money but Frank was strangely reluctant.

"Let's talk," he said.

"Talk costs money," she answered, now the professional.

"How much?"

"Thir . . . ah, twenty dollars," she said.

Frank pulled out his wallet and produced two ten dollar bills. He laid them on the table. Regenia started toward them.

"We talk first," he said.

" 'Bout what?"

"You."

"Me?" Surprised. Regenia studied this slender, slightly built black man who spoke in a high-pitched voice. He was not her usual john. She was used to being considered merchandise more than a human being with emotions to explore. Except for her mother, it had been years, since before her divorce, that anyone had really expressed interest in her on a personal level. She shrugged. Some johns just liked to talk.

"There ain't much to tell. Married too young, couple of kids. Divorced," she said. Frank sat quietly, listening. "My husband beat me. Ran around. I left but there wasn't anything I could do to make a living."

Frank could not help but wonder if her obvious drug addiction began before or after she entered prostitution.

"I didn't want to live with my mother. Me and my cousin, we just sort of drifted over here." She spoke rapidly, punctuating each revelation with hand movements. It had been a gradual descent for the two women, from abusive marriages to boyfriends, and gifts of money, until they became working prostitutes. After only a little time with Regenia, Frank had come to understand that the quick hand movements and excessive body language that normally would be associated with agitation seemed to be her persona.

"My kids?" she did not wait for him to ask. "My kids are staying with my aunt. I got a letter around here somewhere. She wants to adopt them, or something."

The more she talked, the more Frank's fascination grew. Regenia liked her mother, who lived nearby, although she did not see her very often.

"Well, if you're not going to use that," she said, pointing to the two tens on the table. "I sure can."

Frank nodded. She swept the bills into her hands and shot out the door. She was back in a couple of minutes, holding a hit of crack cocaine. She took two or three quick puffs off the little pipe before offering it to Frank, who shook his head.

"We've got to do it now," she said, as a matter of fact. "I've got to go to work."

He left shortly, the twenty well-spent, he thought. Frank drove home in a reflective mood. Was he out of his mind? Maybe? He just knew that he had to see Regenia Moore again.

Frank was up early the next day and out to The Cut. Regenia was not in her room. He wandered the area until he saw her stumbling down the street shortly after noon. Gently he guided her to the car and took her back to the motel. Within seconds she was asleep from either fatigue or drugs, he couldn't tell, since she told him she had worked all night.

It was the first of nearly daily trips he would make to The Cut. Soon he was accepted by the diverse subculture of prostitutes, drug addicts, pimps, johns, and petty criminals that composed the uninhibited area. He was as curious to them as they were to him. He did not drink to excess nor did he use drugs. He was the only straight person on The Cut and therefore the only dependable person. Somehow the collective intellect of The Cut came to understand Frank's unique position in the subculture, and to use it. If someone needed a ride, Frank provided it. If a prostitute found herself stranded ten or more miles from The Cut by an angry john, she could call Frank for a ride home. He never forgot a promise. Occasionally he was called in to referee disputes among the lost souls. Soon everyone had his telephone number. He had nothing in common with these dregs of humanity, yet he possessed an almost uncontrollable interest in their unconventional universe. It was a lifestyle that Frank did not understand, nor could he comprehend his fascination with it.

"I'm the token normal person on The Cut," he teased Regenia, although he found himself trapped in her imperfect spiderweb. The more he struggled to understand, the more enmeshed he became in her life.

"Why are you hanging around here?" Regenia once asked him.

"My dear, I'm an enigma," he said with a smile.

"What's that?"

"It's a puzzling word about a puzzling situation," he said. "I'm a riddle even to myself."

It was not long after that conversation that Frank first heard about Kenneth McDuff. Frank was checking all the regular places for Regenia one night when he stopped by a room in the Sleepy Time Motel rented by a known drug dealer called Porkchop. People seldom had last names on The Cut, unless one was demanded by law enforcement officers.

Regenia had been in earlier, Porkchop related, but she had no money or drugs. Frank decided to wait. Regenia would be back once she made a little money. She always took a hit of crack between johns. Frank had never known of her to service two johns in a row. That was her standard operating procedure—money, then drugs.

"Want a hit, man?" Porkchop asked.

"No, you know I don't do that." Frank was a little irritated. These guys never gave up.

Porkchop shrugged. He was trying to make a living.

"What's new?" Frank asked, settling onto a chair.

"Not much."

Frank nodded his head, "Quiet, huh?"

"Yes and no," Porkchop said. Frank waited sensing a story behind that answer. "We had a big dude in here last night. Crazy guy. Smoking crack."

When the big man got high, he threatened to whip all the

dealers on The Cut and steal their drugs, then kill them all, starting with Porkchop and his friends.

"I eased outside," Porkchop said. He hid his dope in case the big man in the cowboy hat decided to carry out the threat. "I didn't want anymore to do with him. He's nuts. He was sittin' there, calm, then he just went off his rocker."

"What happened?"

"I don't know, man. He didn't whip nobody; but I watched him close until he left. The man scares me. He's crazy."

"Why'd he act like that? The dope?" Frank asked. He wasn't particularly concerned. Incidents like this were common on The Cut.

"He's just crazy. One second he's sittin' there, calm. The next he's all over the room, threatenin' to kill everybody. No reason that I could see. He flipped. Just plain crazy."

Frank wanted to be prepared if he ever met this guy. "What's his name?"

"Kenneth McDuff," Porkchop said. "But you don't want nothin' to do with him."

Within weeks of his arrival on The Cut, Frank began to hear more stories about an abusive big cowboy-type named Kenneth McDuff who roamed The Cut; always neat, always wearing a cowboy hat, always wearing boots, almost always belligerent. Always brutally crazy after a hit of crack cocaine. Always teetering on the brink; polite one second, a violent explosion the next. There was never a warning when the violence erupted from Kenneth McDuff according to the prostitutes and drug dealers.

Once while in a motel room with a prostitute named Jenny Denise Snyder, McDuff attacked a man named Richard and tried to gouge his eyes out.

"It came to a question about the last dope on the table and it was said that I was going to get half and Richard was going to get half, and Kenneth got upset," the prostitute later testified. "Richard was sitting in a chair. I was sitting next to Richard, and Kenneth was laying to the right side of me. I felt him shaking to where he got nervous and I look at him and I seen that he was getting pissed off. He scooted down to the end of the bed and told him: 'You punk motherfucker. I'm going to show you. You think I am a punk motherfucker. I'm going to show you.' "

McDuff leaped to his feet as Richard stood up to confront him. The larger man pushed Richard back into the chair and attacked as Jenny began screaming.

" 'I'm going to put your motherfucking eyes out with my thumbs,' " Snyder quoted McDuff. Jenny tried unsuccessfully to pull him off before bolting from the room. "I thought Kenneth was going to kill him. I left going back towards the highway and the next thing I know Richard was coming towards me. I don't know how he got away from Kenneth."

Although it had only been a few minutes, Jenny added that "He had two big black, purple eyes." The victim was so afraid he refused to press charges.

It was a temperament that had terrified fellow prison inmates and mostly remained under control behind bars. But McDuff gave it free rein in the free world.

One evening Frank found himself in a group that included McDuff, who sat strangely quiet, different from the descriptions of the wild man that Frank had been hearing. *If he is boisterous and loud, it must be when he's under the influence of drugs,* Frank decided as the evening wore on. *He must be like a Dr. Jekyll and Mr. Hyde when he's on drugs.* That evening Kenneth McDuff reminded Frank of a stoic—no laughter, no banter with the group. McDuff watched and listened, a quiet man who seemed absorbed in his own thoughts that night. Frank also noticed that McDuff could not keep his eyes off the diminutive Regenia.

Desperate for more money to buy more crack, Regenia had taken to "peeling" her johns that summer. While a john was occupied in pleasure, often with his trousers still on, the prostitutes on The Cut had become expert in lifting a customer's wallet. Some could even remove the money from the wallet, and slip it back into trousers that had been tossed aside. "Peeling," with its threat of retaliatory violence, especially worried Frank. Regenia had begun the practice because she could not make enough money to support her drug habit.

"You're going to destroy yourself," he told her one night as they lay in bed. He had long since quit paying for her favors. It was a repugnant practice, at least for him, with this woman. He would lend her money, give it to her. Anytime. Anywhere. He would be her best friend, but he could not bring himself to put another twenty on the table after his second night with her.

"You can't keep peeling the johns," he gently lectured. "You're going to do it to the wrong person and he's going to hurt you bad, maybe kill you."

"Don't worry," Regenia muttered sleepily. "I've got a plan."

Frank could not help but smile. "What plan?"

"Well. If anyone ever tries to run off with me in a car, then I'll kick the windshield out," she said, raising her legs and bending her knees to snap her feet forward, striking an imaginary windshield. "Just like that. I'll kick it hard and the windshield will pop out, and I'll run."

When Frank did not respond, Regenia tried to reassure him.

"Me and Brenda talked about it," she told him. Brenda Thompson, another prostitute who was from West Texas; sometimes invited Regenia to spend the night at her house. "She said she'd do the same thing.

"People will see me kicking the windshield. And I'll scream," she said.

"You can't protect yourself on the streets," Frank said, unconsoled by her self-deceptive plans.

Kenneth McDuff was arrested September 1 by the Temple Police Department for driving while intoxicated (DWI).

Three days later he visited the parole office in Waco where he reported that he had been picked up for DWI and admitted that he had been to the lake the day before and smoked a joint of marijuana. Both misdemeanor charges were violations of his parole stipulations.

Parole Officer David Darwin ordered McDuff to participate in alcohol and drug abuse counseling.

TEN

Lorraine "Lori" Bible was born eighteen months before her little sister, Colleen Reed. The pair spent an idyllic childhood on a Louisiana farm near Lafayette, riding horses, feeding the chickens and ducks, playing in the pastures, hunting and fishing with their father. Although they had separate beds the girls slept together more often than not, and when booming thunderstorms rolled across the countryside, the girls would crawl under the bed where Lori would reassure Colleen and rub her back until she was asleep. They shared secrets and occasionally "fought like cats and dogs," which is often the way of sisters who share such an indefinable bond.

Feisty Lori was Colleen's protector. Once, in grade school, an obnoxious boy in a wheelchair had a crush on Colleen. It was his custom to get her attention by banging into the back of her legs with the wheelchair. Soon little Colleen's legs were black and blue. One day, when Colleen cried out in pain, Lori had had enough. Lori plucked the youngster out of the wheelchair by his neck brace, his legs dangling above the ground. She threatened him.

"I just put him down on the ground, and headed for the principal's office," Lori recalls in a husky laugh. "I knew I had had it."

Lori confesses that she was sometimes a "problem child for her parents" and that Colleen was the sweet conformist beloved by everyone.

Their's was an unusual family. When Colleen was born, two

older sisters were in high school about to leave the family homestead. Allen and Pat Reed in essence had two families. Lori was her mother's third child, and her father's first.

Colleen was three years old, and Lori, four, in 1966 when Kenneth McDuff killed for the first time while on parole. Colleen entered kindergarten as Lori went into first grade in 1968, the same year McDuff was sentenced to die in the electric chair on December 3. By the end of 1969, when McDuff had succeeded in dodging three dates with the electric chair, the two children had spent their days gathering eggs, feeding the farm animals, and frolicking in fresh mown hay.

In 1972, when the Supreme Court ruled capital punishment to be cruel and unusual punishment, and McDuff's murder conviction was commuted to life imprisonment, Colleen Reed was nine years old. The highlight of her year was a trip to the zoo in Houston where she saw dangerous animals kept safely behind bars. Lori remembers that Colleen had long curly hair. The girls were paid by their father to count food stamps that came into the bank where he worked as an accountant.

The girls proved to be their daddy's "little boys." Both could "skin a cat" by flipping through their arms on a tree branch. They fished and hunted. They wore blue jeans, and as Lori laughs, "We did all the boy stuff." But as Lori matured away from tomboy activities, the younger Colleen spent a few more months hunting and fishing with Dad.

"He was sure disappointed when she discovered boys," Lori remembers.

Colleen flourished under the love of her family. She was in the eighth grade in 1976 the same year that the Supreme Court reinstated the death penalty and Kenneth McDuff, now safely sheltered from it, was denied parole for the first time on a unanimous vote.

Colleen went on to become a cheerleader and at seventeen graduated high school a year early in 1980, just as Lori had done. Kenneth McDuff was denied parole for the fifth time, but he received one favorable vote. Colleen married her high school sweetheart over Lori's objections, then separated from him; a divorce was final a year later.

Kenneth McDuff was convicted of attempted bribery in 1982 as Colleen settled into college at Louisiana State University where she had decided to obtain a degree in accounting. She would be a bookkeeper, just like her dad.

Colleen moved to Austin in 1989. Lori had moved to Austin at seventeen in 1978 and married Don Bible the next year. They had two sons. The couple divorced in 1986. Lori went to work for real estate developers before she joined the City of Austin real estate staff as a purchaser in 1989.

"She loves this town," Lori told her thirty-year-old fiancé, Jeff Tolson, when she learned that Colleen was joining them in Texas's capital city. Colleen favored small towns with low crime rates, and Austin with a population hovering at 500,000 seemed to fit the bill. It was small enough to have pockets of downhome living but large enough to offer the advantages found in big cities.

However, Lori still worried about her little sister.

"Don't go out at night," Lori warned her sister about nocturnal jogging sessions.

"Nothing's going to happen to me," Colleen reassured her.

Colleen borrowed one of Lori's dresses to wear on her first job interview. She landed a position with the Lower Colorado River Authority as a bookkeeper. She joined the Army Reserves. It had been a happy year for the reunited sisters.

The sisters enthusiastically planned Lori's September 14 wedding to Tolson. Colleen was to be the maid of honor at Lori's second marriage; even Lori's sons would participate. Lori anticipated returning the favor by serving as matron of honor at Colleen's wedding to Oliver Guerra as soon as the two set the date.

What started as a gentle mist turned into a deluge as pregnant clouds dumped torrents of rain the day of Lori's wedding to Jeff. Instead of outdoor nuptials at Zoker Park, the event was moved inside the Omni Hotel where the reception had been planned that Saturday. It was a happy day. The sisters would not let inclement weather spoil their carefully planned event.

But by Thursday Lori underwent an emergency hysterectomy.

"I'm spending my honeymoon in the hospital," she wailed when Colleen visited with flowers and gossip.

"It's okay," Colleen reassured her. "There's plenty of life ahead for both of us."

Regenia was more agitated than ever when Frank answered the telephone shortly before dawn. The police had picked her up for possession of drug paraphernalia and credit card abuse. She needed five hundred dollars bail bond money to pay the required ten percent on a five thousand dollar bond.

"I'll get it back to you," she had pledged. When combined with the extra cash produced by peeling, both knew that hundreds of dollars—even at twenty dollars a trick—slip through the hands of a single prostitute each week. "Don't worry," she added.

So it was that Frank put up the five hundred dollars he had been saving to buy a car at auction. A friend had told him about a late-model automobile that had been in only a fender-bender yet was ruled a total loss by the insurance company. Frank had his eye on this slick vehicle with a bent bumper.

"You'll have the money tomorrow," Regenia pledged when he let her out at The Cut.

What started as a routine driver's license and insurance check in the 1700 block of Faulkner Lane on the edge of The Cut during the early morning hours of October 10 would explode into a major incident fraught with unanswered questions.

Waco Police Department Officer Pat Swanton looked up shortly after midnight to see a faded maroon pickup approaching on Miller Street. The driver slowed the vehicle a bit as it approached Faulkner Lane before it stopped about fifty feet from where Officer Swanton was standing. Swanton played the flashlight on himself so the driver would see his police uniform.

"As I started to approach the truck the driver in the vehicle was looking at me," the policeman wrote in his report. "I noticed in the passenger side a WF [white female]. She put her feet up to the window and started kicking the window on the pickup truck and screaming for help."

The officer speculated that her hands were tied behind her back because he never saw them.

"The driver of the pickup then floorboarded the accelerator and did not care whether we were in the way or not," he reported. "Sgt. [Monroe] Kelinske did have to move out of the road to keep from being struck by the pickup, along with Officer [Donnie] Morgan and I, we also had to move to the side to keep from being hit.

"As he did this we all started shouting 'Police' and yelling for him to stop," Officer Swanton continues in his report. "However, the subject continued southbound on Miller towards Waco drive.

"We all went to our patrol cars and attempted to locate the truck, however, as of that time, we were unable to find the truck anywhere in the area. It is unknown at this point where the subject went."

He described the driver as in his forties, with a ruddy complexion and receding hairline. The driver was wearing a flannel shirt.

"I was unable to obtain any type of LP [license plate] from the vehicle due to his rate of speed," he added.

"Officer [Terry] Meals will be making [an additional report] to this case in reference to information that he received about a female subject [prostitute] being missing for the past several days."

The incident was reported military style as occurring about 00:30 in the morning on October 10, 1991. The officer filed his report at 3:29 in the morning.

Later that night, Frank's fears about Regenia's safety crystallized. He took her to stay with thirty-six-year-old Brenda Thompson. Although Regenia had a standing invitation to spend the night when she had nowhere else to stay, she wanted to check in with Brenda before inviting herself. Frank pulled his car into the driveway of the small home around nine o'clock. The front door was open. The lights were on throughout the house. Brenda's car was in the yard but that was not unusual; she only lived several blocks from The Cut, and sometimes walked to work.

The open house worried Frank but Regenia dismissed it when she got out of the car. "Brenda!" she called several times as she entered the front door, the sound of her voice wafting back to Frank as he heard her go from room to room. It was less than a minute before Regenia came scurrying out the door.

"Man, she's not there. I went all over the house. There was one bedroom that was dark and I stuck my head in it, said 'Brenda,' and I run out. She's not there."

"Maybe she went back to work," he suggested.

"Maybe," she agreed.

"You know how people are," Frank said. "She probably had a chance to make more money."

With a nod, Regenia got back into the car. They rode around and talked for several hours before heading back around 10:30 that night. Everything was the same. Again Regenia checked. No one was at home.

It was not uncommon for people of The Cut to disappear for several days, then resurface. Maybe Brenda had taken off on a trip with a new friend.

Regenia was too afraid to stay by herself, so she spent the night as she had hundreds of others, on the mean streets of The Cut.

Frank had not heard of the roadblock, the maroon pickup or the driver with the ruddy complexion and his hostage. To the best of his knowledge Regenia did not know either.

* * *

Four days later Frank went looking for Regenia. He needed the five hundred dollars he had loaned her several weeks before. The auction was coming up on Wednesday. Previously he had forgiven her her debts, but this time he had his heart set on that car. His steel determination melted when he found Regenia strung out on crack cocaine in a drug dealer's room. He had never seen her more vulnerable.

"Look," he urged in whispered tones. "Just forget the money. Get some rest. Stay off the dope a day. You're going to destroy yourself."

"Don't worry, Frank. I'm fine, I'm fine," she said rapidly, pawing the air, obviously spaced out.

Frank insisted. "You can't protect yourself on the streets like this. Something's going to happen to you."

"I'm fine. Don't worry." She slurred her words so fast they sounded like one long syllable.

"Okay, okay," he knew it was a losing battle. "Call me tomorrow. Call me tomorrow night. I've got something to do. I can't come out. You call me."

"Okay, okay, okay," she said. He turned to leave. "Frank. I'll have the money for you. Tomorrow."

"Sure," he said. "Okay." He knew she would not have it; she probably would not call him. But it was easier to play the game.

You can't be responsible for her, he chided himself on the drive home. *You can come out here each evening and stay until 11:30, then go home and come back at two and go home and come back at six, but you can never protect her, from herself or anyone else.* He understood that crack cocaine addicts, more than any other drug user, lived for the next hit.

"That stuff messes up your brain," he once told Regenia. Frank knew that the limbic area of the brain—the area that controls reasoning—is destroyed by drugs, maybe slowly, but destroyed nonetheless. "It affects your ability to make a decision. You come in off the streets. You've already done anything to get the money for a hit, and you never consider that that hit's gonna be gone in a few minutes and you're going to need more money, soon, for the next hit."

"How did you know?" she asked, surprised.

"It doesn't take a brain scientist to see what you're doing to yourself," he said, sadly. "What about your mama? What about your children? Don't you love them."

"Maybe I oughta stop, just for them," she answered.

"You can't stop for someone else," Frank said. "It has to be for yourself."

When Regenia had not called him on Tuesday night Frank went looking for her. The drug dealers at Sleepy Time Motel had seen her several hours earlier but she had not been back. Her cousin had been working the streets at Faulkner Lane and the Old Dallas Highway where The Cut began when she was accosted by an angry john brandishing a gun and threatening to kill Regenia because she had peeled him of around sixteen hundred dollars. He was driving a dark-colored, old model Thunderbird.

"I'm going to kill that bitch," her cousin quoted the unknown man as saying. A prostitute across the street confirmed the story, adding that the enraged john was asking for Regenia by name. The two women said the man was so out of control that he drove the wrong way on a one-way street.

Tuesday night turned into the witching hours of Wednesday morning until Frank finally returned home for sleep. The best he could do as an amateur sleuth was place Regenia at the Sleepy Time Motel around six o'clock when she purchased drugs from Joe Bob. No one had seen her since. An angry john was the talk of The Cut grapevine. He had been reported cruising The Cut with a gun, threatening to kill Regenia. Did he find her? Frank fervently hoped not.

After a few restless hours Frank was back scouring The Cut until he came across Harley Fayette, a former drug dealer who had become a user and was now reduced to "gofer" to earn a few dollars for his habit. Sure he had seen Regenia. He had spent the evening of October 15 with her.

"Me and Kenneth and Regenia. We drove up and down The Cut," he said. As he recalled it, McDuff spent most of the evening trying to "date" Regenia; like so many in the lifestyle, Harley applied the socially acceptable term to the business transaction between customer and provider. McDuff wanted the services of the petite woman for the whole night but refused to pay the one hundred dollars she demanded.

"How much for a date?" Harley quoted McDuff.

"It'll cost you sixty dollars," Regenia said.

"For one date?"

She nodded as McDuff pulled his red pickup to the curb.

"Get out," he demanded. When Regenia started to leave, McDuff grabbed her arm. "Not you. Get out, Harley."

"Now you've got sixty dollars?" Harley heard her ask. The pickup truck door slammed and Harley watched McDuff wheel it around in the middle of the street in the direction of Texas State Technical College, where the convicted killer lived in a dormitory. Harley estimated the time to be around 8:30 or 9:00.

It had been a little more than twenty-four hours since Frank had begun his search and he had not located anyone else who had seen Regenia on Tuesday. As the hours passed, it became obvious that Harley was the last person on The Cut to see Regenia Moore, with the exception of Kenneth McDuff.

Frank had once asked Regenia who would know how to find her and she had given him her mother's telephone number.

"I had heard of McDuff," Frank said over the telephone to Barbara Miller on Thursday. "The gossip is that he once served time on death row. I don't know exactly why. I've seen him on occasions but I've never had that much to do with him. Not even a conversation. But the word is he has a quick temper."

Frank filled Regenia's mother in on his limited knowledge of McDuff. "I'm worried about her," he said.

"She's disappeared before, then came back," Barbara said wearily. "What do you think I should do?"

"Well, I don't want to scare you but I think you should go to the police," Frank urged.

In light of Regenia's background, Barbara was reluctant to go directly to the police. The mother believed she needed more tangible evidence to get their attention. *After all, she's only a prostitute,* she thought bitterly, reflecting what she believed was the prevailing attitude toward the women on The Cut.

"If she met harm, I'm concerned that she met harm at the hands of McDuff," Frank told the mother.

"Well, then, let's all get together and go out and see him," she suggested.

Frank spent all Friday running down McDuff's dorm number. When he arrived Saturday morning at nine o'clock in the TSTC parking lot, he found Barbara accompanied by Bill Carpenter, her fiancé.

The older couple was standing next to a faded maroon pickup. The front windshield bulged outward on the passenger's side, a pattern of circular striations radiating out from the grim protrusion. Obviously something had hit it from the inside.

"This is what Regenia said she'd do, if she ever got in trouble," Frank said, his hope dwindling. "She told me that the first thing she would do is kick out the front window."

"She told me the same thing," Barbara said, her tone flat.

Frank knew the pair had already assumed it, but somehow it helped to say it aloud. "That's Kenneth McDuff's truck."

They nodded. "Let's do it," Bill Carpenter said.

The three located McDuff's room. Frank knocked sharply on the door. No answer. Again he rapped, prolonged and loudly. Still no answer. The three turned to leave. As they passed the next door it occurred to Frank that he may have been given the wrong number.

"Let's try here," he said. Before he could knock, a tousled head appeared in the first door.

"Whatya want?" the man asked, surly, suspicious.

"Are you Kenneth McDuff?" Frank asked, already knowing the answer.

"Yeah."

The three rushed through the open door, pushing their way into the room as McDuff backpedaled. The room was junky, clothes carelessly tossed aside, chest of drawers hanging open, the bed unmade. Frank noticed a door connecting to the next room where he had started to knock. He moved within a foot of McDuff, peering up into the larger man's face.

"You know Regenia Moore?"

"Yeah, I know her."

"This is her mother," Frank said motioning toward Barbara. "And this is her fiancé. We're looking for Regenia. She's miss—"

McDuff shot backwards a few steps his hands palm forward in a defensive stance, as if Frank was about to throw a punch.

"Don't try to pin that on me!" he exclaimed.

You get more flies with honey than vinegar, Frank thought. *I've got to keep this guy cool.*

"Wait a minute, man," Frank said soothingly. "Pin what on you? Nobody's trying to pin anything on anybody. Just calm down. We just want to find out about her. She's missing. This mother is concerned."

Barbara nodded. "We would really like to make sure she's all right."

Calm enveloped McDuff as swiftly as the agitation a few seconds before.

"They say you were with her. Were you with her?" Frank asked as McDuff relaxed.

"Yeah, I was with her," he admitted. "We had a date."

"What time were you with her?"

"I don't know. Nine-thirty, maybe ten," he said.

That was a later time frame than the one established for the angry john with the gun and it matched Harley's estimate. *I doubt that the man with the gun ever had a chance to find her,* Frank thought. McDuff did not appear to be threatened by the time frame he established.

"What did y'all do?"

"Well, we rode up and down The Cut and I took her back to the motel," he said.

"Where'd you let her off?" Frank wanted to know. "Which side?"

"On the south side," he said; it was drizzling rain and that was where she wanted off.

The location alarmed Frank. Regenia lived on the other side of the motel. Why drop her off, in drizzling rain, where she had to walk to her room when it would be just as easy to drive another fifty feet or so and let her off at her room? He remembered the day he met her. She had instructed him to drive around to the side so they would not walk through the building.

"What did she do, Kenneth, after you dropped her off?"

"She got out of my truck and into a car."

"What kind of car, Kenneth?"

"Oh, I don't know."

"What color car, Kenneth?"

"Oh, I don't know."

"How many people in the car?"

"Ahh. I couldn't see. It was dark."

Everyone in the room felt the tension building with each denial; but, as the tension built for the interrogators, McDuff appeared to become even calmer.

"You're saying that you dropped her off on the south side, not the north side, and she gets immediately out of your truck and into somebody else's car? You don't know the color of the car. You don't know the kind of car. You don't know how many people were in the car."

"No!" McDuff was emphatic, the word rumbling from deep inside his throat.

"And you didn't see her anymore after that?"

"No. I didn't."

Frank looked at Barbara and Bill. Obviously there was nothing else to be gained. After the brief agitation, McDuff had settled into a stoic, almost placid, disposition. *We're not going to get any more out of him,* Frank thought.

"Thank you, Kenneth," he said. "We'll go now."

Back in the parking lot, the red truck with the shattered window drew them like a magnet. Frank touched the striations, tracing them with his index finger.

"We all know he's lying," he said as the other two nodded agreement. "This is the first thing she said she would do." He could not keep his eyes off the broken glass, all the while a mental picture of a violently struggling Regenia replayed over and over in his mind.

Frank believed that Regenia would have insisted on being taken to her room instead of being dropped off on the wrong side of the hotel. He suspected the car was a figment of McDuff's imagination.

"She would never get that close to dope without getting some," he told Barbara and Bill. "Earlier in the day she had peeled a guy and she came straight back and got dope from Joe Bob, and left again. Her habits were almost like clockwork. If she had money she'd go get the dope before she would do anything else.

"I assume that when she left that was when she got into the truck with Kenneth and Harley," he said. "He's lying about everything but the fact she was with him."

"What about the man with the gun," Bill asked.

"I don't believe he had a chance to find her," Frank answered.

"Look!" Barbara gasped.

The men looked up to see a determined Kenneth McDuff striding across the parking lot toward them. Without a word he got into the truck and drove off in an easterly direction.

"We've got to do something," Barbara said.

"Why don't you call the police," Frank suggested.

He had no legal ties to Regenia but the police would listen to a distraught mother. As they discussed what she should tell them, Kenneth McDuff returned in his pickup, parked it from where he had taken it and walked back into the dormitory. He had been gone about fifteen minutes.

Frank would later wonder if their visit had caused McDuff to go check the location of Regenia's body. He would regret not demanding to see what lay behind the door that appeared to connect to an adjoining room. One prostitute would tell Waco police that McDuff used both rooms. He was bedeviled by the thought that a hapless Regenia might have been bound and struggling in the other room.

Barbara went over everything with the police.

"At least question the man," she begged.

She left believing that little, if anything, would be done.

"Frank, they told me there was not enough there to pick up McDuff for questioning," she told him when she called Saturday morning. "She's a prostitute and she's an adult, they told me, and I have to file a missing person report. They say that she may not be missing. She may have just gone somewhere. But she has to be gone seventy-two hours from the time of the report before they can do anything about it."

It had already been more than four days since her daughter was last seen.

Meanwhile, WPD Officer Donnie Morgan, one of the men in harm's way when the pickup plowed through the roadblock, did talk to Kenneth McDuff on October 20, the same day Regenia's mother contacted the police.

"We received some information in reference to a Missing Person, also in reference to the driver of a vehicle," he wrote in his report. "[Concerning] the vehicle which cleared officers out of the road at Faulkner/Miller when we were doing a license check.

"I went to TSTC Campus to Room #118, Sabine Hall and talked to Kenneth McDuff, listed above, and I am positive this is the same person who was driving the truck the night that he ran through our roadblock, making officers get out of his way.

"I talked to Mr. McDuff a short time and then left. Upon leaving, walked outside and saw his vehicle sitting outside, the maroon pickup listed above. It is positively the pickup that ran the roadblock with Mr. McDuff driving on the night in question. Also it is the truck that had the female in it, who was screaming for help, kicking the windshield.

"The truck was positively identified by Officer Swanton, Officer Meals, Officer [Bill] Sims, and I. I am the only one who could identify the driver as being the same one in the truck that night.

"We looked at the vehicle a little bit . . . fading maroon with black side moldings and the passenger side of the windshield is all kicked out, spider-web looking, a lot of beer cans and a lounge chair in the back."

In a supplemental report Morgan added that the floorboard on the passenger side appeared to have been recently cleaned or washed out, as were the floor mats.

Eight days later Officer Michael Bradley submitted a supplemental report.

"After reviewing this case report made by Officer Swanton, I learned that Officer Swanton along with Sgt. Kelinske were conducting a DL [driver's license] check with several other members of the special operations unit in the 1700 block of Faulkner when a PU truck obviously ran through the intersection almost striking Officer Swanton and Sgt. Kelinske.

"I then learned that Officer Swanton along with Sgt. Kelinske stated that they were not in fear of their lives nor were they placed in any fear and this is why an offense report was not made in reference to aggravated assault against a police officer.

"Officer Morgan did find the suspect which was driving the PU truck and the driver of the PU, Kenneth McDuff, was positively identified by Officer Morgan who saw him drive by. The PU which also ran through this DL check was also positively identified by Officer Meals, Officer Sims and Officer Swanton.

"I spoke with Officer Sims and learned that Officer Swanton stated that he was not going to make a supplement report in reference to aggravated assault against a police officer nor was Sgt. Kelinske due to the fact that they were not placed in fear of their lives.

"This case should be referred to Detective Don Lillard's missing person's report. I have spoken with Detective Lillard in reference to this offense and he has received all the information in reference to Kenneth McDuff in the vehicle that he was driving.

"As of this time, this case will be carried as closed."

With the exception of the first report, there was no mention of the screaming, kicking woman in the pickup.

Once again a special fate seemed to protect Kenneth McDuff. Had any of these officers been in fear of their lives and filed a charge of aggravated assault against a police officer, it is possible that Kenneth McDuff would have been returned to prison, since a felony charge of this magnitude might cause his parole to be revoked.

Colleen Reed hosted Lori Bible to a thirtieth birthday luncheon the same day the police visited Kenneth McDuff. The hysterectomy had been a blow to the young woman who had anticipated more children from her second marriage.

"Don't worry," Colleen said cheerfully. "You'll still have mine to love. They'll be the luckiest nieces and nephews around."

The shouting match was in full bloom when Frank pulled onto The Cut a week later. A bulky black woman stood between Tawny Mae and McDuff who was leaning out the window of his faded maroon pickup.

"She ain't gonna git in your truck and you ain't gonna have anything to do with her," Black Hattie was screaming.

McDuff was enraged, spewing obscenities and phrases that had no connection to each other, other than to demonstrate his foul-mouthed fury. Frank was amused and fascinated by the exchange. Obviously McDuff was afraid of the black woman since he remained in the safety of his truck. The fight reminded Frank of a pair of teenage bullies yelling at each other, each afraid to strike the first blow; foul language would be the only ammunition used that particular moment.

Tawny Mae spotted Frank as he parked on the opposite side of the road to watch the fray. Frantically Tawny Mae ran across the street, jumped into the car, and screamed, "Let's go. Let's get out of here."

"It's okay," Frank said, trying to soothe the small frantic woman while keeping an eye on the continuing fight. "I'm not afraid of Kenneth McDuff."

The argument ended, McDuff gunned his pickup onto the road, the wheels throwing dirt and grass and squealing when they hit the pavement. Less than a block away, McDuff wheeled the pickup around. His tires squealed as he raced back and slammed on his brakes, skidding to a stop only a few feet from Frank's car.

"Do you know who I am?" McDuff demanded to know.

Rather than give him the satisfaction, Frank countered, "Do you know me?"

"Yeah, I know who you are," McDuff answered. Perhaps he realized this was the little man who had showed up at his room with Regenia Moore's mother.

"What's up, Kenneth?" Frank asked laconically. *I'm not afraid of you.* "What's the problem?"

"I don't like anybody fucking with me," McDuff growled. "Because if they keep fucking with me, you know what I'll do."

"No, I don't know. What will you do, Kenneth?" Frank kept eye contact with the angry man. Seconds of silence followed.

McDuff started to say something, then stopped, finally blurting out, "You know what I do!" McDuff flicked him off with his center finger.

Frank smiled at the teenage behavior.

"Okay, you've told me what you'll do. Now what?"

Desperate to have the final word in his second confrontation, McDuff blurted, "I don't like people fucking with me."

Before Frank could react, the engine roared in McDuff's pickup and the truck darted down the road, tires squealing until out of earshot. The taillights disappeared to the left.

He's going the wrong-way down a one-way street, Frank realized. It was then that Frank noticed he was squeezing the steering wheel. He relaxed his grip.

"He's a coward," he told Tawny Mae as she began to chatter.

Previously Frank had come to the conclusion that McDuff was a coward because he had never heard of the criminal attacking a man or a large woman. He seemed to prefer the smaller woman. *Ones he can handle,* he thought. The small man was not sure if he had run a bluff or not. His primary rule for surviving on The Cut was to show no fear. Later he would tell Tawny Mae, "I think he saw a problem with me and got out of there. He's a coward."

Tawny Mae had reason to fear McDuff. She told Frank about an incident she had already reported to the police. Only two days after Regenia had disappeared, McDuff picked her up for a date. They went to McDuff's room at TSTC where he insisted on anal sex. She refused and left. Outside he offered her a ride home and she accepted. He drove to a secluded area.

"We can do this easy or we can do this hard, anyway I'm going to get my nut!" he told her and started to take his clothes off. The police report says, "She indicated that she knew what this meant so she took her tights off and he forcefully put her down and said, 'I'll do it slow and easy,' at which point he had anal sex with [the prostitute]." He suggested that he be her man. They could rip off all the other residents of The Cut. No one would be allowed to hurt her.

"He did me in every hole in my body," Tawny Mae told Frank. "I'm so sore I can hardly move."

She showed him a field behind the college. The next day Frank and Bill Carpenter walked the area on the outside chance that they might find a grave holding Regenia Moore. But the cow pasture held no secrets that the men found.

The story would be verified by another prostitute who told police that Tawny Mae also told her that McDuff brutalized her "in every hole I have for three hours" before bringing her back to the corner with a gruff reminder.

"They think I am a civil citizen now. I'm going to give them time to get off my back and then I'm going to show them the real McDuff!" she quoted him.

"McDuff felt like society owed him for all the time he spent in the penitentiary," the police report concluded.

It was a sentiment he echoed to Jenny Denise Snyder, a black prostitute who befriended him.

"Kenneth told me that he has become a good citizen," Jenny told officials. "He wants the people to believe that he has become a good citizen. He's giving them time enough to get off his back and then the real Kenneth McDuff will come out."

Jenny added that he believed prison officials were trying "to make him out—the same words he always used—a punk motherfucker. But he said he wasn't going to let them do him like that because he's a real man."

Kenneth McDuff believed that society owed him for his years in prison, she said, echoing the same words used by Tawny Mae.

Frank continued his search for Regenia. He haunted The Cut even more than he did when she worked the area, but there was little additional information. Several days after she had disappeared, Joe Bob had gathered Regenia's meager possessions, stuffed them into garbage bags and dumped them on the side of the road along with the debris of other people's lives. They lay there several days before Frank retrieved them in a drizzling rain. Nothing had been damaged. He took them to his mother's home and carefully put them in the trunk of an old, unused car, where they remain today.

"You're crazy, man," Harley Fayette told him at the time.

It's more like keeping faith, Frank thought.

The first week of her disappearance faded into the second week. One evening Tawny Mae flagged him down. "This is Roger Jones. He's got something to tell you."

Roger, who attended TSTC with McDuff, had been with his fellow student the weekend that Regenia disappeared. Near midnight he asked Roger to drive to Temple with him. As they passed over a bridge, McDuff turned to him.

"That's a good place to dispose of a body. Nobody'd ever find it," McDuff told Roger as he drove on to a deserted pasture near his parents' modest home in the country.

"Wait here. I'm going to get something," McDuff said. "Don't get out of the truck. There's Rottweilers running loose and they'll get you."

Fearful of the big dogs with the vicious reputation, Roger agreed to stay put. He thought McDuff was going to retrieve a compressor that the pair would pawn the next day. McDuff disappeared into the woods only to return empty-handed about fifteen minutes later.

"Did it seem to you that he was checking something?" Frank asked.

"I don't know, maybe," Roger answered. "He told me he could not get into the garage to get the compressor." Roger added that he had become fearful for his life after McDuff made the statement about dumping dead bodies. He was ready to get back to Waco.

Barbara called the police with this weak lead, desperate to mount a search for her missing daughter. She was told to call the police in Bell County, the field's location. An officer agreed to meet her but later cancelled the date. Undaunted, Barbara, Bill and Roger drove over the countryside in a futile effort to find the pasture that Roger had visited at midnight in the dark. They searched several areas unsuccessfully. Roger was never sure he had found the mysterious field.

As October turned into November, Frank saw McDuff driving up and down The Cut in the reddish pickup with the bulging front window.

He's just daring anyone to catch him, Frank thought bitterly.

ELEVEN

Barbara's Miller's woes were compounded by the death of her mother, a few months after her daughter disappeared. It had been a bitter holiday season, brightened only by her grandchildren. Barbara had come to learn in those months that amid all the recriminations of her life, Regenia had left a legacy of joy through the children. But the joy was tainted by the knowledge that Kenneth McDuff was freely roaming The Cut. This travesty of justice demanded his capture; but she needed proof.

Since the police department was not pursuing the case as actively as she would like, the demand for justice of some kind concerning her daughter's disappearance, and probable murder, began to consume Barbara Miller. She had to do something. But what?

Because Harley Fayette was the last person known to have seen Regenia alive, Frank made it a point to pick up the man whenever he saw him walking along the road and engage him in conversation. One day Harley excitedly told Frank about McDuff's meanderings along the country roads behind TSTC.

McDuff was in a mellow mood, almost reflective, as he participated in one of his favorite pastimes: looking for spots to hide a body. After McDuff pointed out several potential spots, Harley began to fear for his life. Suspicious, he ran his hand under the front seat of the big beige 1985 Thunderbird that McDuff was now driving. He discovered a gun and a strange piece of rope about four feet long. Harley had heard that Kenneth also carried knives in the trunk of the car.

"Stop the car," Harley demanded, suddenly becoming mortally afraid. "Stop the car!"

Harley would later tell Deputy U.S. Marshals Mike and Parnell McNamara that the rope was gray, short, covered with plastic and had a supple feel. The marshals had never seen rope covered with plastic. It puzzled them. No amount of questioning could shake Harley's description. Harley could not identify the rope as being made of cotton, hemp, or plastic.

Instead of stopping as Harley demanded, McDuff increased speed. Seized with fear Harley bailed out of the car, landing with a scraping thud that ripped the flesh open on both arms. Although stunned, he rolled into the big drainage ditch common on farm-to-market roads, hoping to drop out of McDuff's sight. Instead, McDuff slammed the car into reverse, bringing the headlights to bear on the bleeding, limping man.

"What's going on, man?" McDuff asked as he pulled the big car alongside Harley. "Get back in."

"No, man. I'm just going to walk back," Harley yelled.

"What'd I do?"

"Nothin' man," Harley said he replied. "I'm just gonna walk."

And he did, as McDuff drove alongside demanding that he get into the vehicle. Harley walked some six miles to the highway, where he hitched a ride back to The Cut—and safety.

"Why?" Parnell asked.

"There's ghosts on that road," Harley said. "I didn't want to go down that road. There's ghosts in the trees."

The McNamara brothers decided that something terrible had happened on that road; so terrible that it frightened Harley into silence. Unfortunately they would never discover what had terrified the little man. It would remain another McDuff mystery.

* * *

"I've got to have some help. I want to find my baby, and the cops aren't doing anything."

The words were almost whispered in a whiskey voice that was tinged with bitterness and frustration. It was not the first time she had told him this. Stymied by what she considered a lack of concern, Barbara Miller had sought him out three weeks after her daughter had disappeared because he was the detective sergeant in charge of the special crimes unit, a division of WPD that primarily investigated all homicides in Waco.

It was the first time that Special Forces Detective Mike Nicoletti had heard the name Kenneth McDuff. The thirty-four-year-old detective found it maddening that a concerned mother had to inform him that a hardened career criminal had been paroled into his city. He believed the Texas Department of Corrections should have notified him immediately when McDuff enrolled at TSTC.

They should have told us. We were never informed, Nicoletti thought bitterly. *We could have tried to watch him.*

The marshals knew it, but only because a friend called. The police at TSTC knew it, but only because the marshals called. But it would be several more months before the Waco Police Department would receive official notification that a paroled killer was in their midst.

Sergeant Mike Nicoletti was born in Brooklyn, New York, and reared in Remanet, California, where he graduated from high school. He attended McClendon Community College in California before moving to his wife Michelle's hometown of Waco, Texas. He joined the Waco Police Department in January, 1980.

Mike Nicoletti appraised Barbara Miller, a smallish woman with short, chestnut hair touched with gray. Days of worry had made her careworn and dispirited. He admired her spunk. She had confronted the man she suspected to have kidnapped her daughter, then turned him in to the police. Meanwhile, she and a network of friends had tirelessly searched unsuccessfully for Regenia.

He shared her frustration but there was really little he could do. It was not unusual for prostitutes to disappear with a john, sometimes for days at a time. As an adult Regenia was free to come and go, the police in missing persons had told the concerned mother. Also, the department had to wait seventy-two hours before Regenia Moore could be listed as a missing person. Since that report was filed, Barbara Miller kept badgering missing persons until finally she turned to Nicoletti in frustration. He was head of the Special Crimes unit which handles cases of murder. Realistically she did not expect to find her daughter alive so he was the logical person to go to.

After what Nicoletti had learned about the cavalier attitude in missing persons, he believed that her paranoia about police disinterest was justified. Already he had been stopped in the hallway by a fellow officer.

"She's only a prostitute," the fellow officer had said. "What's the big deal?"

"No, she's a woman with a personality, and children, and a mother," Nicoletti answered, each word curtly clipped as he fought anger. "How she makes her money has nothing to do with her value as a human being. All of us have a value."

"Well, I just mean . . ." the officer started. "Well, let's just say that some of us are more valuable than others."

"You can say that if you want!" Nicoletti brushed on past the man before turning to face him. "I pity you your ignorance."

Returning to the present he wondered what it would be like to deal with Barbara Miller's unique problems. Her vulnerability touched his heart, reigniting a silent rage that he had had to subdue in 1986 after he went on a one-man crusade to protest the early release of habitual criminals.

He preached the statistics that affected the Barbara Millers of the world.

"Everyone knows that eighty percent of the crimes are committed by twenty percent of the crooks," he told the news media. "Take care of the twenty percent, those that are habitual

Bob Stewart

offenders, and you're not going to have that eighty percent of the crime."

For a year he sought out the print and electronic news media with the message that habitual criminals should not be released. A series of newspaper articles followed and Nicoletti, although tagged naive by politicians, became a familiar face on local television. Even national television took notice, and he appeared on "America's Most Wanted." He prepared a form letter protesting the parole of habitual offenders. Thousands of the protest forms were printed and mailed to parole officers, especially on high-profile murder cases such as the Lake Waco triple murders, in which three teenagers—two girls and a boy—were stabbed to death in a murder for hire scheme in 1982. Nicoletti could not help but notice the similarities between this case and the 1966 murders by McDuff.

Nicoletti sighed. He was not sure that McDuff was his man, but his gut instinct told him that the ex-convict had had something to do with the prostitute's disappearance. He was amazed that a man with his record had been paroled. It took only a cursory check to discover his murder conviction. No parole and Regenia Moore might not be missing.

"Have you ever heard of a woman named Brenda Thompson?" Nicoletti asked.

"My daughter mentioned her," Barbara said.

"Well, she seems to be missing, too," he said. "What did she say about her?"

"Just that she was nice, and that she spent the night at her house, sometimes," Barbara answered.

"Anything else?"

"Frank might know something about her. I think he mentioned something about going by her house and finding it empty."

"I'll give him a call."

Nicoletti eventually received copies of the missing persons reports on Regenia Moore and the original report filed by Barbara Miller.

I see they finally found them, he thought. *Or finally completed them.*

Another report concerned a routine roadblock to check driver's licenses on October 10. A pickup driven by a large man had plowed through the flimsy barricades half an hour after midnight. A woman with curly blond hair, hands bound, was seen struggling and kicking at the front windshield.

Nicoletti grabbed the file on Regenia Moore to double check the date. She was last seen October 15 with Kenneth McDuff. The roadblock was run October 10. Either someone had made a mistake or it was not Regenia Moore who had cracked the front window of McDuff's pickup. He would have to ask around The Cut. Maybe it was Brenda Thompson in McDuff's pickup.

Nicoletti studied the report. McDuff had run the roadblock thirty-three minutes after midnight on October 10. It had been set up by the Flex Squad, an elite task force designed to operate in high crime areas.

A quick telephone call brought a conference with the men who had dallied in getting these reports to him. They had to face an irate Nicoletti. He believed that these reports should have been passed on to his special crimes unit without delay. It had been more than two weeks since Regenia Moore had been reported missing.

"Here we are the homicide unit and we're the last ones to get the information," he stormed. "This embarrasses me. It should embarrass the whole department."

Nicoletti left the meeting in disgust. Except for what appeared to be a cursory search of The Cut at the time of the incident, there was no follow-up. McDuff and his struggling victim seemed to have disappeared into thin air by the time the officers gave chase.

After a series of interrogations on The Cut over the next few days, Nicoletti confirmed, to his satisfaction, that it was Brenda Thompson in the pickup. One person had even seen her with McDuff that day.

But Nicoletti would not officially receive the cases on Brenda Thompson and Regenia Moore until April 27, 1992, six months after the women disappeared. Redacted police records which removed the names of people other than victims or suspected victims show that Captain Everett January assigned the case to Sergeant Nicoletti on April 27, but the report of the assignment is dated May 8, 1992, several weeks later. Another report dated April 28, 1992, notes that Barbara Miller recontacted the police with additional leads on October 21, 1991.

McDuff "is suspect in a lot of things round here. This guy, no telling what he's going to be good for if he ever gets to talking," Capt. January would later tell a Dallas *Morning News* reporter. "He's just traveling I-35. Any city along I-35 could have him as a suspect in any missing persons or unsolved murders."

Four pretty teenage girls died horribly December 6, 1991, in Austin in a sensational case that would become known internationally as the "Yogurt Murders." The bodies of seventeen-year-old Jennifer Harbison, fifteen-year-old Sarah Harbison, seventeen-year-old Eliza Thomas, and thirteen-year-old Amy Ayers were discovered that day after a blaze was doused at the I Can't Believe It's Yogurt shop on West Anderson Lane. Thomas and Harbison were employees; the other girls were visitors. Each victim had been tied, then shot in the head with a small-caliber weapon. The perpetrators set fire to the building before fleeing. Robbery appeared to be the motive, according to Sergeant John Jones with the Homicide Division of the Austin Police Department. He suspected that more than one person committed the crime. A task force was formed. A $25,000 reward was offered.

Christmas Day found Lori and her family celebrating the holiday with Colleen and Oliver. The children opened presents

Christmas morning at home, then dove into another round of gifts when their Aunt Colleen arrived. The sisters tried to telephone their parents but could not reach them. As they prepared Christmas dinner the sisters compared February schedules. The Neville Brothers were coming for a concert, and they planned to attend, alone; the men were not interested.

"I'll buy dinner," Colleen suggested.

"I can't beat that offer," Lori said.

The evening ended with a family feast prepared by loving sisters.

Also, this Christmas Day, an underworld tough called Bucktooth Billy Brown had a visitor. Kenneth McDuff stopped by the house where Brown was renting a room from a family. McDuff was looking to purchase crack cocaine.

The two made an interesting pair: The fastidious cowboy and the burly three-hundred-pound biker with full beard and a body covered with tattoos. Brown's rap sheet read like a what's what of crime. He has been in and out of jail so often the lawmen joked about a revolving door. But, on this Christmas Day, Bucktooth Billy Brown would be a hero of sorts, and four young girls would never know that a fierce-looking, hulking and bearded biker may have saved them from headline-grabbing deaths.

Four days later Colleen Reed decided to wash her white Mazda Miata at a car wash on Fifth Street. She had gone by the grocery store where she picked up milk and vitamins, then made a quick stop at an ATM machine to pick up a little cash, then on to the car wash. Colleen had just finished soaping the sportscar when a pair of men drove up in a beige Thunderbird.

TWELVE

The scream was so loud it echoed off the buildings. It was a prolonged scream, agonizing, fearful, according to Michael John Goins, who was standing with his brother sixty yards away on the front porch of his sister's home on Powell. It sounded as if the woman screaming had been facing the home, then had turned to face away. The shriek was followed by the heavy thud of two car doors slamming. Immediately Goin's eyes snapped across an empty lot toward the car wash where a big beige Thunderbird crept out of the drive and turned right on Fifth Street, where it slowly proceeded out of sight going the wrong way. It narrowly avoided collisions with two cars.

Goins noted the distinctive round glow of the taillights when the brakes were applied. He and his brother William recognized it as the car that had been going the wrong way down a one-way street only minutes before.

Still uncertain as to what had happened, William and Stephen Marks, the Goins' brother-in-law, jumped into a car and drove to the car wash as Michael and his sister Denise watched from the front porch. The men found a two-door black over white 1991 Mazda Miata dripping soap suds in one of the wash bays. They could find no one around. Obviously the car had been abandoned. The blood-chilling scream told them that someone had been kidnapped.

"Call the police," William yelled when they rushed back to the house.

The search for Colleen Reed had begun.

Goins described the two men in the car as having dark complexions, "but they were white," he stressed. One was tall, the other short.

"No," he said when asked if the men were Hispanic, but the Austin Police Department broadcast an all-points alert for two dark Hispanic males, one tall, the other short.

Most criminals either strike in the dark or take their victim to a hiding place. McDuff did neither. As police scoured the back roads and known "hot spots" of crime, Kenneth McDuff pulled onto Interstate 35. It would become his playground for the next few hours as he turned his automobile into a traveling torture chamber.

Officers worked swiftly to establish if the abduction was a random act of violence or was acquaintance related.

Colleen's fiancé, Oliver Guerra, was immediately contacted by police. He was a suspect; boyfriends usually are. Lori Bible-Tolson would become one when it was discovered that she was the beneficiary of Colleen's life insurance policy.

Sergeant Sonia Urubek took Oliver Guerra's statement when he came into the police office with pictures of Colleen.

The police told Oliver that Colleen's automobile was found abandoned in a car wash, still covered with soap. The keys were in the ignition. Her purse, along with groceries purchased only a few minutes before, was still in the vehicle. The police found a gallon of milk, cat food, and vitamins. The purse contained $19.73 in cash and credit cards. Obviously kidnapping was the prime motive, not robbery.

The next morning Lori went to work as usual without listening to the news. She did not learn Colleen was missing until mid-morning when Oliver called to see if she knew Colleen's whereabouts.

Lori met Oliver at the police station. A distraught Lori told the desk clerk that her "little sister" was missing. The wording set off a series of misunderstandings which ended with Lori standing in the juvenile office.

"No, this little sister is a grown woman," she angrily told confused officers.

Later that afternoon at police suggestion, Lori let herself into Colleen's apartment. The house had been left in the normal clutter of everyday life; a home awaiting the return of its owner. Ever fastidious, Colleen had laid out the clothes she planned to wear to work the next day. Lori did not touch them. Colleen's cat, Mensa, had knocked over a potted plant. Lori righted it, scooping a portion of the dirt back into the container.

She can do the rest when she gets back, Lori thought hopefully, but she found nothing missing. All of Colleen's clothes and cosmetics, any item that might accompany her on a trip; everything was there.

Within twenty-four hours her family assembled at Lori's home; parents, Allen and Pat Reed of Ville Platte, Louisiana, and two older sisters, Mae Rozas of Dallas, Texas, and Anita White of Baton Rogue, Louisiana.

"I'm going to kill him," were Allen Reed's first words. A typical father's reaction Lori thought. The first twenty-four hours are crucial in cases of kidnapping, police told the family. If Colleen was not found swiftly, then each passing hour would erode hope.

Friends and family formed a task force to augment the police investigation. Before the twenty-four hours was up, the first of thousands of posters—perhaps more than 100,000 eventually—were placed across the city.

Life became chaotic for Lori Bible-Tolson. As one day turned into another and family members eventually returned to their homes, Lori would remain the command center. The intense woman could not sleep. She ate very little. Within her very soul, an emotional maelstrom threatened to consume her. Her life was wrapped into one question as she asked herself over and over, *Colleen! Where are you?*

* * *

Bucktooth Billy Brown had been watching the television news about Colleen Reed's disappearance. He called Carmen Garza in Harker Heights, a suburb of Waco.

"You remember that guy you sent down here on Christmas?" he asked. "Don't send him no more.

"And you stay away from him," instructed Billy, whose lady friends praise him as a gentleman. "He's dangerous."

Although still weak from surgery, New Year's Eve found Lori walking along festive Congress Avenue in the shadow of the state capitol, putting up posters of her missing sister. Celebration could wait for Colleen's safe return. In just two days, the search for Colleen had begun to devour her older sister, who somehow felt a sense of failure. She had always been Colleen's protector.

She wondered if Colleen lived. Was she cold? Was she hungry? Lori wondered if she should wish that her sister still be living. Would that wish condemn Colleen to a continuing fate worse than death?

Lori sobbed as she put up the next few posters. She really did not know how to wish for her sister. She certainly did not want her to be dead, but if she wished her alive . . . the thought of what might be happening at that moment was too terrifying to contemplate. Lori wept. She knew one thing, though. She just wanted Colleen back, safe and smiling.

Long-haul truck driver Judy Ann Barton had a rude introduction to Kenneth McDuff only hours after Colleen Reed disappeared.

McDuff and his buddy, Harley Fayette, came to visit with her husband Gilbert only to learn that he had been arrested the day before on a theft warrant after the police arrived to break up a domestic fight between him and Judy.

"He's in jail," she told them before adding, "I can sure use a beer."

"We can fix that," Harley said.

McDuff went out to the car to remove a twelve-pack of beer from the trunk.

"Have you ever seen a set of balls like this on anybody?" Kenneth demanded to know, grabbing his crotch, once he settled onto the couch.

It was the beginning of a bizarre relationship between the truck driver and the convict. McDuff continued to brag, noting that he had just been released after twenty-three years in prison, "six of them on death row," for a crime he did not commit. He boasted that a motion picture would soon be made that would chronicle his fight for freedom and exoneration. His parents had money, he bragged, and it had taken lots of money to get him out of prison.

Anxious to impress this new female friend, Kenneth then gave her a handful of Valium after she admitted using them. Soon the two ditched Harley. Judy detested him; he was always undressing her with his eyes. The day she met McDuff, Fayette had opened a curtain in an attempt to watch her change clothes, Judy would later claim. Kenneth and Judy ended the evening in McDuff's TSTC room smoking crack.

When the pair went to make love, McDuff lay on top of her, his body crushing her into the bed. Unexpectedly, he wrapped his massive hands around her throat, pinning her down, lost in the emotions of the moment.

Panic filled Judy as the big hands began to squeeze the breath from her throat, choking her. She demanded that he let her up, pitching and bucking until he did. He spent the rest of the evening apologizing for her moment of fear. She would later tell police that she noticed a pistol sticking out of one of the boots by the bed. Wisely, she said nothing about it.

Strangely, McDuff would never remove all his clothing during intercourse, she told police. He even kept on his boots.

On a trip to Fort Worth to buy drugs several days later, Judy was in the car when McDuff stole gasoline from several convenience stores. The convict had the license plate rigged to flip up as he gassed up, then he could flip the plate back down after fleeing the scene of the theft. He would pump gas into the car, then lay the nozzle on the ground without hanging it back on the pump. He explained that when the nozzle is put back on the pump it triggers a signal inside that the transaction is complete.

The Fort Worth trip proved fruitless. An angry McDuff drove back to Waco where he ripped off a drug dealer by holding his hand out the window as if offering rolled up bills. Soon as the drugs were in his hand he burned rubber leaving the frustrated dealer at the curb.

"Harley used to talk about how he was McDuff's 'main man' and how they would be ripping off for dope together," Judy would later tell police. "McDuff never did smoke. Harley smoked whatever cigarettes he could bum off of someone. McDuff used to brag to me that he was a 'big guy' in the pen and 'ran' the places that he was at."

On January 3, 1992, just five days after abducting Colleen Reed, Kenneth McDuff asked Judy to join him on a trip to Temple, where the parolee had a court appearance on the DWI charge he had reported to his parole officer the previous September. McDuff decided to stop by his parents' home where he planned to steal Valium and Darvoset from the family medicine cabinet. While his mother prepared hamburgers for lunch, McDuff took a shower. When he told his mother that Judy knew about the movie deal, his mother looked at him with a "kind of strange look," Judy noticed, as if he should not have told his new girlfriend about it. Perhaps she was concerned about her son's inability to keep family secrets.

"McDuff used to talk continuously about how much money it cost him to get out of prison, how many people that had to be paid, lawyers and other people that he didn't identify," Judy told investigating officers at the Austin Police Department. "McDuff would always say that it cost a lot of money, a lot of money; but, his parents had a lot of money. I thought that strange because he never seemed to have any."

What happened next was almost funny. When Addie left the kitchen, Kenneth ordered Judy to serve as lookout as he searched unsuccessfully for prescription drugs. Upon Addie's return, he went to the bathroom as his mother fussed around the kitchen, only to leave as he walked back in.

"Damn," McDuff swore. "The bitch done caught on to me and hid 'em somewhere else where I can't find 'em."

Frustrated, McDuff left the homestead, wandering around back roads until he came to a lake, stopping at a scenic overview by a dam. Judy was drinking a beer. Her new friend abstained since he had to be in court in a few hours. It was a peaceful moment as the pair studied the lake's surface, higher than usual because of heavy rains.

"This would be a good place to dump a body, because the water's so high," he said. "The body would just wash away."

"You're being morbid," Judy said with a slight shudder.

McDuff didn't answer. After a few more minutes McDuff was ready to leave.

The convicted felon received two years probation on the DWI charge. Judy was amazed that the attorney had arranged for McDuff to walk out of court without paying a cent.

Then it was off to a friend's house where McDuff met up with Elroy Jerrold and Boyd Gabriel Obert. McDuff paraded Judy before several appreciative buddies. "Don't she have a nice ass?" he bragged. When one offered to take her in the house, Judy quipped, "Not in this lifetime." After a session with crack, the pair returned to the McDuff home where Kenneth went into the house and returned laughing with several hundred dollars stuffed in his shirt and pants pockets.

"Where'd you get the money?"

"Don't worry about it," he said.

The rest of the day was spent buying and smoking pot until Kenneth McDuff was in no shape to drive. Judy wasn't either, but, she took the wheel in a driving rain when he demanded it and managed to drive back to her trailer in Waco. After another crack session inside the trailer, McDuff's jovial personality turned ugly as he accused her of setting him up. He savagely grabbed her by the hair, forcing her to walk through the rain to the car. There, he demanded that she stand in front of him. Suddenly he jerked open the door on the passenger side, jumped in, slid under the wheel, and took off in a spray of mud and water.

The next day he was back with Boyd Gabriel Obert to rip off drug dealers with Judy's help. As soon as the drugs were in her hand, McDuff peeled out. He hit the curb, dumping beer all over himself. When he yelled at Judy to control the beer, she yammered back, "It's your beer!"

Whack! Her head slammed against the glass of the windshield.

"What the fuck you do that for?" she demanded, her head ringing.

Whack! Again, McDuff's massive hand slammed her head against the front windshield glass.

She tried to leap out of the car, but Obert locked the door.

"Don't ever disrespect me in front of my friends again," McDuff growled. He immediately began to beg her forgiveness, according to her statement, apologizing during the drive to her trailer.

The Marshals McNamara had discovered that McDuff's flash point was well known in prison and The Cut. He was especially concerned about a lack of respect in front of others, which they believed was a holdover from prison culture. Judy had just learned what an inmate told the marshals: "One second he's fine, the next he snaps."

"He must love you," Obert told the dazed woman. He assured her that he had never seen McDuff treat a woman as he treated her.

The pair drove Obert back to Temple, then spent the night in McDuff's TSTC dormitory room.

"McDuff had to have missed a lot of classes at TSTC. He would come over to my house around noon on several occasions and bring a twelve-pack of beer, and wouldn't leave until he drank all the beer and couldn't afford to go out and get more," she revealed. "There was even times when he would show up at my house at 7 a.m. when he was supposed to be in class, and spend the day with me."

He bragged about working as an informant for police in Dallas, Fort Worth, Houston, Waco, San Antonio and Austin. He claimed that he would contact his friends in prison, learn the names of their drug connection on the outside, then turn them over to police. McDuff claimed to have made "hundreds of thousands of dollars" doing this.

"McDuff never thought small about anything," Judy said. "Everything was on a big scale."

Like so many others who talked to police, Judy echoed a familiar refrain: McDuff was always trying to figure out a new or better way to obtain a gun. He also had a weapon that he called his "nigger thumper." It was a piece of round wood with a metal cap on one end and a leather wrist-strap on the other. She described it as a homemade "billy club."

He carried an arsenal around with him: pocket knives in his boots, pistols in his boots, and a "hunting knife" with brown handles and sheath underneath the seat of his car.

All McDuff had to do was check the newspapers or turn on a television set to know that there was no known suspect in the disappearance of Colleen Reed as the media hysteria over her disappearance continued to build.

Michael Goins could not identify the suspects from police mug shots. A Department of Public Safety hypnotist failed to enhance his memory of the two men in the car or help him recognize them in the hundreds of photographs on file.

* * *

To her surprise, Lori's first husband, Don Bible, contacted her with an offer of help. He had known Colleen since childhood, and she was like a little sister to him, too. He took their sons on outings, and as the weeks passed, often worked with the family task force to distribute posters. Sorely needed child support payments began to arrive on time. Tentatively, a destroyed relationship was pieced together until the pair could be friends, again; but no more than that.

Lori was all over the nation's print and television media, as well as tabloid and news shows in January. Each appearance was a plea for help in finding her sister and capturing the monsters who had taken her. An organization was formed called "We Love You Colleen" to help raise money for a search fund. Volunteers took to Austin's streets on January 18 to hand out pink ribbons (Colleen's favorite color) and flyers with Colleen's picture.

Horrendous nightmares began to haunt Lori's sleep. Faceless men would enter her house and stalk her. New emotions swirled about her, as for the first time in her life she began to live in constant fear that something might happen to other members of her family. She drew her boys closer to her, more protective than ever. Although she was on better terms with the boys' father, she still worried about what would happen to them should she be killed or become the next sister to disappear.

Lori became a constant presence at the Austin Police Department, alternately prodding and begging, alternately respected and considered a pain in the neck, but always tolerated by the hardened detectives.

Shortly after the first of the year Barbara Miller hit upon a desperate plan to flush McDuff into the open. She would use the news of her mother's death to bait a trap with a bogus inheritance. First she approached the Waco Police Department with her plan. She wanted to purchase a billboard at The Cut advertising a $15,000 reward for the apprehension of the man who killed her daughter. Barbara did not have the reward money, but she had no qualms about reneging on the deal since she was convinced that McDuff would come forward, and that would be his undoing.

"No," Sergeant Nicoletti told her. "You can't say you have a reward when you don't."

"I don't mind doing whatever is necessary, even lying, to find my daughter," was the mother's curt reply.

"It would be best not to," he urged.

Undaunted, Barbara, Bill and Frank discussed going forward with the billboard but none of them had the money to purchase the advertisement.

"Why don't we just say it's so?" Frank suggested. "Nobody'll know the difference. I can get the word out on The Cut. It'll spread like wildfire. I know it will reach Kenneth. It won't cost a cent, and if anyone other than Kenneth approaches us, we can just say it's rumor."

Agreed and done. That very day Frank walked up and down The Cut, casually spreading the rumor in conversations with prostitutes, pimps, drug dealers and hangers-on. He made sure that Harley and Mike-Mike, another McDuff associate, knew about the bogus reward.

"You guys don't believe me? The obituary is in the newspaper," Frank challenged them to see if Regenia's grandmother had died. "Check it out."

"You should see the greed in their eyes when they hear the words fifteen thousand dollars," he grimly told Barbara that night.

McDuff took the bait in less than forty-eight hours. Harley telephoned Frank for a meeting.

"Kenneth told me that he thinks he knows who did it," Harley said. "This Mexican . . ." Harley let the thought trail off, deliberately trying to set the bait.

Harley would later tell police that McDuff claimed to have bound Regenia and left her with a Mexican, who raped her,

ROBBERY/KIDNAPPING
Victim

Melissa Ann Northrup

D.O.B. 12/8/69   W/F   4' 11"   100 lbs.
Brown Hair   Blue Eyes

Subject Last Seen At 3:00 a.m. 3/01/92
Believed to be victim of Robbery-Kidnapping which occurred
at convenience store in McLennan Co.

Victims Vehicle also missing:*   1977 Buick Regal 2dr.
White/Burnt Orange
Texas LP# 287 XHV

Contact Det. Stroup or Det. Abner (817) 757-5114

Missing persons poster for Melissa Ann Northrup, 22, a pregnant
convenience-store clerk Kenneth McDuff murdered in 1991.

Melissa Northrup's body in the gravel pit.

Edna Louise Sullivan, 16, was kidnapped, raped, and killed by McDuff on August 6, 1966.

Robert Hugh Brand (at left), 17, and his cousin, John Marcus Dunnam, 15, were with Sullivan on August 6th. McDuff killed both boys.

Colleen Reed, 28, was kidnapped by McDuff while she washed her car, then was raped and murdered.
(*Courtesy of Lori Bible*)

(Right to left) 3-year-old Colleen and her 4-year-old sister Lori.
(*Courtesy of Lori Bible*)

(Right to left) Colleen and Lori at September 1991 wedding.
(*Courtesy of Lori Bible*)

U.S. Department of Justice
United States Marshals Service

WANTED
BY U.S. MARSHALS

NOTICE TO ARRESTING AGENCY: Before arrest, validate warrant through National Crime Information Center (NCIC).

United States Marshals Service NCIC entry number: (NIC/ W682016855).

NAME: MCDUFF, Kenneth Allen

ALIAS:

DESCRIPTION:

Sex:	MALE
Race:	WHITE
Place of Birth:	TEXAS
Date(s) of Birth:	MARCH 21, 1946
Height:	6'03"
Weight:	245
Eyes:	BROWN
Hair:	BROWN
Skintone:	LIGHT
Scars, Marks, Tattoos:	SCAR BACK, SCAR ABDOMEN
Social Security Number:	454-72-4658
NCIC Fingerprint Classification:	POAAAAPO18PIAAAA1113

SHOULD BE CONSIDERED ARMED AND DANGEROUS

MCDUFF IS CURRENTLY WANTED BY THE USM WESTERN DISTRICT OF TEXAS WACO DIVISION FOR THE DISTRIBUTION OF LSD. MCDUFF HAS BEEN CONVICTED OF MURDER AND IS BELIEVED TO BE ARMED.

WANTED FOR: DISTRIBUTION OF LSD AND FELON IN POSSESSION OF A FIREARM

Warrant Issued: WESTERN DISTRICT OF TEXAS WACO DIVISION
Warrant Number: 9280-0310-0506-Z

DATE WARRANT ISSUED: MARCH 6, 1992

MISCELLANEOUS INFORMATION: MCDUFF IS A SUSPECT IN THE POSSIBLE KIDNAPPING OF SEVERAL FEMALES IN THE WACO TEXAS AREA. MCDUFF WAS CONVICTED IN 1968 OF THE BRUTAL, EXECUTION STYLE SLAYING OF THREE TEENAGERS IN THE FT. WORTH AREA.

If arrested or whereabouts known, notify the local United States Marshals Office, (Telephone: 817-757-6318).

If no answer, call United States Marshals Service Communications Center in McLean, Virginia. 1-800-3360102
Telephone (800)336-0102: (24 hour telephone contact) NLETS access code is VAUSMOOOO.

PRIOR EDITIONS ARE OBSOLETE AND NOT TO BE USED

Form USM-132
(Rev. 2/84)

Wanted poster circulated in 1992.

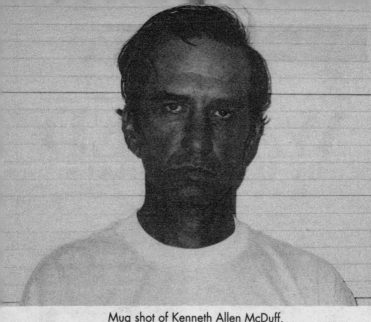

Mug shot of Kenneth Allen McDuff.

Waco narcotics squad file photo of a confident Kenneth McDuff, taken the day he offered his services as an informant.

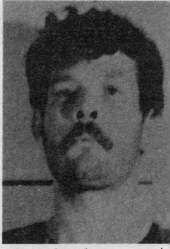

Alva Hank Worley, a convicted felon and McDuff's sidekick.

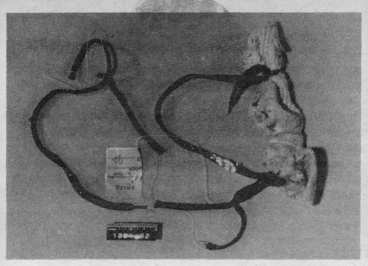

The shoelaces and socks McDuff used to tie Melissa
Northrup's hands.   *(Courtesy of Travis County D.A.'s Office)*

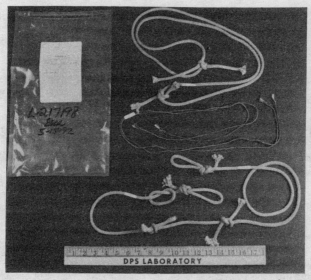

Ropes found in McDuff's apartment with knots similar
to those used to tie Melissa Northrup.
(Courtesy of Travis County D.A.'s Office)

Colleen Reed's car just moments after she was kidnapped by McDuff. The soap suds can still be seen on the ground. (*Courtesy of Travis County D.A.'s Office*)

Daylight photo of the bay where Colleen Reed was washing her car. (*Courtesy of Travis County D.A.'s Office*)

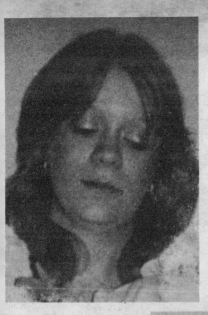

Regenia Moore, a prostitute McDuff knew. He is the prime suspect in her disappearance. (*Courtesy of Frank Pounds*)

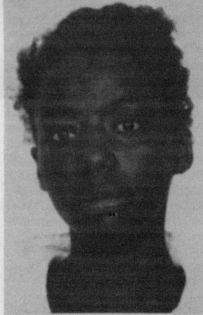

Valencia Kay Joshua, a suspected prostitute, whom McDuff was charged with murdering.

U.S. Marshals Mike and Parnell McNamara flank a hand-cuffed Kenneth McDuff as he is escorted back to Waco, TX.

killed her, and buried her. At least that was the story he instructed Harley to tell Regenia's family.

Obviously it would be natural to lay the crime at a Mexican's
doorstep since the original all-points bulletin for Colleen
Reed's abductors was for two Hispanics. Apparently McDuff
had paid attention to the news.

McDuff told Harley to tell Frank that he knew how to locate
this mysterious Mexican if the reward was legitimate. He
would torture the Mexican, if he had to, to find out where
Regenia was buried. Once he had the information, then he
would dig up the body, and deliver it to Barbara Miller for
the reward.

"But I'm the go-between," Harley told Frank. "You give
me the money and I'll take it to Kenneth. That's the way he
wants it."

"What exactly did he say?"

"He told me that he thinks he knows of a Mexican that
took Regenia off and killed her," Harley said.

Killed her!

Frank believed she was dead, although one secret compartment of his heart stored a hope that defied reason; but Harley's
words stunned him. This was the first time that anyone had
said Regenia was dead; always, she was described as missing.
Suspected dead, maybe, but never discussed as dead with such
finality.

"I can find Kenneth and make him tell me where she is,
and I can tell you, and you can go get the money from her
mother." Harley pressed the point unaware of the emotional
turmoil he had just launched.

"Okay, okay," Frank said. Right then he wanted to leap
across the restaurant table and grab Harley by the throat.

You low-life! You're talking about a special woman!

"And you can give it to me to take to Kenneth," Harley
added breaking into his thoughts. "If the money's real, then
Kenneth can find out where the body is. You give me the
money, and I'll give it to him."

"Why give it to him?" Frank replied coolly. "If we find the body, then you can take the money, hop on the first bus back to St. Louis, where you say you came from, and don't give McDuff nothing. He'd never find you."

"Yeah, man. That sounds like a great idea," Harley said.

The plotters set up a meeting in a few days. Harley was to find out where Regenia's body was located and get in touch.

A week passed without word. Frustrated, Frank found Harley.

"I'm workin' on it," Harley said, reassuringly. "You'll hear from me."

Within three weeks of Colleen's disappearance, Lori's new husband demanded that she get on with her life.

"Pull yourself together," he lectured her. "Colleen is dead. She's not coming back. You have to get back to your life."

Lori listened and dutifully tried to believe. The next day she went back to work, only to leave by mid-afternoon, her concentration gone as her mind wandered, always coming back to Colleen and her unknown fate, her last hours. Horrible, unspeakable acts happened to her sister in Lori's mind.

That night the newlyweds argued over responsibility, both financial and domestic. Lori went to work the next day only to be called to the police station. It was a pattern that would be repeated until she would deplete her vacation time and sick leave, then take days off without pay.

Against all odds, Lori maintained hope that Colleen was still alive. As January turned into February, a distraught Lori began to write poignant letters to her sister.

Dear Colleen,
  It's been twenty-one days. What did I do before? I can't ask again where you are. There are no answers. Oh, everyone has a theory. Boy, have I got stories for you. I have to believe you are alive. But sometimes

the thought of you being alive is too difficult. Are you cold? Are you hungry? What if I'll never know?

I am angry—how dare someone take you—you have a right to freedom.

When you were abducted I disappeared. My life changed. This time the one action of others really changed my life. I will never forget.

The shock came on Monday morning, around 9-9:30—twelve hours after you screamed for help. The police did not call me. Oliver did. He called me at my office. I was working on what I don't remember. Oliver and I met at the police station. After what seemed like an eternity, we talked to a Sergeant [Don] Martin who had been assigned to the case when he came on duty that day. I was shocked by the abduction and outraged that the police did not call me.

Fourteen hours had passed since you had been abducted before I was able to speak to the investigator and find out what had happened.

It was then decided that Oliver would go get pictures of you, and I would go call Mom and Dad, Anita and Mae, and pick up some pictures for the press release. Seventeen hours after the abduction the press had the information. That evening less than 24 hours after the abduction, Mom, Dad, Mae, Wain and family were gathered in my living room. The shock was at it's peak. We cried, watched the news, answered the phone that rang constantly. No one really slept. As fatigue took over, we'd collapse in bed for a few hours. Little did we know this would go on.

The next few days were a blur. We were interviewed in my home by three TV stations and the *American Statesman*. The phone rang incessantly.

Food arrived in mass. Well-wishers and offers to assist poured in.

Nothing that mattered before seemed to matter.

The community reached out.

New Year's Eve—spent at home. Earlier Mae and I put out flyers on 6th St.

By now your face is seen over a large part of Austin and Travis County, Williamson and surrounding counties. Within days of abduction your face is seen over a large part of Central and South Texas.

A week after your abduction we are trying to decide what next. At this point your life has become an open book. A lot of your life is public knowledge—or at least known by family and friends and police who are all so desperately trying to find you.

Mom and Dad leave [Saturday]—six days after abduction, taking cat, Mensa.

Anita leaves next day [Sunday].

Mae leaves later that week.

A fund is set up.

A vigil is held.

The letter, unsigned, was stuck into a growing stack of documents that Lori had begun to collect in a cardboard box in her closet.

Each morning Lori dutifully called the police to report the anonymous tips from mysterious telephone calls in the night from people who feared the law but not the grieving sister. Each day it became routine for her to visit the police station on her lunch hour.

Each day thousands of posters arrived at her home. Posters made up by strangers, posters reprinted by strangers from ones she had put out; sometimes up to four thousand a package.

Colleen's secretary from the Lower Colorado River Authority showed up almost daily with freshly prepared food. Lori's girlfriends took turns keeping the boys when Don was not available.

Lori had never seen such an outpouring of love; yet, she felt strangely alone.

* * *

Three psychics contacted Lori, each claiming to know where Colleen's body lay. In desperation she went to Dallas to meet with one who had vivid descriptions and "auto-writing" supposedly scribbled by Colleen.

"He was so far off it was pathetic," she told Oliver upon her return. The rest of the psychics' predictions were tossed into a second cardboard box.

Three weeks after Colleen's abduction the newlyweds quarreled again.

"I can't do it," Lori told Jeff. "I'm just not ready to go back to work, or to try to live my life without Colleen."

"Do it or I leave," he demanded.

"Then leave," she replied.

She understood Jeff's predicament. They had barely wed when she was forced to have major surgery. The hysterectomy had been life-threatening. She was still recovering from the medical blow when Colleen was kidnapped.

"At least we've had two good months," she said softly. It would be eighteen months before the divorce was final.

Sonia Urubek had just been promoted to sergeant when she was temporarily assigned to the Yogurt Murders task force in early December. Leads began to taper off in the sensational case and before she knew it, although she had spent more than seven years as first a patrol officer and then an investigator in the traffic office, Sergeant Urubek found herself shuffling papers. Her work on the Yogurt Murders had whet her appetite for investigative work.

"There's a high-profile case out there," she told her friend and fellow officer, J.W. Thompson. "I want to be a part of it."

Thanks to Lori Bible-Tolson, she did. Lori had charged into

the office shortly after Colleen disappeared, frustrated and angry. Although there was deep sympathy for Lori, her tirades were beginning to alienate some of the officers. That night Urubek gently soothed the frustrated woman. The night supervisor decided that Urubek would become Lori's contact.

Excited at the opportunity to work on the case, Urubek pulled every document to study it. Her desire to get into the field was frustrated when she was ordered to follow up telephone tips.

In early January the eager investigator noticed that several law enforcement agencies made inquiries to the National Crime Information Center for any records on a man identified as Kenneth McDuff. Urubek read the report from the first inquiry within a week of Colleen Reed's disappearance. The description matched that of the larger man described by the eyewitnesses. She suggested the paroled killer as a potential suspect, but her proposal went unheeded. The Austin police were looking for a Hispanic suspect.

Meanwhile, Urubek reexamined the case. She decided to retrace the perimeter search of the car wash neighborhood by visiting surrounding businesses. When her telephone work was done, she pounded the pavement. Slowly she began to build a suspect list that included several males from Whole Food Market, a grocery store on Lamar Street where Colleen had stopped for groceries prior to the kidnapping. Urubek asked Lori about Colleen's former boyfriends. She spent hours with Lori, trying to probe into Colleen's life and psyche.

On Valentine's Day, Lori came into the station fuming.

Sergeant Don Martin tried to reassure the distraught woman, when Urubek decided it was time to face the facts.

"Lori, we're doing our best," Urubek said, jumping into the conversation. "Do you think we want someone on the loose that kidnaps people? Don't you think we want Colleen back, too?"

Shocked, Lori sat quietly.

"Give us a chance to do our job," Urubek pleaded, an edge in her voice. "Give us a chance to work.

"There are other people who have problems. Your sister's case is not the only one we're working," she said forcibly. "There are other people to consider, too."

It did not appear to help the situation at the time. Lori left in anger.

Kenneth McDuff was busy on February 24, 1992. Suspected prostitute, twenty-three-year-old Valencia Kay Joshua, awoke McDuff's dormitory neighbor by tapping on the window at 3:30 in the morning. She was seeking McDuff. The sleepy student directed her one window over.

Nearly twenty hours later, at 11:30 that night, McDuff was arrested by the Temple Police Department for public intoxication after the ex-con and Elroy Jerrold had gotten into a barroom brawl with a black man.

While going over the original case reports, Sergeant Urubek came to the realization that no one had searched Colleen Reed's apartment.

"Lori, what about your sister's apartment?" she asked in a telephone conversation.

"I cleaned it out weeks ago," Lori said.

"Did anyone go through her things?"

"No, I just came in and stuffed everything into garbage bags," she said. She had put the bulging bags in her attic.

Urubek was shocked that potential evidence had not been collected. She protested to Sergeant Martin. From that time forward, she sensed a real problem with Martin as their relationship began falling apart.

The night of March 1, 1992, when Melissa Ann Northrup was kidnapped from Quik Pak No. 8 in Waco, Mildred Hollins met a tall, rangy man dressed like a cowboy when she left her

hotel room in Temple to visit a nearby lounge. Dressed in blue
jeans complemented by a big belt buckle, western shirt, boots,
and a summer straw hat, McDuff approached her, seeking to
buy drugs. The two walked to a nearby motel where a cast of
characters with names like T-Bone, One-Arm and Darrin, Hollins' cousin by marriage, were already doing drugs. She offered
McDuff a free hit on the assumption that an undercover police
officer would not smoke crack cocaine. Although McDuff had
no money he told her that he had a pair of credit cards issued
in his father's name. They went to a convenience store where
McDuff used the credit cards to purchase eighty-three dollars
in cigarettes with the intent to resell them for cash to buy
drugs.

As the evening progressed, McDuff became more and more
violent.

"He had a knife and he kept pulling it out," Mildred would
later testify. "He kept telling me, he said if he can't get no
crack . . . without money he'll go jack the motherfucker with
the crack." Mildred explained that "jack" meant to rob. "He
said he would kill the motherfucker to get the money for the
dope."

Already uneasy because of his swiftly changing moods, and
the ever-present knife, Mildred agreed to drive McDuff to an
area frequented by drug dealers. When no one offered to buy
the cigarettes, McDuff jumped out of the car, screaming obscenities and threatening the drug dealers.

"He jumped out of the car and that made everybody paranoid because he was the only white person down there in a
black neighborhood," Mildred said in unbelief. ". . . [He]
started cussing and shit. I told him to get his crazy ass back
in the car before he get killed."

McDuff complied, but not before screaming that "he wasn't
no fucking police officer, all he wanted to do was get some
crack and a girl, hundred dollars worth of crack and a lady.

"He told me he don't give a damn about getting killed," she
continued. "He said he'd kill the motherfucker himself. Then

he got back out. I finally convinced him to get back in the car. I didn't want nobody to take the cigarettes."

Mildred Hollins hurried out of the neighborhood, shaken by the incident.

"He's crazy," she told her friends. They were afraid of him, and fearful that he might bring harm to them. They wanted to get rid of this walking time bomb.

Back at the motel, Mildred stole the cigarettes from the car and put them in the room while McDuff smoked another pipe of crack cocaine. She and Darrin concocted a plan to trick McDuff back into his car on the pretense of searching for more dope. Then the cousins planned to abandon him. He had insisted that she drive because he told her he was intoxicated. She let Darrin out several blocks from a friend's house. He walked the rest of the way. After a few minutes, she drove up to Judy's home.

"When I got over there I told him I didn't know if Darrin was coming or not. When I got ready to get out of the car he grabbed me. He told me I was going to Waco with him," she said.

"He asked me, did I want to go to Waco," Mildred remembered. She was putting her high heel shoes on since she would not be driving again. "I wasn't going to go up that far. And he told me, 'Bitch, you going with me.'

"And that's when he grabbed me and we started tussling," she said. McDuff grabbed one of the shoes and began hitting her with it. "He was sitting in back. He never did get in the front when Darrin got out.

"I started screaming," Mildred said, fearful that she was about to be abducted by a man she had come to fear. "And Judy came out the door and cut on her porch light. I opened the door and jumped out. He jumped out the car and ran around and got in and spin off real fast." Obviously he was frustrated and angry she said.

Earlier in the evening she had made an attempt to find him a prostitute.

"Thank God, I didn't find her," she said. "He's weird."

* * *

Fear gripped Central Texas early the next morning when a petite, pretty blonde woman disappeared from Quik Pak No. 8, a convenience store on the edge of the TSTC campus. Aaron Northrup had stayed with his wife until 1:30 a.m. He only went home because Melissa Ann Northrup insisted that her husband get some rest because he was to care for their two children the next day.

Lonely, she called him twice, the final time at 3:35 a.m. Aaron got the impression that a customer had come into the store, so he hung up after she lay the telephone down. He called back ten minutes later. There was no answer. Aaron rushed to the store to find his wife missing. Frantically he dialed 911. Melissa had disappeared. Her car was gone, as was $252.04 from the cash register.

Less than a block away in the dark hours before dawn, Richard Bannister, an aircraft structural repairman, had taken his dog for a walk at the New Road Inn. The motel was several hundred yards from the Quik Pak. Around 4:00 a.m., Bannister met a strange man attempting to manipulate two automobiles at the same time. This tall, ruddy cowboy-type would shove a light-colored Thunderbird forward with a burnt-orange Buick Regal, then get out of the car straighten the wheel of the Thunderbird and shove it forward again. Bannister watched as the man pushed the Thunderbird into the parking lot of the New Road Inn.

"Know a wrecker service?" the man asked.

"No," Bannister replied.

"How about a pay phone?"

Bannister shrugged. The big man drove off, abandoning the Thunderbird.

The disappearance of Melissa Ann Northrup was the talk of Waco radio news that dawn as it would be throughout the state as the news spread. Northrup was the second woman to disappear in two months in Central Texas.

A few days later, Northrup's in-laws would stumble upon Louis Bray as they distributed fliers at a convenience store where Bray worked.

"I don't know that woman, but I know the store," Bray told Bethany Sneed, Aaron Northrup's sister, and her husband Kirk. "A man asked me to help him rob it."

Bray said he lived across the hall at TSTC from a man he knew as Ken. Bray identified him as the man who tried to entice him into helping with a robbery.

A few days later the FBI showed the family a picture of Kenneth McDuff. Aaron Northrup called seeing McDuff's picture a real "head snapper." He had introduced his wife to McDuff, whom he had trained at Quik Pak during the summer.

THIRTEEN

It looked like a routine missing person's report that landed on the desk of Bell County Sheriff's Office Investigator Tim Steglich of the Special Crimes Unit on March 5, 1992. A distraught mother had reported that her son had been missing since February 29 when he left home around eleven o'clock in the morning to mail a package. He had not taken his reading glasses, and this alarmed the worried mother.

Addie McDuff feared that her son Kenneth was dead because he had not returned and had not contacted her since he left home. Deputy Ralph Howell had dutifully taken the information for the missing person's report; but, Deputy Howell was careful to note in his paperwork that Kenneth McDuff had an extensive criminal history and was on parole. Howell had also entered the description of McDuff's car on the missing person's report before sending it electronically to other law enforcement officers across the state.

Investigator Steglich read between the lines of Deputy Howell's report. Many times a "missing person" is a "leaving person." Often a convict will flee his home base rather than risk being issued a blue warrant—so named because of its color—for parole violations. The dreaded blue warrant will send a parolee back to prison, sometimes on a one-way ticket. It is the most powerful warrant in the State of Texas because it is a no-bond warrant. Steglich did not know it at the time, but McDuff's ticket had been punched once too often.

* * *

"Kenneth is dead," the distraught mother told Steglich in a brief telephone call. She insisted that her son was the victim of foul play. "He's not here on this earth any longer."

It sounded more like a statement of fact than opinion. The woman's certainty of her son's death puzzled Steglich. Most parents are hopeful when they file a missing person's report. Hope is the motive behind the report. Most parents cling to that hope, desperately, sometimes irrationally, months, even years, after it has become obvious that the loved one probably will not return home. In the face of apparent foul play, sometimes the hope is simply a desire to find a body, conduct a funeral service, and resume life, to put closure on a painful chapter.

But despite her words, Addie McDuff did not seem to exhibit the normal reaction of a desperate parent. Her statements seemed rehearsed. This was the first of many red flags the perceptive veteran detective would see. It was a dazzling marker, and it worried him.

Tim Steglich was uniquely suited for this case. This was his territory. He was born August 10, 1957 in Temple, but was reared in Bartlett, a small town southeast of Belton, where he now served in the Criminal Investigation Division of the Bell County Sheriff's Office. His dark good looks, topped with salt-and-pepper hair, reminded friends of a young Charles Bronson. Six feet, three inches tall, Steglich played basketball for his high school team, graduated at sixteen in 1975, and spent only one semester in Temple Junior College before moving to Pasadena, Texas, to go to work as a boiler-maker for Shell Oil Company. He had always been interested in police work, so when the Houston Police Department advertised for officers, he applied. Always deliberate, he had researched the reputation of other cities' police academies before determining that HPD had the best.

He reasoned that in a big place a police officer could see

almost anything. At nineteen he was accepted into the academy only to discover when he graduated a few months later that he was too young to buy his own bullets.

Steglich was so inexperienced that during map studies class in the HDP Academy he was asked about the loop. "I thought the loop was something you did with a rope," he said, poking fun at his small-town roots, "not a type of road." The big city was exciting, but within a few years Steglich longed for the simpler life. His wife Vicki, a computer instructor, agreed, and they returned to Steglich's beloved Central Texas.

On March 1, the day after Steglich talked to Addie McDuff, Big Boy Wrecker service was called to tow away a beige Thunderbird found abandoned at New Road Inn, a small motel near Quik Pak No. 8. It had been on the parking lot for five days. McLennan County Sheriff's Office Sergeant Richard Stroup ran a license plate check; the car belonged to a paroled felon named Kenneth McDuff. Suspecting that the vehicle might be involved in the Melissa Ann Northrup case, Stroup put a description of the vehicle on the state electronic message board.

When Steglich read Stroup's dispatch, he saw that the vehicle matched the description of the Thunderbird given by McDuff's mother.

Steglich's eye was also caught by another bulletin issued by the McLennan County Sheriff's Office concerning the March 1 disappearance of Melissa Northrup.

Steglich contacted Sergeant Stroup concerning Addie's missing person report. The pair decided that Steglich should make personal contact with McDuff's parents to find out more about Kenneth's reported disappearance.

It was a bizarre meeting. Addie McDuff dominated more than two hours of conversation, mostly justifying her son and describing him as a misunderstood soul in a cruel world. To illustrate her point, Addie recounted the time a teacher of Kenneth's asked the children to write their names in cursive on a blackboard in a small school and Kenneth printed his name.

The children mocked and laughed at his inability to connect the letters into flowing script, Addie recalled bitterly.

"Kenneth was very resentful," the loving mother told the detective.

But, Addie said, Kenneth had gone on to achieve a 3.64 grade point average at Texas State Technical College. McDuff had received an A in advanced lathe operation, a trade that would require great skill with his massive hands. He had even received an A in human relations.

But even now, Addie continued, her Junior was troubled by small-minded people. He could not find a job because of his prison record. He had to take a polygraph test before being considered by a machine shop in Victoria. Furthermore, Kenneth had been on the verge of being hired by that firm when some vengeful person told the company about his record.

"Kenneth was looking forward to this job," she said. He was on his way to mail the results of the polygraph test when he disappeared. Her son was so sure of getting the job that he had packed his personal belongings in the car in anticipation of moving to Victoria, a medium-sized community near the Gulf Coast about one hundred twenty-five miles southwest of Houston.

"I think . . ." J.A. McDuff, Kenneth's father started to say.

"You shut up!" Addie cut him off, transformed in a millisecond from concerned mother to snarling protector.

Meekly the elder McDuff, obviously in bad health, and perhaps without a grasp of the situation, submissively sank back into the couch as the stunned detective watched.

"What about friends?" Steglich asked.

"No friends that you can contact," she said.

"Anything happen lately; maybe a threat or trouble?"

"He told me that he had been arrested in Temple last week for public intoxication," Addie said. "Didn't you know that?"

Steglich did not answer, making a mental note that public intoxication could be a blue-sheet ticket back to Huntsville.

Instead he asked if he could search Kenneth's room. The mother hesitated.

It was evident to the wily police officer that Addie was trying as hard to get information out of him as he was out of her. She had to maintain control of the conversation. Addie McDuff could not run the risk of her ill husband inadvertently saying something that might harm whatever game plan she was following.

It only took the seasoned officer a few minutes to realize that Addie McDuff was devoted to this fifth child, trying to stand as a shield between this special progeny and a hostile world that failed, or refused, to recognize his uniqueness.

She's trying to set up an alibi for her son, Steglich thought, *but why?*

It was Addie McDuff's role in life to protect Kenneth from the rigors of the world. Dr. James P. Grigson, a psychiatrist who has testified in more than one hundred death penalty cases for the prosecution, believes that some individuals like Kenneth McDuff are sometimes molded through a combination of rejection and obsession—rejection because in some instances the mother does not want to bear the child and obsession because of her guilt. Terrified that the world might discover her true feelings the mother often crosses the line to the obsessive extreme. She coddles the child. He is never wrong. She bears his burdens. She straightens the path. She smooths the rocky road. All the while she is terrified that the world will discover that she never wanted the child and secretly hates it.

"As the child grows, he tries to become Superman," Dr. Grigson says. A child's personality is formed during the first five to six years of life, including the type of work he might do, the type of person he will marry, and the type of family he will have.

"Kenneth McDuff was already suffering from feelings of being unneeded and unwanted, and low self-esteem," Dr. Grigson explains. If a male child is smothered by his mother's obsession, he becomes emasculated. Unable to function in the world around him because of his flawed coping mechanism, his fury builds as he grows older. He becomes a bully on the playground, disruptive in the classroom, and incapable of functioning in polite society.

"School tells him that he is no good because of his failures. He is surrounded by negative attributes that reinforce his bad image. To protect his fragile emotional state, a man like McDuff comes to believe, 'I'm better than the rest of the world. I don't have to conform.' "

Drugs are a convenient escape, Dr. Grigson believes.

"I don't think dope had that much to do with it," says Crawford Long of Waco, one of the McLennan County District Attorneys who eventually would prosecute McDuff. "If there were no dope on this earth, then McDuff would still be killing. He has that dark side."

That dark side would move McDuff into the underbelly of society, a bleak world of fellow misfits where even the pariah will come to consider him a maverick among renegades. Here he will find the weak, the defenseless, the helpless. He can control them, just as his mother controlled him.

In the weeks to come, Tim Steglich would meet many people who feared Kenneth McDuff. But at that moment Steglich stood in the presence of possibly the only person in the world who would ever profess McDuff's innocence and continue to maintain her son's innocence as murder after murder after murder would be revealed.

"Whenever a family member is told the truth, the family says that you are a liar," said U.S. Marshal Service Inspector Dan Stolz, who would eventually head a massive task force searching for the convicted killer. "When they are shown proof, they refuse to talk to you any more."

Addie McDuff had refused to believe her son's guilt in 1966; why would she believe he was guilty now?

In the first interview, Steglich knew little of McDuff's background or his family. What he did sense was Addie McDuff's attempt to manipulate him through a stream of seemingly innocent questions. It would turn into a battle of wits that would last for several months as he deliberately became the McDuffs' connection to law enforcement.

Addie produced a briefcase that McDuff's older sister, Geraldine, had picked up from his dorm room at TSTC. It bothered Steglich that someone had already gone into McDuff's dorm room. McDuff had only been missing four or five days. *Were they removing evidence?* he wondered. *Why go on over there? Why get just the briefcase?* He made a mental bet with himself that the dorm room was already cleaned out. Later, he would read the reports on the murders of the three teenagers in 1966 and realize that Kenneth's older brother had destroyed evidence. He wondered if it was a pattern repeating itself.

The briefcase yielded little: a W-2 form that showed that McDuff had worked for a Quik Pak Convenience Store in Waco in 1991, along with a vehicle title and some other papers. Steglich took possession of these papers. McDuff's room in the family home held a few clothes. There was nothing of substance to aid Steglich in his search for the missing man.

But, the house held something else: an intangible aura that aroused the detective's survival instinct. McDuff's presence permeated the room, as if he had just left the bedroom after spending the night.

Sure. He was just here several days ago, Steglich chided himself. But he knew it was more than that. *I wouldn't be surprised to learn that he's still here, sleeping here each night.*

It was disturbing to consider the possibility that Kenneth McDuff might be lurking about. Steglich had spotted three pairs of binoculars on a coffee table in the living room. Addie McDuff said the spyglasses were used to watch for the postman at a rural mailbox about one hundred yards from the house. *But three pair? In a home for two?* Addie admitted that one pair belonged to Kenneth.

With each visit to the McDuff home Steglich became more and more cautious. He would never be comfortable in that house as long as McDuff remained at large. The criminal's mother could be harboring him at any time, only a few feet away. From that moment forward the experienced lawman walked with his back to the wall whenever he entered the home.

As Detective Tim Steglich was interviewing the McDuffs that March 6, Mike and Parnell McNamara were on their way to meet Assistant U.S. Attorney Bill Johnston for a quick lunch when the marshals passed a pair of FBI agents. They exchanged typical greetings before one agent brought them up short with a question.

"You guys ever hear of a man called Kenneth McDuff," he called after them.

They stopped at the same time.

"Sure," Parnell said. "For a long time."

"We just found a car registered to him at a motel," the agent said, noting that McDuff was a suspect in the Melissa Ann Northrup case. The McNamaras only knew what they had read or heard on news reports about the woman's disappearance.

"Look no more," Mike said. "You've found your guy."

"Really?" The agent would need some convincing. Seldom are cases so easily solved.

"That's the broomstick killer," Parnell said.

"What?"

"The broomstick killer," Mike said again. "We've known about him for more than twenty years."

It was crystal clear to the brothers. McDuff's car was near the scene of a crime. He had killed before. He should be the prime suspect.

The Waco natives excitedly told Johnston about the FBI discovery. Although they ordered meals, the three men hardly touched the food.

"We've got to do something," Mike urged. "Now! If we don't, he'll get away."

They had to have a federal crime to allow them to investigate but so far all they had was a state crime, even if it were kidnapping and possibly murder.

"What's the federal crime?" Parnell asked.

They sat in silence for long moments before Johnston offered a bit of information tucked deep into his memory. He had heard the name McDuff before when a female informant feared for her safety in another case. She told her law enforcement contact that the infamous "broomstick killer" might be called in to deal with her. She identified the broomstick killer as Kenneth McDuff.

His memory jogged, Johnston remembered that Kenneth McDuff had made the mistake of providing LSD to a fellow student in December, 1991, in McLennan County. The men left their meals untouched to search out the student, who they discovered had gone fishing. No problem. McLennan County sheriff's deputies would fetch him back from the lake.

United States Drug Enforcement Administration Special Agent Jay Eubanks questioned the student to determine if the drug McDuff had given him was LSD. It was.

Finally, McDuff had broken a federal law. For an arrest to be made, state law requires a sale of drugs while federal law requires distribution—even a gift without money changing hands.

It was the mistake that the McNamara brothers and Pamplin had waited for.

Johnston unleashed the federal agents by issuing a warrant for McDuff's arrest based on a confidential source who had seen McDuff use methamphetamine, marijuana, crack cocaine, and LSD. DEA Agent Eubanks filed a document quoting the agent as stating that "McDuff dealt blotter paper LSD with a silver palm tree design . . . during December, 1991."

The blotter paper resembled the thin sheets used to roll cigarettes. The design contained the drug. A user would simply lick it clean, or dissolve it in the mouth, to get a potent LSD high. The silver palm was a popular brand in the Austin area.

Johnston was the thirty-five-year-old son of Wilson

Johnston, who served as an assistant district attorney for Dallas County for twenty-five years. Wilson was on the team that helped prosecute Jack Ruby for the murder of Lee Harvey Oswald. As a high school student, Bill Johnston watched his father accompany lawmen on cases in the 1970s, a rare activity for members of the bar, but an example that he would follow.

"We used to worry about my Dad. Sometimes he wouldn't come home at night," Johnston says before ruefully adding, "And I do the same thing to my wife."

In retrospect the men knew they were on the trail of a serial killer. Although they made no connection between McDuff and Colleen Reed's December 29 kidnapping in Austin, the lawmen knew that Regenia Moore and Brenda Thompson had disappeared from The Cut, and the FBI agents had identified McDuff's car as being near the Quik Pak where Melissa Northrup disappeared on March 1.

When the marshals left the federal offices just off Interstate 35 in Waco, Parnell told Mike, "This is going to be a cakewalk."

"We'll have him in two or three days," Mike agreed clutching the drug warrant in hand.

The search for Kenneth McDuff and his victims began that evening. Officers of the police department and sheriff's office quickly formed a team and fanned out to search a field near the Quik Pak for Melissa's body. The next morning the Department of Public Safety provided an airplane that flew over a cow pasture behind TSTC, but none of the searchers discovered anything awry.

That same evening "America's Most Wanted" ran a picture of Colleen Reed and a video tape at the end of the show requesting help in the search for the missing woman.

A spokesman from "America's Most Wanted" called Sergeant Don Martin later that evening. Out of twenty-five tips, one offered promise. A dead white female had been found in West Virginia, but a follow-up proved to be fruitless.

* * *

Three days after the initial contact, Addie was back on the telephone to Steglich. She had learned that Kenneth's car had been found in Waco and towed into storage. Furthermore, she related, Kenneth had been seen getting into another car that strangely resembled the missing vehicle Melissa Northrup was driving.

Steglich was incredulous. "How did you learn that?"

"I got a telephone call," she said. Steglich said nothing. "From someone I don't know," she added, "a white male . . . a man . . . about ten o'clock."

I wonder if that man could have been Kenneth? Steglich immediately thought. Steglich knew it was not uncommon for a criminal—especially a serial killer, if that's what McDuff was—to return to the scene of a crime out of a compulsion to watch the police investigate.

Addie went on to explain that the caller, who said he was in Victoria, Texas, told her that Kenneth left because of trouble with his parole officers.

The concerned mother reiterated her belief that her son had not voluntarily left and was dead or "tied up where he can't get away."

The next morning Sergeant Stroup would confirm that no information had been released about the McDuff car other than to police officials. *Either Mrs. McDuff is receiving inside information,* Steglich thought, *or she had spoken with Kenneth.* Stroup and Steglich agreed that Steglich should continue communicating with the McDuff family.

Later, on March 9, Steglich was contacted by Parnell McNamara, who informed him that a federal warrant had been issued March 6 for the arrest of McDuff on charges of selling LSD.

Inspector Steglich returned to the McDuffs' two days later. In the garage he discovered a maroon pickup truck. The glove box yielded a repair bill showing that the front windshield had been replaced. Steglich ran a license plate check. No match. But the vehicle description matched that of the pickup reported in the Waco roadblock incident October 10, 1991, when a white female was seen tied and kicking the front windshield.

Steglich took a stab in the dark when he went back into the house. Maybe McDuff had brought Melissa Northrup to the family home. "Does he have a girlfriend?" Steglich asked.

Addie did say that her son brought a girl to the house several months before, but she did not resemble the missing woman.

The detective told U.S. Attorney Johnston in a telephone call that the second visit raised more questions than the first. He had seen boots, binoculars, and a book opened to a section on machine shops, the topic of McDuff's study at TSTC.

"It's like he has just left the room," Steglich told Johnston. "I believe McDuff is there."

McDuff's TSTC records confirmed his 3.64 grade point average. The records showed that McDuff had made an A in oral communication, and a C in industrial safety. His technical skills were high, but Steglich suspected that most of those skills were obtained during two decades in prison. It amazed Steglich that McDuff had obtained a student loan for eight hundred dollars. It disappointed him that the school's attendance records were improperly kept. The records could have proven invaluable in documenting McDuff's whereabouts, but more often than not the convict was listed as present in classes he did not attend.

Perhaps the most bizarre item in the packet was a situational test McDuff had taken for a story he had read. The questions required McDuff to answer true or false or with a question mark:

1. A man appeared after the owner had turned off his store lights.
2. The robber was a man.

3. The man did not demand money.

4. The man who opened the cash register was the owner.

5. The store owner scooped up the contents of the cash register and ran away.

6. Someone opened a cash register.

7. After the man who demanded the money scooped up the contents of the cash register, he ran away.

8. While the cash register contained money, the story does not state how much.

9. The robber demanded money of the owner.

10. The story concerns a series of events in which only three persons are referred to: the store owner, a man who demanded money, and a member of the police force.

11. The following events in the story are true: someone demanded money, a cash register was opened, its contents were scooped up, and a man dashed out of the store.

"False" was McDuff's answer for questions three, five and seven. The rest he answered "true."

He ought to know the answers, Steglich smiled to himself. *He's actually done those things.*

A few days later the harried McNamara brothers revised the number of days it would take to catch McDuff. They anticipated it might now take several weeks. Several weeks later as leads poured in, the men realized they needed help.

As overtime hours began to pile up, they turned to Warrant Supervisor Sam Williams in San Antonio. Williams contacted U.S. Marshal Service Inspector Daniel Stolz, who, although assigned to the home office in Washington, D.C., lived in Houston, with his wife and three children.

Stolz, too, comes from a long line of lawmen. As a child he

heard the stories about his grandfather, Texas Ranger Marcelo Dougherty, who enforced the law along the Rio Grande in South Texas. Stolz was born December 30, 1952, in San Antonio. His family moved to Long Beach, California, when he was a child. After graduating from junior college with a degree in criminal justice, at twenty he joined federal law enforcement by becoming a correctional officer guard, eventually graduating to his present position with the U.S. Marshal's Service.

Since joining the marshal service, Stolz has worked with the Organized Crime Drug Task Force, an assignment that has sent him undercover to Colombia, Hong Kong, the Philippines, Thailand and Honduras as well as other countries in Central and South America. He and Inspector Michael Carnevale—a friend and fellow officer who was more like a brother—had the reputation of being two of the best trackers in the United States.

The team was winding down a federal task force program called Operation Gunsmoke when Stolz was contacted by the McNamaras. Stolz would see to it that equipment and funding for hundreds of hours of overtime would be channeled into the search for McDuff. Within a matter of days, lawmen from police departments, sheriff's offices, and state and federal agencies would band together in the search. A master at planning, Stolz elected to remain in the background.

Stolz ordered a psychological profile on McDuff on the theory that such a profile would indicate what bars to hit or what family members to question.

"I have a theory that history repeats itself," Stolz told Mike and Parnell McNamara as the task force was formed. "When he killed in 1966, his older brother hid him in a barn. I believe he is somewhere around Waco. We need to find the fugitive, then the bodies."

On March 11, Sergeant Sonia Urubek received a telephone call from McLennan County Sheriff's Office Lieutenant Tru-

man Simons concerning a Thunderbird found abandoned at a
motel in Waco.

"Look at this, J.W.," Urubek said. She had been attempting
to bring J.W. Thompson into the McDuff investigation. The
officer felt she needed an ally. She also knew that people were
drawn to even-tempered Thompson, who had a calming influence on those around him. A native of San Antonio, Texas,
the forty-seven-year-old Thompson had recently been promoted to sergeant, and to homicide. As far as Urubek was
concerned, the report matched the description of the car seen
leaving the scene of the Reed kidnapping.

"The guy the car is registered to is even a convicted murderer," she stressed, noting a federal warrant had been issued.
The report also mentioned his burglary convictions. "J.W., the
guy that took Colleen is Kenneth McDuff," she said, a bit cha-
grined that she had suggested him as a suspect as early as January 6.

Urubek asked law enforcement officers in Waco to fax details
and a picture of McDuff. Intrigued and not a little bit excited,
she asked Simons to send her the information on the murders
in 1966.

This is the guy, she thought when she finished reading the
files. She could not deny the combination of investigation and
instincts that produced the conclusion. Urubek approached her
supervisor.

"This is the best lead we've got," she said. "I want to look
at that car. I don't want to wait. I've really got a feeling about
this."

She had learned that Bureau of Alcohol, Tobacco and Firearms (ATF) Special Agent Jeff Brzozowski was going to run
a federal search warrant for a gun the next day. He had invited
several state and city law enforcement organizations to ob-
serve. The supervisor suggested that Sergeant Martin be called
in since he was in charge of the case.

"This is my tip," Urubek said. "I want to work it."

Both Urubek and Martin went to Waco the next day.

* * *

Sergeant Urubek stared at the closed garage door. She felt the thrill of discovery tinged with the fear of failure. If the car belonged to McDuff, then the evidence had to be protected. She glanced at Martin. He seemed unconcerned. As they waited, the McNamaras and Johnston brought Urubek up-to-date on their search for McDuff. The men were happy to share the thrill of the chase with this inquisitive woman. It was nice to have someone interested in their quest.

Urubek had reread all the reports. Her finely honed instincts had caused her to suspect this to be the car. After talking to the marshals and U.S. attorney, she was nearly certain it was the vehicle in the Reed case, and she had not even seen it, yet.

But she had visualized it in her mind. As unobtrusively as possible, Urubek asked Brzozowski to help her conserve possible evidence in the Reed case as he searched the vehicle for a gun.

"Could you be careful?" she asked. "Some of this might have evidence that will connect this car to Colleen Reed, and we might want to get our own search warrant."

"Sure. Fine," the cordial ATF agent said. "No problem."

The officers stood in a line in front of the big aluminum garage door. The anticipation was akin to opening a Christmas present.

As the vehicle came into full view Urubek first noticed the light color of the car.

That's right.

She saw that it was a Thunderbird.

That matches!

Slowly she walked to the rear of the garage to study the taillights.

They appeared to match!

"This is it. I know this is it," she told Sergeant Martin.

He was not as sure as she was.

What are you talking about? she wondered. *You haven't even looked!*

Flushed with anger, Urubek stepped to the rear of the Thunderbird where ATF Agent Brzozowski was preparing to inventory the contents. At that point she decided to ignore Martin.

Urubek was careful to document the search. She had already written down the names of all the law enforcement representatives there, as well as the names of Big Boy employees. She spied a bent straw cowboy hat on the back seat of the car.

Brzozowski spread a large blue plastic tarpaulin on the ground. He carefully began placing items onto it as he searched for a gun, the reason for the search warrant. The tarpaulin secured the integrity of the evidence for the Austin Police Department. Urubek watched as clothing was unfolded and placed on the crisp, clean plastic: wrinkled and unwashed shirts, soiled underwear containing hair and blood that could yield forensic clues. It looked as if someone had dumped the contents of a chest of drawers into the trunk then threw dirty clothing on top. When finished, Brzozowski and another officer carefully lifted the tarpaulin, and its potential clues, into the trunk so nothing else would be disturbed.

Careful not to touch the car herself, Urubek was concerned that the vehicle might be contaminated by the curious lawmen surrounding the vehicle.

Just back off, she pleaded in her mind. *Don't touch anything.*

Texas Ranger John Aycock, a blood-splatter expert, field tested a spot on the driver's side door. It proved to be blood. A spot on the brim of the crumpled straw hat also tested to be blood.

Just stay out of the car, Urubek thought. *Don't touch it.*

Had the men known her secret thoughts, she might have encountered trouble. Instead, she kept her patience and their good will. Within a few minutes the officers were through.

"Could I seal the car?" Urubek asked. No one objected, so she placed sticker tape over the trunk seams and door jambs, then initialed each strip. It would be impossible for anyone to enter the car without breaking the seals.

"We're going to get our warrant, and we're going to get this guy, too," Urubek told Bill Johnston.

During lunch, Urubek asked Sergeant Stroup if anything had been taken out of the car. Stroup nodded—McDuff's billfold for one thing, and some papers. Urubek and Martin went through the items seeking any connection to Austin. Parole Board Commissioner Helen Copitka's business card, offering her services as a consultant, and a hand-drawn map to a house in Dell Valley were among the items found in McDuff's wallet.

On the drive back to Austin, Martin decided to follow up on the map; Urubek got Helen Copitka's business card. She noticed that Sergeant Martin appeared interested in the day's developments.

Sergeant Urubek called Lori Bible-Tolson at work the morning of March 13 and told her that Kenneth McDuff's automobile had been located. The police officer was seeking samples of Colleen Reed's hair, skin, saliva, body fluids—anything that could be used in scientific testing to match against potential evidence in the car.

On her way to meet the police officer, Lori stopped to tell Jeff Tolson about Sergeant Urubek's request. Although the two were separated, a familiar argument developed over responsibility and money.

"I don't have time for this," Lori warned. "I'm too upset about giving her Colleen's things. I've got to go."

Jeff was leaning on the door of the car, refusing to back away. Anger enveloped her frustration as Lori slammed the Jeep into gear and Jeff leaped backward as the vehicle jerked forward. She spun out of the driveway leaving a stinging trail of gravel and dirt.

Urubek had been pleased to learn that Colleen's possessions and personal items had been packed in plastic garbage bags.

Inadvertently, Lori had picked the best possible way to protect evidence. Colleen's possessions had been uncontaminated except, possibly, for the brief time it took to pack them.

Urubek walked into an emotional maelstrom that night. Lori was mentally unprepared to handle her sister's possessions. Some people allow themselves months, even years to heal, before going through personal possessions of a loved one. Lori lost that option because her sister was a victim of random crime. She sobbed gently as she picked through Colleen's purse, putting her sister's hairbrush, toothbrush and lipstick into separate bags.

Urubek was carefully going through one bag when she came across a hairbrush.

"Did you use this?" she asked, holding the brush containing strands of dark hair.

"No." Lori shook her head, fresh tears coursing down her face. Urubek was forced to distance herself from the woman's grief. It was a technique she had to learn as a patrol officer investigating traffic fatalities. To do otherwise would have destroyed her emotionally and professionally.

"I just wanted to cry with her," Urubek later told J.W. Thompson, "but I couldn't. I had to remain focused on the need to collect evidence to use later on."

The search turned up unwashed underclothing that held body secretions unique to Colleen and her blood type. Hair was discovered on unwashed outer garments as well as in the hairbrush. Washcloths were carefully bagged and tagged for body secretions. Urubek collected any item, no matter how insignificant, for later use as evidence.

Back at the station, Oliver Guerra brought in clothing from his apartment. Urubek carefully stored everything in the evidence room. Eventually these personal items would be used to establish DNA evidence as Travis County district attorneys prepared their case.

* * *

Lori answered the telephone to hear Sergeant J.W. Thompson on the other end.

"I just wanted to check on you," he said.

"I'm doing fine," she assured him.

"I know it looks bleak," Thompson said, "but we'll find her, Lori, and we'll bring her home."

Urubek felt she might be able to get more information from Helen Copitka if she made the telephone call as a potential client rather than a police officer.

"What kind of counseling do you do?" Sonia asked.

"A little bit of this and a little bit of that," Copitka replied.

"Like marriage counseling or psychological counseling?" Sonia prodded.

"Well I've done some of that," she said.

Quietly the McNamara brothers placed a telephone call to "America's Most Wanted." Would the popular television show be interested in broadcasting information on Kenneth McDuff?

Sure, they were told, as long as the broadcasters could tag Kenneth McDuff as a serial killer and quote the brothers. Based on their knowledge of the case at the time the McNamaras had to decline. Technically, the federal case was not a homicide investigation. The only federal warrants were for drug and gun possession, and those were tenuous at best.

The program needed justification to call him a serial killer. The men could not strike a bargain with the popular television series, so the request was dropped.

Fourteen

Sergeant Sonia Urubek decided to make another telephone call to Helen Copitka, this time as a law officer.

"Have you ever heard the name Kenneth McDuff?" she asked.

"I think I counseled him and his wife back in eighty-nine," Copitka said.

"We're talking about Kenneth Allen McDuff?" Urubek asked, knowing that McDuff had never been married.

"Yes. In 'eighty-nine, him and his wife."

And he was in prison that year, Urubek thought before saying it aloud.

"I must be mistaken," Copitka said. "I must be thinking about someone else."

"Would you double check your records?" Urubek asked.

Copitka agreed. "I'll call you back."

Because she was working nights Urubek had to drop the McDuff case, specifically her quest for a search warrant for McDuff's car. It would become Sergeant Don Martin's responsibility. Although Urubek was concerned that he would not follow through, Martin did get the warrant, and he and J.W. Thompson would serve it on April 2.

On March 17, Deputy U.S. Marshal Mike McNamara asked Investigator Tim Steglich to assist in gathering intelligence for a search warrant to be served at the McDuff homestead.

* * *

Lori continued to write letters to her missing sister.

Dear Colleen,

I still wonder where you are. Are you dead? Alive? Hurting? Happy?

I am questioning everything. I wish you were here. I wish I knew where you are!

I have tried to go on with my life. But my life is a mess.

Jeff and I are separated. Everyone wants to know why. The answers don't come easy.

I am in a recovery program. I wish you were here to help me sort out truth from fiction.

Quietly, Mike and Parnell McNamara visited a relative of Kenneth McDuff's. The family member told the brothers that McDuff boldly bragged about killing women with his hands. McDuff often dug two graves in one day in anticipation of his murderous work. After their use, he would camouflage the graves with brush. The informant said that McDuff offered to kill anyone that family member selected for assassination. The only problem, McDuff had said, was that he did not want to dig three graves in one day. It simply was too much work.

"It is so bizarre, so crazy," the relative had said. "I just really did not think he was serious."

It had become a familiar refrain. McDuff's boasting was so outlandish that even a family member found him hard to believe.

Lawmen descended on the McDuff homestead before noon on March 19 at the beginning of a twenty-four-hour period that would solidify their case. Steglich, the McNamara brothers, Johnston, ATF agents Brzozowski and Wayne Apelt, all arrived to search the house and grounds. Within minutes of their arrival, an angry Addie McDuff drove up.

"Don't hurt Junior!" she exclaimed rushing into the house. "Don't hurt Junior!"

"How can we hurt someone who is dead?" Parnell McNamara whispered to his brother. Steglich grinned.

The woman's plea certainly justified the search warrant since the lawmen believed it was possible that her son although reported missing, was staying there. It certainly conflicted with her adamant contention that her son was dead. Steglich had told the other lawmen that he almost felt McDuff's presence in the house whenever he visited the family.

It was one of the strangest homes the McNamaras had ever visited. Not one photograph decorated the home. No pictures on the wall; no family snapshots; none of the children.

This home is stripped of personality, McNamara thought as he wandered around.

Parnell took advantage of a few minutes with McDuff's father as Addie followed the searchers to the garage where they examined the maroon pickup with the repaired windshield that Steglich had discovered. In a side pocket the officers found a well-creased map of the City of Austin; the first concrete connection to the city. Slim, at best, but still a connection.

Parnell visited with John McDuff for a few minutes before asking the question burning in his mind.

"Did your son do it?" Parnell asked the old man as the rest of the law officers searched the grounds.

"Ya wouldna found out if ya ask 'em," J.A. McDuff said. "If ya ask 'em if he done it and he told ya something, you couldn't believe it."

Then he asked the marshal a strange question.

"You afraid of anything?"

"Yes, sir, I am," Parnell replied.

"I ain't afraid of nothin'," J.A. McDuff asserted. "But, if you don't like anything the best thing to do is be quiet."

The marshal believed he knew one source of power the old man feared. Whenever Addie was around, old John was quiet.

"Don't frame Junior, like you did before," Addie pleaded with the officers as they left. "He said he didn't do it and I know he didn't do it if he says so."

The posse decided to visit Elroy Jerrold, a known McDuff associate, in Temple. On the way to Temple, U.S. Attorney Bill Johnston revealed that he, too, had found a few minutes alone with J.A. McDuff.

"If you find him, kill him if you want to," Johnston said McDuff's father told him. It sounded to the veteran barrister as if the feeble old man was giving his permission.

The search was a defining moment for Johnston, a tall, handsome man with unruly black hair. Always, he wore a dress suit on the raids, in contrast to the lawmen who favored rugged blue jeans and boots and jackets emblazoned with the name of their law enforcement department.

On this day, Johnston reasoned with the McNamaras.

"Tell me," he asked rhetorically. "How many serial killers were in Austin in late December in 1991?"

"One?" Parnell ventured.

"Okay," Johnston continued. "How many serial killers were in Austin in late December in 1991 driving a light-colored Thunderbird?"

"One," Mike answered as Parnell nodded; no question this time.

"How many serial killers were in Austin in late December in 1991 that liked to kidnap short, dark-haired women?" Johnston continued.

"One," the men answered in unison.

The litany continued as they drove north along I-35. By the time they reached Temple, U.S. Attorney Bill Johnston smiled.

"I've convinced myself, and you two, that he did it," he said. "Now we have to prove it."

The brothers nodded. From that point forward they never

doubted that McDuff was involved in the Colleen Reed disappearance.

Janice Worley Jerrold said her husband Elroy was not home. The officers explained their mission.

Janice revealed a distinct distaste for her husband's running buddy. She mentioned that her ex-husband, Alva Hank Worley, was an associate of Kenneth McDuff's. The officers should go see him, she suggested.

Worley was living at Blooms Motel on the southern edge of Belton. Steglich recognized Worley's name as that of a small-time punk and drug user who did not cause a lot of problems. But it was the first time that law enforcement officers heard the name Worley in connection with Kenneth McDuff.

Janice gave the officers the names of several local beer joints her husband favored. They immediately began a surveillance along several blocks of dives, looking for Elroy Jerrold whom they planned to arrest on misdemeanor charges. They did not have to wait long before Jerrold showed up. He spoke freely about McDuff, whom he had known in prison. The last time he had seen McDuff was when the two had been arrested for public intoxication and fighting in Temple shortly before midnight on February 24.

The McNamara brothers took Janice's suggestion to interview Alva Hank Worley. As Steglich continued to talk to Elroy Jerrold, the marshals drove to Bloom's Motel, where they landed on Worley like a ton of bricks.

"You know something, and you're not talking," Parnell snarled when Worley proved a reluctant interview.

"We just want to find Kenneth McDuff," Mike said, softer. "Tell us where he is?"

"I don't know," the small man insisted.

"You know what he did to a little girl in Fort Worth . . ." Parnell started as Mike finished, ". . . in 1966?"

"I know he was in prison for something," Worley said. "Murder . . . something like that."

"But a sixteen-year-old girl?" Parnell asked. "A baby!"

"And two teenage boys," Mike added. "He shot them in the head. Boys!"

"Then he raped the girl in every way possible," Mike continued. "He had a pointed broomstick and a Coke bottle."

"And then he used that broomstick to choke the life out of her," Parnell added. "He got on top of her and pushed the stick against her throat and pushed and pushed and pushed until there was no more life in that little girl's body."

"We want to get him," Mike interjected. "You know that two women are missing. Colleen Reed, the woman somebody snatched out of a car wash, and Melissa Northrup is missing. She's pregnant, Hank. If we find her dead, that's like killing two people.

"We know of one prostitute that he's killed, and two others who are missing," Parnell said.

Worley's reaction to the horrible news from 1966 was not normal. He showed no horror, asked no questions. It convinced the marshals that Worley had secret knowledge of something. Both agreed that he was strangely unresponsive to their concern about Colleen Reed or Melissa Northrup. He did not ask for details. They noticed that his face was placid, not like a person who had just heard something horribly offensive; especially the father of a teenage girl.

"He knows what has happened. He doesn't need to ask questions," Mike said later, as Parnell nodded.

"He's very nervous," Parnell told Steglich.

"Very nervous," Mike agreed.

The brothers had acquired a target, someone they believed knew some dark secrets, if not McDuff's whereabouts.

Worley did give them the name of Carmen Garza, a known drug dealer in Harker Heights.

Steglich rode with Mike and Parnell McNamara, Bill Johnston, and Jeff Brzozowski late that night as they went from one McDuff associate to another seeking Carmen Garza. Each contact sent them to yet another stale pool hall. But patience and shoe leather are often the keys to success as officers winnow fact from fiction. Finally they ended up in Harker Heights, a suburb of Waco, where they approached Carmen Garza at her trailer home. They showed her the picture of Kenneth McDuff.

"That's Macs!" she exclaimed, excitedly. "That's Macs."

"Macs who?" Parnell asked.

"I don't know. I just call him Macs," she said.

"Do you know where he is?"

"No, Billy told me to stay away from him." Carmen paused before dropping her little bombshell. "This is about that girl in Austin, ain't it?"

"What do you mean?" Mike asked calmly, his pulse pounding. No one had said anything to her about Colleen Reed or a missing girl, let alone Austin. The brothers had just asked if she knew McDuff.

"That girl somebody got right after Christmas," she said. "Billy thinks Mac's done it."

Parnell feared that Carmen should have been able to hear his heart pound, it was racing so fast. The lawmen were reasonably sure that McDuff had taken Melissa Northrup. He had been seen within a hundred yards of the Quik Pak the night she disappeared. But there was nothing tangible to link him to Colleen Reed. Carmen's simple statement could be the thin string that would tie the killer to the Austin victim.

"Billy who?" Mike asked.

"Billy Green," she said, "Billy. A guy with one eye. McDuff was with him Christmas Day. I sent him to Billy in Austin, to buy drugs."

No one had successfully placed McDuff anywhere near Austin, much less four days from the date of the crime. Coupled with the indirect implications of the creased Austin city map, it was the second time that day that McDuff had been tied to the city.

"But Billy didn't like him much," Carmen went on. "Said he was crazy and that I was to stay away from McDuff."

Billy Green, Parnell thought. *Bucktooth Billy Green!* He looked at Mike who nodded. It had to be the same man they had arrested several times on federal warrants. She told them he was currently staying in Dallas after illegally leaving a half-way house for convicts.

Although it was nearly two o'clock in the morning, Mike and Parnell immediately called Warrant Supervisor Sam Williams, a supervisory Deputy U.S. Marshal in San Antonio, to alert him to developments. The marshals were concerned that Brown might disappear by the next morning, so Williams gave the men clearance to go on to Dallas.

The lawmen secured a warrant for Brown, who was now a fugitive for leaving the halfway house, then drove to Dallas with Johnston where they planned a raid on Brown's current address with the help of fellow Deputy U.S. Marshal Larry Gunn.

When the Dallas duty sergeant found out what house was to be raided he refused to let his men participate. "Get the SWAT team," he insisted. The men Brown was staying with were outlaw bikers. The Dallas sergeant believed a specially trained team was needed to handle the raid. His instincts were right.

As SWAT team members entered that house shortly before dawn, a desperate fistfight broke out before the occupants were subdued without gunfire or injury to either side. Although the incident seemed to last an eternity to the participants, the fight was over in a few short minutes. The McNamaras had just located Bucktooth Billy when they heard a commotion behind them.

"Get in there!" the marshals heard Bill Johnston snarl after the donnybrook.

They looked up to see a prisoner enter the house, hands held high, followed by Johnston, who was now armed with a shotgun. Fearful of becoming so involved in the hunt that he would disqualify himself as a prosecutor and become a witness, Johnston had stayed in the marshal's Suburban. He had spotted a man watching the action from a car parked across the street, so he had taken no chances that the watcher might ambush the assault team.

With Brown safely in the van, the weary team started back to Waco. The four rode in silence for a time.

"Parnell, I know y'all didn't come all the way to Dallas to get me 'cause I run off from a halfway house," Brown said sullenly.

"You're exactly right, Billy," Parnell answered. "We didn't come all the way to Dallas to get you because you ran away from a halfway house."

Parnell paused for effect, before adding, "We're going to try to charge you with capital murder."

By now the officers were beginning to suspect that Brown had been with McDuff when Colleen Reed was kidnapped.

"We want to know what you know about Kenneth McDuff," Mike said.

The implication angered the husky man.

"I don't hurt kids and I ain't into that, and I'll tell you whatever you want to know," Billy said. "I had nothing to do with it."

He poured out his story, one that confirmed what Carmen had told the men. McDuff had been in Harker Heights at Carmen's house on Christmas Day looking for drugs. His bizarre attitude caused Carmen to become fearful, and she sent him to Austin, even though Brown had instructed her not to do so when he called earlier that day.

Bingo! We've got an eyewitness to his being in Austin on Christmas Day, Parnell thought. It was the third time that day that McDuff had been tied to the capital city.

"He's nuts," Brown said, interrupting Parnell's thoughts. "He's spooky."

"That's a big hurdle," Parnell said aloud. "Maybe Austin will take McDuff more seriously now."

Brown told the lawmen that he believed McDuff had abducted Colleen. It was a conclusion based on knowledge and assumption.

"The news reports said he was driving a big car with rounded taillights," Brown explained, although technically the taillight cover was flat and only appeared round when the brake was applied. "And, they said he went the wrong way on a one-way street. That did more to convince me than anythin' else. I didn't doubt it, then."

Brown went on to explain that McDuff arrived that Christmas Day spewing obscenities and talking death. "All he talks about is killing: women or crack dealers," Brown explained.

Brown, who had already run away from the halfway house, was renting a room from a couple with a small child, a boy.

"Where's Billy Brown?" McDuff said walking past the landlord and into the house, uninvited.

The one-way conversation that holiday centered on crack dealers: blowing their brains out and robbing them. Soon McDuff was giving gory details of the murders of women and digging graves for them.

"He said he loved to dig graves," Bucktooth Billy said. The McNamara brothers exchanged silent looks. They remembered their visit with McDuff's relative who had said something similar.

The landlord sent his wife and child from the room when McDuff begin to describe his technique. He would wait until a drug dealer was half-way out a car before shooting him so the victim fell forward out of the car. That way the killer would not blow brains and blood all over the interior of the vehicle. McDuff refused to be quiet or talk about another subject.

"Whenever I've been around him, that's all he wants to talk about is killing people," Brown told the officers. "The man's weird."

Brown talked McDuff into leaving the house. Once in the car, McDuff charged the wrong-way up one-way streets. Austin is peppered with these streets and Brown said McDuff seemed obsessed with driving the wrong way on as many as possible.

Needing gas, McDuff stopped at a convenience store, filled up the car tank, then laid the nozzle on the ground and took off.

"That's the way you steal gas," McDuff told him.

What happened next irritated even a criminal as hardened as Brown. The McNamaras believe that Brown is one of the most physically tough men they have ever met.

"He likes a good old-fashioned barroom brawl where he

takes on three or four people," Mike laughs. "But, he's not a bully. He is good to his girlfriends and hangers-on. Carmen describes him as a gentleman. That's hard to believe when you look at his big biker image. He's one of the most frightening looking people you'll ever see."

But most people draw the line somewhere. Brown knew his code. The McNamaras believe that he has never lied to them.

"He'll tell you 'I don't lie. If I'm caught, I'll admit it. But I don't lie about nothin'," Mike quotes him.

McDuff spotted a pair of black girls in their early teens rollerskating down Congress Avenue as he and Brown rode around Austin.

"Let's get 'em," McDuff suggested.

"Hell, no, man, I'm not into that stuff. I've got girlfriends," Brown snorted. "That's nuts. I'm not going to do anything like that."

"Let's grab 'em and get outta here," McDuff said.

Brown said McDuff was looking at the girls "with a real weird look in his eyes."

"I don't know for sure if he said 'use 'em up' or not, but I told him no, I had girlfriends for that."

Later McDuff spotted two attractive white teenage girls at a pay telephone at a convenience store closed for the holiday. Brown estimated their age to be around sixteen years old.

"How about them?" McDuff said. "Let's get them."

"No, man, I told you I ain't into that," Brown said, growing angry at the continued suggestions.

Silence. McDuff sat there staring at the girls, transfixed; unable to take his gaze off them. After several minutes Bucktooth Billy broke the silence.

"Whataya doin'. Let's get on outta here."

"We can get 'em," McDuff tried again. "We can get 'em and go."

"I got no need for little girls," Brown reiterated. "I got girlfriends for that."

Brown spoke up again after a long silence. "I told you to get outta here. Let's go."

McDuff put the car in reverse, never taking his eyes from the girls. He slowly backed the car into the street, still staring at the girls. McDuff eased the car into drive and slowly turned it onto the street. He did not take his eyes off the girls until they were out of his sight.

Brown had already decided he wanted no contact with McDuff. After this visit he was sure.

"Why, Billy? Why didn't you call someone when you suspected McDuff?" Mike asked.

"I was on the run," Bucktooth Billy said. "I knew if I called anyone I'd be caught. I don't know. That's why, I guess.

"I regret it," he added.

By the time Brown finished his story a golden Texas dawn had dropped a hazy glow on the first greenery of early spring. It was a beautiful, peaceful sight. Yet Parnell McNamara could not help but wonder how many graves slipped past the window of the Suburban, and how many innocent victims had died that night.

The men had been up twenty-four hours. They had their first concrete proof that McDuff was a suspect in the Reed abduction.

With a sigh, Parnell turned to his brother and Bill Johnston, a vision of those four little girls, innocently skating and talking on the telephone that Christmas Day, going through his head.

"Life can be so fragile," Parnell said.

The next day Detective Tim Steglich received a telephone complaint from Addie McDuff. She said that during the home search the McNamara brothers had deliberately changed the hot and cold faucet handles on all the fixtures in her home in an attempt to harm her.

"I'll talk to them about it, Ma'am," Steglich said, barely able to conceal the roar of laughter building in his throat.

Austin Police Department Sergeant Don Martin placed a telephone call early in the morning on March 20 to Steglich as the marshals and Johnston made their way back to Waco with their prisoner.

Martin confirmed that McDuff was now a bona fide suspect in the disappearance of Colleen Reed. Steglich had heard the news broadcasts about the woman who had been kidnapped from a car wash in Austin, but it was the first time her name had been mentioned in connection with Kenneth McDuff.

This thing just keeps growing, Steglich thought. He was amazed. Kenneth McDuff's name kept popping up at every twist and turn of the fledgling investigation. Steglich spent the rest of the evening searching for known associates of Kenneth McDuff.

A few days later, Steglich was invited to the U.S. Marshal's Office in Waco. It turned out to be the organizational meeting for one of the most massive manhunts in the history of the U.S. Marshal's Service. A handful of dedicated officers would spend the better part of the next six weeks searching for the elusive McDuff. Also attending the March 24 meeting were Austin PD Sergeants Don Martin, and J.W. Thompson. Martin explained that witnesses had seen a tall man and a short man in a light-colored Thunderbird at the car wash when Colleen Reed was abducted. He asked Steglich to find John Roberts, a short man who was a known McDuff associate and who lived in the Temple area.

Mike and Parnell McNamara told Sergeant Martin about the Austin map found in McDuff's car. They suggested that Alva Hank Worley might be a suspect. Martin noted in his police report of the meeting that the map contained an ink line that started at Highway 183 and ran through the city until it ended at Ashdale Drive, only a few blocks away from where the four teenage girls were killed at the yogurt shop in December 1991. The street name was circled.

The next day Steglich located Roberts, who recalled a scary incident when the men decided to "score some dope." McDuff gave Roberts three hundred dollars to purchase drugs, then became angry when he decided his buddy did not get enough dope for the money. Roberts said McDuff pulled a pistol before the evening ended. He listed McDuff's best friends as Clement Burch, Elroy Jerrold, and Boyd Gabriel Obert.

As Steglich interviewed Roberts that March 26, a man who decided to take a shortcut across a cow pasture behind TSTC in Waco discovered a buzzing mass of green blowflies covering the partially decomposed head of a corpse in a shallow grave. Brush and boards had been scattered over the grave in an attempt to conceal it.

The only evidence found with the unclothed body of a young woman was a haircomb under her torso. She obviously had been in the grave for weeks, buried face up and covered with three to four inches of dirt. Her face was injured but authorities suspected that the damage occurred when a cow's hoof knocked in the thin covering over the grave.

Sergeant Richard Stroup of the McLennan County Sheriff's Office at first thought the corpse was that of a black woman. But he recalled that a prostitute named Brenda Thompson had disappeared in October, so he penciled in that information before the body was taken to the Office of the Medical Examiner in Dallas county. He could find out her race and notify the Medical Examiner. He suspected homicide.

A subsequent search of the pasture turned up a length of fine wire, about four-feet long, pliable and braided together. It had been covered with plastic. Mike McNamara suspected it might be the plastic-covered "rope" that Harley Fayette had discovered under the front seat of McDuff's car.

When he joined the search, Bill Johnston discovered what appeared to be an unused open grave. Soil was carefully piled to one side of the shallow indentation. Cut underbrush lay nearby.

"Remember what we were told?" Mike asked Parnell.

"About McDuff digging graves in advance?" Parnell answered.

"Yes," his brother replied. Grimly, Parnell nodded as he looked across the large cow pasture.

Who else is out here? he wondered.

As sometimes happens, a divorce does not end a relationship. Sometimes it continues on with no apparent rhyme or reason. Although Janice said she had no use for her ex-husband, Hank still considered her a friend, someone in whom he could confide. Shortly after New Year's Day he had called Janice with a mysterious message. He had to tell her something, but not on the telephone. Hank indicated that it was about McDuff. The meeting had to be face to face. She was not interested and declined, she told Steglich. She and Hank were going through a child custody battle. Fearful of hurting her case, Janice terminated most of her conversations with Hank within minutes.

Obviously Janice Worley Jerrold had reason to believe that Hank knew more about McDuff than he would admit, so Steglich decided it would be wise to stay in contact with her.

She insisted that Steglich ask Worley about the telephone call when the sheriff's detective checked with her that morning.

Mike and Parnell McNamara eased the big four-wheel drive Suburban to a stop in front of Bloom Motel that night. After a few minutes the window blinds flickered in Worley's room. They sat quietly for more than half an hour before Hank Worley opened the door and looked out at them. Mike smiled and waved. Parnell tipped his hat. Worley slammed the door.

Fingerprints were taken from the unidentified woman found in the cow pasture. She was described during the autopsy as being a well-developed black woman with abundant curly black hair. The medical examiner also took swabbings for pow-

der-residue analysis, blood, hair and a set of fingernail clip-
pings to keep on file. The fingerprint records were given to
the McLennan County Sheriff's Office.

Meanwhile, Janice's current husband stonewalled officers.
McDuff was a good fellow, Elroy Jerrold told Steglich.
McDuff never did or said anything about abduction or killing.
As did Janice, Elroy told the investigators about their rescue
of McDuff and Worley around Thanksgiving 1991, only he
added a titillating fact. The Jerrolds had picked up the drinking buddies at a convenience store just five miles from the
store where Melissa Northrup was last seen alive.

Steglich was amazed at the lives of these people who
claimed to dislike or even hate each other, but who continued
to run in a pack.

The McLennan County Sheriff's Office sent the dental records of Melissa Ann Northrup to Dallas on March 30 on
the outside chance that the corpse might be the missing convenience store clerk. The cautious lawmen would not leave
one stone unturned. It had already been established that the
dead woman was not the missing prostitute Brenda
Thompson.

What was Worley's secret? Was it real or was it born in a
druggy haze? Intrigued by Janice's suggestion, Steglich
stopped by Worley's motel only to find him gone. He left his
telephone number with the manager.

When Worley returned home that night he found the
McNamara brothers patiently waiting for him.

"Whataya want?" Worley snarled.

"Just tell us what you know about McDuff," Mike said.
"Did he take Colleen Reed and Melissa Northrup?"

* * *

The corpse of Valencia Kay Joshua was identified by her fingerprints on March 31. Officers discovered that the suspected prostitute was last seen knocking on the window of Kenneth McDuff's dormitory room on February 24.

In July, Waco Police Sergeant Mike Nicoletti would discover a prostitute who had talked her way out of a deadly situation in early February when McDuff raped her and began choking her with his massive hands.

"She started sweettalking McDuff and told him that he didn't have to get rough with her and McDuff stopped choking her," Nicoletti would report.

A few weeks after the incident, the woman saw Valencia Kay Joshua in a car with McDuff. She was crying. "I just want to go home!" Joshua begged. The prostitute warned Joshua not to trust McDuff because of what had happened to her.

"A couple weeks later she heard that [Joshua's] body was found buried at TSTC in the woods," Nicoletti noted. The prostitute would identify a picture of Joshua as the woman she had seen crying in McDuff's car.

Valencia's hair, meanwhile, was found on the plastic "rope." Murder charges were prepared to be filed against Kenneth McDuff in Joshua's death.

No matter when Steglich stopped by the motel, day or night, Worley was gone. He never returned the officer's telephone calls. Janice said Worley would be attending a hearing on April 8 for custody of their fifteen-year-old daughter Chelsea.

The days passed slowly for Frank Pounds, who continued to haunt The Cut looking for information. Harley Fayette would drop tantalizing hints but deliver no information. The trap was ready, all the amateur sleuth needed to do was spring it, but McDuff had been too cautious so far.

Frank began to pick up rumors that the Waco Police Department was looking for Kenneth McDuff for questioning in the death of Valencia Kay Joshua.

Within hours of the rumor, McDuff disappeared from The Cut, frustrating the trio of amateur detectives who believed that they had come tantalizingly close to springing their trap.

It was shortly after the discovery of Joshua's body that Sergeant Mike Nicoletti discovered yet another mystery within a mystery. Valencia had come to Waco with a friend, another prostitute known only by her street name. That friend had disappeared, nameless and unknown. Nicoletti could not locate the friend, nor find out her real name. Like Brenda and Regenia, she has just disappeared into the dark Texas night.

"As far as I know, she's dead somewhere, too," he said.

The career officer was frustrated by the narrow focus of the police department. He believed that WPD failed to look at the big picture as he saw it. This unknown prostitute would increase to three the number of women missing from the often brutal streets of The Cut. There might be even more. Was there a serial killer stalking this quiet community? Did he deliberately strike in the subculture of The Cut? Nicoletti knew that The Cut was a place where a disappearance might go unnoticed for days. It was a marketplace where a prostitute was no different than a piece of meat to be sold and used; not someone's daughter, not someone to be missed.

Waco Police Department had been tantalizingly close to McDuff. Nicoletti learned that the convict had visited the narcotics squad offering to be an informant. The officers had taken Polaroid pictures of a grinning McDuff for the department files. McDuff had arrogantly suggested that the police reveal the names of all known drug dealers in the Waco area.

Armed with that knowledge, McDuff offered to inform on the drug dealers.

Cautious police officers declined to give him the names, suspecting that McDuff was trying to run a scam. He had a reputation on The Cut for stealing narcotics from drug dealers, often handing them a rolled up one dollar bill, instead of a twenty-dollar bill, then roaring off in his pickup truck, drugs in hand.

Ironically, the officers would turn over these pictures to the U.S. Marshal's Service to be used on wanted posters.

Tim Steglich studied the new batch of wanted posters the day they arrived. He could not believe what he perceived. Obviously, a dark overcoat had been hung on a coat rack and McDuff was inadvertently seated in front of it for the photographs.

From that day forward the veteran lawman could not look at the photographs of a wickedly smiling McDuff without his eyes wandering to what appeared to be the black-hooded specter of death rising up behind the serial killer's left shoulder—the Grim Reaper.

Early in April the Austin City Council declared that April 26—Colleen's birthday—would be "Colleen Reed Day."

Family and friends were gathering in Austin to plan a birthday memorial for Colleen when another young woman disappeared. Lori rushed to the police department to counsel the family. Fresh wounds just beginning to heal over were wrenched open again. Lori was joyful when the contrite young woman turned out to be a runaway and returned home after twenty-two hours.

"Who cares?" Lori told irate friends who felt manipulated by the girl's apparent bid for attention. "She's safe."

Early the next morning Lori left for work a little early. She drove aimlessly for about an hour, searching the faces of the women walking the streets, to work, to school, to the activities of everyday life. She did not find Colleen. She never did, but somehow she could not quit searching. Her little sister could have amnesia. *Well, she could!* she told herself.

The special task force that sprang from Operation Gunsmoke spent the early days of April in surveillance of the McDuff homestead. They dropped by beer joints and assorted dives seeking McDuff associates. Several patrons reported seeing McDuff in past months, but not the last few weeks.

Steglich had a meeting with his boss, Bell County Sheriff Dan Smith. The search for McDuff had become almost a full-time job for the conscientious investigator who was juggling the McDuff case with his regular load. Sheriff Smith told his employee to do what he had to do. It was too late in the game to pass Steglich's portion of the case to someone else. Steglich had amassed a great deal of knowledge concerning McDuff, so he was given "a pretty free hand to do what I wanted to do."

Once again the McNamara brothers stopped by Hank Worley's motel. They sat there for more than an hour with the motor running but he did not come to the window or door. Perhaps he did not see them, they joked.

Deputy Steglich met Alva Hank Worley in the hallway of the courthouse prior to the child custody hearing April 8. Worley agreed to give him a statement following the hearing.

"What do those marshals want?" he asked. "They're bugging me. They're always hanging around."

"You ought to know." Steglich shrugged, and left, silently amused. *That's good. They're getting to him.*

Worley arrived at the Sheriff's Office at 10:30 that morning. Steglich established that Worley had a ninth grade education and could read and write English before beginning the statement, which he typed on an old manual typewriter in his office:

At 10:30 a.m. o'clock [sic] on the 8th day of April, 1992, at Bell County Sheriff's Department in the City of Belton in Bell County, Texas, prior to the making of the statement below, I was warned by Investigator Tim Steglich, the person to whom this statement is made and who identified himself as a peace officer, (1) that I have the right to remain silent and not make any statement at all and that any statement I make may be used as evidence against me at my trial, (2) that any statement I make may be used as evidence against me in Court (3) that I have the right to have a lawyer present to advise me prior to and during any questioning (4) that if I am unable to employ a lawyer, I have the right to have a lawyer appointed to advise me prior to and during any questioning, and (5) that I have the right to terminate the interview at any time. I understand all of my rights as stated above, but I do not wish to consult with a lawyer and I do hereby knowingly, intelligently and voluntarily waive the above rights prior to and during the making of the following statement and without being induced by any compulsion, threats, promises or persuasion make the following statement in writing:

My name is Alva Hank Worley. My date of birth is December 2nd, 1957. I live at Bloom's Motel, room #12 in Belton, Texas. I do not know the telephone number to the motel. I am currently working for Adam's Drywall which is in Belton. We are now working a job in Round Rock on some schools. In about October of 1991, I met a man named Kenneth McDuff. I met him through Elroy Jerrold. I was living at the S & S Trailer Park near Belton at the time, and Elroy brought him over there one day. I did not see him for 2 or 3 weeks after that. He had told me he was in school at the time in Waco. At that time, Mac was driving a beige T-Bird, but when I first met him he was driving a maroon pickup, I think he said it was his Dad's. The pickup did not have a camper on it at the time. Me and Mac used to ride around and drink beer. We went to Poor-Boy's, the He Ain't Here, and Dundee's club to drink, also. I usually rode with him. I do not have a car. One time, I went with Mac to Waco to score some speed. I think he went to a relative's house. This might have been in November or December. The house we went to is next to a beauty shop. He went in and got the dope, then we left. We went down LaSalle where the whores are, and he told me he gets dope from them. He had intended to get the dope from one of the girls on the street, but no one was out that particular night. We were talking about the whores, and having sex, and things like that. He then started talking about a girl that worked at a convenience store that he went into all the time. He said she knew him from him going in there so much. He mentioned she knew him pretty good. He said she was a "damn good looking girl." I don't remember exactly how he said this, but he said he "would like to take her." I understood this to mean kidnap her. When Mac gets tilted, he talks like that a lot. He said this store was pretty close to the college, but we did not go there. After we finally got the dope, we started heading back, and the car broke down. We parked at a convenience store, and I called my ex-wife, and she and Elroy Jerrold came and picked us up. I think they took me home, and Mac went with Elroy. I think before that trip to Waco, I went to Austin with Mac and a guy named Indian. I think Indian lives in Temple, and I had never seen him before, and I have not seen him since. Indian directed Mac to a place in Austin, on the north side, maybe near Round Rock. Mac seems to know his way around Round Rock and Austin very well. We could not score any dope that time, so we came back. In December

Mac told me he had beaten somebody real bad. He did not say if he killed them, he said he just "left them laying." I do not know if this was a man or a woman or what. He said he beat them with a tire iron. He always carried it around with him. Mac had a big interest in guns, and he was always asking me where he could get one. I do not know if he ever got one or not. He always said his Dad had a lot of guns. Like I said, when Mac was tilted, he talked about "taking" women and "using them up." I understood this to mean he would kill them. We would be riding down the street, and we would see a girl, Mac would say something about "using her up." This statement is true and correct to the best of my knowledge.

Investigator Steglich has typed this statement for me.

(Signed)
Hank Worley

When Worley went to leave, Steglich handed him a business card.

"I think there may be more to it than this, Hank," he said. "If you ever want to talk, just give me a call."

FIFTEEN

A state trooper who had met the grieving Reed family when Colleen was kidnapped called Lori early the morning of April 10.

"They have a suspect," he said. "A guy named McDuff. Kenneth McDuff. You better pray that it's not him." He went on to explain that McDuff had murdered three teenagers in the 1960s. "If it's him, then your sister is dead."

There was a long pause. Lori did not know what to say.

"I'm very sorry," he said.

Lori did not think she was capable of the range of emotions that filled her that day: anticipation, then excitement that finally there was a suspect, then an even greater sense of loss because she had heard the finality in the trooper's voice.

Janice Jerrold verified to Steglich that she and Elroy picked up McDuff and her ex-husband when McDuff's vehicle broke down around Thanksgiving 1991.

Dan Stolz visited a bar McDuff was known to frequent. He shook down a known associate of the serial killer. In the man's side pocket were twenty-two small-caliber bullets.

"Explosive devices," Stolz exclaimed, running a bluff. "Man, you're going to be arraigned for carrying explosive material in your pocket. You're going to go to trial, then to jail."

Immediately the suspect agreed to plea bargain on current charges that Stolz did not even know existed. He would plead guilty if the marshal would drop the bogus charges of possession of explosive devices.

Agreed and done. Stolz marched him to jail.

"I wonder how many hundreds of people are going to jail because of Kenneth McDuff," he wondered aloud, chuckling at the recent byplay. "He's going to be one of the most hated inmates in history."

Stolz knew that the task force dragnet was sweeping up the flotsam and jetsam of the underworld just as it had happened that night.

At least that's a positive, he thought.

The McNamaras found Worley barbecuing on an outdoor pit. They walked him aside as Chelsea watched from a distance.

"We know you know something Hank," Mike began. "How can you protect someone like that."

The marshals had to be careful not to accuse McDuff of something they could not prove so they decided the best course of action was to stick with the 1966 murders, especially the brutalization of Edna Louise Sullivan.

The men took turns firing questions, leaving no room for answers.

"Do you know what McDuff did back in 1966?" Parnell asked.

"Do you know he killed two boys, shot them in the head?"

"And the girl. He had a broken, pointed broomstick he used on her."

"He ripped her up inside."

"And she was crying for her Daddy," Parnell insisted. " 'Daddy, help me.' But her Daddy wasn't there to help her."

Then Mike delivered what he hoped would be the mental blow that would break Worley.

"How would you feel if that was done to your little girl?"
No reaction.

"And McDuff is still out there, an animal among thousands
of little girls," Parnell said.

The experienced lawman paused, glaring into Worley's eyes.

"Hank, I cried when I read about it, it was so horrible,"
Parnell said evenly. "I couldn't believe any man could do that
to a little girl."

"He's a mad dog, and you ran with him," Parnell added.
"And you have a sweet, innocent daughter. Think about that,
Hank."

"Think about it when you go to bed tonight," Mike said.

"Think about it and see if you can sleep," Parnell added.

"You want somebody like that loose?" Mike asked, nodding
his head toward Worley's daughter. "You want her to meet
Kenneth McDuff?

"Think about it, Hank. That sweet little girl in 1966, her
insides torn up by a broom handle, calling for her Daddy, naked on the ground in front of those car lights," Mike paused,
before he commanded, "You have a daughter. He used that
broom on her in every way he could, and all she could do was
whimper for her daddy. Then he put that broom across her
throat . . ."

"Stop it," Worley pleaded, throwing his hands over his ears.
"Stop it. I didn't do nothing."

The marshals waited.

"You've got the right man," Worley said in reference to
Kenneth McDuff. "I'm telling you, you've got the right man,
but you've got to know I can't tell you any more. He'll come
back and kill me."

"What did Kenneth do?" Mike questioned.

Silence.

"What did he do?" Parnell demanded.

Tears formed in the corner of Worley's eyes. Both officers
believed he was on the verge of breaking.

"Was Elroy with him?" Parnell took a stab in the dark.

"No. Elroy wasn't with him, but you've got the right man," Worley insisted. "You've got to go. He'll come back and kill me. I tell ya you got the right man!"

"Where were you when you saw him last?" Mike asked.

"The parking lot," Worley replied.

"You're his buddy. You run with a man that'll do horrible things to a little girl," Parnell bore in.

"Stop it," Worley demanded.

"Who was the girl?" Mike asked. "Who was with him?"

"He was with some girl and she asked me to help her, but I didn't want to have anything to do with her, because I didn't want to get involved with him," he said. He could not remember who else was there or the location of the parking lot.

"Tell us," Mike shot back, offering a picture of Melissa Northrup. Worley looked at the picture, startled. His composure began to return. The McNamaras did not realize that he had expected to see someone other than Melissa.

"That's not her," he said, tipping his hand before swiftly adding, "I never seen her before."

Now the marshals were startled. Since Worley had mentioned the convenience store and the good-looking girl in his recent statement, they naturally suspected him of helping McDuff kidnap Melissa Northrup. His reaction to the picture had been as animated as it had been flat when they first broached the subject of Colleen Reed several weeks before.

"How about her?" Mike asked, holding a picture of Colleen Reed. Worley took the picture and studied it for long seconds, then gave it back to Mike. The officers waited. Sometimes silence was an ally. Worley reached for the picture and studied it again, his face now placid.

"Never seen her before in my life," he said calmly, shaking his head.

But the emotional dynamics of the past few minutes had convinced Mike McNamara. *You're involved. I know it. I don't know which girl, or both, but you're involved.*

Mike turned to leave, then wheeled on Worley. "McDuff is

a kid killer, Hank. A kid killer! I want you to think about that tonight after Chelsea is safely tucked into her bed. He's a kid killer. I want you to look over at your daughter."

Worley stood with downcast eyes.

"Look at her right now!" Mike demanded. "You picture her on her knees in front of those lights, naked and defenseless."

Worley refused to turn toward Chelsea.

"I just want you to try to remember if McDuff ever met Chelsea," Mike said before turning to Parnell. "Come on, let's get out of here."

"I thought that he might be hiding McDuff," Mike told Parnell as they drove off. "But I don't think so. I think he was with McDuff one of those nights."

"I think you're right," Parnell said.

A federal grand jury returned an indictment against McDuff for possession of a firearm by a felon on April 14. If convicted it would mean fifteen years to life. The drug charge for distributing LSD, for which he was already indicted, carried a penalty of up to twenty years. The federal dragnet was closing. It was decided to go public with McDuff's name at a press conference the next day.

The pressure on Alva Hank Worley continued to build. The McNamara brothers contacted his boss in the drywall business to solicit help. He agreed to talk to his employee.

Anxious to keep the heat on Worley, a team of U.S. marshals, including Stolz, Mike Carnevale and the McNamaras, decided to go to Belton to talk to him. While they were there, it was decided to make another round of known McDuff associates at their favorite bars. After asking Steglich to accompany them, the marshals decided Tim Steglich should talk to Worley alone, since the suspect seemed to open up in one-on-one conversations with the easy-going Steglich.

Late that evening Steglich contacted Worley outside his room at Bloom's Motel. Already on edge, Hank became increasingly nervous under Steglich's questioning. Beads of sweat began to glisten on his forehead as the questions hit home. Nervous energy kept him in motion. The veteran investigator read the suspect's body language. By now Worley was sweating profusely, constantly moving his head, unable to stand still.

"Well, I know a little something about some of the things Mac done," he said, cautious.

"Some things?"

"You know."

"No, I don't know. That's why I'm asking you," Steglich replied, patiently waiting.

One of the first rules of interrogation is to keep the subject's attention. Under the circumstances it was difficult to keep Worley focused. By now the pair had walked around Steglich's patrol car several times and crossed the parking lot.

Hank, you're lying to me, Steglich thought, so he planted himself in front of the man, cutting off his rambling and forcing the sweating, troubled man to establish eye contact. Worley was stopped in his tracks.

"What things, Hank?" he persisted.

"Things," Worley said. "Things that hurt someone."

Steglich waited.

"Mac hurt somebody . . . bad," McDuff's sidekick added. "Real bad."

"Will you go to the office with me, and talk some more?" Steglich asked, ready to get the nervous man into a controlled situation. Besides, Steglich thought, the marshals might have better luck.

But after several hours, it was obvious to Stolz, Carnevale, and the McNamaras that Worley was not talking that night. He maintained that be did not know where the man was staying unless it was with his parents.

"We might as well release him," Stolz suggested during a

break in the interrogation. After several hours the investigators had made no progress. It was time to either take Worley back to the motel or arrest him. Based on their knowledge at the time, Worley was not a suspect in Colleen Reed's disappearance, nor technically was he in custody. He was free to walk out anytime.

"We know he's done something, or knows something," Carnevale agreed. "But there's nothing we can do now."

"We have to be patient," Steglich added.

The ride to the motel was quiet, each man was exhausted by the emotional strain of the past few hours. Once again, Steglich gave Worley a business card.

"If you need to tell me anything, you need to do it now," the officer warned. "You need to do it pretty quick. Things are starting to roll here. Things are going to be automatic when it gets started.

"You could get caught in a steamroller."

Austin Police Department Sergeant Don Martin made it official in a telephone call to Steglich the morning of April 15.

"Kenneth McDuff is a definite suspect in the disappearance of Colleen Reed," he told Tim. Since Worley matched the description by eyewitnesses of the smaller man seen in the car, he could be considered a suspect, also. His recent statement, actions and attitude marked him as a suspect.

"I told Worley that it was going to start rolling," Steglich told Martin. "I'm just surprised that it's happening so soon."

Martin was careful to note that the Reed case was still listed as an abduction, nothing more. Over the next few days Steglich would continue to document the instances of McDuff's drug use by contacting known associates.

The next day U.S. Marshal's Service Inspector Mike Carnevale held a press conference calling for public cooperation in locating McDuff who had failed to report for a meeting with his parole officer.

"He's a very dangerous man," Carnevale said. "We want him off the street. That's why we're asking for the public's help."

U.S. Attorney Bill Johnston said a federal grand jury had indicted McDuff on Tuesday April 14, with the felon charge of possession of a firearm.

Several leads kept pointing the task force to a tiny community fifty miles southeast of Waco. Rogers is a collection of small homes only one step removed from shantytown. Wood-burning-stove pipes stick out of unkept houses. Discarded appliances and rubbish dot the town's weed-filled yards.

"This place is straight out of *Deliverance*," Mike whispered to Parnell. "Or *Tobacco Row.*"

Parnell had to grin at that description.

Stolz, Carnevale, and Johnston, along with Deputy U.S. Marshal Jerry Lowry on surveillance, joined the men for the raid. All the officers wore dark jackets with identification emblazoned on the back, with the exception of Johnston, who wore his trademark suit. Before the raid could be launched, someone slipped "Dueling Banjos," the theme song from *Deliverance* into a patrol car cassette. Pandemonium erupted as the first distinctive notes blared out of the vehicle's loud speaker.

"Turn that thing off!" Danny Stolz yelled. Too late. The men came charging into the neighborhood, rousting people out of their homes as the banjos dueled.

"Hit the ground and don't move," the officers were yelling as the homes emptied of men, some bearded, some tattooed, some toothless, most burly. All had a menacing look.

One man in red longjohns complied, the flap of the underwear flying down to reveal milk-white buttocks. A prison veteran, he never moved, lying exposed in the cool morning air for minutes until the officers got to him. "I didn't want no trouble," he said. "I do what I'm told."

The McNamara brothers spotted a familiar face: Jevon Williams, an old-time thug known for his violence, although he always insisted that he never beat women or children. He had been reared in the same area as McDuff, and at one time the pair had been buddies.

"We're looking for Kenneth McDuff," Mike said.

"Why d'ya want him," Williams said, revealing few teeth.

"He killed some kids."

"Kids?" Williams was surprised. "I knowed he was in prison for killing, but not no kids."

"He did," Parnell added. "Shot two boys, tortured a little girl about sixteen, then raped and killed her. We think he may have taken that woman—Colleen Reed—over in Austin."

"He killed some kids?" Williams asked again. "I always hated him. Took him food on death row.

"I started to kill him then," Williams added. "Smart-aleck sonofabitch. He killed kids?"

"Where is he?" Mike asked.

"Hell, I don't know," Williams said. "I started to kill that kid killer when he was in prison. I wish I had now."

"You don't have any idea where he is?" Parnell pressed.

"No, but I'll tell ya this: If I find him, I'll kill him for ya," Williams offered.

"I think it would be better if you didn't," Mike suggested, secretly amused. "Just give us a call."

"Naw, I'll kill that kid killer," Williams said.

"Just call us," Parnell encouraged.

Williams's was not a unique reaction. The men were discovering that the people who knew McDuff best were often repulsed by the man. They also discovered that most of his friends did not know he had been on death row for killing teenagers.

"When we tell them that he brutalized children, that turns most of them off," Mike told Stolz as they rode back to Waco.

"A lot of people knew that McDuff was in prison for murder. And that put him in the top echelon in their eyes, until they learned he was a child killer."

Although underworld figures live by a deviate code, most draw the line when it comes to children. A child molester or killer is universally despised, so the McNamaras effectively used the 1966 murders as a weapon that encouraged informants to step forward.

Without exception, McDuff's associates said that the man talked constantly about drugs, guns, and killing people.

"We found him to be despised, universally," Parnell said. "We've found no one who would say anything good about him."

As it sometimes happens, a break in a case comes from an unlikely source, and is often the result of many hours labor by many police officers.

When Judy Dupuis, Hank's sister, called Tim Steglich to say that Hank was waiting to speak to him, the veteran officer was out the door immediately. Worley was not the type of personality to check in unless he had to. He had not called once since Steglich had been showering him with business cards. Alva Hank Worley definitely was not a caller.

Judy said Worley would be waiting at his motel room for the police officer. And he was there, standing outside, talking to his daughter when Steglich wheeled into the parking lot. Hank walked over, opened the passenger's side of the squad car, and bent over to peer across the seat, locking eyes with the detective.

"McDuff's the one that took the girl from the car wash in Austin," he said, a toneless statement of fact mingled with undertones of relief. "We . . ."

"Don't say anything else," Steglich commanded as Worley tried to continue, puzzled by the detective's reaction. "Don't say another word!"

Finally! The detective felt a rush of adrenalin. He was not totally surprised at Worley's accusation because he had suspected that Worley harbored additional information. He knew when Judy Dupuis called that Worley was ready to talk; but not this fast. A blunt accusation; immediately blurted out, was unexpected at that moment.

"Get in your car and let's go to the Sheriff's Office," Tim instructed.

"I don't have a car."

"Then get in."

"Can I talk to my daughter?"

Steglich, himself the father of three daughters, nodded; then watched the pair in earnest conversation. He could not help but wonder what was being said between the father and daughter. *What could be said,* he thought, coming to the conclusion that Worley would not tell her the whole truth. *That will come later . . . as it probably will with us.* He knew there was much more to be told.

Worley tried to talk several times during the brief trip but Steglich, careful to protect the man's legal rights and the integrity of the case, hushed him or changed the subject each time. Obviously Worley had direct knowledge of a crime, but he had to be read his legal rights.

"I couldn't do anything about it," Worley said, bursting to tell his story.

"Not yet, Hank," Steglich said, bursting to listen to it.

The conscientious inspector wanted no mistakes. He knew he would have to be patient. Worley would have to be allowed to unwind his story at his own pace but under the proper setting.

"I have to get this shit straight," Worley said as they approached the Sheriff's Office. "I am not sleeping at night."

Nor are half the lawmen in Texas, Steglich thought, turning his face to hide the half-smile that sprang to his lips at the irony of the statement.

Simultaneously the McNamaras were meeting with a biker they had accosted several days earlier at a bar.

"You know Hank Worley," Parnell growled.

"Yeah," the biker said.

"Then you better tell him to get into the ,U.S. Marshal's office and tell him everything he knows," Mike suggested two days ago.

Earlier in the day the biker had driven up from Austin to meet with the officers.

"Worley was with McDuff," he told them. "He told me that."

Mike grabbed the telephone. Steglich had to know so he could bring Worley in for questioning.

Little did he know that Steglich was at that moment doing just that.

Sixteen

Inside the sheriff's office Steglich checked the time. Five forty-five. It was April 20, 1992. He read the suspect his rights, flicked on the tape recorder, then asked him to briefly give a summary of the statement he wanted to make.

"I was with McDuff when he took the girl from the car wash and Mac had sex with the girl," Worley said. It was enough to send Steglich to the telephone to contact the Austin Police Department but neither Sergeant Don Martin nor Detective J.W. Thompson was available, so Tim asked one of the patrol deputies to try to contact either of them as he took Worley's statement.

"Tell them he's ready to talk, and I'm going on without them," he instructed.

The telephone rang. It was Mike McNamara.

"You need to go get Hank Worley," he said. "We've got a guy that will testify that Worley was involved with the kidnapping of Colleen Reed."

Steglich turned sideways in the chair and put his hand up to the telephone to muffle his voice.

"I've got Worley right here, right now, and he's talking up a storm," Steglich whispered. "I don't know exactly what he's going to say, but he's talking and I'm taking it down."

He then told McNamara that a telephone call had been placed to Martin and Thompson in Austin before the conversation ended.

Mike laughed as he hung up the telephone.

"If that doesn't take the cake," he told his brother. "Worley's talking to Steglich. Right now."

Parnell grinned. The brothers knew it was the beginning of the end.

In Belton, Steglich was on thin ice since Worley was free to leave at any time. The investigator had to get something on paper, so he put an old typewriter on his desk, rolled a statement form into the machine and began to type. Steglich had intentionally not read the official kidnapping report on Colleen Reed. If he found a suspect, he did not want to unintentionally lead him.

Steglich established the basic information, the who, what, where, why and when of the incident; what vehicles the suspects and the victim were in; descriptions of people and places; and approximate times. Steglich asked for details of what the pair had done prior to going to Austin, including the names of people who may have seen them and what route they took to Austin. All these were facts that would be laboriously checked over in the coming weeks to verify Worley's story.

Worley noted that he had previously given a statement April 8, and that it was the truth, but he had information to add to the statement.

As Worley dictated and Steglich asked questions, the horrified detective heard the story, for the first time, of what happened after Colleen Reed disappeared the night of December 29, 1991. The statement would take all night to produce over several sessions as the detective painstakingly asked Worley questions designed to jog his memory and trap him in any obvious falsehoods.

My name is Alva Hank Worley. I am 34 years old. My date of birth is December 2, 1957. I currently live at Bloom's Motel, Room #12 in Belton, Texas. On April 8th, 1992, I gave a statement to investigator Tim Steglich of the Bell County Sheriff's Department about Kenneth McDuff. All that information in that statement is the

truth, but I do know about something that Mac did that
I need to tell you about.

Back in December, about 2 or 3 days after Christmas,
Mac picked me up at my sister's house. My sister is
Judy Dupuis, and she lives at the S & S Mobile Home
Park outside Belton, Texas. He picked me up about 6 or
7 at night. I do not remember if it was on a weekend or
a work day. We ran around together at that time, and he
did not say where he was going when he picked me up.
We went to Love's Truck Stop near Temple, and he got
gas. I don't know if he used a credit card or paid cash.

We started going toward Austin, and it was just kind
of understood we were going to Austin to get some speed
or coke, whatever we could find.

Worley interrupted the statement to explain that while he
favored speed, McDuff liked crack, hence the street nickname
of "Crack Mac."

We stopped at a Conoco truck stop on Interstate 35,
on the northbound side of the highway, past Jarrell. I
bought a six pack of Budweiser Longnecks. We had already drank a six pack or better before that. Mac drove
on to Austin, and I thought we were going down to the
U.T. campus to get the dope, but Mac drove downtown,
and drove around because we had beer left. He would
not let me get anymore beer after the second six pack;
I do not know why. I know we went down 6th Street,
and in that area. I remember we got a hamburger at Dairy
Queen, I think on Congress. I remember streets were
real lit up at that time.

Steglich wanted to know if Worley meant that the streets
were lit up from street lights or Christmas decorations.
"Christmas decorations," Worley explained before returning to
the statement.

We rode around and ate. Mac was just driving, and he pulled into a car wash, right into a bay, and I thought he was going to wash his car.

I need to explain that we were in Mac's cream Ford Thunderbird. It was about 8:30 or 9:00 p.m. when he pulled into the car wash. This car wash is pretty close to downtown. I could see some of the big buildings. I know it was a pretty good size car wash; a six or seven car bay. We were not on a main road when we pulled in there, he got there off an alley, or a small side road. After he parked the car in the bay, Mac just got out. He did not say anything. He walked around the front of the car, and over to the next stall. I had noticed a woman washing her car when we pulled in, and she was the only other person there. I thought he was going to get change from her or something.

You can do better than that. Get change? It was all Steglich could do to keep his composure. He had heard numerous stories, but this was both chilling and stupidly clumsy, almost laughable except for its tragic theme.

He was only gone maybe 30 seconds. When he came back, he had the girl that was washing her car by the throat. Her feet were off the ground, and she was kicking like hell. She was screaming, 'Not me, not me.' He told her, 'You're going with me.' I noticed he had tied her hands together with some string or something like that.

He took her to the driver's side of the car, and he shoved her in the backseat. Her hands were tied behind her, I think. She was still saying, 'Please let me go, please don't let this happen to me.' I was stunned, I did not know what to say. He got in the driver's seat, and drove off, but not real fast, but fast enough to get away from there in a hurry. I think we went to the right on the road that runs in front of the car wash. I don't know

if it was a one-way road or not; a lot of Austin right
there has one-way streets. The kid was asking me to help
her, and I reached back there one time to untie her. Mac
told me not to untie her. I did not argue with Mac. He
is much bigger than I am, and I am afraid of him. There
was no way I could have done anything about what happened to that girl. He would have hurt me bad if I had
interfered. We headed north on the Interstate. All this
time the girl was trying to get out of the backseat. Mac
had laid her down when he put her in, and she could
not get up. She just kept begging for her life. Mac kept
north on the Interstate till about Round Rock, and he
pulled over on the shoulder of the Interstate. He got in
the back seat with the kid, and he told me to drive. I
slid across the seat. He told me not to open the door. I
started driving north on the Interstate. I told Mac I was
going home. While he was in the backseat with the girl,
he raped her. I know he was screwing her because the
car was moving too much.

"Didn't you look?" Steglich interrupted the statement,
knowing that normal human nature would almost demand a
peek.

"No."

"What about the rearview mirror?" the investigator asked.

"I did not want to look back. I had already seen more than
I cared to see," Worley answered before adding that McDuff
struck Colleen Reed several times as she apparently tried to
fight back.

Returning to the statement, Worley repeated:

I did not want to look back there, I had already seen
more than I cared to. I remember he told her to take her
clothes off, so I don't know if he untied her. He was
telling her, 'All you have to do is fuck.' He was trying
to put in her head that if she would just fuck, she would

be turned loose. She was saying she would do what she
was told. She was trying to buy time was what she was
trying to do. Mac had his shirt off, and I believe he had
his pants down. I do not know if the kid was facing up
or down when he raped her. I remember he made her
give him a head job. I remember that because he almost
choked her. Mac had hit her several times in the head
when he first got in the back with her. He was forcing
her head down on him and she was choking. I was just
driving, and when I got to the Stillhouse Hollow exit, I
decided to get off there to go to my sister's house. He
was just sitting back there with her after she gave him
the head job. Mac told me to pull over when I got to
the dam at Stillhouse. I pulled over near the spillway,
near the trailer houses there. I moved over to the passenger seat, and Mac got the keys out and opened the
trunk. She was quiet at that time, and he had to force
her into the trunk. That was the last time I saw that girl
or heard anything about her. Mac drove to my sister's
house. I asked him what he was going to do with her,
and he told me, 'I am going to use her up.'

"What does 'use her up' mean?" Steglich asked.
"I don't know," Worley shrugged. "Use her up."
"But what does it mean?"
"I guess he's gonna fuck her some more. I don't know."
"What else?"
"I don't know," Worley said in exasperation. "Maybe . . .
maybe it means he's gonna kill her. Yeah. He's gonna kill her."
He started the statement again:

He told me, 'I am going to use her up,' . . . and I
knew he meant he was going to kill her. He asked me
if he could use my knife. He knew I had my pocket-knife
with me. I told him he could not have it.
I knew I was close enough to my house at that time

that I could jump out of the car if I had to. He also wanted a shovel so he could bury her. He did not say bury her, but what else would he have wanted with a shovel? I told him I did not have one. He said he could get one at his Dad's house.

A knock on the door stopped the interrogation. Steglich received the message that Don Martin and J.W. Thompson were on the way from Austin, a solid hour away. Steglich checked his watch. Six forty-five.

I can't turn back or stop now, Steglich thought.

"Then what happened?" he asked, returning to the typewriter.

We did not talk much more, and he drove me to my sister's house. He did tell me to keep my mouth shut. I told him I didn't see shit. I do not know which way he left when he left the house. I went in the house, and that was the last I saw of McDuff, and I have not talked to him since that day, either. That day, Mac was wearing blue jeans. I don't remember his shirt. I know it was cool that night, because I was wearing a sweater. The girl was wearing pants, blue I think. I can't remember what kind of shirt she had on. I know she was not wearing a watch, because I noticed that when I tried to untie her. I think she was wearing white tennis shoes, also. I do know Mac had his tire tool with him, but I don't know if he did anything with it. I also remember he said he could not turn her loose because it would get him into all kinds of shit. That was part of the argument I had with him when he first put her in the car. Mac had some stuff in the car that night. There was some of his clothes, or somebody's clothes in the floorboard. He had a big ghetto blaster, and it was in the backseat. He put it on the rear deck when he got in the back with her. When Mac got her out of the car at the spillway to put her in the trunk, she did not have any clothes on at all. There is one part that I left out that I need to get straight. I pulled over at the Amity exit off the Interstate so Mac could put on his clothes. I pulled over on the service road, and we all 3 got out. He did not want me and her in the car alone. While he was putting on his clothes, she was begging me to help her. She said that if I stayed with her, he would not bother her.

We were standing near the front of the car. That is the part that bothers me the most, and I did not want to say it a while ago. I knew there was nothing I could do for her, and I told her that, and she just kind of accepted it. I told her I couldn't do nothing with him. One other thing; when Mac was in the back seat with her he burned her with a cigarette, I guess near her pussy, because she screamed, and I saw him put his hand down that way. I believe we did get to the spillway by going down Amity Road, not by the Stillhouse exit like I originally said. I have had a hard time with this since it happened, and I have wanted to tell someone about it. Today, my boss, Jim Adams talked to me, and told me I should tell the truth about everything, and I decided to call you [Steglich] because I said you would be the only one I would work with.

(Signed)
Hank Worley

Steglich nodded. *Either he's trying to con me or my work paid off.* But it was of little importance to the officer. He knew that that statement was the beginning of the end for Kenneth McDuff.

It was 7:45 p.m. The men had been working on the statement for more than two hours. Steglich had Worley initial each sentence in the preamble stating that he understood his rights and the right to an attorney. Then Worley signed the document.

"My boss told me to tell the truth," Worley said again. "So I did."

"All the truth?" Steglich inquired.

Worley hesitated. "Sure."

"How about something else to drink?" Steglich offered.

Worley declined, but he had run out of cigarettes.

"What does McDuff smoke?" Steglich asked, curious to know everything there was to know about the quarry.

"He doesn't smoke."

"But you just said that he put out a cigarette on Colleen Reed," Tim countered.

"He did, but them was my cigarettes," Worley said. McDuff demanded the cigarettes, puffed them to a cherry glow, then tortured his captive, sometimes inserting the fiery mass into her already brutalized vagina, Worley explained. At times the red glow lighted up the interior of the car as it sped down Interstate 35.

It was with great difficulty that Tim Steglich purchased cigarettes for Worley out of a nearby machine, but he was determined to treat this man with courtesy. He also brought him something to eat.

Tim was glad when Martin and Thompson arrived a few minutes later. Accompanying them was ATF Agent Charles "Chuck" Meyer, an acknowledged expert in interrogation.

Steglich decided to take a rest.

"Maybe it would be a good idea for one of you to talk to him," he suggested after the men read the statement. "A change of pace."

It was decided that Martin and Thompson would interrogate Worley who apparently did not consider it strange that the Austin policemen asked him to retell his story. He could have ended the session whenever he wanted, but a man used to dealing with the law is used to answering questions.

The men began the interrogation as the McNamara brothers and U.S. Attorney Bill Johnston arrived from Waco.

It was a gathering of the principle investigators—to this

point—most involved in the case, with the exception of Sonia Urubek. Although she was the first Austin police officer to promote McDuff as a suspect back in January, she would not hear about this session until the next day.

The interrogation turned into a shambles only a few minutes after Martin began the new round of questions. Hard-nosed and frustrated by months of misty leads, Martin came down hard on Worley, and the suspect fought back. Soon the men were yelling at each other. Martin demanded to know the location of Colleen's body.

Outside the men heard the angry exchange punctuated by pounding fists on the bare table.

"We've got to get them out of there," Meyer urged, fearful that Steglich's carefully cultivated goodwill with the suspect was being destroyed by the quarrel.

"He might demand termination," added Mike McNamara, fearful that this tenuous lead to McDuff might vaporize.

A knock on the door stopped the session. Meyer and Steglich took over. After a couple of hours, Worley decided he wanted to add to his statement.

It was a few minutes after midnight when Steglich once again began typing.

"April 21, 1992. 12:05 a.m. Addition to statement of April 20, 1992," the document began after the standard acknowledgement that Worley had signed on the two previous documents. This statement was brief and illuminated what happened when Worley stopped the car on Amity Road.

> I did not say exactly what happened when I stopped the car at Amity Road. When she was standing at the front of the car with me, she had no clothes on. I pulled my pecker out of my pants, and I put it up against her pussy. It was wet, and I do not know if I ever got it in, I was not much in the mood for that shit. I did not even take my pants down, I just pulled it out the front. I did

not ejaculate. I kept it up against her for just a minute,
then Mac put her in the trunk of the car.

At the end of the last sentence the detective typed a series
of slashes to the end of the page, then drew a diagonal line
from right to left across the bottom of the page so no one
could add to the statement. Worley initialed and signed the
document.

"He's lying and confused," Steglich told Meyer. "Why don't
you talk to him a little bit, then I'll come in. You can get him
to trust you."

Meyer talked to the suspect briefly, then Worley agreed to
take the men to the spot on the gravel road where McDuff put
Colleen in the trunk of the car. Steglich was not surprised to
discover that it was almost across the street from the McDuff
homestead.

By 3:35 a.m. Worley was ready to make a third statement
to clear up discrepancies or misunderstandings in the first two
statements. Steglich once again manned the typewriter as
Thompson and Meyer joined them. Worley began again, and
made fourteen changes in the story he had first told less than
twenty-four hours before. It took three hours for him to give
the new, more detailed statement. While Worley smoked in the
interrogation room, the officers went over the changes:

1. The suspects ate at the Dairy Queen instead of
driving around. Worley placed the location of the
Dairy Queen on Congress Avenue.

2. The car wash was one block south of Sixth Street.

3. McDuff drove twice around the car wash.

4. Colleen Reed was the only person in the car wash
and she was washing a small, light-colored car.

5. Worley heard McDuff's voice and he came to the
car carrying Colleen by the throat. He still denied any
"hands-on" participation in the kidnapping.

6. McDuff left the driver's side of the car open. Wor-

ley was still hesitant about exactly where he was at this moment.

7. The victim's hands were not tied behind her back.

8. Worley got in the backseat.

9. Colleen told McDuff to go to MoPac, a four-lane bypass of the city.

10. Worley took over the wheel while McDuff got into the backseat.

11. Worley described the area where they stopped near the McDuff homestead.

12. McDuff raped his victim in the vagina and the rectum, then bragged that "her ass is tighter than her pussy."

13. Worley added that the feisty woman had scratched McDuff's eyes. The convict had retaliated by slapping her after exclaiming, "She tried to hurt me real bad!"

14. Worley claimed to have challenged McDuff over what to do with the girl and that she begged Worley to stay in the backseat and have sex with her to protect her from McDuff.

"With each telling Worley becomes more and more of a hero," Steglich said derisively as the officers nodded in agreement. "Now he even challenges McDuff. He lies to him about the shovel and knife. The girl is begging him to stay with her. He's even arguing to protect the girl."

"I'm not so sure he didn't help put her in the car," J.W. Thompson added.

Steglich took Worley back to the motel in the early dawn where the suspect talked to his daughter. The officers seized a knife in the room. Worley was placed into custody and taken to a holding cell in Belton County jail. By 4:30 that afternoon he would be charged with aggravated kidnapping and placed on $100,000 bond.

Steglich would get three hours of sleep over the next four

days, mostly from catnaps, as the investigation now focused on the hunt for Colleen Reed's body.

Lori Bible was called to the police station in Austin where Sergeant Don Martin told her that a suspect was under interrogation but she could tell no one until it was official.

Lori had asked for as much warning as possible so she could prepare herself for the announcement. The police observed that courtesy, but there was also a practical reason. Lori had so many contacts in law enforcement that she would have found out about Worley within a matter of hours.

Lori went straight home and locked herself into her house, fearful that she might blurt out the news. Already stretched taut by the torturous days of wild musings, concern and worry, she decided her home needed a spring cleaning. She became obsessed with making her home sparkle. Working through the day she scrubbed and cleaned until the house glistened. The boys found her trying to sing and dance as she pushed the vacuum cleaner. Then, she mowed the yard. She weeded the garden. She washed the dirty clothes, then wished for more. She rearranged the clothes in the closet after taking each piece off and repositioning it on a hanger. She sought any physical release as she waited to hear the name of the man suspected of kidnapping, maybe even killing, her kid sister.

Still and all, she was terrified. The officers said they only had one of two suspects. The man who had taken Colleen was walking the streets. Would she be next?

Triumphant, a bleary-eyed J.W. Thompson greeted Sonia Urubek that morning as she came in to work.

"What are y'all doing here," a puzzled Urubek asked.

"Sonia, you were right!" Thompson exclaimed.

"What do you mean?"

"We've been to Belton, talking to a man named Alva Hank Worley, and he said that McDuff kidnapped Colleen."

Thompson paused. Urubek understood what he was saying. She was still working her way through the reality that she suspected McDuff before anyone else and had not been invited to participate in the payoff.

"What happened?" she asked.

"It was McDuff," Thompson said. "Worley was with McDuff the night Reed was kidnapped."

"J.W., why didn't you call me?"

"Don called and told me to meet him at the station," Thompson said. "We left immediately."

"I still should have been called," she said, anger rising in her voice.

"Sonia, just calm down. It's just as well that you weren't there. This guy, Worley, he has a thing about women."

Urubek understood, but she did not believe it. *A woman would not have kept him from talking,* she thought. She held her peace with Thompson. She believed he was trying to take the sting out of what appeared to her to be a slight. In retrospect she would be pleased that her instincts had been proven true. But, it was a slight she would never forget.

Almost as if to add insult to injury, it fell to her lot to draw up the arrest warrants for aggravated sexual assault and aggravated kidnapping against Worley.

Meanwhile, there were a couple of other tasks to perform. Sergeants Don Martin and Thompson helped prepare a probable cause warrant for Worley's arrest. The men were joined by Urubek and Travis County Assistant District Attorneys Mariane Powers and David Counts in preparing a press release. The police officers insisted that the release remain unspecific. Too many undercover officers remained in the field searching for McDuff; knowledge of their work would be life-threatening. The officers decided that there should be no public knowledge of Worley or his accusations against McDuff. The document was sealed in 147th District Court.

Between the time the document was approved and released, details contained in the probable cause document, which had been sealed, nevertheless began to be broadcast in television special reports. When J.W. Thompson heard the news, he immediately called Inspector Dan Stolz of the U.S. Marshal's office.

"What are you guys doing over there?" Stolz demanded to know.

"I'm sorry," Thompson said.

"You don't have to tell me anything," Stolz snapped. "I just know there are a lot of people in the field, and a lot of people in danger."

When Thompson tried to explain, he was cut off.

"I don't have time to talk to you," Stolz said. "I have operatives in the field at this moment and I'm pulling them out."

There would be long, anxious hours before Stolz could enjoy the knowledge that the case had been broken.

Within hours Lieutenant Gerald Raines of the Austin Police Department began organizing a mounted patrol to search for Colleen Reed's body in the area near the McDuff home. By the next morning, April 22, a dog handler for the Texas Department of Corrections, was contacted to bring highly trained cadaver dogs.

Meanwhile, the Department of Public Safety authorized a helicopter sweep. The choppers were equipped with infrared heat detectors designed to detect gases given off by decaying flesh. Several hot spots were immediately detected but searches of them proved fruitless.

With all this activity came dozens of reporters to surround the Sheriff's office in Belton, all eager for exclusive breaks on the sensational story.

Worley was confronted by law officers at 4:15 that afternoon.

"We haven't found Colleen Reed's body," Steglich said without preamble.

"I don't know what he did with her," Worley said. "But she should be near there."

"Show me again," Steglich instructed.

The men had to sneak out of the Sheriff's office in downtown Belton. Worley lay in the floorboard of the squad car as Steglich drove. First they went to where McDuff took over the driving near the Amity exit. The suspect feared that McDuff may have hidden Colleen's body near his sister's trailer in an effort to implicate him.

"He might want to make me look responsible," he told Steglich.

"It makes more sense to me that it would be near his parents' house," Steglich replied.

The men spent the rest of the afternoon driving the back roads in a vain effort to jog Worley's memory. As it had been with Roy Dale Green more than two decades earlier, all small country roads tend to look the same in the dark.

That evening Janice Jerrold telephoned Steglich with some news. Hank Worley had told a mutual friend that McDuff had killed a girl around the first of the year by hitting her in the head as she begged him not to beat her. Worley had said McDuff disposed of the body by setting it on fire after covering it with brush, the friend told Janice.

It was not an uncommon method, Steglich thought. Bodies are sometimes disposed through submersion in water or earth or through burning. Either method will destroy evidence; sometimes all of the evidence, or large quantities of it.

But when confronted with his alleged words Worley maintained he did not know what had happened to Colleen Reed. He vehemently denied any suggestions that McDuff set fire to brush heaped over the woman's body. Steglich surmised that the mutual friend, a chronic alcoholic, was told about McDuff burning her with a cigarette. Perhaps his hazy intellect heard a different story.

Assistant U.S. Attorney Bill Johnston decided that Worley should be arraigned. At 11 p.m. he was transported to Killeen where he appeared before a judge. It was past midnight when the lawmen returned with Worley.

"This day has lasted six days," a weary Steglich quipped to his wife in a telephone conversation before he went back to a pile of paperwork. He grabbed an hour of sleep before dawn, then resumed the hunt for Colleen Reed.

With Worley's arrest came the public knowledge that Kenneth McDuff was the prime suspect in Colleen's disappearance. Also came the general belief that Colleen Reed was probably dead.

Colleen's U.S. Army Reserve Unit volunteered to join in the search. Due to the clamoring media, her family was asked to stay away from the site where the police anticipated finding the body. Sergeant Thompson recruited a police academy class to join him in the muggy spring heat.

The leads continued to mount that morning. Detective Stroup called early on April 23. He had discovered Roger Jones, the TSTC student who had told Frank Pounds about McDuff's strange trip into the countryside a few days after Regenia Moore had disappeared. Although the lead had been rejected by law officers in October, it was eagerly followed in April. Roger accompanied officers to the concrete bridge where McDuff had suggested a body would disappear in the murky water below. It was a mile from the J.A. McDuff residence. He recounted the scary stop in the middle of a pasture where McDuff said he was to retrieve an air compressor to hock at a pawn shop. The nervous man admitted that it seemed to him that McDuff had already disposed of a body in one of these locations. Roger was concerned for his safety. McDuff had an evil temper, he said. He was a likeable person one moment, a raving terror the next.

The law officers spent the evening and most of the night in beer joints, searching for any McDuff associates who might know his whereabouts. No luck. The prime suspect in the bru-

tal murders of Colleen Reed and Melissa Northrup had disappeared. But if any of his buddies knew where he was, they
were not talking.

The cadaver dogs arrived early Wednesday morning, April
22, 1992, as Steglich, with the help of Thompson and Meyer,
prepared to once again sneak Worley out of the Sheriff's office.
The team planned to retrace and videotape the route McDuff
and Worley took the night Colleen was killed. Electronic and
print media surrounded the building. Dozens of eyes watched
each exit.

This time Steglich used the jail's sally port to whisk Worley
into a police van with tinted windows. With the suspect lying
back in the seat, the men eased the vehicle through milling
newsmen.

"I know it's their job," Steglich told Thompson as they drove
through the crowd. "But it's still very disturbing."

Thompson nodded agreement. "It's hard to get your job
done."

"You wish you could tell them to let us do our thing, then
we'll tell you what happened," Steglich sighed.

The officers watched the changing scenery on Interstate 35.
Each was wondering how many other women McDuff had
taken onto the interstate to rape as a buddy drove aimlessly.

"It's normal for a serial killer to just drive," Steglich said
breaking the silence as the driver left the freeway to pilot the
van to the spot where Worley last saw Colleen Reed. "The
highway system is his bloodline."

"It's how he lives," Thompson agreed. "He can go from
point to point, virtually unnoticed."

"They love that travel," Steglich added. He suspected that
there was more to it than just means of transportation, or even
a method to elude capture by committing crimes miles apart.

Both men knew that serial killers would get into a car and
drive several hundred miles in one direction, then backtrack

past the point of origin and go several hundred miles past that, then abruptly change directions again.

An automobile becomes a part of the killer's personality; few serial killers are without some means of transportation. An emotional bond exists between a serial killer and his vehicle that seems to make the inanimate object an extension of his persona. And although McDuff mistreated the car—Worley had told Steglich that McDuff routinely drove more than eighty miles per hour—he would later grouse about its treatment in a storage facility.

"What kind of a man is McDuff?" Thompson asked Worley.

"He's a nice guy, easy to talk to," Worley said, then paused. "Until he falls off the deep end and does weird things."

As the lawmen intensified the search, McDuff associates were starting to come forward to tell of hours they spent prowling the back roads of Central Texas with a man who raved about killing and drugs and guns. These predatory prowls cast a net over a sizable chunk of the state. Several associates came forward to state that McDuff would cross a creek or stop by a lake or pass a wooded area only to comment that a body hidden in any of these areas would be hard to find. The McNamara brothers were already alerting hundreds of small cities and townships in Central Texas, soliciting unsolved cases that could match McDuff's method of operation.

The men stopped at the Amity exit where McDuff took the wheel of the Thunderbird, and the gas station where McDuff had ripped off gas earlier in the afternoon the day of the kidnapping. The men went to the car wash where Worley demonstrated the abduction.

A little later, when the men exited the van on the country road near the McDuff home, Worley dropped a little bombshell.

"When he hit her, it sounded like a tree breaking," he said. "It sounded like a gunshot."

"A gunshot?" Steglich was immediately interested; McDuff had used a gun on the two boys in 1966.

"Maybe . . ." Worley seemed about to backtrack.

"What do you mean maybe?" Steglich demanded. "It was or it wasn't."

"Well, I don't know."

"Was there a gun?" Thompson joined in.

"No!"

"Are you sure it wasn't a gun? If it was a gun, tell us it was a gun," Thompson said. He felt as if something might have slipped from some guarded spot in Worley's memory. "We're not lying to you, don't start lying to us now. If it was a gun, tell us."

"No!"

"Come on, Hank." Steglich was weary from lack of sleep. "You know what a gun sounds like. You know what a gun looks like. Was it a gun?"

Steglich thought it unusual for Worley to compare the sound to that of a gun. A breaking branch would crack; a pistol makes a popping sound.

"I didn't see no gun," Worley insisted, then changed the subject. "She was probably dead when he put her in the trunk."

The men let the subject drop, but it would always bother Steglich that first Worley was alleged to have mentioned fire as a means of disposing of the body, and now he compared the sound of McDuff's hitting the woman to a gunshot. Worley may have a conscience, but how much truth were they getting out of him?

The pudgy suspect explained that the torture had been so intense during the long car ride that Colleen's screams had echoed off the car interior, hurting his ears at first. But as time passed her voice became hoarse and her screams lessened until they became low, barely discernable moans. When McDuff inserted a glowing cigarette inside her after he struck her, she had no reaction to the burning tobacco, not even a moan.

Thompson noticed that Worley was crying as he added the ugly details to his statement. It would be the only time the officer saw him cry, and the only time Worley would mention a gun or its sound.

"Did you help him put her in the trunk?" Steglich asked.

"I ain't touched no dead body," Worley said. He was becoming agitated, shuffling around, apparently trying to control the fight-or-flight syndrome that comes with an adrenalin jolt.

"You didn't help put her in the car?" Steglich asked, again somewhat surprised at Worley's unexpectedly strong reaction. Worley said McDuff grabbed the apparently dead women by the hair and lifted her into the trunk. He was contradicting his previous statement that McDuff had walked her to the trunk of the car by grabbing her hair.

"I ain't touching no dead body for nobody," he said, shaking his head vehemently. Worley's intense reaction was enough to make the law officers suspect that he was telling the truth about that.

By the end of the day they had videotaped the route and Thompson decided he wanted another statement in light of some of Worley's revelations.

At 7:10 that night, Steglich set up the typewriter and the men took Worley's final statement. It was a rehash of the first three statements with a couple of important additions. Worley admitted that he held Colleen captive in the backseat by pushing her against the side of the car.

He then gave a vivid description of what might have been Colleen's murder.

Mac got out and took his shirt off. He reached in the car, and grabbed her by the hair, and dragged her out. She did not say anything. He pulled his pants down about to his knees. He put her on the hood of the car, over on the driver's side. She was sitting up. He was standing near the front tire. He had her legs on either side of him. He started having regular sex with her. He was pulling and pushing her. He then grabbed her by the hair of the head and jerked her off the car. He put her on her knees.

He told her, 'I want another head job.' She started giving
him another head job. She was on her knees facing the
car door. I am not sure but I think she bit Mac's dick,
or she did something to make him mad. He said, 'I'll
kill you, bitch.' He pulled his hand all the way behind
himself, and he hit her so hard I heard a loud pop or
crack. I had started backing away from him. It almost
sounded like a big tree breaking. I was sure he broke
her neck. She fell backwards toward the weeds, and her
head bounced off the ground. She did not move at all.
Her whole body was limp. I think she was dead at that
point. I had been standing at the back of the car on the
driver's side. Mac was out of control. I could not believe
what he had done. I told him he should have let her go.
He reached back in the car and got a cigarette and my
lighter. He got a good fire on the end of it, and he put
it on her pussy. He did that 3 or 4 times. She did not
move or scream. Every time he did that he would take
a hit off the cigarette to get a good fire on the end of
it. The last time he put the cigarette in the area of her
pussy. I did not see the cigarette after that.

There is one point I need to get clear about when Mac
put her in the trunk of his car. He picked her up by the
hair, and he carried her to the trunk, and put her in. She
was not moving at all, and her legs were dangling off
the ground. She did not make any noise at all. All the
way to my sister's house I did not hear any noise from
the trunk or back of the car.

Worley would not tell his story again until he went to court
to testify against his former buddy and hero.

Once the statement was completed at 9:40 p.m., Worley was
charged with aggravated sexual assault. Bond was set at
$250,000. He told the officers that the final confession was
"the absolute truth."

But Worley had a question for Thompson.

"Since I'm helping you, do you think you could get me probation?" Hank asked.

Astounded, Thompson studied the man for a moment and thought, *He really means this!*

"No. I think probation is out of the question," Thompson answered evenly, hoping that he did not betray the surprise and disgust in his voice.

Bleary-eyed and exhausted, Steglich finally went home to bed for his first extended rest in four days.

The cadaver dogs failed to find anything in the search for Colleen Reed and were withdrawn on April 25.

U.S. Marshal Services Inspector Dan Stolz sent word to the troops.

"We've got to concentrate on finding McDuff and quit searching for bodies," he said. Ever practical, the twenty-year veteran of federal law enforcement believed that the bodies of victims would be recovered when McDuff was apprehended. The task force divided into two parts: one seeking McDuff, the other seeking the victims.

SEVENTEEN

Ironically it was a fisherman who discovered the body of a badly decomposed woman floating in a gravel pit in southeast Dallas County on April 26. It was a fisherman who had discovered the dead teenage boys near Everman in 1966.

The body was clothed in a dark denim jacket, a purple shirt, and a white brassiere. The denim jacket had been pulled down from the back and over her arms, in effect becoming a restraint that pinned the arms back. A twenty-five cent piece was discovered in the left jacket pocket.

The victim's hands were bound behind her back with a combination of shoestring and a single white sock with a pink insignia. Her legs had been tied together by what appeared to be black shoestrings.

It was a gruesome autopsy for the medical examiner. The body cavity was split open, and the torso's lower organs and portions of the internal organs were missing. The medical examiners discovered the hyoid bone in the victim's neck to be broken into three pieces, an injury reminiscent of the damage done to Edna Louise Sullivan with a broken broomstick in 1966.

The medical examiner noted that death was caused by homicidal violence, listing three reasons:

A. Body found in water by fisherman.

B. Ligatures around wrists and ankles.

C. Advanced decomposition.

It would be only a matter of hours before an alert Sergeant

Richard Stroup saw a report on a "floater" found half a mile away from the area where Melissa Ann Northrup's car had been discovered near the small community of Combine. A telephone call confirmed that the body matched the description of Northrup, as did the clothing. Arrangements were made to send dental charts the next day for positive identification.

In Belton, Worley signed a consent form to provide semen, blood, hair, and saliva samples.

As Melissa Northrup's body was being fished from the rock quarry, the Reed family gathered for a memorial service in honor of Colleen's twenty-ninth birthday on April 26. Three trees were planted in her honor in a park next to the Rosewood Recreation Center in the Boggy Creek Green Belt. Pink bows were distributed to the guests.

"We're just going through these kinds of activities to keep going on," Lori Bible told the news media. "I encourage reform of the parole system because my sister was so badly violated. We have to get this man off the street."

Melissa Ann Northrup's body was positively identified the next day, April 27, with the aid of dental records.

Shocked at the brutal death of his wife, Aaron Northrup said, "I know Ken McDuff. I trained him for Quik-Pak. He was weird. I thought maybe this guy needs some help, but the parole board especially knew that and let him go."

The man the parole board let out of prison was released from the only real world that he understood, according to Dr. James Grigson, a psychiatrist known as Dr. Death because he has testified for the prosecution in more than 155 death penalty cases.

"In the penitentiary he will follow the rules," Grigson said. "Most of the time people like him get along fantastic in a system. They are likeable, easy going, and they use the system to their benefit."

Dr. Grigson says a person with the severe anti-social behavior found in a deviant sociopath exhibits warning symptoms such as a disregard for the rules; disrespect for personal property; sadistic behavior in inflicting pain on women, then killing them; overwhelming desire for self-gratification; and lack of conscience.

Also, it is typical for these killers to have a weak-willed sidekick who can watch and appreciate the special powers of the sociopath, who enjoys bragging about his deeds. Sometimes the psychopath will kill his sidekick.

The killer is usually fixated on his mother.

"I've interviewed so many who praise their mother," Grigson explained. "Often they are not aware of their anger [toward their mother]. There is no thought of revenge aimed at the mother as he kills.

"There is an absolute sexual pleasure in killing women," he said. "He wanted to see the fear in the women through his power and domination."

The killer becomes a con artist by assuring the victim that the victim will not be killed if she cooperates.

Perhaps the most chilling aspect in Dr. Grigson's analysis is the aspect of pleasure as enjoyed by a psychopath. Most people have empathy for any creature in pain. A person sees a dog hurting, and it touches his heart. A person sees a complete stranger hurting, and it doesn't give pleasure.

"It is a difficult concept, but a psychopath's pleasure comes from inflicting pain. Imagine, if you will, any normal, pleasurable emotion—perhaps the sight of your child, or the fun of planning a vacation, or the thrill of accomplishment," Grigson explained. "Then layer those normal emotions over his activities."

The killer is experiencing the emotions of normal pleasure during the horrible reality of death and destruction.

"It is almost incomprehensible to a normal person that he

could get the same type of experience from torture or pain," he explained.

"There is absolute sexual pleasure in killing women," Grigson continued. Yet, the killer is unable to achieve a normal sexual climax, so he rapes, and causes his victim to perform sodomy, over and over. "If he achieves sexual satisfaction, then it is at the time of the death of his victim.

"He is in no hurry to finish his pleasure. Like a child with an ice cream cone, he wants to savor the moment and make it last," Grigson said.

In McDuff's case, Dr. Grigson believes "The pleasure came in 'using her up.' Degradation, fear, total dominance—this was all part of 'using her up.' When it ended, the pleasure ended."

Grigson suspected there would be no trophies as in the Jeffery Dahmer case. "If there can be no more pain, there is no more pleasure," he explained. "The trophy is the memory, and nothing can compare to that. That party's over."

"McDuff wanted out of prison for one reason," Grigson said. "He wanted to kill more women, small women who should be easy to control.

"That's hard for the average person to understand," Dr. Grigson added. "He was biding all that time to get out to kill more women."

Investigators would study the statement made by Judy Ann Barton to Sergeant John Jones of the Austin Police Department. She gave police an insight into McDuff's sexual habits, a topic which both fascinated and repulsed the veteran investigators.

Judy stated that McDuff never undressed when the couple had sex. "McDuff always wore most of his clothing, including his boots," she said in contrast to Worley's assertion that McDuff undressed completely to rape and torture Colleen Reed.

"Maybe he was evidence conscious," J.W. Thompson suggested after reading Barton's statement. "No hair or fluids on his clothing."

Apparently McDuff had learned his lesson in 1966 when he attempted to burn or bury soiled clothing, only to have his bloodstained underwear admitted as evidence in court.

Once he penetrated Judy with his fingers before she was prepared for sex. Although she protested the pain, he insisted that it would feel better in a little bit.

"I told him to get out of me, and he did," she said.

"McDuff never did complete the sex act; he could not come."

Judy went on to explain that McDuff "would fake it. I believe that McDuff couldn't come unless he was screwing you in the other end [behind]."

In contrast to what he did to Colleen Reed, Judy said that her lover did not like oral sex, "either giving or receiving. He said it was degrading and disgusting for a woman to have to do that to him. [He] . . . was more interested in my holding and playing with his big balls than anything else."

Her lover slept with all his clothes on but wanted her to "sleep without panties and with my nightgown pulled up. I refused." When he went to shower at TSTC, he entered the shower alone, carrying his clothes, and emerged fully dressed.

Once McDuff suggested having anal intercourse and she refused. He never asked again, although another time he asked her to stand on a suitcase and bend over. She suspected he was simulating anal intercourse.

When she learned that McDuff had been sleeping with a woman with a bad reputation, Judy became fearful of disease, and she ended their sexual relationship.

"When I told him, it seemed like . . . [he] didn't care."

Inspector Stolz and Captain John Moriarty of the Texas Department of Criminal Justice called Teresa Arnold in for an interview in Dallas.

"Close those legs. It won't do you any good here," Stolz barked when the seductively clad woman arrived for the interview apparently intent on distracting the men. She wore a micro-miniskirt with a revealing low-cut blouse.

She can't even bend over in that thing, Stolz thought. The blatant attempt at seduction angered him. It was obviously a ploy that had worked for her in the past.

"We're trying to find your Daddy, and I bet you know where he is," Stolz said, threatening to charge the pretty blonde with aiding and abetting a fugitive.

She denied knowing his whereabouts but was willing to discuss her unique relationship with the man she identified as her father. Teresa told the lawmen that McDuff was kind and nice, at first. Then he became possessive.

"He wanted to control me," she said. "Sometimes he would act as if I was his girlfriend instead of his daughter."

This bothered her, she said, as did his propensity to order her around. She admitted that he had asked her to go to Las Vegas as a prostitute. At first she agreed, then later backed out.

Teresa admitted that she smuggled contraband—drugs and money—into prison to her father.

The family that commits crime together, stays together, Stolz wryly thought.

"You know," Stolz told Moriarty after the interview. "I get the impression that she is a woman who has been abused. I feel sort of sorry for her."

Sergeant Don Martin called to ask Steglich to help man the telephones when the search for McDuff received national publicity that coming Wednesday on NBC-TV's series "Unsolved Mysteries."

Later that day a nurse collected body fluids and hair samples from Worley in Belton. She certified that all the fluids came from Worley, with the exception of the semen, Steglich wryly noted in his report.

* * *

At the height of the search for McDuff, Mr. and Mrs. Jack Brand, parents of Robert Brand, one of the 1966 victims, reduced the complex parole board issue to human terms.

"He was out on parole when he killed our kids," the dead boy's father said in a story carried by the Associated Press. "They are going to have blood on their hands, those people who turned him loose."

Lori Elmore-Moon of the *Cleburne Times* obtained an exclusive interview with the reclusive couple who vividly recalled the tragic days in 1966.

Steglich drove to Austin on April 29, three days after Colleen's birthday, for the national broadcast of "Unsolved Mysteries" which focused on her disappearance. He answered a few telephone calls, but, although hundreds were received, leads from the telecast would eventually prove fruitless. The broadcast did, at least draw national attention to the search for Kenneth McDuff.

Steglich met with Lori Bible and returned to Belton with an armful of photographs of her little sister.

Before a task force session the next afternoon, Steglich went over Hank Worley's first statement taken on April 8. He zeroed in on Worley's recollections of McDuff's description of a short woman at the convenience store near TSTC. Steglich took a few minutes to talk to Worley but he could add nothing to what he had already told the officer. All the evidence pointed toward this being Melissa Northrup.

At the meeting, the task force team created a profile, of sorts—perhaps more of a litany of tendencies—to help analyze their prey. The men found the following traits in McDuff, most of them compatible with a general profile of a serial killer:

    1. He had an accomplice.
    2. He lived within two to three hours of the dump site.

3. He enjoyed anal intercourse, a favorite form of prison degradation.

4. He abducted his victims.

5. He habitually visited prostitutes.

6. His preferred method of murder was strangulation.

7. He bound the victims' hands behind their backs.

8. He was always looking for a gun.

9. He was always looking for crack dealers to rip off.

10. His victims were left nude.

11. His victims were small—four foot-eleven inches to five foot-five inches, one hundred to one hundred and ten pounds.

12. He was very evidence conscious.

13. The victims' bodies were hauled in the trunk of a car.

14. He tried to cover the graves with debris.

"I know that these don't fit each case, but there are certain aspects that do fit all the cases," Parnell told the men. "This hints at what to look for."

Captain John Moriarty of the Texas Department of Criminal Justice distributed copies of a thirty-nine-page report entitled "The Sexually Sadistic Criminal And His Offenses." The document had been published in the *Bulletin of the American Academy and the Law,* and outlined an alarming number of characteristics that Worley had attributed to McDuff in Worley's confessions.

Investigators offered cases for consideration from such varied cities as Temple, Mesquite (near Dallas where the body of Melissa Northrup was discovered), Waco, Austin, and Huntsville in East Texas. All the sites were within several hundred miles of Waco. As the lawmen studied missing persons reports from across the state, the list of suspected victims began to grow.

Among those attending the session was U.S. Marshal Mike

Earp, a distant nephew of legendary U.S. Marshal Wyatt Earp. He was one of the U.S. Marshals brought in by Stolz.

"We've got to be careful we don't lay every unsolved mystery at McDuff's feet," Marshal Stolz warned. Stolz had already made a decision to turn the heat up on McDuff so he put in a request to the home office in Washington for "Red October," a state-of-the-art communication center.

Although it looks like a big semitractor trailer, "Red October" receives its nickname because its interior resembles the inside of the high-tech submarine featured in the motion picture. The ominously black command post rumbled into Waco the last week of April to set up near the county courthouse.

"I don't think in all his life that McDuff would have ever thought that he would have so much pressure put on him as we have been able to do, once we got started," Stolz said.

"McDuff thinks he isn't going to get caught," Mike told Parnell as they watched the high-tech apparatus come to life. "But he's ours now."

As April drew to a close, the family of Colleen Reed attended a memorial mass at Saint Catherine of Siena Catholic Church.

Texas Governor Ann Richards added a $1,000 reward through Texas Crime Stoppers to an already existing $5,000 put up by Melissa Northrup's employers.

Burly, bear-like Sheriff Larry Pamplin was concerned about his family's safety. "I was told that he threatened to kill my family," he said in a television interview. "He is a very violent, very vicious person who has no conscience.

"Kenneth McDuff enjoys the torturing more than the murders. The murders are just to cover up the crimes," the sheriff explained. "History has repeated itself."

It appeared that every new media report attempted to explain two mysteries: The inner workings of Kenneth Allen McDuff and why he was paroled.

The national publicity generated by "Unsolved Mysteries" encouraged the Texas authorities to make another venture into the world of reality-based television on Friday, May 1. This time Marshal Stolz arranged for Lori Bible-Tolson to appear on "America's Most Wanted." The popular program was created by John Walsh, whose son Adam was kidnapped in Florida in 1981. Adam's headless body was found shortly afterwards in a canal. The case was never solved, and his father became a crusader, championing the cause of missing children. The television show was created in 1988 to help bring criminals to justice.

J.W. Thompson helped sort through the leads that poured into the studio the night of the May Day airing. No help came that Friday night. McDuff still eluded capture.

In a poignant interview Lori revealed that she had obtained copies of Worley's confession.

"My imagination would run wild," she said, struggling to keep her composure. "But never did I dream—in my worst nightmare—never was it as bad as what really happened to her."

Kansas City Police Sergeant J.D. Johnson received a telephone call at home Sunday morning from Gary Smithee, a long-time friend who had watched "America's Most Wanted" on Friday. Smithee said he believed a fellow employee whom he knew as Richard Dale Fowler might be the missing fugitive. The informant and Fowler both worked for a private trash hauler in Kansas City, Missouri. Longview Waste System had hired Fowler on March 19. Smithee knew that Fowler lived in an apartment in midtown Kansas City.

McDuff's affinity for prostitutes would prove his undoing. First thing Monday morning, Johnson contacted Willey's Refuse for the birth date of Fowler. The police officer ran a computer check for the name of Richard Dale Fowler. He discovered that Fowler had been arrested on April 10 in a decoy prostitution sting. Fowler had been charged with solicitation after approaching an undercover police officer. A single fingerprint of his right index finger had been taken. The McLennan County Sheriff's Office sent a fax containing a complete set of fingerprints to Kansas City. The print matched. Richard Fowler and serial killer Kenneth Allen McDuff were one and the same.

Sergeant Johnson and five other officers decided to capture McDuff by ambush. He set up a six-man surveillance team that would work undercover as truck inspectors. They set up a fake inspection site to stop trucks for what appeared to be a routine check. Sergeant Johnson wanted to minimize the chance of McDuff's escape or injury to arresting officers.

McDuff was scheduled to be on trash truck No. 103 at 1:00 p.m. when it arrived at 85th and Hickman Mills Drive, a secluded trash dump. The officers flagged the vehicle to a stop when it appeared at 1:30 that afternoon. McDuff leaped from the passenger side only to be thrown to the ground where officers placed handcuffs on him.

"We had the guy out of the truck, in handcuffs and on his way in less than sixty seconds," Johnson said in an article in the Kansas City *Star*. "Everything was just perfect."

"We wanted to make sure the location we picked was isolated in the event of trouble, because McDuff was reported to be armed and dangerous," Johnson said. During the arrest, however, McDuff was "totally passive. He was congenial. But everything was in our favor. There were two officers there with shotguns; there was no opportunity for him to be argumentative."

Johnson said the trash dump site was selected to keep McDuff "in an open area [rather] than go in a building after him."

The two other men in the truck said that McDuff had asked them if they could help him get a gun.

At first "Fowler" denied he was McDuff, but later admitted his identity.

As jubilant Task Force members flew to Kansas City aboard

a departmental flight arranged that afternoon by Stolz, U.S. Deputy Marshal Michael Carnevale held a press conference in Waco.

"Let me first say, thank God, that the hunt for Kenneth McDuff is over," he began.

"At 1:30 p.m. today, Kenneth Allen McDuff was arrested in Kansas City, Missouri," he said triumphantly, officially ending weeks of searching by the special Task Force composed of federal, state, and local law enforcement officers. "He had been living in Kansas City for the past two to four weeks. We've had hundreds of leads and we've been following each one at a time."

"He was basically an animal . . . who had to be taken off the streets," Marshal Earp added.

EIGHTEEN

"This is the most fun I've ever had without getting drunk or taking my clothes off," goes the old cowboy joke, and it fit the occasion. The mood on the airplane was nothing short of euphoric as members of the Task Force travelled by jet courtesy of the U.S. Marshal's Service.

The departure was so fast that some of the men boarded the airplane without expense money; food and lodging was secondary compared to being a part of the team that fetched McDuff back to Texas.

Deputy U.S. Marshal Parnell McNamara, Assistant U.S. Attorney Bill Johnston, Austin Police Department Sergeant J.W. Thompson, Texas Ranger Joe Wyle, and ATF Special Agents Jeff Brzozowski and Charlie Meyer were among the men on the airplane. Although they had shared months of hard work on the same case, some were meeting for the first time.

"This has been like chasing a ghost," Parnell told Johnston as they boarded the jet. "I just want to get there and make sure it's him."

The U.S. Attorney nodded in agreement. Had McDuff been a corpse, Parnell would have wanted to stick a pin into it to make sure he was dead.

The lawmen arrived in Kansas City, around 11:00 p.m., checked into a hotel, and immediately held a war council in Johnston's room.

It was decided to interview McDuff at the Blue Springs federal holding facility immediately. McDuff was ushered in at 2:01 a.m., May 5, 1992. For the first time some of the men stood face-to-face with their elusive quarry.

Sergeant J.W. Thompson produced a blue card. The officers were going to be especially careful with this man. His days of slipping through the cracks of justice had come to an end.

J.W. Thompson read the suspect the Miranda Rights as ATF Agent Charles Meyer and Texas Ranger Joe Wyle listened.

Once finished, Thompson asked McDuff to initial all seven paragraphs and sign the back of the card to verify he had been read his rights.

"I'd like to talk to you men, but I ain't gonna sign the card," McDuff told Thompson.

With a shrug, the Austin police officer dated and signed the card himself, then added the names of Meyer and Wyle as being present. The officers were surprised that McDuff was willing to talk to them instead of asking for an attorney. Each one was anxious to hear what the fugitive had to say.

McDuff was a sorry sight to Thompson. Since the killer had dropped from sight in early March, Thompson estimated that he had lost about sixty pounds from being on the run, compared to the pictures that he had seen. That made his hands appear even bigger, his wrists stockier. He was still dirty from working as a trash collector, his clothes soiled. Thompson noticed that McDuff's features were drawn; he guessed from the weeks of stress.

"What are you here for?" McDuff asked.

"Distribution of narcotics and possession of firearms," Meyer countered as the mind games began.

McDuff became aggravated with the officers. He claimed never to have used narcotics and denied ever having a gun. He immediately began to probe the officers for information concerning the charges although the Kansas City police had already told him about them. McDuff made no mention of the more serious homicide charges. It was as if they did not exist.

His story was simple. McDuff claimed that he fled Waco about four days before his graduation from TSTC because he feared that his parole officer David Allen Darwin would issue a blue sheet on him and cause his parole to be revoked. McDuff had been arrested in Temple for public intoxication. He believed that that arrest could send him back to prison. The convicted murderer claimed that he feared he might fail a urinalysis for drug use if he kept the March 3 appointment. He considered the situation, he said, and as he drank large amounts of beer, the more obvious it became that there was only one solution: He had to flee. He acknowledged that the night he left Central Texas was the night that he met Mildred Hollins, the woman who claimed he tried to abduct her in Temple.

McDuff decided to cross into Oklahoma but he could not remember how he did it, he told the officers. Then he told them that he was refusing to give details of that trip because he did not want to get anyone in trouble.

When pressed, McDuff would not waver from his story that night. The officers would never learn how he got out of Waco, or how long he may have been there before fleeing.

However, at his trial for the murder of Melissa Ann Northrup in February, 1993, McDuff would weave a tale that involved a mystery man, a tattooed drug dealer, and a period of riding the rails.

McDuff claimed he met a man named Al in a Temple bar. McDuff decided to sell his car to Al for $1,500, and purchase Al's car. It was stolen but had a legitimate license plate. McDuff believed he would elude capture in the stolen car since the license plate was "clean." McDuff followed Al to an apartment complex in Waco where his new friend failed to get the money to complete the transaction. So the pair left with Al driving McDuff's car. Not far from Quik Pak No. 8, near New Road Inn, McDuff's car broke down. Al hitched a ride to get jumper cables and never returned. Subsequent investigations would fail to turn up this mysterious man.

McDuff started pushing his alleged broken car with Al's vehicle. (When officers attempted to start the car after its discovery, it fired up without trouble.)

While he was manipulating both cars, McDuff said he fell down, crushed his straw hat, and skinned himself. (Officers found blood on the hat and in the car.) He met Richard Bannister in the parking lot of New Road Inn but claimed it was nearer to 4:30 a.m. than 3:30 a.m.

The convicted killer said in testimony that he started walking toward the main office of the motel to telephone for a wrecker when he made a crucial decision.

I'm going to leave McDuff right here, he says he thought. "That's my thought, I am leaving him here. And I walked over to my car and took the money out of my wallet and just throwed my wallet in the car." The convicted killer had decided to start over again.

He drove Al's car back to the TSTC dormitory where he lay in bed the rest of the night considering the situation. He decided to go to San Antonio, about two hundred miles to the south on Interstate 35. There, he purchased fake identification for twenty-five dollars from a big man with tattoos whom he met on the side of the road. He discarded the Arkansas driver's license because the physical description did not match him, but he kept the Social Security card of Richard Dean Fowler, who turned out to be a real person who had lost his identification.

McDuff learned that his new buddy was a drug dealer and he accepted the offer of a ride north. The unnamed drug dealer drove toward Austin along a meandering trail through rural areas before the vehicle had a flat tire. A highway patrolman offered help, then became suspicious and checked McDuff's identification before letting them go. Then it was through Austin to Fort Worth and onto the highway toward Wichita Falls. The buddies had more car trouble as the radiator started leaking. The car heated up. The pair limped into a truck stop where McDuff hooked up with a long-haul trucker leaving his unnamed friend hunched over the leaking radiator.

McDuff said he did not know where the truck was headed. "I had no specific plans, period. My only plans specifically

was not to be in Central Texas on Tuesday," McDuff testified
at the trial.

The black truck driver let him off in Lawton, Oklahoma.
From Lawton the fugitive caught a bus to Oklahoma City where
he spent his first night in a burned-out house. It was almost
identical to the story he wove in trial testimony in 1966. Then,
McDuff had testified that he slept in a burned-out building
while Green was supposed to have killed the three teenagers.

But during the interrogation that night in Kansas City he
told the police officers that he spent the first two nights in
Oklahoma City sleeping under a bridge near the railroad tracks
before going to a rescue center.

McDuff told the officers in Kansas City that he teamed up
with yet another unnamed stranger who suggested they go to
Tulsa to join the carnival. This stranger was proficient at se-
curing food stamps and knew the best places to stay. McDuff
said he worked for the carnival for several days assembling
rides. Nights were spent in a newly acquired sleeping bag.
After several days a photographer started taking pictures of
the workmen. McDuff believed the photographer took too
much of an interest in him, snapping too many pictures for a
newspaper article. Spooked, he told his employers he had to
go to the bathroom. Instead he gathered his belongings and
left for fear a reporter might recognize him. McDuff remained
in the area, now sleeping at rescue centers.

After two weeks, he decided to ride the rails to Florida;
perhaps Miami or the Florida Keys where he could disappear.
But he, and another unnamed buddy, leaped onto the wrong
train, which wound its way through Arkansas and into Kansas.
He attempted to jump from the train in one town, but it was
travelling too fast. McDuff complained that he suffered se-
verely from the cold because he had only light clothing.

*I guess when you go on the run you don't have much time
for planning,* Thompson grinned to himself at the image of
the nasty killer huddled in a cold, barren railroad freight car.
The Austin detective studied McDuff as he talked. *Can I be-*

lieve him? Thompson asked himself. *Who knows? At least we're getting his story. I don't know if I'll ever be able to believe it.*

The fugitive managed to get off the train in Kansas City. It was a nasty spill in which he tumbled head-over-heels, he told the unsympathetic detectives. When he stopped rolling, McDuff looked up to see a man he believed to be a railroad detective walking toward him. Hurriedly, the convicted killer walked off in a different direction for a mile or so. No one questioned him.

He stayed two to seven days at a rescue mission in Kansas City before obtaining a job and moving into the apartment. The Reverend Steve Kmetz of the Kansas City Rescue Mission told officers later that week that a man identified as Richard Dale Fowler stayed at the mission from March 15 to March 26.

The hunted killer told the detectives that a man at work had said that "I look like a guy on 'Mysterious Mysteries' ['Unsolved Mysteries']. I asked him if there was a reward.

"I'll split it with you," McDuff said he joked with the fellow employee.

But it was enough recognition to cause McDuff to become concerned. His face had been on national television Wednesday night when his case was featured on "Unsolved Mysteries," then "America's Most Wanted," called attention to the missing serial killer on Friday. It was too much publicity, and too much of a coincidence that his co-worker would tease him. McDuff told the officers that he had decided he would not leave Kansas City until Wednesday. He did not explain why he picked that date, but he was captured on Monday, two days before his planned departure.

Soon McDuff was bragging to the officers. He considered himself a true, traditional convict, not a wimp like modern inmates.

McDuff denied belonging to any prison gang. He did not need the protection of a gang, testimony to his image among the inmates. Proudly he told the officers that he could make his own brew in prison using yeast and honey, that he sold marijuana, that he cheated a fellow convict out of money over a dope deal, and that he never lost respect from fellow prisoners. Respect was an important issue with McDuff. Thompson could see the prison subculture rising to the surface with each brag.

"I'm nobody's punk," McDuff said, alluding to the men who provide homosexual sex for cell block bosses. "Inmates are in and out. They don't do hard time like the convicts."

He was especially proud of his ability to "fight with the best of them." McDuff was consumed with his tough guy image. He even ventured back to his teenage years to brag; he stood up to the principal, he drove a motorcycle. To Thompson the criminal sounded like a tough teenager trying to boast his way out of trouble.

Thompson viewed McDuff as being trapped in a time warp. The more he talked, the more it became apparent he was living in the late 1960s when he had first been arrested. McDuff had lived more than two decades in a prison culture, suspended in time. His rare contact with the outside world was through television or family visits, neither of which would promote emotional development. When he returned to the general population he did not emerge mentally into modern times; his emotional growth was stunted. This phenomenon was apparent in this interview since McDuff dwelled on life as a teenager. It was the first time Thompson had viewed the phenomenon up close, and it was fascinating. He remembered his discussion with Steglich the day Worley retraced the route he and McDuff had taken after kidnapping Colleen Reed. They had explored McDuff's time warp, a teenager trapped in an older body because his social development had been stunted.

The officers let McDuff ramble about the state of the prison system for a few minutes before pulling him back to the reason everyone was up at three o'clock in the morning. By now Texas Ranger Joe Wyle realized it would be hours before the men reached the topic that interested him, so he left the room.

He thinks we're here because he jumped parole, Thompson suddenly realized. *Or that we want him for some minor crime.* The veteran officer was amazed that McDuff believed he was important enough for lawmen to come that distance to retrieve him for some secondary violation.

Parnell McNamara joined the interrogation as Meyer began mentioning the names of people McDuff knew. Parnell threw out the name of Alva Hank Worley. McDuff first said the name was familiar, Worley might be an acquaintance; but, eventually he admitted he knew Worley.

"You can't believe anything that Worley says." McDuff danced close to the subject, trying to find out what the officers knew.

"About what?" Chuck Meyer asked innocently.

"Austin. I never did anything in Austin," McDuff said. "I've never been to Austin. I never did any robberies."

The lawmen paid attention. What robberies? They had never mentioned robberies? McDuff may have tipped his hand to other crimes but the lawmen did not pursue the topic. They were interested in murder.

"The guy who told us you've been there said he went with you," Thompson ventured.

"Not me. I've never been there."

"He took and passed a polygraph examination. He said you were there."

"Never been there."

The men were careful not to mention the crime but used parts of statements made by Worley and Bucktooth Billy to bait McDuff. Again, the officers mentioned going to Austin. They revealed that they knew that McDuff and Worley had eaten hamburgers at the Dairy Queen. They were careful to walk the thin line between giving or receiving information. The men even added a few false items in hope that McDuff might take that bait and tell them that the information was not true. He did not.

"We know you were in Austin," Meyer insisted, turning up the heat. "We know you were with Hank."

"What about Christmas?" Parnell McNamara wondered.

To Thompson's trained eye, McDuff's ruddy complexion began to drain.

"We know you were in Austin." Parnell continued.

"No, I wasn't."

"Yes, you were. You were with Billy. Bucktooth Billy."

Uncomfortable, McDuff shifted his chair back a few inches, subtly trying to escape the intense questioning by putting a small distance between himself and the hunters. Parnell scooted his chair forward a few inches, erasing the gap.

"Billy told me you were there," Parnell bore in on his quarry.

"No. Not me," McDuff said, again inching his chair backwards. This time Meyer eased his chair forward, keeping the same distance between interrogator and subject.

"Worley says you were in Austin," Meyer insisted as a strange ballet began to unfold. With each question, McDuff backpedaled, pushing his chair away from the inquisitors who relentlessly followed his lead by moving forward.

"I'm a loner. I don't hang out with anybody," McDuff insisted, again easing his chair backward only to have all three lawmen move their chairs forward.

Soon McDuff had literally backed himself into a corner, his chair flush against the wall; he could flee no longer. He was surrounded by the three lawmen who had followed him across the room. It was as if the whole chase had been reenacted in miniature during that interrogation.

Cornered, McDuff reached the point of not wanting to talk anymore. He went into total denial. With each question concerning Austin, Thompson noticed that McDuff's complexion continued to pale until it became ashen gray.

We're talking about something you don't want to talk about, Thompson thought. It was apparent that finally, McDuff had come to realize that the lawmen had come to Kansas City to bring him back to Texas to face murder charges.

You didn't expect that, Thompson thought.

"You were in Austin, driving down Sixth Street with Hank, weren't you," Meyer asked.

"Wrong guy, not me," McDuff answered coolly.

"You went to a car wash," the officer suggested.

"Wrong guy, not me," McDuff said.

It was the only answer McDuff would give during the rest of the interrogation. Within a matter of minutes he evoked his right to an attorney.

The interview ended at 4:41 a.m.

"Did you notice that not once—not one time—did he ask us what crime he was being accused of in Austin," Thompson asked Chuck Meyer.

"Certainly not your normal reaction," Meyer acknowledged. "Most people want to know what's going on. He didn't."

"He didn't need to," Thompson replied.

"He already knew," Meyer nodded in agreement.

The next day a warrant was filed by the McLennan County Sheriff's Office in Waco charging McDuff in the murder of Valencia Kay Joshua, the twenty-two-year-old black woman found in the shallow grave in a cow pasture near TSTC. Sergeant Stroup told reporters that it was a coincidence that the murder charges were filed the day after McDuff's capture.

It had been determined that the murder weapon was the four-foot length of plastic-covered wire that the McNamaras believe Harley Fayette described as a "plastic covered rope." Later in the month the sheriff's office would announce that the hair that had been found on the body of the victim matched that of hair samples taken from Kenneth McDuff.

In Kansas City, J.W. Thompson was one of the officers who searched McDuff's apartment. They found two sets of shoelaces, one set frayed as if cut, and two cotton-braided ropes that were tied in various knots as if the killer had been practicing.

* * *

Texas Ranger Tommy Ratliff added Denise "Jan" Mason, a twenty-eight-year-old Austin prostitute found dead January 17, 1990, along old Manor Road in Travis County, to the list of suspected McDuff victims. She had been strangled and beaten. She was known by the street name of "Crystal," and her death bore a resemblance to other Central Texas cases. It was under investigation by the Travis County Sheriff's Office.

Sergeant Mike Hughes of the Temple Police Department said that McDuff was a strong suspect in the disappearance of Verna Blunson, a twenty-eight-year-old Temple homemaker and mother of two children, who left her apartment July 19, 1991, while her husband was showering. She has not been seen since.

In Missouri, Sheriff Ralph Rider of Camden County, listed three potential cases in his state: Trudy Darby, a forty-three-year-old convenience store clerk in Camden County who disappeared January 19, 1991; Cheryl Kenney, a convenience store clerk who disappeared February 27, 1991; and Angela Hammond, who was last seen at a telephone booth in April, 1991, talking to her boyfriend who heard her abduction over the telephone.

A spokesman for "America's Most Wanted" said that McDuff's capture was the two-hundred-eighth time a wanted person had been apprehended after the fugitive was the focus of a show segment. Since the show started in 1988, James Breslin said, a total of four-hundred-sixty-nine reenactments had aired.

Although maligned as sensational, reality-based shows such as "America's Most Wanted" were praised in the aftermath of the arrest.

"So far we have found these shows to be very successful," said Gerald Anerberg, head of the National Association of Chiefs of Police in a Fort Worth *Star-Telegram* story. "Police officers like them because they help catch criminals and they often put the officers in a better light."

Kansas City residents who had had contact with McDuff were shocked. Fellow employees, his landlord, his boss, all described him as quiet, unassuming, even dull. He was a man lacking personality, most said.

"I had no idea," Barbara Haman, his landlord was quoted in the Austin *American Statesman*. "I watched 'America's Most Wanted' Friday, and it never sunk in . . . Thank God it did with someone else."

Haman said McDuff paid her fifty-two dollars a week for a one-bedroom apartment in Clyde Manor. He had been referred there after staying at a local shelter for the homeless. His possessions were in a pair of plastic garbage bags. All his utility bills were current. Except for his brief encounter with the undercover police officer posing as a prostitute, McDuff appeared to have been a model citizen in his host state.

"He was not a problem, not aggressive. There was no display of any kind of attitude," said Bill DeRoss, his employer.

But there was one person who was not too surprised after the Texas contingency swept into town. McDuff's roommate at the apartment told authorities that McDuff bragged about his prowess as a killer.

"He told me that he was good at killing with his hands, and that he had his own private graveyard," the former roommate told Parnell McNamara.

And, as had happened with other McDuff acquaintances, the roommate found it difficult to believe the convicted killer's brags because they sounded so absurd.

"You think he's just talkin'," the roommate said.

When law enforcement officers arrived, however, the tall tales acquired the ring of truth.

* * *

As Steglich worked at his desk to catch up on his neglected workload, a woman being escorted down the hallway saw Kenneth McDuff's picture. "That's the man who tried to keep me in the car," she said.

"What?" Steglich asked.

"We call him Cowboy," she said. "That's because of the way he dresses."

And then she was gone.

Steglich found out that the woman's name was Mildred Hollins and made a mental note to question her. McDuff was in custody. The session could wait until he had caught up on paperwork. He had spent so much time on the McDuff hunt that his other cases were suffering.

Steglich would continue—on and off—to gather evidence for the Colleen Reed case for months. Three days after the arrest he met with members of Hank Worley's family. They said Worley had indicated as early as December 31, two days after Colleen's kidnapping, that something was going on, and had kept asking family members rhetorical questions about seeing a woman injured. He had been encouraged to call the police.

Sergeant Sonia Urubek called Steglich about green carpet fibers found in the trunk of McDuff's car. Green fibers had been found in the hair of Valencia Joshua, the woman found buried in the pasture behind TSTC. Steglich had seen green carpet tossed into the underbrush near the Colleen Reed murder site, so the next day he gathered samples to send to Urubek. Neither investigator expected the tests to prove fruitful since green is the most frequent color of dumped carpet found along country roads. Subsequent tests would show the fibers did not match. It was just another of many small leads that the officers had to follow to bring a case to successful conclusion.

Still gathering evidence to document McDuff and Worley's travels on December 29, Steglich checked with a convenience store on I-35. The clerk remembered an incident near the end of December on a Saturday or Sunday. Weekends were the only days he was working nights, so it had to have been one of those days. After filling his tank, a man in a Thunderbird put the gas hose on the ground, leaped into the car and sped off. The cash register showed a shortage of $15.37. The hose on the ground was a McDuff trademark. The clerk did not report the incident to the police.

Deputy U.S. Marshal Parnell McNamara looked out the window of the federal department's jet as it approached Waco Regional Airport. Across the aisle sat a solemn Kenneth McDuff, clad in white T-shirt, green fatigue pants, and black wing-tip shoes. Parnell was nervous. He did not want to lose this prisoner to a crazed family member or a fringe-element lunatic out for revenge in Texas. Threats against McDuff's life had been made in telephone calls to the McLennan County Sheriff's Office, so everything had been done to ensure McDuff's safety.

"We want to keep him alive . . . at least for a little while," Parnell said in ironic reference to an anticipated execution date. No one on the jet doubted that McDuff eventually would be tried, convicted of murder, and sentenced to death by lethal injection.

As the airplane approached the airport the pilot called for Bill Johnston to come to the cockpit. He saw more than two-hundred people lined up on the tarmac outside the hanger.

"Do you want to land or keep on going," the pilot asked Johnston, who later learned that this was the largest crowd to ever assemble at the airport.

"I guess we'd better land," he said. "There are a lot of people waiting for Kenneth McDuff."

Assistant U.S. Marshal Mike McNamara was among those who watched from the ground as the pilot nosed the plane down. The aircraft rolled to a halt at Texas Aero, a service building away from the main terminal. Dozens of agents in raid jackets, some carrying automatic weapons, surrounded the platform as McDuff stepped out into the bright Texas sunshine. Swiftly as possible, he was escorted a few feet to the waiting squad car. Hands and feet shackled by chains, all McDuff could do was shuffle along.

"Did you kill anyone?" a reporter hollered at him.

"No!" McDuff said.

Within seconds, a caravan of eight vehicles left the airport amid a crowd of cheering on-lookers who had come out to get a glimpse of one of Texas's most famous killers, perhaps the most vicious in its history.

The crowds worried the McNamara brothers. Their apprehension increased when the squad cars, some with lights on and sirens wailing, encountered an even larger crowd at the U.S. Courthouse.

"Reminds you of one of those old-fashioned lynch mobs you hear about," Parnell said, a bit grimly.

"No kidding," Mike answered.

"Let's go," Parnell said, throwing the door open as the crowd tried to surge near.

"Did you kill Melissa?" David Northrup, Melissa's brother-in-law screamed at McDuff. "Did you kill Colleen Reed? Are you going to confess?"

The pleas fell on unsympathetic ears as did the questions by local television media. McDuff looked up once when asked by a reporter if he had killed Colleen. "No," he said.

"Did you kill Melissa?" Bethany Sneed, Melissa Northrup's sister-in-law, screamed. McDuff grimaced but said nothing.

"I hate him!" Bethany screamed. "I hate him. He's evil. I want to see him fry."

"He doesn't look like a killer" said David Northrup, Aaron's brother, as the lawmen safely escorted McDuff into the courthouse for arraignment. "But who does?"

Roy Greenwood flipped on the evening news. Grim-faced U.S. Marshals surrounded a tall, rangy prisoner. Greenwood had only seen that face one time, but he recognized it immediately. The veteran attorney listened with growing consternation as the reporter detailed the murder charges against Kenneth McDuff.

Greenwood would tell a friend that if he had had any twinge of guilt for his role in getting McDuff the stay of execution in 1970, which kept him alive to kill again, he would always remind himself that Supreme Court Chief Justice Hugo Black had also issued a stay of execution for McDuff.

Two stays in one day! Greenwood was still amazed at McDuff's incredible lucky streak.

Mildred Hollins, a pretty, petite woman with raven hair, had already been in prison for forgery, pimping for prostitutes, prostitution, and drug charges. She was ready to tell her story when Tim Steglich arrived May 18, several weeks after she saw Cowboy's picture on his desk.

"That guy's crazy," Mildred said. She told Steglich about the night McDuff met her, T-Bone and One-Arm, his bizarre threats when they went to buy drugs, and his attempt to kidnap her. It was the same night that Melissa Ann Northrup disappeared.

She would later state under oath that she testified against McDuff because she wanted the streets safe for her sister and daughter. It was the only time Mildred had seen McDuff until she testified at his trial.

"That guy's weird," Mildred repeated when she ended her story.

Steglich shook his head in amazement. He considered the street characters who populated his daily life to be off center, "weird," to use Mildred's description.

How much more scary must a Kenneth McDuff be to strike fear in these people? People that civilians would consider scary themselves? he wondered.

Yet again, the families of victims faced disappointment. Elated that the search was ended, they anticipated learning the fate of their missing loved ones, perhaps even a confession from the lips of the accused killer.

But Kenneth Allen McDuff maintained his innocence. The whereabouts of the bodies of Brenda Thompson, Regenia Moore, and Colleen Reed would remain a mystery.

Colleen Reed's family petitioned to have her declared dead in June, 1992. Once the petition was granted, Lori sold Colleen's little sporty white Mazda Miata found in the car wash. She closed Colleen's bank accounts, including the one the kidnap victim had used only minutes before she was seized. Then, Lori attended to the necessary paperwork that officially ended Colleen's participation in day-to-day life.

NINETEEN

Sergeant Sonia Urubek decided to recontact Helen Copitka, the former parole board member whose card was found in Kenneth McDuff's wallet in his car. The officer drove to Copitka's residence on Bangor Bend where she called the house from her patrol car. It was May 25, almost three weeks after McDuff had been arrested. The line was busy. Urubek went to the door. She got no answer. Back in the car she dialed again. The line was busy.

Idly turning the card in her hand, Urubek noticed that directions of some sort were written on the back. On impulse, she decided to follow those directions. When she reached the end of detailed written directions Sonia found herself at a small strip center. Astonished, she stared at the I Can't Believe It's Yogurt Shoppe where the four girls had been murdered the previous December. She reread the directions. She had made no mistake following them.

Stunned, she considered the situation. If Kenneth McDuff followed the directions on the back of the card, then he would arrive at a location where a horrible crime had been committed.

The business card was the second artifact linking McDuff to the immediate area of the horrendous murders of the four teenage girls. The McNamaras had given APD Sergeant Don Martin a city map with a route traced in ink that ended several blocks from the shop.

It seemed to the veteran police officer that the McDuff case just kept burgeoning outward like the mushroom cloud of an atomic bomb with its deadly fallout.

Immediately, Urubek found Sergeant John Jones, the officer in charge of the Yogurt Murders investigation, and showed him the card with the instructions. Jones asked her not to go back to Copitka's house until she heard from him.

"It seemed almost natural to pull into the parking lot from where I was," Urubek told J.W. Thompson later that day.

Copitka's business card was discussed by APD officers over the next several weeks until it was decided she should be asked to testify before the Travis County Grand Jury.

No action would be taken until June 28 when Sergeant Jones and ATF Agent Meyer visited Copitka in the morning and returned at noon with Sergeant Urubek to serve the grand jury summons. Copitka remembered Urubek's original telephone calls but said she did not connect the telephone calls to Kenneth McDuff. The former parole board member said she was counseling another Kenneth about marriage and mistakenly thought this Kenneth to be the subject of Urubek's inquiry. She acknowledged that she worked as a paralegal for William T. "Bill" Habern, an attorney hired by the McDuff family to evaluate their son's chance of parole. Habern could not help McDuff. She informed them that the lawyer had the only McDuff file.

Copitka denied ever handing McDuff a business card, although she said that one might have been included in correspondence. She told the officers that she has been working as a consultant on her own since 1985.

The next day a nervous McDuff declined to voluntarily submit a semen sample. The request had probably triggered a fear in the murderer that Colleen Reed's body had been found. He did not know that the APD wanted to check his semen against a sample discovered on the Thunderbird's upholstery. He refused the request.

* * *

Later that summer of 1992, ATF Special Agent Charlie Meyer invited Waco Police Department Sergeant Mike Nicoletti of the Special Crimes Unit to join him on a July 10 special flight to Lubbock to interview Harley Fayette, who was being held in that West Texas city's county jail. Meyer knew that the Waco detective was still investigating Regenia Moore's disappearance the previous October.

Nicoletti was especially interested in hearing Fayette's story since he was one of the last people seen with Regenia. Meyer wanted to talk to Harley about McDuff's weapons possession and drug use.

Harley's tale was chilling and more detailed than what he told Frank Pounds. He was with McDuff when the killer picked up Regenia at a motel on the New Dallas Highway several miles from her usual hangout.

Nicoletti surmised that Regenia had moved to the new location because her pimp had been arrested. The pimp's arrest could have had a bearing on what had happened that night. Several prostitutes had told Nicoletti that Regenia had refused to accept McDuff as a customer after several brutal sessions with him. The women said that not only did McDuff demand anal sex of Regenia, but that she complained his physical size caused pain during intercourse. Her pimp had told McDuff to leave her alone, one informant said.

Harley said that he, McDuff, and Regenia spent the evening cruising the treacherous streets of The Cut the night she disappeared. They drank, they used drugs, and Harley said that Regenia became more and more spaced out. Like Frank Pounds, Harley said he had never seen Regenia as out of control on drugs and alcohol as she was that night.

When Regenia decided she needed more cigarettes shortly before ten o'clock, McDuff pulled into a convenience store.

"I'm going to fuck her, and use her up, and then I'm going to leave her on the road," Harley said McDuff told him in the course of the conversation as the pair watched the attractive woman through the pickup's broken windshield.

"He dropped me off," Harley told the lawmen, "and I never saw her again."

Nor did anyone else, Nicoletti thought. *Except for Kenneth McDuff.*

"Did you have anything to do with her disappearance or death?" Nicoletti asked the criminal. McDuff had an accomplice in the 1966 murders of the three teenagers, and in the kidnapping of Colleen Reed. Harley fit the prototype, a weak personality similar to Roy Dale Green and Alva Hank Worley.

"No. I swear it. I didn't." The reply was quick, defensive.

"Why is it I don't believe you?" Nicoletti said. But the impact of the rhetorical question was lost on the small, fidgety man. As other officers had before him, Nicoletti had come to the conclusion that there might be several men walking free who were not as weak-willed as Green and Worley.

"I believe in listening to everyone, then corroborating or discrediting their story," he told Harley. "Until someone proves himself unreliable, then I'll listen."

Nicoletti knew that many cases were solved through information provided by the unfortunate dregs of society.

Just because someone's a dope addict or somebody's a prostitute or a pimp doesn't mean that they are not necessarily telling you the truth or don't have the facts, Nicoletti reasoned to himself as he bitterly considered the nature of what would have been Regenia's malevolent death at McDuff's hands.

" 'Use her up' appears to be one of McDuff's favorite sayings," Nicoletti told Meyer on the flight back.

"Do you think Mrs. McDuff knows where Colleen's body is?"

Captain John Moriarty's question came as the lawmen approached the McDuff home on Cedar Creek Road on July 27, 1992.

Tim Steglich considered the question before answering.

"I don't think so," he said. "Unless she found out by accident. McDuff knows where he made his mistakes in the past.

"The fact that one person knew where the body was was one person too many," he said, referring to the Fort Worth case. "He learned his lesson. Hank Worley may know, but he's never going to tell."

Steglich paused. "I wouldn't be surprised if Addie does, but I don't think so."

The missing women were always foremost in the lawmen's mind. Whenever they gathered it was a topic that had to be discussed. Too many families still wondered about their child's final moments. Too many families needed closure through a dignified service. Too many families needed a quiet place to go where their loved one lay in peace.

"I wish we could find her," Moriarty said.

Steglich understood the wistfulness in his friend's voice, but he was also a realist.

"I don't know that he will ever talk," he said. "And if Worley's involved in the killing, he sure won't. His conscience only goes so far."

It was July 27, 1992. McDuff had been apprehended in early May. Since then Internal Affairs Captain John Moriarty of the Texas Department of Criminal Justice had been spearheading an investigation, along with U.S. Attorney Bill Johnston, into alleged bribery within the parole system. After parolee McDuff's torture and killing spree the collective conscience in Texas demanded an easy answer and bribery fit the bill. How else could a hardened killer be paroled?

Moriarty wondered about that, himself.

Even McDuff's illegitimate daughter had gone on television to detail an expensive bribery scheme she claimed to have overheard at a birthday party in the McDuff home.

Moriarty wanted the McDuffs' side of that story so he enlisted Tim Steglich's help to set up the interview. Steglich had remained the liaison between the McDuff family and law enforcement. Addie had called him a few days earlier to complain that mysterious people were shining bright spotlights into her home. Her husband had erected plywood barriers over the windows that faced the road. Addie also complained that mysterious people had been following her. She asked Tim for a meeting. Moriarty's request came at a perfect time.

Moriarty, always plainspoken, got right to the point after the introductions. And so did Addie.

McDuff's mother denied any knowledge of bribery in a long interview that included a denouncement of Teresa Arnold.

"I never did figure that she was Kenneth's daughter . . . still don't. She's not!" Addie said.

"[Teresa said] we was all going to get together and pay a parole board, but that was simply a lie," Addie insisted. "There weren't no such . . . meeting or nothin'."

The parents insisted that they paid an attorney named Bill Habern to represent their son, but they never paid any bribe money. They acknowledged that Helen Copitka worked for Habern.

Captain Moriarty had learned that some Parole Board members would serve a term of office, then enter private practice as a consultant. For a fee ranging from $1,000 to $2,000, the former parole board member would petition his old friends who remained on the board on behalf of a convict up for parole. With the Texas Department of Corrections demanding that one-hundred and fifty prisoners be paroled each day to keep the prison system in compliance with federal regulations there was an ocean of eager clients and their families willing to pay almost any fee, perhaps even bribery.

The thought of bribery was not unknown in McDuff's case, Moriarty reminded himself. Kenneth had already been convicted of trying to bribe a parole officer in 1982. He received a two-year sentence for the attempt. It did not keep him in jail. Through a technicality, two years that he had earned in good time went toward the sentence, thus erasing it. Had the new conviction been added to the end of his life sentence, he would have been ineligible for parole.

In effect, he got away with attempted bribery which allowed him to eventually murder again, Moriarty thought as a litany of the dead women flashed through his mind. He shuddered at the thought.

The family kept returning to their rejection of Teresa Arnold during the long interrogation. McDuff's father launched into a story Kenneth told them after visiting Teresa in Bryan. She told Kenneth that her ex-husband had beaten her. She wanted her newly discovered father to warn her ex-husband against future beatings.

He let the couple vent their anger against Teresa before once again bringing them back to the present topic. The couple repeated that they had only paid attorneys to work on Kenneth's case with the exception of Bill Habern, and he was a parole specialist as they understood it.

The couple denied paying a guard to smuggle cash into McDuff and were horrified at the thought of smuggling drugs to their son.

"I went to visit Kenneth, not go down there to stay," Addie quipped.

"Okay," John chuckled, bringing the interview to an end.

Addie McDuff and Steglich left the room to get a briefcase in Kenneth's room. Moriarty visited with Kenneth's father who continued to try to convince him that Kenneth was innocent of the 1966 murders. He stuck to the family story. Kenneth had lent his new car to Roy Dale Green. Kenneth was asleep on concrete in the burned-out hulk of a former pharmacy.

"What do you think about the current cases?" Moriarty asked.

"I don't know a thing about it," the elder McDuff said.

"Okay."

"But, I don't think that he would kill anybody. That there's like you've got a dog . . . you don't know what that dog's gonna do when you're not there."

"Right," Moriarty said quietly. It was the closest that anyone would ever get to a family admission of guilt.

Addie McDuff was uneasy when she discovered Moriarty talking to her husband. It turned to rage when she discovered the topic.

"Now, Mama," J. A. McDuff insisted, "you don't know what he was doing out there . . . when he wasn't here."

"You shut up," she angrily demanded. "Kenneth did not kill anyone."

Steglich suspected that the old man knew there were severe problems but at this point in his life, ill and aging, he had no control. Also, Addie was in better physical condition.

On more than one occasion Addie had tried to convince Steglich that her son did not do drugs, never sold drugs, and never hurt anybody.

"Nobody was as good as him," she told the officer, insisting that her son ran off only because he was fearful of getting into trouble over his parole violations. Often the officer had trouble staying awake during the long, rambling diatribes.

"So, that was just a big lie . . . [they have] tried to [tie] him with everybody that's been killed from the time they think they can and I'm telling you, he didn't kill nobody . . . not ever! He just wasn't the type to go around killing people. And when he was young, he had girlfriends . . . they'd come on our porch at night looking for him. And he had no reason to ever kill anybody for any reason. I'm not making that up, 'cause like I said, I will not lie for nobody. No, sir, this world's not my home.

"It's too bad," she said, shaking her head.

Addie blamed the U.S. Marshals for being responsible for the probing lights into her home, specifically the McNamara brothers.

"I'll check into it," Steglich said, inwardly amused. "I'll put a stop to the lights being shined through the window."

The McNamara brothers seemed to be the source of all the McDuff family woes, according to Addie, from switching faucet handles to shining the probing lights.

TWENTY

Gary Smithee received $5,000 reward money for his part in the capture of Kenneth Allen McDuff in Kansas City.

Most Crime Stoppers tipsters remain anonymous but Smithee went public to encourage others. "The public needs to get involved in this stuff, and if, you know, one person comes forward, maybe it will encourage other people to come forward . . . to get some of the criminals off the street."

Colleen—
    "It's been almost a year. I look at your pictures, as everyone does.
    "I miss you!
    "Remember when the 4 girls were killed.
    "You never thought it'd happen to us—but it did.
    "You probably know this. Jeff & I split up. He has the divorce papers ready.
    "I saw his new girlfriend. She's the opposite of us. She's tall, She's blonde.
    "Remind me to tell you a story . . ."

Lori Bible's letter to her late sister trails off into a series of dots.

A memorial service was held December 30, 1992, to honor the memory of Colleen Reed. Three hundred and sixty-six pink ribbons were pinned to a tree to mark each of the days she had been missing.

A little over a month later, Kenneth Allen McDuff was brought to trial in Houston in February, 1993, for the murder of Melissa Northrup.

Lori Bible testified on February 2, 1993. It was the first time she saw Kenneth Allen McDuff. She could not take her eyes from his massive hands.

McLennan County District Attorney John Segrest and his assistants, Crawford Long and Mike Freeman, carefully put the case together. "We have to work it perfectly," Segrest warned the men.

The facts built a convincing but circumstantial case:

- Richard Bannister had seen McDuff pushing his car while driving another vehicle at 3:45 a.m. He could not identify it as Melissa's car. Assistant DA Crawford Long spent hours agonizing over this bit of evidence. Was it Melissa's car? He suspected it was. If so, was Melissa in the trunk of her car? He would never learn the answers. Another mystery in the Kenneth McDuff saga.
- McDuff's car was found in the New Road Inn parking lot only a few hundred feet from the Quik Pak No. 8 where Northrup worked.
- Melissa's 1977 Buick Regal was found abandoned on March 5 about a half mile from where her body would eventually be discovered in east Dallas County.
- McDuff's head hair was found on a coat Northrup was wearing when her body was found. His head hair was also found inside her automobile. Charles Linch of the Southwest Forensic Institute testified that the root clumping in McDuff's hair were Negroid in feature. He said that he had never seen a Caucasian with that type clumping.

The revelation in court caused McDuff to publicly protest. "He has a strange relationship with blacks," Freeman observed. "He hates them, yet he runs with them and sleeps with black prostitutes." On reflection it made sense to Freeman since McDuff would seek the people he considered inferior to boost his sagging self-esteem.

- The time sequence was crucial. All the attorneys had was a woman's disappearance and McDuff was known to be in the area.
- Two eyewitnesses would testify, however, that they saw Melissa Northrup with McDuff; one saw her screaming for help and beating on a window as her automobile pulled onto the freeway, and the other saw her crying in the company of a large man on a lonely road near a Dallas lake. No eyewitness, however, could positively place McDuff at the Dallas lake where Melissa Northrup's body was found.
- Louis Bray, a fellow student at TSTC, said McDuff tried to entice him to rob Quik Pak No. 8. Bray said McDuff described a pretty young girl. Also, McDuff told Bray how a body could be chained, the stomach slit open and tossed into a lake, never to be seen again.

Prosecutor Freeman, who has done missionary work in Russia, is a member of the Church of Christ and a graduate of Abilene Christian University.

"Pray for us," he asked members of the Crestview Church of Christ, his home congregation, as the trial began.

With only a few days remaining, the attorneys produced a dramatic witness. Publicity generated through extensive media coverage caused Shari Robinson, a Seagoville woman, to step forward. Robinson testified that she had given Kenneth McDuff a bowl of beans about 9:00 p.m. on March 1, the day Melissa Northrup disappeared. Muddy and unkempt with dirty smudges on his face and hands, a stranger had knocked on her door seeking food.

"He said that he was hungry and him and his old lady had just had a fight," Robinson testified. He told her that he had lost his job.

As her husband watched from the living room, pistol at the ready, Robinson prepared the food. The stranger ate the beans on the porch, then left.

Robinson said she came forward when she recognized Kenneth McDuff from his television image as the tall, rangy stranger. Fearful for her safety, her family encouraged her to remain silent. But, she could not.

"I remember how good I felt," said Crawford Long. "Not only did we have McDuff near the scene, but now we have him near where the body and the car were found."

Long, a graduate of Baylor University, has successfully tried three other death penalty cases, and would use his summation to eloquently call Kenneth McDuff "Everybody's nightmare; the monster that comes out of the dark and jerks innocent people off the streets and takes them out and slaughters them."

"It was like prayers had been answered," Mike Freeman added. "That sealed our case for us, and it happened in the closing hours of the trial."

Since the state had a circumstantial case, the law allowed it to use evidence of other crimes to prove the criminal identity of the accused.

Freeman carefully worked out nineteen points of similarity between the abductions of Northrup in Waco and Colleen Reed in Austin.

1. Both times McDuff was driving the cream-color 1985 Ford Thunderbird that is registered to him.
2. Both offenses were committed in the darkest hours of the night.
3. Both victims were abducted.
4. Both victims were young, white females.

5. Both victims were in their twenties.

6. Both victims were alone at the time of the abduction.

7. Both women have never been seen alive again.

8. Both abductions were from a public place.

9. Both women were short in stature and small framed.

10. Both women were brunettes.

11. Both women were bound.

12. Both women were taken to another county.

13. Both were placed where their bodies were not likely to be found.

14. Both purses were left at the scene of the abduction.

15. Both victims were sexually assaulted.

16. Both abductions took place along Interstate 35.

17. Before both abductions McDuff was known to have been looking for drugs and a prostitute.

18. Both abductions were from major cities.

19. Shoelaces were used to tie both victims.

The list of similarities was not used in the trial, but much of it can even extend to Edna Louise Sullivan, the 1966 victim. She, too, was a small, young, white female whose purse was left at the scene of the abduction. She, too, was taken to another county in the dark hours of the night where she was sexually assaulted, killed and her body hidden in a place where it might not be found.

Because both the Reed and Northrup cases were similar, District Judge Bob Burdette allowed the McLennan County prosecutors to use testimony by Alva Hank Worley about the night Colleen Reed was kidnapped.

The judge accepted the similarities that both women were short, white and in their twenties. Both were kidnapped at night after being caught alone in spots not far from Interstate 35.

Furthermore, both were taken to remote locales with their hands bound by shoelaces.

"Up until Worley hit the stand," McDuff whined as deputies led him back to jail, "I would've been acquitted."

Roy Dale Green was called on to recount the night he fell under the evil influence of Kenneth McDuff.

Although Lori Bible, who had by now dropped her hyphenated name, attended the trial to testify, she also appeared in support of Brenda Solomon, Melissa Northrup's mother. Andy Kahan, the Mayor's Crime Victim Director for the City of Houston, attended every session to help the families. Frank Pounds also attended every day of the trial.

McDuff sat emotionless during the trial until Sheriff Larry Pamplin was called in to testify concerning the convict's character. A chill filled the room as Pamplin took the stand, never taking his eyes off McDuff, who seemed to shrivel under the steady glare.

"Get him out of here," McDuff hissed at his attorneys, according to Freeman who heard the whispered command.

"Obviously Pamplin struck fear in his heart," Freeman later said with delight.

It took the jury of eight men and four women only an hour to convict McDuff of Melissa Northrup's murder and then sentence him to die. The guilty verdict was immediately appealed, as are all death sentence verdicts in Texas.

Yet another crazy quirk of justice surfaced in 1993 after McDuff had been indicted by the Travis County Grand Jury in Austin for the murder of Colleen Reed.

It was discovered that the grand jury foreman had been indicted years before for passing a bad check. All indictments—including the one against McDuff—were thrown out because of an 1876 law that does not allow people to serve on juries if they have been "convicted of or who may be under indictment for theft or any felony." The law was designed to keep horse thieves off juries in frontier Texas since horse stealing was a hanging offense in the 1800s. Eventually McDuff was reindicted and his trial was moved from Austin to Seguin on a change of venue.

There was a collective sigh of relief in the law enforcement community since it appeared McDuff might, once again, manipulate his way out of legal jeopardy.

Deputy U.S. Marshal Michael R. Carnevale, died at age forty-four on July 5, 1993, in San Antonio, Texas. Although knowing that he was dying of cancer, Carnevale continued to work the long hours necessary to help bring McDuff to justice. It was his last significant case after years of working with Stolz as a tracker for the U.S. Marshal's Office. Thanks to the work of the McLennan County District Attorney's Office he had the reward of seeing Kenneth McDuff convicted of the murder of Melissa Ann Northrup and sentenced to pay the ultimate penalty.

Since McDuff had already escaped the death penalty for the 1966 murders, Travis County District Attorney Ronnie Green stepped forward with a plan to try McDuff for Colleen's murder as a "safety net," although there was no body.

It appeared that the legal system had learned its lesson. McDuff was originally convicted for only one of the three 1966 teenager murders on the theory that he could only die once in the electric chair, why convict him on three separate murder charges? It was good theory, but it did not work.

This time McDuff would not escape so easily.

"It's like the old mad dog," Green told David Counts, the assistant district attorney who would prosecute the case along with Buddy Myers. "We've got him surrounded. He's not going anywhere, so everyone needs to take their shot."

In February, 1994, Travis County prosecutors took their shot.

Melissa Northrup's mother attended the trial to support Lori, who sat front and center, only a few feet from an alternately surly and smiling McDuff.

"I could have taken a pistol and killed him without harming anyone else," Lori said, venom dripping from every word. "But you don't do that."

The state victim assistance program assigned a counselor to help her through the trial. Lori went a month without pay from her job as a real estate purchaser for the City of Austin and had to hire a baby sitter to stay with her children while she attended the trial. "I'll be paying for that trial for a long time," she said ruefully.

State witness Alva Hank Worley balked at testifying the first day of jury selection, unhappy with the life sentence deal he cut with the prosecutors. He also feared Lori Bible.

"She'll never let me get out," he said, apparently thinking of future parole hearings.

"I told him to take that to the bank," Lori said.

Worley eventually plea bargained to reduced charges in September, 1994, and is now in state prison.

In an attempt to discredit Worley, McDuff claimed that his sidekick admitted to committing the Yogurt Murders of four teenage girls in Austin only three weeks before Reed was abducted. McDuff made reference to burning flesh and rituals in a curbside press conference on the way into the building.

Kenneth Allen McDuff was convicted of murder with malice in the death of Colleen Reed in a trial in Seguin, Texas. He was sentenced to death by lethal injection although the prosecution had no body to prove that a murder had even been committed.

The verdict came one year to the month after his conviction for the murder of Melissa Northrup. It took the jury less than three hours of deliberation to convict him, mostly on Worley's testimony that the pair raped and tortured Colleen Reed before McDuff drove off with the promise to "use her up" still ringing in Worley's ears.

"A little bit of justice has been served," Bible said as she awaited the penalty phase of the trial after McDuff was convicted of her sister's murder. "Death or life at this point, I don't care. As long as he is never free again. I don't want that man ever, ever to hurt another family again."

During the penalty phase of the trial, prosecutors brought in Roy Dale Green again. Green served seventeen years in prison for his portion of the 1966 crime.

They also brought in former Tarrant County District Attorney Charles Butts, who successfully prosecuted McDuff for the murder of Robert Brand in 1966.

If pupils were bullets, I'd be a dead man, Butts thought as he took the witness stand under McDuff's steady stare. Butts had been called to testify about McDuff's character.

Butts recalled stories about McDuff's bestiality—one in particular, although it had been a story hard to believe. Butts had been told that McDuff routinely used Ben-Gay as a lubricant when he raped women.

It was a weird day. Roy Dale Green embraced Butts like a long-lost relative, exclaiming, "Mr. Butts. It's so good to see you."

"It's good to see you, again, Roy Dale," Butts replied, startled by the greeting.

"This man treated me good," Green said excitedly.

"We would have been in a bad way without you," Butts replied.

Butts believed that McDuff possessed a peculiar bent toward women. Something in his background made him want to hurt women. McDuff did not want to rob them, he wanted to humiliate and destroy, Butts said. It was a built-in program that was loosed again and again. McDuff had spent his parole doing what he liked to do the best, killing women. Butts hoped that McDuff would be stopped permanently, and he was pleased to have a tiny part in it. "His character is very bad," the attorney testified.

Mike McNamara, Parnell McNamara and Sheriff Larry

Pamplin, who seemed, once again, to provoke fear in McDuff, also testified.

"I expected it," was McDuff's terse reply when the jury convicted him, then sentenced him to die. He angrily struggled with deputies, shouting his innocence and demanding that they not touch him.

"The system failed us once," said Lori. "Colleen was three years old when McDuff murdered those three kids near Fort Worth.

"If it takes ten death penalties to make sure that he never walks free again, that's what we're going to do."

Reed's former fiancé, Oliver Guerra, said that if lethal injection was the only way to keep McDuff out of society "then so be it."

As it was in the Northrup case, the death penalty verdict in the murder of Colleen Reed was appealed.

Prosecutor David Counts suspected that the appeal process would take seven years, "perhaps as many as fifteen," before the death penalty was carried out.

"If he dies before the year 2010, I'll be surprised."

McDuff's case is unique in several ways. He is the first person ever sentenced to die by two different methods of execution. In 1966 he was sentenced to die in the electric chair. Now he faces death by lethal injection.

Not only has he been sentenced to die by two different methods, but he is the first Death Row inmate to be issued two separate Death Row numbers in the State of Texas.

Also, the case is atypical because he is the first Texan to receive three separate death sentences for three separate murders which occurred at different times; 1966, 1991, 1992. Most multi-death sentences come from a single incident such as the famous Luby's Massacre in Killeen, Texas, when George Hennard drove a truck through the window of the restaurant then shot and killed twenty-two people and wounded twenty-three people in one incident.

McDuff is now on death row, legally ordered to die for the deaths of Melissa Northrup and Colleen Reed.

As he was led out of the courthouse in Houston after receiving the death penalty in the Northrup trial a reporter asked him what was going to happen.

"I guess I'm gonna die . . . apparently," he said, offering a sly, quirky grin. "We all do, you know."

There is a certain warped irony here since technically he is still going to thumb his nose at the law whenever the deadly chemicals enter his arm. Now, Kenneth Allen McDuff has been ordered to die: twice! Even his death at the hands of the state will be an ironical, final act of impertinence, although one beyond his control, because he cannot die twice.

TWENTY-ONE

Colleen Reed's parents filed a civil lawsuit in December, 1993, alleging that McDuff's premature release from prison led to their daughter's presumed death. It named several current and former parole officials, alleging that they released "highly dangerous killers such as Kenneth McDuff out into the public without good reason." Before it can go to court, the State of Texas must first grant permission before it can be sued. "If we are successful," Lori Bible says, "it will be the first time in the history of the state."

The questions in the McDuff case linger, some still unanswered:

- Just how was a man convicted of murdering a teenage boy, and sentenced to die in the electric chair, ever allowed to leave prison on parole?
- A man also accused in the death of another teenage boy who had been shot in the head?
- Much less a man who had sexually molested a teenage girl, brutalized her, raped her and strangled her to death with a broom stick?

As the hunt for McDuff intensified in 1992, a hue-and-cry arose across the state over slack parole laws that would release a convicted killer who once faced the death penalty. At that time,

Lori Bible was seen on television across Central Texas, and on national news, urging a change in parole laws. She wrote letters to the people who voted to free McDuff. She testified at investigative committee meetings.

It became public knowledge that several former board members—Helen Copitka and Dr. James Granberry to name two—had brokered their services and knowledge of the parole board to inmates seeking parole. Although it was legal at the time, some legislators felt it was ethically questionable.

The investigation by the Federal Bureau of Investigation, the U.S. Attorney's Office, and the Texas Department of Criminal Justice into the circumstances surrounding not only McDuff's release but the release of other prisoners proved fruitless, although Dr. Granberry was eventually convicted for perjury before a federal grand jury.

It was learned that Granberry had testified in Federal Court in Austin that he had only worked a few cases as a parole consultant. Under oath he said that he no longer represented convicts seeking parole.

"What the truth was is that he had handled many more than a few cases," U.S. Attorney Bill Johnston says. "Actually, three or four times the number he stated. And at that time—the day before he testified, and a few days afterwards—he was working with the family of a prisoner to get the prisoner out. He perjured himself, we thought."

Granberry was charged and subsequently pleaded guilty to a single count of federal perjury on April 29, 1994, Johnston said. He was placed on five years probation and sentenced to stay in a half-way house and perform 150 hours of community service. Granberry is the highest state official ever convicted of a felony crime, Johnston says.

"Ironically, those half-way houses are places that convicts come on the way to parole," Johnston added.

Johnston said that Dr. Granberry offered to cooperate with the FBI although he still received the maximum sentence available.

Although Granberry voted to release McDuff in 1989 there are no charges or public allegations of wrongdoing by him in that case. Confidential sources say that Granberry's conviction of perjury was part of a plea-bargaining agreement in which he turned over evidence against other former parole board members.

Granberry testified against Frank Eikenberg, a former parole board member. Granberry told the grand jury that Eikenberg was providing him parole board records so that Granberry could make money helping the men get out of prison. The grand jury in Anderson County indicted Eikenberg in April, 1994, on charges of felony misuse of official information. The case has not yet come to trial and no further charges have been made against him.

"The reason our office became aware of parole consulting questions is that we were looking for McDuff and we began to hear about these people," said Johnston. But the subsequent investigation by the state and federal agencies would prove frustrating. "It was like jello. You'd find something and try to pick it up and it would dissolve. Too many people didn't want to talk to you."

Helen Copitka, whose card was found in McDuff's automobile, testified before a Travis County Grand Jury.

John and Addie McDuff were never charged with the crime of bribery. No criminal charges were ever developed, Captain Moriarty says of the investigation.

The state legislature sought to plug up the leaky system. When McDuff was released in 1989 and 1990 it required only two of three votes for him to be paroled. Today, a new law demands that the entire eighteen-member parole board of the Division of Pardons and Paroles must vote on the release of a person convicted of capital murder. Previously, only three members had to be present for parole procedures. Twelve members—a two-thirds majority—would now have to approve the release of an inmate convicted of crimes punishable by death or life in prison. The new law is known as the "McDuff Rule."

"We had a former board member who I think might have stacked some panels, and I think that we had some prior situations where there was some calling around in setting up those panels," State Representative Allan Place of Gatesville, the bill's sponsor in the House of Representatives, said in a Houston *Chronicle* report. "Without having any hard and fast proof of that . . . let's just go ahead and make the entire panel hear it. They're going to have to have all eighteen vote on this deal."

Soon Texans began to learn why the state's crime rate was rising. As more and more people were sentenced to jail, more and more hardened criminals were released onto an unsuspecting public. It became a revolving door that had cost an unknown number lives, just as Detective Mike Nicoletti had predicted years before.

Ruiz v. Estelle, a landmark federal case which declared that Texas prisons were overcrowded, started the 94.5 percent capacity ruling. Texas governors ordered the release of prisoners to comply with this ruling and it eventually led to the release of men such as Kenneth McDuff.

"It was not an easy decision," Chris Mealy said in an interview with the Associated Press in defense of his vote to parole McDuff. "It was the best that could be made at that time. Something happened to McDuff from the time he was released until the time he decided to commit new crimes.

"For that, we all are responsible. It is society's responsibility to take some ownership for that. Unfortunately, no one will take that other than [to] point fingers at the parole board."

Granberry took a more defensive stand in a television interview about the McDuff case. "I don't have a crystal ball. I don't know what that fellow would do."

Granberry would claim that he never saw the "Dear Jim" written by Jackson. He said the letter was automatically referred to Bettie Wells, a staff lawyer who authorized McDuff's parole reinstatement after reading the letter.

Therein lies the rub, according to Andy Kahan, the Mayor's Crime Victim Director for the City of Houston. The most that should have occurred when Jackson wrote his "Dear Jim" letter was a reopening of the hearing. That's all the attorney requested in both the letter and the petition.

"Now, the ghost of McDuff will haunt this state forever," Kahan says, noting that McDuff was one of sixty-eight former death row inmates to be subsequently paroled.

Perhaps the best illustration of the issue would be found in David Allen Darwin's testimony during the Melissa Northrup trial. Darwin, who had been a parole officer four years, was the District Parole Officer to whom McDuff reported, along with approximately eighty other convicts. In testimony introduced by the defense, Darwin outlined the conditions of McDuff's parole, which included abstinence from alcohol and drugs and associating with other convicted felons.

After McDuff told the parole officer about the DWI incident and admitted to smoking marijuana, both crimes that could result in prison sentences, he was ordered to receive counseling through a drug and alcohol rehabilitation center.

"Mr. McDuff came to my office and he made me aware that he had just recently been arrested for DWI in Bell County the weekend before," Darwin testified. "And also he informed me that the next day after the DWI that he had gone to the lake and smoked a joint of marijuana. It was at this very time that we imposed these special conditions and also requiring him to enroll in drug and alcohol rehabilitation."

Darwin received monthly progress reports from the rehabilitation center. The state official testified that McDuff participated in urinalysis testing for the presence of drugs about "every other month or so."

Darwin said he was unaware of the February 24, 1991, arrest in Temple for public intoxication a little more than a week before McDuff's next scheduled monthly meeting on March 3.

"Hypothetically, on March the 3rd, 1991—and you had been informed or had learned of the arrest for public intoxication in Bell County and he had shown up testing positive, in other words, having shown that he consumed narcotics within a certain period of time—would you have initiated revocation procedures?" court-appointed defense attorney Mike Charlton asked.

"I would say very possibly," Darwin answered.

McLennan County District Attorney John W. Segrest hammered away at Darwin's leniency. Citing the DWI arrest and admitted drug use, Segrest asked, "Now, any parole condition is going to include, 'Don't break the law again?' "

"Right, yes sir," Darwin answered.

"So when he was paroled from the prison he was told not to break the law?"

"Yes, sir."

"And both of these were criminal offenses that he reported to you?"

"Yes, sir; right."

"You did not seek to revoke his parole and send him back to the penitentiary?"

"No sir, not at that time."

After going over McDuff's counseling, Segrest got to his first point.

"DWI, a fairly serious criminal offense?" Segrest said.

"Well, any—yes, sir."

"Especially if you're on parole, it's serious?"

"I think it's serious for anybody."

"Isn't it true that because of the crowding problem in the penitentiary . . . that you do not revoke people for what they call technical violations?"

"Well, possibly," Darwin acknowledged. "Anytime a releasee commits a crime it's reported to the Board and the Board makes the final decision on anything."

"Isn't it highly unusual to send anybody back to the pen without a new conviction for an offense?"

"Yes, sir."

Segrest contrasted the penalties for public intoxication—the only penalty is a fine—to DWI, which can result in a prison sentence in Texas, and smoking or possessing marijuana, which can lead up to a six-month prison sentence.

Then he honed in on the issue of revoking McDuff's parole.

"Mr. Charlton asked you a hypothetical question, if you wouldn't send Kenneth McDuff back to prison for DWI, you wouldn't send him back for smoking marijuana. You really believe that you would send him back for getting drunk and getting arrested?" he asked.

When Darwin said that the Board would be responsible, Segrest probed deeper.

"Generally they don't send anybody back to the pen for public intoxication or a dirty urinalysis?" Segrest asked, pounding the point home.

"Not just for that, they don't."

McDuff had no reason to run from the parole officer in late February or early March if he feared being sent back to prison for parole violations. He had already dodged the serious offenses.

"The chances of him going back to the pen were real slim. Is that correct?" Segrest asked.

"More than likely, yeah."

Darwin had gone from the position of believing it "very possible" that McDuff's parole would be revoked for public intoxication under defense questioning to believing it to be "more than likely" slim when questioned by the prosecution.

McDuff had lived a charmed life until he was arrested in Kansas City, and part of that good fortune had to do with a prison system that paroled him twice after he had been sentenced to die in the electric chair and his date with death commuted to life imprisonment. He was also under parole supervision that did not revoke his latest parole for criminal offenses of DWI and drug use.

Each time he slithered through the system, new victims were added to a growing list, until he went on a rampage beginning in September, 1991, and subsequently three women died, and two—possibly three—disappeared, and are presumed dead, all with known connections to Kenneth McDuff.

Had his parole been revoked for any of his known criminal offenses, most law enforcement officials believe that some of these women would be alive today.

McDuff killed three teens in 1966. Add the murders of Melissa Northrup and Colleen Reed to the list for a total of five victims. He is a prime suspect and has been charged in the murder of Valencia Kay Joshua, whose body was found in a shallow grave in February, 1992. He is a prime suspect in the October, 1991, disappearances of Brenda Thompson and Regenia Moore.

Five of his eight suspected murders occurred after his second parole in 1990.

After his arrest officers projected McDuff as a suspect in half a dozen more cases in Texas, plus three more in Kansas.

"There's no telling how many more victims are out there, perhaps dozens; maybe a hundred or more," says Parnell McNamara with a sigh and sad shake of his head. "He fits the profile of a serial killer that roams within a three-hundred-mile radius of his home."

Out of the chaos has come reform and a positive program to keep violent parole offenders off the streets. Ironically, the parole reform has been tagged the McDuff Laws.

"A lot of prisoners are going to hate McDuff," says Captain Moriarty, who has been promoted since McDuff's capture. "His actions have caused the laws to be changed and affected the prison population. Many of the men will not get out as early as they would have without the McDuff Laws."

In November, 1993, a one billion dollar bond proposal was approved in a statewide election as a measure to help protect Texans from violent crime.

"The bottom line is not that this bond issue is going to cost one billion dollars . . . the bottom line is there are literally going to be hundreds of Texans who are not murdered," said Ken Anderson, Williamson County district attorney and president of the Texas District and County Attorneys Association.

He cited "everybody's nightmare, Kenneth McDuff," who had already been sentenced to death that year for the sexual assault and murder of Melissa Northrup.

Under new criminal justice system reforms, Anderson said, McDuff would not have been eligible for parole until 2007. The minimum time served for convicted capital murderers under the new law is forty years before the criminal would be eligible for parole. Anderson is careful to note that it would be forty years of "day-to-day" serving—no accrued good time—before a prisoner convicted of murder with malice could be considered for parole. In most instances that will insure a virtual life imprisonment.

The custom of parole commissioners leaving the parole board and moving into private enterprise as consultants has been outlawed.

"We're going to lock up the worst of the worst for a lot longer," he said. The one billion dollar bond issue was to finance correctional facilities, including a 22,000-bed state jail system for non-violent offenders, mental health and youth facilities which would free more space for violent felons in prisons.

Violent parole offenders are now the target of a special governor's task force. U.S. Attorney Bill Johnston was astonished to discover that violent parole offenders often fell through the cracks of criminal justice, as had Kenneth McDuff. Moriarty explained to him that although these violent criminals often broke parole within days of release there was no mechanism in place to return them to prison other than routine law enforcement should they be apprehended by a city, county, state or federal officer.

Immediately, Johnston contacted Texas Governor Ann Richards. She formed the Governor's Fugitive Squad, a task force composed of three officers from the Texas Department of Public Safety and two officers from the Internal Affairs Office of the Texas Department of Criminal Justice. The men were challenged to scour the state for Texas's Ten Most Wanted violent parole violators. The task force had a narrow focus that would include hundreds of suspects: The quarry had to have been on parole and committed a violent crime.

Within twenty-four hours of the press conference that launched the special task force, Captain Moriarty captured the first fugitive with the help of the Wise County Sheriff's Office in Decater, Texas.

Since then, Moriarty has been promoted to major, and is no longer a member of the task force, although he supervised the TDCJ force that, under the administration of Governor George W. Bush, has been renamed the Texas Fugitive Apprehension Unit.

"Deep in his heart he doesn't think he's going to die," Peggy Dorris said of Kenneth McDuff. Dorris, a forty-six-year-old registered nurse certified in adult psychiatry and director of Health Services at the McLennan County Jail, cared for McDuff during his stay in Waco.

"The reason he has not told where the bodies are located is

simple, really," Dorris said. "He is not through. Being captured, going to jail, these are only sidelines until he can get started again."

Dorris found McDuff to be "more grandiose than delusional. He knows what he wants, and he is impulsive about what he wants." She found McDuff's actions while incarcerated in Waco to be "animalistic in some respect," noting that he is "driven by primitive needs" in his search for instant gratification. Cordial when events were going his way, he exhibited waspish temper tantrums when he was denied even the most inconsequential request.

Dorris was especially intrigued by McDuff's lack of emotional tone. "He never experienced small emotions," she explained. "They were magnificent. Grandiose is a good word."

Dorris believed his emotions needed powerful stimulus to be experienced.

"I don't think he could have an emotion unless it was to the extreme," she explained. "Several times I believe he asked for something he could not have so he could become enraged.

"With most crack addicts the hook is the euphoric, almost orgasmic high or rush," she said. "I don't think he felt that same high. I think it took something much stronger than that."

She never saw him cry, but he did laugh, and it was generally at inappropriate times.

Although he claimed to despise prostitutes, he often bragged about the number he had used. Dorris believed he was testing her, playing mind games, to see how she reacted.

"He could turn his emotions quickly when he played mind games," she said. "And if he could evoke any emotion in you, then he believed that he had won."

She recalled McDuff's smile.

"I can see it to this day," she said. "It was not a wicked smile, or evil, just quirkish. It said, 'Gotcha.'

"He was like the fox in the hen house when it came to other inmates," she said. "They were in awe, and fear, of him."

He conned several of his fellow inmates out of money by promising them drugs or alcohol.

"It never occurred to them that he couldn't come through on

his promise," she said. McDuff was in isolation several yards from inmates in other cells. "I'd listen and laugh to myself as he talked to them. I remember thinking that there's a fool born every minute and he knows how to work them."

Although he claimed the system mistreated him, McDuff liked to brag about his knowledge of the system, "although he would discredit himself."

In all her memories, his hands stand out. Big. Strong.

Trained in psychiatric evaluation, Dorris found McDuff more normal than psychotic.

"I did not see any clinical psychotic symptoms. There were no delusions, no hallucinations and no depression.

"He knows what he's doing, even when it is bizarre or abnormal," she said.

On March 21, 1995, Lori Bible lent her support to an important piece of Texas legislation—Senate Bill 38, sponsored by J.E. "Buster" Brown—which would allow the families of murder victims to witness the execution of the person who killed their kin.

Lori indicated that although she did not desire to witness McDuff's execution she would like to have that right.

"It would just make me feel better," she said.

Lori met the parents of Jennifer Ertman and Elizabeth Pena, two Houston teens who were raped and killed when they stumbled upon a gang initiation while taking a short cut home one night. Randy and Sandra Ertman and Adolfo and Melissa Pena launched the drive for the new law, which passed the Senate 28-0. Randy Ertman is the only one of the four parents who says he will be at the execution if the law passes the House of Representatives.

Subsequently the attempt to change the law failed, but the persistent parents pressed their case before the Texas Board of Criminal Justice on September 14, 1995, after they learned the ban was TBCJ policy and not law. Kahan read Lori Bible's name into the record in support of the policy change. The next day the Board voted 9-0 to approve the policy change, subject to a ruling from the state attorney general's office which was given the next week. Victims' families now have the right to witness the murderer's execution.

ATF Special Agent Charles Meyer and Austin Police Department Sergeant J.W. Thompson still have a mission. They want to bring peace to the grieving families touched by murder and a closure to the aching void in the lives of families whose children have disappeared. Periodically the lawmen make a trip to Huntsville to visit Kenneth McDuff.

"If they can have a place to go, to know where their loved one is buried; sort-of a homecoming," Thompson says of the families, "then, maybe there can be peace."

The two lawmen believe that Colleen Reed was buried by Kenneth McDuff after she was killed. They are not sure when she died. In his final confession, Worley said he believed Colleen died when Kenneth McDuff struck her. However, during Melissa Northrup's trial, Worley changed his testimony, stating that he believed that Colleen Reed was alive when McDuff lifted her limp body into the trunk of the Thunderbird. Worley's change in testimony might have been a ploy to keep himself free of legal entanglements that would make him an accomplice to murder, which he would be if she had died in his presence. There is no statute of limitations on murder.

The officers wonder about Worley's description of the blow as a loud "crack," the sound of a breaking branch or of a gunshot. There are hundreds, perhaps thousands of questions to be answered, and no telling how many grieving families.

The officers can list the names of women who are known McDuff victims or were last seen with him. Brenda Thompson, Regenia Moore, Valencia Kay Joshua, Melissa Ann Northrup, and Colleen Reed. Five for sure, and perhaps another four; Sarafia Parker, Verna Blunson, Denise Mason, and the unidentified prostitute whose disappearance Nicoletti documented in Waco.

And, there is the haunting case of the Yogurt Murders. In accusing Worley, McDuff seemed to have information that only a

murderer would know. Meyer and Thompson convinced McDuff
in December, 1994, to take a polygraph test concerning the Yogurt Murders. He passed, according to an experienced ATF examiner. But McDuff also tested truthful in 1977 when he denied
knowledge of the murders of the three teenagers in 1966.

Meyer says that through a mishap, McDuff's attorney received
the Yogurt Murder file during discovery on the Northrup case.

"He's read every report," Meyer says.

The ATF agent also believes the two maps—on the business
card and the Austin city map—lead to a two-block area where
McDuff was working a narcotics deal with a known drug dealer.

In subsequent interviews with Thompson and Meyer in December, 1994, and February, 1995, the convicted serial killer
came to the verge of revealing the location of not only Colleen's
body, but bodies of other victims. The three men developed a
"speculative language" which allowed McDuff to talk in some
detail without outright self incrimination.

"Kenneth, you know that if a body is thrown into a river or
left lying on the ground that it will be destroyed," Thompson said
in February, 1995. "Dogs or wolves or other animals will attack
the body and scatter it. It won't remain together, and can never
be completely recovered."

"Well, I would speculate that would not be the case," McDuff
said.

"She's in the ground?" Meyer asked.

"I would speculate that she's probably in the ground," McDuff
said. "I would speculate that Colleen Reed's body might be found
in one piece."

"You mean she's buried somewhere?" Thompson probed.
"That's the only way the body will remain together."

"I would speculate that if I were a police officer I would find
her in one piece. I would speculate that she is buried," McDuff
said. "Of course I wouldn't know, but I'd speculate that."

One day McDuff agreed to take the men to areas where the
three could "speculate" that bodies might be buried. But the day
Thompson and Meyer arrived for the "speculative" drive,
McDuff refused to go.

"A man's got to do what he's got to do," McDuff said, looking up with tears in his eyes. "I'm not going today."

The show of emotion astonished the lawmen who had never seen anything in McDuff's eyes but seething anger or a cagey intellect hiding behind a flat persona.

"Why, Kenneth?" Thompson asked, puzzled and not a little frustrated. "We had an agreement."

"I'm just not going with you."

Baffled, Thompson studied McDuff for long seconds. It had taken a great deal of work to get the prison system to agree to this excursion, and only then because of the outside hope that the bitter grief of the victims' suffering families might be laid to rest.

Thompson suddenly had an insight.

"I know why you're not going, Kenneth," he said, a challenge in his voice.

There was no response.

"It's your mother," Thompson offered. McDuff sat stoically, his face blank. "She's the only person in the world who believes your stories and you want her to believe. She's the only person who will stand up and tell the world you're innocent."

Silence; a stony stare.

"You don't want to disappoint her," Thompson continued. "You'll never admit anything until she's gone. And when she's gone, I'll come back here, and get you, and you'll take me to where those girls are."

McDuff stared at Thompson. The tears had gone, now replaced by the killer's mask. He said nothing; no denial, no acknowledgement.

But for one brief moment, Thompson and Meyer had had the rare opportunity to look beyond the crimson veil into the heart of a mother's son.

"You know, there's a strange thing about McDuff," Thompson would later reflect. "You can talk to him and he's like your favorite uncle. He appears to be the nicest, funniest guy in the world. He has the biggest, happiest laugh; but there's something there that's very, very evil."

Then the veteran police detective defines the essence of Kenneth Allen McDuff, perhaps better than the psychologist and psychiatrists who have interviewed the sociopath.

"Prison is McDuff's world. Anything outside prison is fantasy, and he can live it anyway he wants to."

He did, too.

EPILOGUE

Until McDuff is executed, Lori Bible believes that she lives under a death sentence of sorts. During the murder trials in Houston and Austin, the attractive woman caught McDuff staring at her with cold, dark eyes.

"He wants me dead so bad. If he ever gets out, he'll come after me," she says with conviction.

Although it has been several years since the disappearance of her sister, Colleen's presence still permeates Lori's life in Austin. Recently Lori passed a business where years later a poster bearing her sister's picture is still prominently displayed in the front window.

Stunned at first, she recovered in time to toss a cheery greeting. "Hi, Colleen," she called out as she continued on her way, her cherished memories of a younger sister now her only companion.

Prosecutors have asked Lori Bible if she will meet with Kenneth McDuff. They believe it might spur him to reveal the location of Colleen's body. The day she was asked to do this, Lori wrote her sister a letter.

Dear Colleen:
 Have I got stories to tell you. They asked me to meet McDuff. Maybe it will spur his conscience and he'll tell us where you are. I doubt it, but I'm willing to try. One day I'll get a call and I'll go. It might not be today, or tomorrow. It might be next week or years from now, or the night before he dies. But when they call, I'll go, little sister, and maybe, then, we can bring you home.